P9-DTA-510

SISTER TIME

Baen Books by John Ringo

The Legacy of Aldenata Series
A Hymn Before Battle by John Ringo
Gust Front by John Ringo
When the Devil Dances by John Ringo
Hell's Faire by John Ringo
The Hero by John Ringo & Michael Z. Williamson
Cally's War by John Ringo & Julie Cochrane
Watch on the Rhine by John Ringo & Tom Kratman
Yellow Eyes by John Ringo & Tom Kratman
Sister Time by John Ringo & Julie Cochrane

There Will Be Dragons
Emerald Sea
Against the Tide
East of the Sun, West of the Moon

Ghost
Kildar
Choosers of the Slain
Unto the Breach
A Deeper Blue

Princess of Wands

Into the Looking Glass
The Vorpal Blade with Travis S. Taylor
Manxome Foe with Travis S. Taylor (forthcoming)

Von Neumann's War with Travis S. Taylor

The Road to Damascus with Linda Evans

with David Weber:
March Upcountry
March to the Sea
March to the Stars
We Few

SISTER TIME

JOHN RINGO &
JULIE COCHRANE

SISTER TIME

This is a work of fiction. All the characters and events portrayed in this book are fictional, and any resemblance to real people or incidents is purely coincidental.

Copyright © 2007 by John Ringo & Julie Cochrane

All rights reserved, including the right to reproduce this book or portions thereof in any form.

A Baen Books Original

Baen Publishing Enterprises
P.O. Box 1403
Riverdale, NY 10471
www.baen.com

ISBN 10: 1-4165-4232-9
ISBN 13: 978-1-4165-4232-2

Cover art by Clyde Caldwell

First printing, December 2007

Distributed by Simon & Schuster
1230 Avenue of the Americas
New York, NY 10020

Library of Congress Cataloging-in-Publication Data

Ringo, John, 1963–
Sister time / John Ringo & Julie Cochrane.
p. cm.
ISBN 1-4165-4232-9 (hc)
1. Sisters—Fiction. 2. Human-alien encounters—Fiction.
3. Life on other planets—Fiction. I. Cochrane, Julie II. Title.
PS3568.I577S57 2007
813'.54—dc22

2007030472

10 9 8 7 6 5 4 3 2 1

Pages by Joy Freeman (www.pagesbyjoy.com)
Printed in the United States of America

For Miriam

And, as always:
For Captain Tamara Long, USAF
Born: May 12, 1979
Died: March 23, 2003, Afghanistan
You fly with the angels now.

CHAPTER ONE

Tuesday 10/12/54
Chicago, USA, Sol III

The dark figure dropping over the edge of the building could have given lessons in camouflage to a Himmit. Well, almost. Actually, the bodysuit and balaclava she was wearing owed rather more of their stealth abilities *to* the Himmit than the reverse. The rappelling rope was more conventional, as were the multivision goggles. A clever observer, had she been observed, would have noticed that the better gear was old, and the cheaper gear new, suggesting that the agent or her employer had seen better days.

She stopped at the thirteenth floor, fourth window from the north end. The tool she pulled from a clip on her web gear was something like a monomolecular boxcutter. Working with a fluidity that belied the complexity of the task, she clipped a line to the rope above her, deftly secured the two suction cups of the complicated apparatus to the window, tightened them down, and excised a wide oval of the thick glass. She pulled the glass piece free and allowed it to dangle, swinging her feet through the hole and slipping inside.

The room she entered was dusty from extreme disuse, and she wouldn't have braved it at all if the threadbare carpeting hadn't been there—perfect for hiding footprints that otherwise would have been glaringly obvious. The carpeted cubicle walls, now a moth-eaten, mottled gray, had the occasional rusty bolt showing through the cracked plastic. The dusty, crumbling particle board contraptions that used to pass for "desks" for corporate underlings dated the room as being part of the postwar surplus office space. The phenomenon made the middle floors of skyscrapers in most major cities very convenient for people in her profession but, despite its drabness, it did tend to trigger a certain wistfulness for a world she'd never really gotten to know. Still, it was eerily silent, beyond the muted traffic sounds coming through the hole in the window, and that was creepy enough that she'd be glad to leave it. She was careful to touch as little as possible as she shrugged off her gear and went rummaging through for the props for the next stage of her mission.

If the stealth suit was high-tech and inconspicuous, the little black dress she pulled from her back pouch was neither. The only modern convenience was the very light antiwrinkle coating that enabled the minimal silk sheath, with its skirt that flared out below her hips, to look as perfect as if it had just been pressed. Still, the dress was tight and she had to wiggle a bit to shimmy into it and get her ample cleavage positioned for maximum effect. She frowned down at her chest, grumbling a bit about the overendowment she'd gotten stuck with when they'd lost the slab in the Bane Sidhe split.

Her employers had steadfastly refused to surgically alter them, pointing out the futility as it was hard-coded in her body nannites; they would only grow back inside a month. Besides, the doctors were unwilling to afflict her with the scars such primitive field surgery would undoubtedly leave. She harrumphed at them silently as she pinned her silver-blonde hair into a smooth chignon at the nape of her neck and spritzed it with good old-fashioned hair spray. She slipped a gold and diamond torq-style watch, which was unusual in having a digital instead of an analog readout, around her wrist. *Damn, gotta hurry. Not quite a minute until the guard reaches this floor again.*

In the past few years, rejuv had gone from being a mark of social shame to an outlet for conspicuous consumption among the glitterati. Hence, all but minimal makeup was out of fashion. Chances were very good that *she* would be taken for an authentic twenty-year-old. Most black market jobs were incomplete, missing at least the individual fine-tuning that was necessary for the full effect. They left subtle signs that the gossips were quick to notice and comment on. Her rejuv, done in better times, was perfect. A light coating of lip gloss, a pair of clear Galplas high-heeled sandals that looked like cut crystal and felt like a medieval torture device, and she was ready to go. Well, almost. She tucked a small egg-shaped device with a pull ring into her cleavage. The body her own DNA originally built never would have been able to hide it. *I swear I could hide a truck in there. Geez. Not like I really* need *to be able to blend in with a crowd or anything, not like sticking out like a sore thumb with this attention-getting look isn't a mortal hazard for an assassin. And thank God my "real" work has been light enough since I came back to work that they can divert me more often to fluff missions like this one.*

Her rappelling gear and other nonessentials got bundled into the pack and clipped onto the line outside the window. She looked down, and down, and down to the street below and shuddered. *And Tommy wanted me to exfiltrate the same way? Hell, no! Crawling around outside some skyscraper like a freaking fly was bad enough once, I'm not doing it twice in one night.* She pulled her eyes away from the dizzying downward view. *God, that's a long drop. Besides, who tries to catch party-crashers* leaving *the party? And this way I spend about half as much time slinking around places in the building where a party guest, even a lost and tipsy one, has no business being. Okay, and I don't get out much. Sad, Cally, really sad. Maybe I ought to make time next month to take the girls up to Knoxville to the zoo. Maybe I ought to get back into character and get my mind on the job.* She shook herself slightly and got back to work.

Two sharp yanks to the line and the pack began ascending out of sight—now it was Harrison's problem. Once she got the glass oval seated back in the window, she took a ballpoint pen out of her evening bag. The pen extruded a thin line of silicon-based adhesive and nannites around the cut piece. The window would heal in about a day. After that, it would take a very sophisticated forensic analysis to tell that there had ever been any damage. Well, okay, there was a slightly larger bead of goo where she'd had to shake the pen. Damn thing was almost empty. Still, it was the next best thing to untraceable. When she was done, the pen went back into the tiny evening bag with her lip gloss, a pack of Kleenex, a comb, an assorted handful of FedCreds, and the ubiquitous slimline PDA that nobody who was anybody went anywhere without. The decoy nanogenerator code keys were in a hidden pocket. It wouldn't pass close scrutiny, but then, as she wasn't on the guest list tonight, neither would she.

She'd chosen this office because the suite had an internal stairwell access, and the door was right outside this one. The office door was ajar, and she ghosted through the opening without needing to lay a finger on it. The door to the stairs was another matter. She opened it with a tissue, crumpling it and tucking it back in her purse. As she climbed the stairs to the thirty-second floor, she glanced briefly at her watch and sighed, slipping off her shoes so she could pick up the pace without sounding like a herd of elephants.

The last half flight of stairs, she froze, foot halfway down onto the next stair. Talking in the hall. The Darhel was late leaving his room. The sound was muffled enough that without her enhanced hearing she wouldn't have heard it at all through the heavy stairwell door. With enhancement she still couldn't make out the words. Just that it sounded like a command, followed by the shrill, piping acknowledgment of an Indowy servant. After a few moments she heard the bell of the arriving elevator, and she strained to hear the opening of the doors, and their closing.

Cally glanced at her watch, *Damn. Time's gonna be tight.* She crept the rest of the way up the stairs, pausing to slip her shoes back on before opening the door and stepping out into the hallway. This part of the building was immaculately maintained. The carpet was new, and the walls smelled of fresh paint. She passed a picture of a lighthouse, in a gilt frame, as she counted three doors down and retrieved the gas grenade from inside her dress.

The Posleen had reduced Earth from a thriving civilization of five billion down to about one billion refugees, barbarians, and Galactics' lackeys. The six-legged carnosauroid aliens were immune to every hostile chemical agent the humans or Galactics had been able to envision. Likely, they were immune to quite a few things nobody but the half-legendary Aldenata had envisioned. Fortunately, the Indowy were more vulnerable. Particularly, they were vulnerable to the general anesthesia agent in the grenade. She opened the door just long enough to toss it in, pulling it closed and waiting outside.

Nonlethal and scentless except for a vanishingly faint chemical-lavender smell, the gas was harmless to humans and persistent enough to be readily detected later. The thing she liked best about it was that one of the breakdown products was a common Darhel allergen and tended to give them a *very* nasty rash—about three days later. She watched the second hand on her watch tick off thirty seconds before going in.

Inside, one of the first things she noticed was a holographic display that sat on an antique mahogany table. In a display of vanity excessive even for his own species, this Darhel apparently traveled with his own portrait. The silver-black fur would have been salt and pepper except for its characteristic metallic luster. His fox ears, cocked forward aggressively, had been embellished with the lynx-tufts that were the current fad in Darhel grooming. His cat-pupilled irises were a vivid, glowing green—she would be willing to bet they had been digitally retouched. They glinted in the middle of the purple-veined whites of his eyes. The most prominent feature, however, was row of sharp teeth, displayed in a near snarl. Again, they had obviously been retouched to make the light appear to sparkle off their razor edges. He was draped in some kind of cloth that was, no doubt, hideously expensive. His angular face combined with the other features to make him look like a fatally charismatic cross between a fox and some sort of malignant elf. Half a dozen Indowy body servants were portrayed clustered in subservient postures around his feet.

Other than the gratuitous display of self-adoration, it was a stereotypical Darhel suite. A thin layer of gold covered practically everything that could be gilded, worked in intricate patterns. Piles and piles of cushions were covered in muted colors of an expensive Galactic fabric ten times softer than silk. Some of those cushions were now graced with the small, green, furry forms of sleeping Indowy. One of them had been unlucky enough to fall on the floor. It had curled up into a ball and she stepped over it as she searched for the all-important, hideously expensive code keys that were the goal of her raid.

The drawer was one of several hidden in one of the false columns ornamenting the room. She assumed it was the one with the expensive bio-lock worked into the hatch. Her buckley might have been able to convince it she was the Darhel owner. Or it might not. Fortunately, this Darhel had neglected to consider the hinges, which were delicate, of a Galactic material far too strong for most brute force, and exposed. The screw holding one end of each pin took the normal Indowy hourglass head. She unscrewed the top of her pen, selected the right size bit and—

"Cally O'Neal, I see you." The soft voice behind her was soprano, but not nearly high enough to be Indowy. The blonde cat burglar whirled and froze in mid strike, staring at a thin girl in Indowy mentat's robes, her brown hair pulled back in a tight bun . . .

"Michelle?" Cally asked, her eyes blinking rapidly in surprise.

Since Cally had been officially dead for over forty years, including as far as she had been aware to the knowledge of her only sister, seeing the mentat was, to say the least, a bit of a shock. Especially in the middle of an op.

"What the hell are you doing here?" Cally hissed. "And that Indowy greeting was in very poor taste, you know. 'I see you' sounds like we're playing hide and seek."

"Is this a bad time?" Michelle could have been slightly miffed. In all that serenity, it was hard to tell.

"Hell yes, this is a bad time!" Cally hissed. "I'm kind of in the middle of an op here. And could you please keep your voice down!" Despite feeling totally surreal from the interruption, the underdressed cat burglar couldn't help drinking in the sight of her long-estranged sister. "Waitaminute—you knew I was alive? How the hell did you get in here, anyway?" she asked.

"The physics is . . . complicated. You know, Pardal is going to be very displeased when he finds those missing."

"Fuck Pardal. Personally, I wouldn't mind if it sent the bastard into lintatai." The thief fitted the screwdriver into the tiny hinge.

"Fine, don't listen to me," Michelle sighed, "but don't do it that way. You'll break it. Someone put a lot of time into that drawer. Why don't you just use the manufacturer's override code?"

"Oh, I don't know. Maybe because it's a hundred random characters of Galactic Standard? What do you mean I'll break it?"

"Those aren't hinges. They're purely decorative. And breakable. Also alarmed. If you attempt to remove them the real door will lock somewhat permanently. Besides, the code's not quite random." She rattled off a string of Galactic syllables with a glibness that made Cally's tongue ache in sympathy.

"How? Nevermind. Could you repeat that again, only slower?" She fiddled with her PDA for a moment, "Buckley. Give me a Galactic keyboard and pretend to the drawer you're an AID."

"It wanted to tell me. It likes me." Michelle gestured faintly towards the drawer, then began repeating syllables, pausing briefly after every group of five.

"The keyboard's rather pointless, you know." The buckley's conversational tone made Cally twitch a bit, as did the fact that it was talking again. "I understand Galactic perfectly," it said.

"I told you not to talk."

"Yes, but when you spoke to me directly I presumed you wanted that to override the earlier instruction."

"Buckley, is your emulation up too high again?"

"Of course not," it answered indignantly, "and don't reset it until after the mission. You know it'll all go wrong without me. Not that it won't anyway." It sounded smug. She hated it when the buckley got smug. Whenever it was too happy, sure as hell she'd screwed something up somewhere. Michelle reached the end of the long code, and the door slid open soundlessly as the buckley finished feeding it the correct characters. Damned if the hinges weren't ornamental, after all. And the inner door was solid plasteel with very expensive subspace traction locks. If she'd triggered those the thing would have become more or less a single piece of material.

"Okay, thank you for helping me get into this thing," Cally said, checking to make sure the code keys were actually in the compartment. "Now go away. I have an egress to effect and I don't need the distraction. Nice chat. Catch me some other time."

"I did not just come to nag you. It is business. I wish to engage your team's services for a mission. Are you available three weeks and two days from now?"

"If the money's right and it doesn't go against our core objectives, we are," Cally said. "But I did mention I'm on short time here, right?"

"Neither of those things should be a problem. Shall we talk terms?"

"Oh, jeeze," Cally sighed. "Fine. Whatever. We're expensive."

"I had assumed as much," Michelle said calmly.

"If you have that much backing, I need to know who you're working for," Callly said.

"This is primarily a personal venture. Although it is of course in the larger interests of Clan O'Neal and all the clans."

"Personal? How much do you make?"

"Quite a lot, but I presume you mean money. Whatever I ask for."

"Whew." Cally whistled softly. "Want to come over to the side of Good and Right?"

"As members of the same clan, I thought we were already on the same side. For the rest, now is neither the time nor the place for this discussion."

"Well, thank you for finally agreeing with me!" Cally snapped. "Can you meet me at Edisto Beach tomorrow at seven? I'll take a walk after dinner. We can talk privately. I can bring Granpa. I'm sure he misses you as much as I do, and we can iron out the details together."

"Please, it would be inappropriate to distract my clan head when he has such weighty policy matters to meditate upon as he does at this time. I would take it as a personal favor if you would grant me a private meeting between us to handle the negotiations." She vanished, not giving her sister time to reply.

And it was a good solid vanish. One moment, sister. Next moment, air. Cally had enough experience of holograms to be pretty sure she'd been dealing with a real human. There had been a faint smell of perfume, something extremely light. Her nose was tweaked high enough that she'd caught a faint odor of body as well. Not funk, just the smell any human gave off. Traces of heat, a breath. Michelle had been standing right in front of her and now was not. Cally waved her hand across the space for a moment, then shrugged. She didn't have time for this.

She lifted the code keys out and put them carefully into her purse, replacing them in the drawer with the identical-looking but worthless decoys. Each single-use key, when plugged into a nannite generator, would trigger it to make enough fresh nannites to fill an Indowy journeyman's Sohon tank. Among the Darhel, they were the diamonds of currency.

Manufactured *very* carefully by the Tchpth, with multiple redundant levels of control to ensure that the makers could not self-replicate and did indeed self-destruct precisely on schedule, the nannite generators were the underpinning of virtually all Galactic technology. The use-once key codes that safely activated those generators were obtained from the Tchpth by the Darhel and traded amongst themselves and to the Indowy for all the necessities and luxuries that comprised the Galactic economy. They were too useful to be allowed to sit idle for long, but they were the ultimate basis of both the Indowy craftsman's wage and the FedCred.

Darhel actuaries had been in business for a thousand years by the time humans were counting cattle on tally sticks. They knew to a fraction the worth of code keys and where the nannites were flowing throughout the entire Galactic economy.

They weren't used to being robbed.

Cally suppressed the temptation to hum as she pressed the button on the inside of the door to close it. The fancy lock probably had recorded that it had been accessed with a manufacturing code, but that just added to the mystery for the Darhel. She lifted the edge of a cushion and kicked the empty gas grenade shell underneath. She wanted it found, just not right away.

I don't know what the hell to think about all that. I'll think about it after I'm out. First things first. She hurried to the door as one of the Indowy began to twitch. *They'll be awake any second now.* She glanced at her watch again. She'd made up time on being able to just close the drawer instead of reassemble it. Thank God.

After letting herself out of the Darhel's suite, getting out was a simple matter of taking the elevator to the second floor and schmoozing her way through the party. As with a lot of places, there was a lot more effort put into keeping unauthorized people from getting in, than keeping people from getting out.

The party was the kind of glittering affair that had been attended by national-level movers and shakers back in the twentieth century. It would have had diplomats, politicians, major league bureaucrats, and the occasional celebrity or industrialist. This party still had movers and shakers, but while some of the attendees were officially diplomats, the interests they really represented were one or another Darhel business group. There were a few more celebrities than would have been in attendance before, outside of fund-raisers. As artists had throughout history, they clustered where the opportunities for patronage were. Whatever else they were, the Darhel were not stupid. They understood the value of good public relations. People in the entertainment industry knew the value of a FedCred. As a business arrangement, it generally worked out rather well. In show business, people who didn't think so tended to be conspicuous by their absence.

Wow. That's the first time I've seen a champagne fountain done in real life. Clever to have floated it over the water garden. Jewels and gold lamé had enjoyed something of a revival. The room was alive with potted trees and draped greenery. Floating lights resembling mythical will o' the wisps made the ballroom look like something out of a materialistic reinterpretation of *A Midsummer Night's Dream.*

Cally shrugged. She was a realist. As long as a collaborator didn't actually get innocent people killed, he'd have to be into some pretty heavy-duty stuff to merit her professional attention. She didn't think of operations like the one tonight as professional assignments. Sending her out to steal was a little like having an attorney take out the office trash. If your employer asked it, and cash flow was tight, and you could spare the time from your real job, you did it. But it wasn't her real job. Cally O'Neal's real job was killing people. And once she'd thought she wasn't bothered by that at all. Now she knew she was, sometimes. And that it was better that way.

As she eeled her way between one overly large matron and a rather sticklike pruny one, Cally couldn't help observing the effects of bad rejuv jobs from incomplete drug sets. *Okay, so there* are *worse things than backaches and blouses that gap at the buttons.*

". . . and so my therapist said not to worry, Martin's just entering a third childhood, and *I* said I'd had enough of this midlife crisis crap the first time and . . ."

There are definitely worse things. She snagged a glass from a tray carried by a balding, forty-something man in an ill-fitting tux. *Including being stuck in a dead-end job like waiting on these bastards.* She jumped as a hand groped her butt and glanced back to see a man who looked like a seventeen-year-old geek in a tuxedo disappearing into the crowd with his matronly wife on his arm. *Case in point.*

A slim socialite with the tight face characteristic of good old-fashioned plastic surgery caught her arm. Cally suppressed her reflexes, turning a blinding but polite smile on the woman.

"Gail? Is that *you*? Why the rumors said you weren't due back for at least another two weeks. It looks *fabulous.*" The woman chattered at her, not pausing to wait for a response, "Where *did* you get the full set, you naughty girl, you. Oh, gawd, and the boobs look *great*! A bit over the top, perhaps, but you always were the drama queen, weren't you."

"It's so good to see you!" Cally piped in a bright, cheerful generic Chicago accent, noting from the woman's eyes that she was probably too blitzed to even notice that Cally wasn't this "Gail," whoever she was.

"God, I almost didn't recognize you, but I said from across the room, *no* two girls could walk like that. Blonde really suits you. A bit dated, perhaps." She plumped her own fashionably chestnut curls into place. "But I always say you should wear what looks good on *you* and to hell with little things like fashion. I'm never daring enough to do it, though. Anyway, you look *marvelous*! Oh, is that Lucienne Taylor-Jones? I just *must* speak to her! Kiss kiss, must run!" The woman weaved off in the direction of an eighteen-year-old looking, red silk-clad grande dame on the arm of an apparently sixteen-year-old uniformed man with a pair of stars on his collar.

Cally grinned privately at her "friend's" back. *There's always one. But it makes it easier to get to the door.*

Another female hand, this one with an electric blue and white French manicure, rested lightly on her arm as she wove towards the door at an oblique angle. "Love the dress, darling. It reminds me of something from Giori's Fall collection. Did you by any chance notice where they've hidden the Ladies'?"

Cally hadn't, but she had memorized the floorplan of strategic parts of the hotel and business center. "Right over there behind the Birdwell sculpture." She pointed across the room to a gaudy confection of Galplas and cobalt blue glass, formed to resemble yards of lace draped over a Shaker chair.

"Ah, I see the sign now. Good eye for art, by the way, and thank you." The woman left her, hurrying as much as the crowd would permit.

As she passed a waitress in a tuxedo that was just a hair too tight for her hips, Cally drained her champagne and added the empty glass to the woman's tray. Another tray she passed had Oysters Rockefeller, and mission or no mission, she couldn't resist taking two. Three would have been conspicuous. Not that she wasn't anyway. She could feel the male eyes on—well, on her everything, really. Rounded butts were apparently the thing, courtesy of some starlet or other. And the captain she'd been impersonating when the slab went away had also been not quite wasp-waisted, but close enough. In the little black dress she'd checked out from Wardrobe, it showed. *Goddamn conspicuous slab job.* She simpered past some guy with a Kirk Douglas chin and a martini, who moved just enough to be standing way too close, resisting the impulse to spike him in the instep with her heel. It didn't help that her last stolen weekend with Stewart—she still didn't understand why he insisted on her using a name that had been an alias in the first place and wasn't even his current one—had been damned near six months ago. Between that and the overcharged female juv hormones, which must have been somebody's idea of a bad joke, she was getting downright cranky. *Well, a secret marriage* sounded *romantic at the time.*

She carefully didn't sigh with relief when she finally reached the door. She nodded to the door attendant as she slid past a couple who were presenting their invitations, and ducked out of the building through a fire exit. Holding her PDA up to her ear, she pretended to be dictating a voicemail to a friend, rounding a corner before telling her buckley to page the team.

A few moments later, an antique limousine pulled up and the rear door opened. She climbed in, gratefully slipping off the evil high heels and massaging her sore feet. The glass between the driver's seat and the passenger compartment lowered slowly. A man in a green and black chauffeur's uniform that contrasted nicely with his properly spiked red hair glanced up into the rearview mirror and met her eyes. The slight bulge in his cheek and the faint but unmistakable whif of Red Man tobacco was out of character for a chauffeur, but didn't surprise her in the least.

The two other men in the car couldn't have looked more different if they'd tried. Harrison Schmidt was slightly too handsome, on his worst day, to be a field agent. If he wore the right clothes to make his triangular frame look paunchy, and with the right makeup, he could look nondescript enough to get by in a support role. They tried to keep him from having to do so, since if he lost concentration his native dramatic flair tended to get in the way. He simply refused to alter the windswept, golden-brown hair that could have made a holo-drama hero die from envy. But his talents for obtaining or making virtually anything they needed, regardless of the circumstances, made him a valuable addition to the team.

"Oh, don't tell me you went in with your hair like that!" their fixer said.

"What's wrong with my hair?" Cally put a hand to her hair and looked around at the interior of the car trying to find a makeup mirror.

"Nothing, if you like split ends. And when you wash it you

really need to work through a little mousse while it's still wet. And a hot oil deep conditioning treatment once a month. My hairdresser has an herbal shine rinse that works wonders. You need it, hon. And if you can possibly avoid it, no more color changes for you until you can let it grow out enough to trim the damaged hair off." He flicked a nearly invisible speck of dust off his immaculate, charcoal-gray sweater.

"This *is* my natural color. Well, now, anyway," she said.

"No, dear, it's been bleached and dyed *back* to your natural color. Not the same at all. When you were first back from sabbatical it was all fresh and not that bad, but the years of chemicals have taken a toll. Honey, you have *got* to start taking better care of it if you want to be able to pass at parties like this one."

Tommy Sunday coughed into his hand, looking at Harrison.

"Dude, you're blind. Cally, ignore him. You look gorgeous as always, okay?" he said.

Tommy Sunday was a large man. He seemed to crowd the back of the limousine all by himself. His hair was so dark it was practically black. In an earlier time, he wouldn't have looked out of place among a pro-football team's defensive line. In fact, his own father had played. It was part of the reason he was such an avid baseball fan. Oh, he'd long since made peace with his father's memory, but the love of baseball had stuck. Cally was sure that he would be eager to get back to base as quickly as possible tonight, entirely out of a dedication to professional efficiency, and having nothing to do with game three of the World Series being due to start within the next half hour. Personally, she didn't think the game had been the same since they let Larry Kruetz get away with betting on baseball. Sure, the only incidents they could prove were on games in the other league, but she suspected the commissioner's leniency had more to do with the Rintar Group owning a majority stake in the St. Paul Mavericks.

"Now, if we go ahead and get the post-op review out of the way, we can all get home quicker. Everything went okay, right?"

"I got the keys, if that's what you mean. And a line on another job. Hey, where's my stuff?" Cally said.

"What? Run that job bit by me again." Papa O'Neal said, glancing sharply at her in the rearview mirror

"Your other granddaughter sends her love." Cally lied. Michelle hadn't, actually, but she would have, of course, if she had had more time. Or at least the Indowy social facsimile thereof. She suppressed a slight grimace. In many ways it was harder to deal with the Indowy-raised humans than it was with any of the other races of aliens. You expected the Galactics to be alien. And you could always tell the Indowy-raised at a glance. They either wore robes like Michelle's, or street clothes of a particular shade of green that no other human would ever wear. She was surprised they hadn't developed a fabric with active chlorophyll.

"Michelle? Michelle's there?" He started to turn his head and turned it back as he felt the car begin to drift.

"Was. She seems to have figured out the trick of getting places without crossing the space in between," Cally answered drily. "She left before I did. Vanished, actually. Either a very good cloak of some sort or teleported."

"You're joking," Tommy said, shaking his head. "Tell me you're joking."

"About my sister?" Cally asked. "Or her vanishing. Neither. That girl has some answers to cough up."

"What did she want that was worth breaking cover after this long?" Papa asked. He looked surprised and puzzled. No wonder. This was the first personal contact any of them had had from Michelle since they "died." Cally couldn't sort the rest of the jumble of emotions out from his face. Hell, she was having trouble sorting out her own.

"She wants to hire us. I don't know what for. I'm supposed to talk to her again tomorrow night. Did you know she's apparently rich as Croesus?"

"What, she's talking about *personally* hiring us? To hell with that. How is she?" Granpa asked.

"She's . . . very Indowy. But seems to be healthy and everything. Could use some extra food in my opinion. She was in mentat's robes, like always." They had gotten a hologram a year through Indowy sources until the split seven years ago. Since then, it was more like a hologram every two or three years, whenever the O'Neal Bane Sidhe—and she still winced at the organization's new name—could get an operative close enough, on some other business, to sneak a picture. It didn't really matter. They could just replay the old holograms. She never changed.

"My stuff?" she prompted Harrison again.

"All the gear's in the trunk," Tommy said.

"But you got my shoes out, right?" She dangled the high heels from their straps. Her look spoke volumes.

"Uh . . ." Tommy hesitated. His experience of women frustrated with painful shoes had taught him that he usually wanted to be far, far away. Women did best with cute shoes when they only wore them long enough take them off—or at least didn't walk on them much.

"Sorry, darling. Forgot. I always find the grav belt a tad awkward." Harrison looked like he really was sorry.

"You wouldn't have had to wear them in the first place if you'd gone out the same way you went in," Papa O'Neal grumped.

"I told you, Granpa, I flew the friggin' thing way up to the top of the damned building, and I didn't trust it not to give out then. No way was I gonna do it twice if I had a choice. What kind of moron thought it was a good idea to fly around hanging from some stupid belt?" She examined the shimmering pink nails of one hand. "Besides, you know I hate heights."

"The only fatalities flying the belt have been either from sabotage or a direct hit in combat." Her grandfather shrugged, apparently wise enough not to say anything more on the subject.

Cally regarded it as a mark of extreme dedication to her job that she'd let them talk her into this mission at all. Never again. And it was high time she thought about something, anything else.

"Excuse me, y'all. I've got to check in or Morgan and Sinda will pout at me." She looked down at her PDA to dial, but the phone on the other end was already ringing, reminding her that she really needed to turn the buckley's intelligence emulation level down before it crashed itself.

"Buckley, you didn't call directly, did you?" she asked.

"What do you think I am, stupid? No, when they catch us all and kill us, it won't be my fault. Can I give you a rundown of our current tactical vulnerabilities?"

"Shut up, buckley."

"Ri—" It cut off as hundreds of miles away a phone was answered.

"Hello?" A soft female voice answered. Cally still marveled that the voice didn't sound even a little bit harried.

"Hi, Shari. I'm done for the evening and thought I'd call in. How are the girls doing?"

"Sinda's out like a light. She really wore herself out in Aunt

Margret's dance class. Morgan's almost finished with her homework. I'll get her."

Seven minutes later, the limo turned into the parking lot of a vintage car dealership, pulling around back to park. Its four occupants piled out and into the building, taking the hidden elevator in the back of the broom closet down to the tunnel. In the small antechamber at the bottom, they carefully hung their dress clothes on the cleaning rack and racked their shoes and equipment. Cleaning was no longer a euphemism for precautionary destruction—not always. Things tended to be figleafed with a new look and reused as much as possible. It wasn't terribly safe, but then it wasn't a safe business. She tucked the small evening bag inside a pocket of a larger purse that had already been prepped.

Cally and Harrison got the makeup table to themselves for a few minutes while Tommy ran the standard post-op checks, downloads, and scrubs on the surveillance equipment and Papa dictated the post-op report into his PDA. By the time they were ready for their own turn at the table, she and Harrison were through. She smiled gratefully as he ushered her over to a stool and went to work on her neck and shoulders. Certified massage therapist was not on the list of desirable secondary skills for operational team members. It should've been, and Cally was personally grateful for the luck of the draw that had put Harrison available for field assignment just when Granpa was filling the vacancies on the team left by her sabbatical and Jay's timely demise.

She knew the rest of the team, while glad to have her back, still missed George Schmidt. She could understand that. George was a damned good assassin and field man. Unlike his more flamboyant brother, he could blend into a crowd easily, either as a shortish, nondescript man or a teenage boy, if he chose. He had needed the brotherhood of being part of a working team to pull him through that awkward and painful grieving time after losing his father-in-law to the enemy, and then his wife to a sudden and severe infection bare months afterwards. Everyone agreed that her grief had weakened her system, and in the immediate aftermath of the organizational split of the humans from all but a small remnant of the Indowy and other galactics, the O'Neal Bane Sidhe had discovered quite unpleasantly just how much their internal emergency medical services had relied on access to the slab. Sherry Schmidt had been one of the casualties of the chaos.

It was good for George to have had Harrison to get him over the hump of anger, where you just wanted revenge and wanted to kill any and every enemy culpably connected with your loss. Assassination was one job where you couldn't be impersonal forever and stay sane, but you couldn't let it get too personal, either. It was like walking a razor's edge all the time, while accepting horrible danger and risks of loss. Not many people could do it. She'd never figured out if she was supremely lucky or supremely unlucky that she could.

By common consent they let Tommy and Papa leave first. Harrison didn't follow baseball, and she wouldn't have been able to stay for the game, anyway. Seventeen minutes after they left, she slid behind the wheel of her ancient, primer-colored Mustang. One of the things she liked about Harrison was he understood her need to drive her own car now and again. A natural gearhead, he had restored, enhanced, and carefully tuned the car so that it had more power than your average police interceptor, but had artistic rattles and clinks. The ever-so-slight smoke out the exhaust that implied (falsely) that it would soon need a ring job was the perfect finishing touch. The best part was that she could turn the special effects off, taking her baby out on a nice open stretch of road to listen to the engine purr. She didn't get to do it often enough, with one thing and another. Still, she could feel the power under her right foot, and that'd do for now. They drove out of the city in silence, watching the stars come out as they got beyond the smog belt. In Indiana she turned up a dirt road between two cornfields and followed it around to the back of a grain silo, where she hit the garage door opener and drove into the vehicle elevator.

Underground—far underground—she parked it in her reserved space. One benefit of the split was plenty of parking. She waved Harrison off to whatever his evening plans were and went to turn in the night's take.

The Base had none of the graffiti and vandalism which so dated the various Sub-Urbs. Still, whether it was the smell of the air or dark lines in the little places that dirt gathered no matter how carefully you cleaned, there was an atmosphere of age about the place. After seven years it still seemed so empty she almost expected it to echo. Her black tennis shoes, of course, did nothing of the sort. As she walked from the south elevator to the workroom administration corridor she noticed someone had gotten creative with the Galplas again. The design wasn't bad at all. It appeared to be a rather interesting cross between Celtic knotwork and early circuit board. And the murals, probably done by the children, of Indowy engaged in daily tasks were pretty well done. She just wished they'd chosen a background color other than puce.

The Indowy she passed on the way were all people she recognized by name. Even after so long, they still traveled the corridors in pairs or triads where possible. She had been told it helped to cut the risk of agoraphobia.There had been initial talk about establishing breeding groups in the Base, but for some Indowy reason no one had explained to her it hadn't happened. Maybe it still would. She didn't know and for some reason had always felt it would be rude to ask. Instead, once or twice a year when a Himmit scout ship came through another one of Aelool's people would come inside, or two or three from Clan Beilil.

The other operatives had, in a way, had more time to adjust to the change. Since she had been home with the girls, not on base, for most of the past seven years, it always hit her as a shock to see the emptiness of Earth's central Bane Sidhe base since the split. It was very hard not to take that split personally, as centrally located in the whole mess as she had been.

First, her decision to kill the traitorous Colonel Petane, who had been partly responsible for the death of a Bane Sidhe team that had saved her life. The assassination had not only been without orders, but she'd done it after the leadership of the Bane Sidhe, the entire Bane Sidhe, had gone to considerable lengths to make her and Granpa think he was already dead. They had considered him an intelligence asset, and never revisited that decision after he turned out to be basically worthless. In retrospect, she agreed he was not only a fucking traitor, but a harmless schmuck. It wouldn't really have hurt anything to leave him alive. At the time, however, she had been truly livid at the deception that had deprived her, and Granpa, of giving their input to the decision.

That was the moment when the building tensions in the Indowy about how to relate to humanity, or whether they even wanted to relate to a species of carnivores that could and did kill other sophonts, finally started to come to a head. Clan Aelool and Clan

Beilil had had deep and recent experience with extreme clan-wide blood debts. Debts of honor, and debts of vengeance both. While Clan Roolnai and the rest of the clans had seen the assassination of Petane as a dangerous repeat of Granpa's assassination of someone on his own personal "better dead" list in Vietnam, and a sign of the fundamental homicidal instability of humanity, Aelool and Beilil had taken the view that Team Conyers had saved the clan head of Clan O'Neal, the O'Neal himself, in saving Michael O'Neal, Senior. This had made the blood debt to Team Conyers a much graver matter, and the concealment of Petane's continued existence an offense against Clan O'Neal as a whole. Aelool and Beilil, victims of the worst of the massacres on Diess, apparently felt the guilt of this offense the most keenly, feeling the strongest debt to Clan O'Neal because of the actions of her father on Diess. They had, after much internal discussion, taken the mostly private position that Cally had been acting on behalf of Clan O'Neal to discharge a debt the clan owed to Team Conyers.

The Indowy concept of loyalty, called loolnieth, did not translate very well into English or any other human language. The loyalty was all up chain to the clan. The mere idea of down-chain loyalty to individuals was, by Indowy standards, perniciously insane. It made perfect sense, applied to their species. Individuals were overwhelmingly plentiful, and clans were few. The only protection the vast majority of individuals had for their safety and the safety of their offspring *was* the security of the clan as a whole. Additionally, the Indowy breeding groups precluded anything like the human nuclear family.

Another facet in the split had been that the Indowy Aelool had, by far, the greatest understanding among his people of humanity as a species. He understood, in some small sense, why human reproductive patterns dictated that loyalty that did not go at least partly down chain as well as up was disastrous to any tribe that adopted it. He understood why a social convention that was insane for his own species was not only sane but necessary for humanity, especially its predominant surviving variants. In his understanding, he was as rare as humans who truly understood why Indowy loolnieth worked—for Indowy. It was not, as some in the cyberpunk faction supposed, a corrupt and dishonorable reaction to oppression by the Darhel. It was not some Indowy feeding others to the tiger in the hopes that the tiger would eat them last. Instead, it was just another example of the truism that aliens are alien.

In retrospect, she'd had to admit that lack of human understanding of the Indowy had been as much a cause of the Bane Sidhe split into the Traditional Bane Sidhe and the O'Neal Bane Sidhe as the reverse. Perversely, it made her feel better to acknowledge that. She certainly hadn't been responsible for human misunderstanding of the Indowy, whatever else she might have done.

The final break, the break that had resulted in the other clans packing up their delegations and leaving Earth, also cutting themselves off from any human agents the Bane Sidhe had managed to cultivate off Earth, had also revolved around her. According to the majority faction of the Bane Sidhe, her capture on Titan Base had presented a neat solution to the problem of a renegade agent and was best left alone without risk of further exposure for the organization or expenditure of organization assets. Loolnieth owed no allegiance to an individual operative, however occasionally useful.

The Indowy Aelool, Father O'Reilly, Granpa, and the entire leadership of what would become the O'Neal Bane Sidhe realized that if Cally had been abandoned to torture and death without even an attempt to determine if rescue was feasible, especially if a component of the decision was her personal inconvenience, the ability to retain and recruit human operatives would have been compromised to the point of destruction. The operatives that could have been recruited would have been mercenaries with little loyalty to the organization and would, every one, have represented horrendous risks of exposure. The cyberpunk faction would have bolted outright, drastically reducing the ability of the Bane Sidhe to operate on Earth. The cyberpunks had signed on with the Bane Sidhe back during the war, but they had always harbored extreme reservations about the Indowy and had never truly integrated with the noncyber operatives. Cally had been admired and respected in the cyber community largely because she was admired and respected by Tommy Sunday. The O'Neals and Sundays had forged strong ties over the decades, including the development of Edisto Island as a unique refuge for the human resistance. When it was impolitic to ask for a close friend or family member, a completely trustworthy one, to be taken in by the Bane Sidhe itself, the Edisto operation had smuggled many to new lives.

None of that had mattered to Granpa or Tommy at the time. They would have pursued any feasible extraction plan to save her. However, the larger political calculus had meant that the next time she saw the Base, the other side of the split was mostly packed and gone. Aelool and Beilil had taken the position that the O'Neal was making a decision as clan head to preserve a vital asset of his clan, and had also pointed out the "as yet" tiny size of Clan O'Neal and the corresponding magnification of the value of each member. Cally thought that may have been just an excuse, out of blood loyalty from the Battle of Diess. If so, she could live with that. Loyalty was loyalty.

She shook herself out of her reverie as she passed an Indowy with a bay mare, about six and a half hands and clearly gravid, headed down to the trotting ring. Obviously "travelling in pairs" included their equine pets. Hey, whatever worked. It wasn't like they were going to run short on corn any time soon, and hydroponics easily turned out everything else.

She passed through workroom administration and back into equipment supply. Someone had obviously reported her presence, because Aelool and Father O'Reilly had preceded her and were standing next to a machine she hadn't seen before, chatting. It was a plain gray cube with beveled edges. Small seams outlined shapes on its surface that were probably panels of some sort. Other than shape, the thing it most reminded her of was the slab. God, she missed the slab. She rubbed the small of her back with one hand as she took the small evening bag out of her purse, opened the pouch, and handed it over.

Father O'Reilly took it without comment and placed one of the keys against a matching shape where it clicked into place, only to click back out almost immediately as a beep nearly too high for human ears sounded and a spate of Galactic Standard appeared in the air above the device.

"Cally, *what the hell did you steal?*" Father O'Reilly asked, looking at the readout.

"*Me?*" she spluttered. "You're the one who told me to! I followed that ops plan to the letter." *Well, okay, the ops plan did not say get the drawer's override code from your Michon Mentat sister, but it's the thought that counts.*

Aelool's ears had turned in slightly and shoulders tightened in the expression Cally had learned to interpret as "pensive."

"It is not a disaster. It is simply not useful to us at this time." His tone said not useful ever.

"What's wrong with it? It was where you said it would be. It looked just like the holograms in the briefing. Is it broken or something?" *Okay, bad enough that I have to stoop to being a cat burglar. Money's tight, I know that. But I would like to at least not be blamed for someone else's bad intel.*

"Cally O'Neal, it is not that it is broken. And it is not your error. It is that our generator is only authorized to read and execute level three and lower code keys. One of many redundancies in a system designed with the best of intentions to prevent dangerous industrial accidents. It is unfortunately also useful as a tool of political control." Aelool explained patiently, "These are simply more powerful keys. Almost certainly level fours, or perhaps even level fives."

"But you sounded like they aren't worth anything. It seems like we could at least fence them. Can't we?"

"No. It is that we cannot use them ourselves and they are too overheated to fence." He sighed.

"Too hot?" she echoed.

"Isn't that what I said?" He cocked his head at an angle in a questioning gesture he'd copied from humans and other terrestrials.

"More or less. So it was a busted mission after all. Sorry. Other than that, is there a problem?" Cally would have been the first one to admit that the business side of the organization was not her forte.

"The Darhel will not be happy. But it was a low budget mission and a small cost to us. And Darhel happiness has never been one of my priorities." His face crinkled, amused.

"You lost *what?*" The Epetar Group executive suddenly understood why the useless, decayed, folth of an underling, Pardal, had insisted on a meeting without any Indowy body servants and had meticulously searched out and disabled the spy devices from rival groups that tended to accumulate over time. He began his breathing drill and spent a few moments making sure he had himself under full, tight control before continuing.

"You have delayed *shipping,*" he said coldly, raising a hand to forestall interruption by his hapless subordinate. His clear displeasure did nothing to detract from the hypnotic, melodious tones for which his species was renowned.

"You will explain to me how any Darhel, however incompetent, can contrive to lose six level nine nanogenerator code keys in a single night. You will explain this in detail. You will pause when necessary to control yourself and you will *not* go into lintatai before you have completed your explanation. Afterwards *feel free*."

CHAPTER TWO

Kieran Dougherty was not a tall man. Not to put too fine a point on it, he was downright short. At least, he thought so. When he was on the ground. Which was one reason he liked to fly. The gray-eyed man with short, straight mouse-brown hair and an extensive collection of freckles liked to fly the way retrievers like to swim. The biggest design flaw of airplanes, in his opinion, was that they usually had to land to be refueled. The other options were unfortunately beyond the resources of his organization at the moment. Still, he could accept that, just as he could accept that an old and perpetually restored puddlejumper was a lot less conspicuous than something with a lot more range and capability. Besides, he liked prop-driven planes. You could really feel the air in them. Not that he would have turned down something newer and fancier, mind you. He stopped daydreaming and focused his full attention as he began his descent for Charleston. Any way you cut it, his worst day flying was still better than a day stuck on the ground.

As he slid into the pattern, Schmidt strapped into the copilot seat beside him and looked out the window at the city lights as they came in. When he wasn't talking to the tower, Dougherty kept his mouth shut. He knew Schmidt was listening to the engines. It wasn't by the book, but damned if Harry wasn't the best aircraft mechanic he'd ever had. The guy loved engines, and was almost psychic in his ability to detect anything that wasn't quite right with "his" bird. He was pretty damned good with the other stray aircraft they had to cope with now and again on this crazy job, too.

After landing, he got Lucille into the hangar and left her to Schmidt while he went outside for a cigar, waving goodbye to Cally and Papa as they wheeled a couple of carefully anonymous black and gray bikes out the back door, mounting up and disappearing through the chain link fence, hair and faces hidden under the ubiquitous black helmets. Charleston airport was salty, and sandy, and the air was thick with cold moisture that smelled like rain. Wind blew sand against his cheeks and he had to squint to keep the little bits of grit out whenever the wind shifted. He took deep drags off the Cuban cigar, staring at nothing and wishing he was still in the air. He finished it and dropped the butt in the ashcan by the door before going back in to hear Harry's update on his aircraft.

"So how is she?" He looked over to Schmidt, who was whistling as he pulled on a coverall and got his toolbox out of its locker.

"Well, she sounds real good. I should be able to just go down the list and have her all checked out before I leave tonight." He pulled a wrinkled and oil-stained piece of paper out of the box and spread it out neatly on the rolling cart where he was beginning to lay out the well-used and carefully cared-for tools in their precise places. Harry didn't really need the list, he was just a touch obsessive. Dougherty could understand that. It was one reason he trusted the other man to work on Lucille. On the other hand, Dougherty had a personal life, sort of, when he wasn't in the air. Since he'd been assured he wouldn't get to fly again for at least seventy-two hours, he was eager to go make the acquaintance of the pitcher of stout that was calling his name. Maybe even find a girl with the right combination of looks and loneliness. And a no expectations of permanence. A few minutes later he waved cheerfully to the security guard, leaving the airport in search of beer and women. Song was optional.

Cally shared a lane with Granpa on their way home. She still missed her little apartment, but she wouldn't trade the girls for anything, even if motherhood did mean moving back home. Oh, she hired one of Wendy's granddaughters to play nanny whenever she expected to be gone for awhile, but there still needed to be someone to watch over all the details and make sure everyone got where they should be on time and all the bills got paid. If Granpa was Clan O'Neal's patriarch and clan head, Shari had matriarchy down pat. The O'Neal Bane Sidhe hid their headquarters in a Himmit-camouflaged mini Sub-Urb deep under Indiana. The Clan O'Neal hid its headquarters in plain sight in a sprawling farmhouse, in the swampy pine woods of Edisto Island.

Technically bounty-farmers, living under various names and identities, the O'Neals and the Sundays, their immediate in-laws, and assorted Bane Sidhe waifs and strays had kept the area on and around the island swept clean of all but the occasional stray abat, the pests, for at least twenty years. It would have been inaccurate to call the clan self-sufficient on the local land and sea. They had a source of working capital. The Clan O'Neal men (by now the Sundays were regarded as a cadet branch) who planned to work for the Bane Sidhe tended to seek training, and find it, in the armed services. While Fleet Strike and Fleet remained the primary armed forces of the Galactic Federation, the various United States and Canadian military organizations still remained. Missions tended to be against pirates or insurgents. Or the U.S. military "loaned" units to Fleet or Fleet Strike, or other Galactic interests, for specialty functions. To limit the problems associated with being off-planet and unavailable, the O'Neals tended to gravitate to what was still called counterterror special ops. Large parts of the country on both coasts still lay in ruins, but the United States was no more able to survive without the rest of the world now than it had been prewar. The war itself had been a special case, but strategic resources from overseas were as important now as they ever had been. In modern times, counterterror really meant protecting those strategic resources and the trade lanes that served the many single-export colonies.

The clan members' service in the military provided excellent training while continuing an honored family tradition, albeit under assumed identities. It also brought hard currency into the Clan community. Their pay covered goods and services that the island community couldn't make or grow for themselves. It stretched the dollars from the small cash crops some of the women grew each year. Low-country agriculture had been a hand-to-mouth proposition long before the war, and the O'Neals didn't go in for tourism, great beaches or not. Still, shipping by moonlight was an old and revered tradition along the North American coastline. A couple of what she still thought of as "the kids" had quite a talent for it.

Having grown up with just Granpa, and then having lived alone for so long, Cally still felt vaguely claustrophobic if she stayed too long in what had become a happy, if chaotic and often quarrelsome, jumble of aunts and uncles younger than she was mixed with all sorts of cousins, grown or growing. Not to mention various people relocated by the Bane Sidhe, who needed to live someplace anonymous for awhile. Without the slab, that added up to a good little small town, even though a number of kin had wrapped themselves up in very sincere identities and assimilated into the outside world. The Clan was careful to turn in enough Posleen heads for bounty, maintaining the illusion that the area was still infested. This brought in a little hard currency, but they were having to go farther and farther afield each year in search of prey.

Cally and Papa's drive didn't take as long as it could've, once they'd navigated the tunnel under the Charleston Wall. The O'Neals kept the track between Charleston and Edisto well maintained, but took pains to make it look dilapidated. When they got on a good patch of straightaway, they could really open up the engines and make some time. It would have been suicide without the buckleys running IR watch for whitetail deer. With them, it was merely foolhardy. But fun. Well, except for a bug that hit her helmet's air-intake and sieved into her mouth, leaving her spitting what tasted like grass the rest of the way. You took the good with the bad.

It was predawn by the time they got home, the sky turning slowly from blue-gray to gold. The sun wasn't up, and neither were most of the kids. One of the girls coming out to milk her cows waved to them as they pulled into the packed sand and shell driveway. They wheeled the bikes into the shed behind the house, racking the helmets neatly on a set of carved wooden hooks. As Cally climbed the cinderblock kitchen stairs and trudged down the creaky pine hallway to the add-on Granpa had built for her and the girls, she knew her ass was dragging. All that way and all that work for nothing. What a night. She checked that her shades were pulled down and sealed tight before shutting her door and going to bed, shedding shoes and clothes on the way. As long as it stayed dark, her body would neither know nor care that it was daytime out there. She needed at least a good six hours before she was going to feel human again. She patted the washcloth on her nightstand where Shari had left it. That was thoughtful. The sheets smelled faintly of lily of the valley as she snuggled between them and shut her eyes.

The grass was wet under her feet and her sneakers squelched loudly as she snuck through the trees, hunting rats. The twenty-two rifle in her hand was pointed upwards, away from any non-targets. Oh, God—she ducked as an owl flew past right in front of her face, a struggling rat between its claws. A rat with a human face. Oh no, not the faces again, I hate the faces. A twig broke next to her and she jumped, inadvertently pulling the trigger. The shot echoed loudly in the night. A woman beside her in an antiquated nun's habit sneered, "Stupid girl! You had your finger on the trigger. Now they've got you for sure." She tried not looking at the face, but the glazed eyes and tongue hanging out drew her own eyes upwards. And then she could hear the hissing growl and the thud of clawed feet behind her. The horses were coming for her. She dropped the rifle and ran and kept running, down the empty Galplas corridors, spattered and rust brown. There was a door and she didn't want to go in it but she had to hide. The door swung open and another one of the faces leered out from the darkness. "They'll kill you just like you killed me. But come in, come in. I was such a scumbag, I deserved it. You'll be in such good company, won't you, Cally?" Her T-shirt was plastered against her in cold sweat as she turned and ran again. They were closer now. Quick, into a ventilation shaft! And she was over the edge and falling, and the faces were in the walls again, going past as she fell, and she tried to scream but she—

She was sitting up in bed, her breath coming in gasps. The T-shirt she'd slept in was cold and wet on her skin. She grabbed her washcloth, burying her face in it and shuddering. *That was a bad one. They told me the dreams might come back when I started working again, but damn. What time is it, anyway?* She looked over at the alarm clock and groaned. *Only nine-thirty? Ah, hell. Might as well get up. No way I'm getting back to sleep after that.*

She pulled on a robe and a pair of big, cushiony slippers that had been fuzzy once upon a time, and wandered into the kitchen in search of coffee and breakfast. She yawned, feeling her back pop as she stretched out the kink that had somehow worked its way into her spine.

Shari was in the kitchen. Slim, her hair the gold of the dune grass on the beach, Cally's step-grandmother looked twenty-something, like all juvs in their first century. She'd been a middle-aged mother back in the war when Cally was just thirteen. Both women had old eyes—eyes that had seen too much. Shari's were more motherly and less haunted. The kind of mother's eyes that didn't miss a thing. She was loading her breakfast dishes in the dishwasher when Cally came into the kitchen. The O'Neals had to be careful to keep it quiet, but electricity was damn near free. When you had friends who played with antimatter almost as an afterthought, power for basic household needs wasn't a problem. Raising the kids to understand and follow blackout rules on the electric lights could have been rough, if they hadn't been doing it all their lives. To satellites or aircraft, what few there were, Edisto Island looked like just another war-wasted and not-yet-recovered stretch of wilderness. Well, it *almost* was. Secretive clannishness had, by now, become a set of ingrained habits. The O'Neals had learned some hard lessons about survival and had adapted and copied a few tricks from their Galactic friends. In a pre-Posleen world, Clan O'Neal would have been a flock of very odd ducks. In the modern world, they were survivors.

"You're up early. Not another nightmare?" A frown crinkled Shari's forehead as she pressed a mug into Cally's hands, "I just fixed a fresh pot. Carrie said you got in about milking time this morning."

"Yeah, she was just going out. The kids are at school?" Cally yawned again, pouring a mugful of the wonderful-smelling fresh, strong coffee, but neglecting to pollute it with cream or sugar. It didn't matter how many times they told her it was hard-coded, she was convinced she was keeping just a little of the extra weight off her thighs and chest by watching what she ate. She split a bagel and dropped it in the toaster.

"Mmm. I expected it would be almost time for them to get out and come home by the time you and Michael woke up. Pam works so hard on her lesson plans, it's a shame to have the girls miss a day. So, 'fess up, how long's it been since you went to confession?" Shari asked.

"Uh . . . a few months, I guess." Cally hedged. Actually, it had been more like eight months, since she'd gone back to work full time and been taken off of the six-monthly courier run to the Moon. *Dammit.*

"Go to confession. I'm not Catholic, but even I'll agree it does you more good than that fancy Bane Sidhe shrink ever did. Here," she said, putting a box of cornflakes and a bowl on the table. She turned to grab the milk. "Still can't see why you like that stuff when I've got cheese grits in the crockpot. It's not like you have to worry about your arteries. Go to confession." She must have thought Cally's pensive expression was disagreement because she shook the wooden spoon in her hand towards the younger woman. "You're my friend, Cally O'Neal, and I won't have you getting all shredded up inside again. It was bad enough when you were pregnant with Morgan. Go or I'll . . . I'll sic Michael on you!"

"All right, all right already. I'll go. Last thing I need is Granpa nagging." Cally said, crunching her cereal and wincing as the sound echoed in her skull against her headache. *God, I really needed more sleep.*

The younger woman was halfway through her breakfast when the door opened. A largish pile of dirty white fur and drool came bounding in, scattering sand across the clean floor. As Shari pulled the joyfully maniacal dog off of Cally and ushered it back out the door, she glared at her husband, who was shaking out his own shoes off the edge of the steps.

"Sorry, honey. He got past me again. Nagging about what?" Papa O'Neal looked sheepish as he shut the door behind the dog. He shook his head, looking for someplace he could politely spit. Shari handed him a mug and a broom.

"Good morning, Granpa. I thought you'd still be in bed." Cally said, brushing sand off her lap.

"When you're older and wiser, you'll have the sense to take a nap the day before a night job." Papa O'Neal sometimes seemed to forget he didn't look a day over twenty-five.

"Yes, Granpa. We all know the elderly sometimes need an afternoon nap," she said, brushing her hair back behind one ear. It was a habit from the Sinda persona she had never quite dropped.

"Elderly, hah! Who had the aches and pains last time we met in the gym?" He grinned, dodging as she took a swipe at him, and began to sweep.

"What were you thinking about for dinner tonight?" she asked Shari, pointedly ignoring Granpa as she drained her cup of coffee.

"I thought I'd make a crab and chicken casserole Pam came up with and get rid of a few leftovers. Why? What's on your mind?" Shari finished loading the dishes and started the machine.

"Just wondered if there was something I could fix to help out."

"If you could make something for dessert this afternoon, I'm sure the kids would like it. I could use something sweet myself." Shari took a cloth and began wiping down the counters.

"That works. I need to go down to Ashley's for some stuff. I can get the kids and make the weekend incinerator run if you want," Cally offered, glancing at the nearly full can.

"Thanks. Um, Mark's spending the night with Lucas. The keys to the truck are on the hook," Shari said absently, preoccupied with slapping away the hand that was playing around the belt loops on the back of her jeans. She wasn't slapping very hard. Cally smothered a grin and grabbed up the bag and the keys as she scooted out the door, reminding herself not to get back *too* quick.

Years ago, when she was a teenager freshly home on summer break, she had ridden cross-country with Granpa in a dusty red pickup truck from the School, in Idaho. They came back through all of the midwestern rear area country, until they met up with Shari in Knoxville, where she'd been filling the shopping list. It seemed Granpa had shamelessly used the slab and about a dozen different identities, with some judicious palm grease, to buy up the bounty farm allotments for all of Edisto Island. Even back then, she could easily imagine him going through all the changes, because it still looked strange as hell to her to see him with red hair and all young and everything. He probably would have kept on buying until he'd owned half of Colleton County if Father O'Reilly hadn't gotten concerned and ratted him out to Shari.

Still, even the Bane Sidhe had had to agree that the possibilities were useful. And it was already a done deal by the time they'd realized what he was up to. Granpa got to keep his island, but the price for Cally was that her first summer home from school had been spent hunting Posleen and getting a crash course in low-country construction. Typically, Papa O'Neal had spent his free time during her first year of school in a combination of shady trades of Galtech goods from the Rabun Gap cache—those he didn't plan to keep for himself—and brushing up his construction skills doing day labor jobs.

The hardest part had been sweeping the island once they got there. Satellite shots showed the bridge was intact, but they hadn't known much else. And at the time Edisto Island was very nearly as far as anyone had penetrated into the Lost Zone. The ride in the back of truck, on the first load of mostly cinderblocks, ammo, and the bare necessities, watching the treeline for feral Posleen, had not been fun. Not fun at all. She'd gotten five of them, and that was just on her own side. The large, ochre, centauroid reptiles had to be the most repulsive things she'd ever seen.

She'd thanked God that Granpa had decided that speed was more important than profit and had put off taking the heads and hauling them on the truck to the first bounty outpost at Spartanburg. They were repulsive enough lying dead on the pavement leaking yellow ichor into the ground. Having that stinking mess in the truck right next to her would really have been too much, wrapped in a tarp or not. He'd sprung for the rental fee for a really big truck for that one, bringing down most of the parts of the house. Most of the parts of Granpa and Shari's house were, of course, Galactic materials. Extruded and formed to spec, they could laugh off a direct hit by a hurricane. And over the next couple of centuries, they probably would.

Sensors and scanners for civilians hadn't even been a dream in some bright boy's head that soon after the war. Making do with the Mark I Eyeball when a Postie just might have picked up a railgun from somewhere wasn't quite as terrifying as being in a bunker too damned near ground zero of a nuclear explosion, but it had been close. The worst part of the ride had been whenever they crossed a Postie bridge. She'd known they were structurally sound, of course, but the reminder of *organized* and technological Posleen had rubbed salt in memories that were all too fresh.

The first month on the island had been a hot and muggy hell, especially to a girl who'd recently acclimated to the Idaho mountain air. Sister Gabriella had really believed in PT, so at least she hadn't been out of shape. Standing her watch at night, stalking Posties from one end of the island to the other, bit by bit, in the day had been tiring and tedious. It wasn't that there were a whole lot of ferals. There weren't. Fleet and Fleet Strike and all the rest had done their job, and, once the God Kings were gone, the ravenous hunger of the feral Posleen normals had done even more. It was just that Posties, even single isolated feral normals, were so terribly nasty. At least she'd gotten to vent her frustration at the heat and the mosquitos and the sand in everything whenever they'd actually found a Posleen. Granpa didn't care, he'd just let her vent, as long as she didn't give him cause to scold her for wasting ammo. She didn't. Well, not more than once. And she'd had a really bad morning that day.

Shari's kids had stayed at a Bane Sidhe safehouse back in Knoxville that summer. Cally hadn't blamed her one bit for keeping them out of it. They hadn't been trained for any of this. She had. Well, she'd lived with Granpa during the war, which had amounted to the same thing. By the time they'd finished clearing the island, putting up the cinderblock and earth-berm-reinforced guardshack had been nothing. Guarding the bridge for the three days it had taken Granpa and Shari to bring back the big truck of building materials from Knoxville had been interesting. Before they left, she had helped Granpa and Shari load up the rotting but still identifiable Postie heads in the back of the pickup. Another nasty job.

Granpa had helped her run the line of tripwires connected to alarms back and forth across the bridge. It was still a day and a half before she could convince herself to take the time to sleep. In the end, only one of the moronic, leaderless feral normals had happened along and actually tried to cross the bridge. Then had come the icky task of chopping it into pieces she could carry and dropping them over the side of the bridge and down into the water. She pitied the aquatic scavengers that had to dine on the thing, but she could hardly leave it on the bridge to rot and attract more. And then she'd had to wrap the head and keep it so they could take it in for the bounty later. She'd made sure it was downwind.

After Shari and Granpa got back, having brought Billy to ride high sentry and help out, they'd reviewed the island looking for the best place to build. On a plot on the landward side, next to a big bay, Shari had found an old bit of street sign that had somehow survived the scavenging. It had said "Jungl" on the only bit that was left. Granpa had laughed and said that was home for him. The name had stuck, and even all these years later everybody still called it Papa's Jungle House. When they didn't call it Mama's house. Cally still couldn't figure out quite how it had happened, but over the decades Shari had somehow become honorary mother or grandmother to the whole island, whether the kids or grandkids or—hell, the relationships were all too confusing—were hers, or not.

When she was out and about, Cally could still see what she regarded as the O'Neal touch in the layout of the island. Everything was downplayed to any potential observer on land, sea or overhead. Trees and brush and dunes broke up vertical outlines and while planted fields were impossible to hide, a whole lot could be done with roofs and netting. Between irregular overhangs and creative use of vegetation, most roofs couldn't be distinguished from the air. Hiding, of course, wasn't the point. Obfuscation was enough. With so many people moving into the Lost Zones, the purpose was to make the O'Neal compound seem just one more group of poor but independent bounty-hunters.

The houses of O'Neals and Sundays were not showplace houses, designed to be artistic, designed to be seen. Rather, they were designed to fade into the background. Shrubbery and vegetation around the houses wasn't planted to artistically enhance, but to blur straight lines and obscure. A prewar Green would have loved it. All so artistic. All so earthy. All so . . . deadly.

Cally savored the smell of the salt on the brisk fall air as she walked across the road from the parking lot to pick up the kids. The olive drab pack on her back, brought along for the groceries, helped block the wind. She'd worn her shooting glasses to keep the fine, blowing sand out of her eyes. The school was only about a klick from the house, and right across from the small building that served as a local barter market and grocery store. She wouldn't even have driven if there hadn't been the trash to haul. Ashley Privett, Wendy and Tommy's oldest, had made a good business out of selling baked goods when she'd first arrived on the island some years ago, and over time had evolved into a sort of barter grocer, keeping track of what came in from whom and selling on consignment.

After the BS split, Cally had figured out a way to stretch her shrunken salary by using half her personal baggage allowance on each trip between home and base carrying something abundant one place and scarce in the other. Consequently, her pack was about half full with jars of soy sauce, corn syrup, four quart jars of moonshine, and some bagged popcorn. Bringing corn to the low country would have been like bringing sand to the beach except for the relative difference in price, and that the Indiana popcorn popped a lot better. She'd gone out with two pounds each of roasted coffee beans, baking chocolate, cane sugar, homemade cigars, a pack of vanilla beans, three bottles of rum, and a bolt's worth each of indigo denim and unbleached shirt-weight oxford cloth. Her market for stone-ground hominy grits had gone out in the first year, after one of the women on the cleaning crew on Base had figured out how to make it herself. It had been a niche market, anyway. Besides, cloth was better. There was always a market for blue jeans. She supposed she was technically a smuggler, among other things. Not like it mattered. Assassin, smuggler, thief, but not a drunk—it's kind of hard to become an alcoholic when your blood nannites break it down before you ever feel the effects. Not a brawler—well, mostly. Not a rapist—she'd heard it *was* technically possible, but it wasn't to her tastes or her needs, even if she had been celibate for months now. *Dammit.*

That was the worst thing about getting back on the team. Her six-monthly regular courier slot to the moon would be given to someone else on light duty, and she'd have to find some other way to arrange time with James. Okay, Stewart. And of course she couldn't explain why she wanted to keep the courier route. She couldn't even ask to keep it. She'd been lucky to get it in the first place. James had been on Earth for conferences twice since Morgan was born. Unfortunately for her love life, she was probably going to have to wait until he could get down here again. Anything less wasn't an option. In forty or so years' work for the Bane Sidhe, she'd had enough casual sex to last multiple lifetimes. She'd denied it often enough, even to herself, but she'd been looking for "the real thing." Having found it, she was hardly going to settle for less. Oh, if the fate of humankind was at stake, she wasn't going to be a prude, but she'd also determined to say no to plans that involved her as a honey trap if it was just a matter of getting information faster or cheaper. Sure, sometime faster or cheaper might mean life was on the line. But more frequently than not, it wasn't. Motherhood was an excuse for saying no. It sometimes meant they weren't happy with her, but under the circumstances, she could live with that.

Still, it was good that Granpa owned the island free and clear.

Before the split, her pay had been enough to keep a footloose single girl in beer and skittles, but hadn't been anything to write home about. Since the split, if she hadn't moved back home, she'd be struggling to make ends meet for herself, let alone the girls. It frustrated James that he couldn't help, of course. But in her business, having more money than you ought was dangerous. Bosses were understandably paranoid about who else might be paying their covert operatives, and for what. Fortunately, since the smuggling was almost a public service to the organization, it was honest income. Enough for a bit extra for Christmas and birthdays, anyway. Saving the world was great for warm and fuzzy feelings, but the pay sucked.

She kicked at the sand and a bit of some scrubby creeping plant with one foot, frowning as the sand in her sneaker reminded her of the hole she had worn through the sole. Still, living in the next thing to paradise was a nice compensation on its own, thanks to Granpa. And if paradise was gritty and placid and boring, those were what made a good place to raise kids. Even if the Bane Sidhe had made her into a thief. At least every mission she went out on to steal something was one mission where she probably could manage not to kill anybody. That was something, wasn't it?

She shoved her hands in the pockets of the olive drab windbreaker she'd pulled on over a faded red T-shirt and jeans. The fall wind was starting to cut right through the holes at her knees and back pocket. Time to patch this pair. She stepped over a dried palmetto frond that had gotten blown together with spanish moss and downed leaves.

The external walls of the little schoolhouse were plastered with tabby and screened with vegetation; the thin sheet of Galplas that surfaced the roof had been tuned to a camouflage pattern Shari had done up on her PDA. The windows, while clear, had been coated with a thin film that kept the sunlight from glaring off of them, although they still admitted daylight and allowed the children to see out. On the side closest to Granpa's and Shari's was one of the small concessions to color that the teacher and some of the mothers had insisted on—the children's flower garden. Currently, there was a small carpet of pansies peeking mischievously out at the afternoon sunlight. It was another reason Cally picked up the kids herself in the afternoons whenever she could—the flowers were nice.

Most of the kids were out on the obstacle course by now. Well, okay, there was a seesaw and a rope swing, when somebody wasn't climbing it. The monkey-bars and tower and such were all kid-sized, and the kids tended to attack everything from the cargo nets to the tower in no particular order, substituting random, chaotic enthusiasm for the single-mindedness of adult PT. Still, the O'Neals and Sundays and various children of Bane Sidhe families were the only children she'd ever seen play hide and go seek in ghillie suits. At four, Sinda hadn't quite gotten the idea yet. She was sitting under the tree happily weaving flowers and bits of brightly colored construction paper into the new section of loose, unbleached cotton netting Granpa had given her last week.

"Mommy!" Morgan yelled, dropping off the rope swing and running across the packed sand. Sinda, whose head had jerked up as soon as she heard her sister cry out, wasn't far behind her, having left her netting behind her on the ground. Cally crouched down and spread her arms, catching one girl in each, and enjoyed the best moment of her day.

"Did you two have a good day?" she asked, looking into one set of green eyes and one set of brown ones. Sinda's honey-blonde hair hung around her shoulders in curls. Morgan's straighter and shorter brown hair looked like she'd been rolling around in the sand.

She braced herself for impact as a little red-haired girl, liberally daubed with fingerpaint, crashed into the three of them. "Aunt Cally! Aunt Cally!" she squealed.

Cally picked up three-year-old Carrie, who was actually technically *her* aunt, weird as that was, and planted her on one hip. "Hiya, squirt!" she said.

"Come look at my Billy suit, Mommy!" Sinda started dragging her over to the now brightly decorated piece of netting, while Morgan said something about her books and ran inside.

Cally looked down at the netting as her four-year-old pulled it over her head like a scarf and preened at her. "It's a very colorful ghillie suit. The most colorful one I've ever seen," she said.

"Do you just love it?" Sinda asked.

"It's very pretty. But isn't it going to stand out when you play hide and go seek with the other kids?"

Sinda's forehead wrinkled a bit. "I could hide in the flowers!"

"Every time?" Cally said.

Sinda nodded cheerfully. "I like flowers. They're my favorite."

"Okay. Are y'all ready to go to the store?" Cally asked as Morgan came back, a blue denim backpack slung over one small shoulder.

They walked across a path that had bits of pavement, indicating it probably had once really been a street, to the store. Privett's Grocery was a weathered gray pine building, almost a shed, really, with a mud-brown roof of Galplas tiles and a couple of windows with big, gray, storm shutters latched open against the walls. A bright splash of color came from the fresh fruits and vegetables displayed in wooden carts on the front porch. The carts were obviously new, the boards the golden white of fresh, unweathered pine.

As soon as they got in the door, Carrie started struggling and Cally put her down. The girls drooled over the assortment of fudge behind the counter while she swapped her trade goods, incoming for outgoing, and picked out her own groceries. Shari's cabbages hadn't survived this year, so Cally grabbed a head of cabbage for coleslaw, and a bottle of lemon juice that must have been put up last year. A pitcher of lemonade would be a nice treat for everybody. She got each girl a small piece of fudge wrapped in rice paper, fighting the temptation to buy one for herself. Christmas was just around the corner, and it was going to be tight this year. Besides she *was* making brownies for dessert. Halfway down the steps she turned around and went back for the square of fudge. It was definitely getting to be time to do something about her salary.

CHAPTER THREE

Granpa was quiet as he fought with the tie-downs on the tent-roof thingy they were putting up over the picnic table. Cally knew it said gazebo on the box, but she'd seen plenty of gazebos in Indiana—white, wooden, merry-go-round buildings without the ride. This was just a square tent roof with four poles and top to bottom mosquito netting. She got the zipper to work and zipped the mosquito netting from bottom to top outside her pole, moving on to the next one. Shari was grilling some hotdogs for the little kids, and had a shrimp boil going for the adults.

Cally had really hated having to tell Granpa that "our" meeting with Michelle was really *her* meeting with Michelle. She'd felt like she'd just taken away a kid's Christmas candy. He hadn't said much, then or since. She'd passed on Michelle's excuse, and cringed when he'd tried to wave it away as "no bother" to him as Clan Head. From the way Michelle had sounded, it hadn't seemed like she'd show unless Cally was alone. Granpa didn't understand, of course. She didn't, either, but she wasn't the one being left out. Telling him had been just awful.

Soon they'd gotten the netting down, which was more to stop the blowing sand than anything, all sensible mosquitos having decided to stay out of the cold, or whatever it was mosquitos did. She looked at her watch and threw a side-glance at Granpa. Neither one met the other's eyes. She looked up at Shari, whose eyes plainly said she didn't want to be involved.

"I guess it's about that time. I'll be back in a bit," Cally said. Granpa just grunted in reply. *Not gonna be a real relaxed dinner, is it?*

Cally picked her way through the tall grass to a set of ancient railroad-tie stairs and started down onto the beach. She looked out at the waves hitting the shore and sighed, futilely trying to tuck her hair behind her ears. The wind insisted on blowing it right into her face. She dug an elastic band out of her jeans and pulled it back in a ponytail. It made her look about sixteen. Twelve, if it hadn't been for the boobs, which she still considered overwhelming. She sighed, but it wasn't like anyone but family was here to see her. The impression of adolescence was complete as she walked down the beach, scuffing her feet in the sand.

"Where are you going?" The voice came from behind her and Cally jumped, spinning around in a crouch.

"Ack! Don't *do* that!" Cally clutched a hand to her chest and looked back up toward the girls, letting a breath of relief out that they were still sitting at the table and maybe hadn't noticed anything unusual. "You didn't just appear out of nowhere, did you?"

"Please give me credit for some sense. I came in behind that pile of rubble." Michelle gestured at the crumbling remains of some cinderblock structure or other. "I only walked down when I saw you. So it seems I am finally at a beach with you."

"Yeah," Cally said. There was an uncomfortable silence. "Before we get into the mission, real quick, can I ask you a question about nanogenerator code keys?"

"Your employers do not have the capability to make use of the keys you stole." It wasn't a question.

"Right. Our people say they're level fours and would be difficult to fence," Cally said.

"The current price of six level four code keys would be sixty thousand seven hundred and forty-eight point zero nine seven FedCreds as of close of business at the Chicago Trade Consortium. I would be willing to pay that amount for the keys you took from the Darhel last night. Do you agree to carry my offer to your employers? It would be an arrangement of benefit to Clan

O'Neal." If possible, Michelle's voice was even more expressionless, and she stood still in her mentat robes. They should have been blowing in the wind, but weren't. The wind wasn't allowed to so much as ruffle her hem, and Cally was suddenly aware of the sand in her own shoes and the blowing wisps of ultra-pale blonde hair that had escaped from her ponytail.

Michelle had clearly inherited her height from their father and Granpa. Her petite five foot nothing had an almost boyish slimness that made her sister feel awkward in her own tall frame. If she could have seen herself through the eyes of others, the unlikely assassin would have realized her comparatively small waist and Scandinavian features made her look more like a nineteen-nineties calendar girl than the chubby teenager she imagined. If Captain Sinda Makepeace had been anything, she'd been strikingly attractive. Cally's physical appeal had not suffered from being stuck in the other woman's semblance when the Indowy and Tchpth yanked the slab off Earth. Unconsciously, she arched her back and stood straighter in a seven-year habit designed to minimize her imagined defects.

"Okay, we'll sell you the keys. My bosses will probably be thrilled I found a safe buyer. Now, what couldn't you tell me last night?" Cally asked.

"I could have told you all of it. But you seemed rushed." Michelle said. Cally looked for any sign that she was making a joke, but couldn't see one. Perhaps Indowy-raised mentats didn't have anything as mundane as a sense of humor.

"First, you need a way to reach me with questions about the mission. There must be some kind of indicator you can set somewhere for me to see. I can not watch you every minute of every day—I have work I must do. I would prefer a day's notice in advance of a meeting, if possible. This is your specialty, is it not? Do you have any suggestions?"

"Um . . . lemme think. There are several message boards on the Perfect Match singles site on the web. When I need to meet you, I'll place a message on the pre-date board. The message should be from MargarethaZ, capitol 'M,' capitol 'Z,' no spaces. It should go to whoever you are. Say . . . Apollo555. I'll post it the day before I need you, or include the word 'diamond' if it's an emergency and I need you sooner. You can find me, right? And check that I'm alone? If we don't have to set up a code for meeting time and place, it makes it a lot less complicated and a lot harder for anyone else to twig to."

"Do I need to know what a singles' site is? Never mind, I am sure it will be clear enough. MargarethaZ, Apollo555, and diamond. I will remember." Michelle nodded. "Here is a broad outline of the mission. I have a colleague, a fellow mentat, who has recently acquired an obscure piece of very old technology and developed it into a problematic device. It is a device which should not remain in his keeping. I wish to hire your team to obtain the device and deliver it to me so that I can arrange safe storage for it. The priority is, however, on removing the device from the possession of this colleague. If a choice comes between damaging the device or failing to remove it, it is the removal which absolutely must be done to complete the contract."

"Okay. Are we supposed to just waltz in and take whatever this is?" Cally asked, her brow furrowing. "I presume you have a full description, location information, some background. Any recon data you have would be nice. Come on, I'm going to need the most complete information you can possibly give me for us to plan and execute this mission. First of all, what the hell is this device? What does it do, and what does it look like?" Cally glanced quickly up to where the candlelight was silhouetting the girls, glad that Morgan appeared to be putting their dinner things back in the packs.

"It is a discontinuous, partially automated, multichanneled, medium-range harmonic resonance inductor. I have a datacube for you with full external specifications, a very abbreviated overview of its known and theorized capabilities, and the location of the facility where it is being used." Michelle said, "Of course, you must absolutely avoid any direct confrontation with—"

"Whoa. Back up a second. It's a discon-what? What does it do, in plain English, please."

"I was speaking plain English. The best way I can describe the action is that it affects the brain, in this case of human subjects, stimulating and analyzing the internal signals for report and, if desired, overriding the internal voluntary muscle commands and other processes with replacement sequences of the operator's choosing."

"What, like reading minds? You're shitting me."

"Excuse me? What does excrem—nevermind. In a very nontechnical and imprecise sense, that is probably a workable functional estimate. Although it would be a mistake to overlook the capacity for control."

"It's a mind-raper."

"The process is reported to be quite unpleasant for the subject, yes."

"You're telling me this monstrosity really exists? Yuck!" Cally shuddered. "That's vile. That's really, really vile." She rubbed her hands up and down her arms, hugging herself. She almost thought she could feel the goosebumps.

"That is an adequate nontechnical description of the device's function. One reason I chose to hire your team for this mission is convenience of location. The research facility where the device is located is outside the Great Lakes Fleet Base. Obviously, they will have some sort of human security arrangements in addition to the automated systems. Your people are going to have to determine what those are and be prepared to deal with them. You must avoid any direct confrontation with the other mentat, Erick Winchon. You will need to use a time when Erick Winchon is absent. He has periodic absences from the facility, you'll need to determine his schedule and use one of them." Michelle paused, taking a deep breath. "The deadline for this job is January 15 of 2055, Earth time. By that date, I must have in my possession either the device itself or conclusive proof that it has been destroyed. The proof must be sufficient to pass a rigorous inspection by a Galactic Contract Court."

"What can you tell me about how the device is protected and guarded? I'll need the blueprints of the facility."

"Much of that you will have to determine yourselves. It is what your team does, is it not? I will, of course, get you any information I can without exposing my actions."

Cally rubbed her chin, thinking. "One of the classic ways of working this kind of mission involves a switch of a replica for the target item to postpone discovery of the theft. I need not only the external specifications of the device but everything you can tell me about the device itself and how it's used and when and by whom so that I can get a convincing replica made, if that's even possible. We'll do our research thoroughly, but the more you can tell us about the device, the better chance we have at constructing a convincing replica. The other solutions I can think of are all more complicated. That would mean more expensive, with more chances for something to go wrong."

"I do not think your organization could build a cosmetic replica that would fool the security systems or the lower level employees. I will build a facsimile of the device that should deceive anyone but another mentat. I will deliver the facsimile to you before the first opportunity to acquire the device arises." Michelle pressed a datacube into her sister's hand. "Hug your girls for me." She folded her arms closer in, a gesture that had immediately preceded her disappearance from Pardal's suite before.

"Wait!" Cally said.

"Yes?" The tightness in the mentat's arms loosened fractionally.

"You said you'd get us information if you could. If you have anyone inside, that could be vitally important. That's the biggest risk of the entire mission—it can take months to get a man inside a secure facility, or more. As I understand it, we don't have that kind of time, but we need that kind of subtlety to pull this off. We can work without it, but it sure would be a big help."

"I have a worker there who owes me a significant favor. He cannot help directly. It would place his actions too close to both violence and breaching his word. The favor owed is large, but not that large. I do not see how he could help you. He works off the main site, in their personnel department." There was a long silence as she thought, the wind off the sea at last ruffling a few stray tendrils of hair from her severe bun.

"Could he get you a list of any job openings? They've got to have vacancies, coming open feet first. Operations like these always do. If he could influence hiring decisions by losing some resumes or bumping ours to the top of the list, that would really help."

"Possibly. Do you have any idea how difficult it would be to 'lose' an electronic resume? Not to mention several. I will do what I can."

Cally placed a hand on Michelle's arm, only to take it back for no reason she could name, just that the mentat seemed somehow more withdrawn than before.

"There was something else?" her sister asked.

"Granpa was pretty hurt that you wouldn't see him, you know. Telling him was hard. I'd at least like to know why." She shoved her hands into her jeans pockets and stared out to sea.

"The split in the Bane Sidhe has created political difficulties between myself and the Indowy." Michelle didn't even twitch. Cally found it irritating.

"Oh, don't tell me you're shutting out Granpa because of your job. Do *not* tell me that." She fixed her sister with an icy, gimlet stare.

"You do not understand. I remind myself that you do not understand," Michelle said.

"Damn right I don't!"

"You need resources. I am, for now, able to help you. I can only keep the access to help you by avoiding the O'Neal. No, allow me to finish. Of course I want to see Grandfather. At present, I am what you might call 'in limbo,' but I am balanced upon the edge of a knife. It is for me as if the split had not yet taken place. I have not yet been officially informed of the change in clan policy and alliance by my head of clan, or an immediate ancestor, or his designate. I can pretend official ignorance. Among Indowy, this would be impossible. They would never go so long without a meeting. But humanity's asocial nature has the Himmit, Darhel, and Tchpth precedent. It is viewed as different but not insane. Clan O'Neal may desperately need my resources at some point. Once I meet with Grandfather, I must then confine my future dealings to Clan Aelool or Clan Beilil, and my resources will be greatly reduced. For myself, I would be well enough. But at the cost of greatly increased risk to the survivability of Clan O'Neal. The Indowy know that I must know, yet they know that the resources serve my clan. And so they cannot decide whether I am being supremely honorable, or supremely dishonorable. The thought is distressing to them, so they ignore it, waiting for the dilemma to resolve itself. Which may happen either by reconciliation of the O'Neal with one or more major clans, which is highly unlikely, or by my meeting with my clan head. I must maintain this delicate balance until our clan is secure. I admit that my understanding of the value of what it is that you do is limited, but I believe we both understand that loyalty requires personal sacrifices. As our estrangement through the years has been. Please believe me that this is a most regrettable sacrifice and convey my apologies to Grandfather for the necessity."

"Wait!" Cally said again, sensing that Michelle might be about to pull her vanishing act. "Michelle, I've gotta ask. Yes, this mind-raper thing is obviously a problem, but you've made contact after an awfully long time and you haven't done a lot of blatant things in the past to save the world. There's something different about this, and I have to know what it is."

"That does not concern you." Michelle's face could have been carved of stone.

"I can't do my job without the whole story. I *won't* take my team into this without all the background. We can keep it between us, but I'm responsible for my people. Now give." She made a come-on gesture with one hand, fixing her eyes on the mentat's face. Everything about her posture, ratty jeans and blowing hair or not, suddenly screamed "professional." It was a nonnegotiable demand.

"Very well. It was my project, for the Darhel group that holds my debts, when Erick stole the technology. They are holding me personally responsible." She shrugged beneath the enveloping robes, agitation betrayed by a slight fluttering of her hem as some of the wind finally got through.

"Wait a minute. How can you still be in debt and afford us, the code keys, all of that? I'm lost. This makes no sense." Cally said.

"I have disposable income. That is not the same thing as being out of debt. We never get out of debt. Even appearing to try will get your debts called in then and there. Every tool and tank I have is deeply mortgaged, as are the tools of everyone else. When I die, the equipment will revert to the Epetar Group to pay the debts. Unless the debt is called in beforehand, as it will be if I do not at least remove the device from the hands of the rival group."

"So what if they do call your debts? You can teleport. Just move on. Disappear. Let them take the damned tools and go to hell. It's not like it hasn't been done before. Just because you were raised by the Indowy doesn't mean you have to sit there and starve to death. We're human, not Indowy. You have to know there's no way we'd just leave you to your fate like they would one of theirs."

"Yes, *I* can teleport. The possibility of which is a secret held by few, and worth more than my life. My daughters cannot, and the Epetar Group also holds *their* debts. If you fail, I will let my debts be called and you certainly will leave me to my fate, for their sake and for the reasons you would not understand. But no, I would not wait to starve. There are quicker ways." The Michon Mentat squared her shoulders. "This discussion is pointless. You, and the very few who must know, can, at least, keep a secret. I have risked worlds and more on that decision—far more than I should. You must justify my trust," she pronounced.

"For the moment, we will presume my offering price for the code keys is acceptable. Here." She pulled a brown cloth bag out of her robes from somewhere, though for the life of her Cally couldn't see where, and thrust it into the blonde woman's hands. "Grandfather can carry out the next step in the dealings. I do not understand the purpose of the . . . work that you do, but you *are* quite effective at it and you will not fail. You will succeed at retrieving the device, or, if necessary, you will destroy it. It is an obligation to serve Clan O'Neal which you will understand. So the question of failure does not arise, does it?"

This time, she did vanish, leaving Cally staring at a pair of indistinct footprints, already being erased by the blowing sand. She shivered in the cold wind, sand stinging her face, as she turned and walked back up the beach. Summer was definitely over.

Michael O'Neal, Senior, sat on the comfortable but patched living-room sofa trying to talk some sense into his most lethal granddaughter. He was pretty proud of how she'd turned out. A real survivor. Deadly, but ethical. Sometimes too damned moral for her own good. Like now.

"I don't want a frickin' bonus, I want a raise!" Cally hissed over her shoulder at him as she poured a fresh cup of coffee. Two bright dots of color on her cheeks showed more real emotion in this family squabble than she would have ever revealed in the field. Shari had fastened the dark blue, denim nightblinds over the windows to keep the electric light from leaking out into the darkness. Clan O'Neal, and its Sunday branch, were meticulous about not displaying more wealth and development than they ought to have. Most bounty farmers had electric enough for their scanners, but little generator power to spare for other applications, even if their homes had been wired for it. None had buried antimatter plants with community power transmission. For bounty farmers who were not O'Neals, "burning the midnight oil" was not just a figure of speech. Cally leaned back against the counter, cupping the warmth of the mug in both hands. She gave Shari a tiny headshake, obviously warning her not to intervene. Michael O'Neal, Sr., was making extra effort to be reasonable. He didn't feel reasonable. *She calls in after all these years and I don't get to speak to my own granddaughter. What, does Michelle think I've got leprosy or something?*

"This is professional," he said. "You take your pay when and how you can get it. That's the business we're in." Papa opened the gray and blue salt-glazed jar on the counter next to the fridge, hand hesitating between the familiar red and white foil pack and the leather pouch with Billy's Cuban-Salem blend.

"It's bad enough becoming a thief for a cause. I'm not going to turn into a common thief just because Mommy needs a new pair of shoes. Granpa, if we don't have some principles, we're no better than the damned Darhel," she said.

"What, you'll kill people for a living but you're too good to profit off a raid? A raid of that Darhel enemy you're so busy despising, little girl." He could tell the ironic, mocking edge to his tone lit a slow fire under Cally's temper. Good. She needed to be shaken up a little.

"Well, *that's* below the belt!" Her hands were fisted at her sides as she tried to control herself, but her voice was rising.

"Could you two keep it down! The children!" Shari backed out of the room, closing the door to the den as an extra buffer between the kitchen and the kids' rooms.

"You aren't making a dime off the theft; you're making a commission on a sale," Papa said.

"Okay, so now I'm a fence?" Cally said.

"A frickin' barbed wire one," he muttered under his breath, as he turned and spat into a chipped blue mug with no handle.

"What?"

"Nothing. Look, we live in an imperfect world. We *are* working to make it better. If you agree to the commission, I'll use it as leverage to work on a raise. We all agree that a raise is necessary and fair. If you want it to happen, I need bargaining chips." Her grandfather spread his hands, the picture of reason. Stir her up, then calm her down.

"So you're trying to tell me you're not actually going to do this ten percent thing?" she asked skeptically.

"I can't bargain with a bluff. Hey, I'm not just using this as an excuse to get around you. Holidays are coming up, you know. I'll ask for the raise first. If they won't see reason, we take the commission to get through their thick skulls so the next time I bring it up, they're not so pigheaded," he said.

She still didn't look happy.

"What, you've got a better way to get through to them?" As

he asked, looking her in the eye, he could practically see her playing Christmas in her head. If he let even a flicker of triumph show in his eyes, she was going to dig in her heels. He kept a poker face, leaving her nothing to think about but a bare tree and empty stockings. She drank her coffee, probably playing for time. Besides, good coffee was too expensive to waste. He waited, watching, until finally she sighed and set the cup down.

"Against my better judgment. But if they offer a raise instead, and it's at all reasonable, we take it. Whether the numbers match up or not," she said.

"You're going to get all stubborn and noble over that, aren't you? Fine. I'll be leaving money on the table, I just know it, but fine. I swear, I never should have let you spend all those years with nuns. Went and turned you into a dewy-eyed idealist," he groused.

"And any part I take of it goes for the girls," she said.

"Fine." As she left the kitchen on her way to bed, he let a tiny quirk at one corner of his mouth get through. She was stubborn. Just like Mike had been. Always saw sense eventually, but you sometimes had to get her attention with a two by four first.

Cally got into her red, Tweety-bird nightshirt, frowning at the narrowness of the twin bed in the small room. Quite a change from her apartment in Charleston. At least she'd been able to keep some of the art from her walls. Even added a print. Okay, so the picture of the surfer catching a wave at Malibu was a cheap reprint of a digital file. Still, it was nice having it. It was a small, tangible reminder of her time with Stewart on Titan Base seven years ago. She got a fresh washcloth from the pile under the nightstand and picked up the buckley to set her wake-up call.

"Psssst. You've got a message," it said in an exaggeratedly soft voice.

"Why didn't you beep me?" she asked.

"It's a *secret* message," it said.

"Well, yeah, buckley. I'm an assassin. I do get a few of those. What message?"

"Yeah, but this one's *really* secret," it said. By now she wanted to throttle him.

"Buckley, what's the message? Is it from . . . him?"

"Say, 'pretty please,'" it prompted.

"Buckley, give me the damned message," she said.

"If you're not going to be polite about it maybe I won't."

"Buckley!" she hissed. "Do you want me to load a Martha emulation on top of you? This place looks pretty drab. I could use some affordable decorating tips. Buckley, what's 'raffia'? Does it come in purple?"

"All right, all right. It's from him. He's making a trip to Charleston. Can't stand another minute without you, apparently."

"Text, voice, or holo?"

"Encrypted text."

"Buckley, if it's encrypted, how do you know what he said?"

"I didn't say it was very well encrypted. Well, it sort of was, but you guys are way too gooshy in your choice of decryption keys. And if *I* can decrypt it, would you like an estimate of how quickly your bosses can decrypt it in various scenarios? I can give you a full set or just the basic dozen run-downs."

"Shut up, buckley."

"Well, that's gratitude for you."

"Buckley, please just display the text."

"Right."

Thursday 10/14/54

The building looked harmless enough. Windowless on the lower floors, it squatted, a giant rectangular block, northeast of a small city on Lake Michigan. Convenient to a good beach on the lake, and several smaller lakes for the recreation of the employees, the surface of the building was simple pink brick, from base to top. The dark, mirrored windows that ringed the top floor looked out at the world with guarded impassivity.

The signs in the ample but mostly empty parking lot, and large aluminum letters on the side of the building, announced it as the Institute for the Advancement of Human Welfare. On each side of the building, raised brick beds and dense boxwood hedges separated the front parking lot from the back of the building.

Through the front door, a large middle corridor went halfway through the building. Well-tended ficus trees flanked a central security desk where solidly-built guards took pains to keep their guns concealed beneath the jackets of their cheap, maroon suits. On each side, there was a glass-fronted office with white lettering on the double doors. The one on the left identified itself as Altruism Research, the one on the right, Kindness Care. Against the glass walls inside the offices to the right, one could clearly see the generously laden shelves of a newsstand and gift shop.

Behind the guards, a brass- and granite-fronted bank of elevators led to the rest of the building. A thin strip of brass, practically invisible until one got past the security desk, outlined the card readers to the side of each elevator.

Behind the building, loading docks allowed trucks to back right up against garage-style doors that were exactly the size of the rear of a semi trailer. Thick black weather-stripping insured a strong seal between arriving truck and building. To the side of each loading dock door, cement steps led up to painted white steel doors with security card readers to the side.

An entrance from a separate road wound down to the subterranean parking deck at the rear of the building, which bore large signs reading, "Employee Parking Only." At the deck's combined entrance and exit, a guard occupied a small, heated booth. The gates into and out of the deck also had card readers, though nobody who was not an employee ever saw them. An elegantly domed conservatory stood at ground level on top of the parking deck. Inside, ornamental plants from several worlds graced professionally designed beds along silver-sanded footpaths, winding in to a Galplas water feature. Carefully crafted to resemble lichen-encrusted granite, the salt-water pool and fountain had at least a dozen colorful species of tropical fish.

The burial of a parking deck was unusual at this latitude. Although parts of the building were clearly of Earthtech materials, legacy of whatever occupied the building before the institute, the deck was a recent addition—pure Galtech, top to bottom. From top to bottom the warmth of the surfaces and an overengineered drainage system kept the deck operational year round—access road and all.

The man and woman walking in the garden did not work in the front offices of the building. They were an odd contrast. The man presented an image that was conservative to the point of functional invisibility. Almost everything about him was bland, from the hairspray-glazed newscaster spikes in his thinning blond hair, to the gray tailored jacket and pants, to his plain brown dress shoes. The exceptions were his eyes, which were a disconcertingly frosty blue, and his ruby and onyx tie clip, stark against the charcoal gray tie. The eyes and ruby burned, oddly paired fires against the man's drab, brown shirt and pasty skin.

So thin he was almost gaunt, his slightness combined with his short stature to give the impression of an ice-carven gnome in a suit. He kept his elbows in closely when he walked, as if he had grown up spending much of his time in crowds. Which, in fact, he had. Growing up on the Indowy planet Haithel, he had been accustomed to crowds and crowds of the green-furred Galactic working class. The Indowy family who raised him carefully schooled in the Path, cautioning always against human barbarisms. To their quiet pride, he studied the Sohon techniques with diligence, energy, and phenomenal talent. Reaching legal adulthood at age twenty-one, Erick Winchon continued study, driven by some unsung inner need, despite clear serenity and a fanatical devotion to the strictures of the Path. By Earth's 2042, he had become one of only three human mentats in known space. Meticulously modest, he avoided every appearance of attention-seeking.

The woman, on the other hand, clearly had no objection to attracting attention. She wore her hair in a simple but eye-catching classical style, shoulder length black hair drawn back in a lime green headband and worn with bangs. The headband matched her green suede suit, teamed with a black leather corset and vinyl go-go boots. She walked just a little too close to him, arching her back to give him a perfect view down the front of her corset. He appeared more interested in the data on her clipboard.

"So we've got progression in the food series down to a week?" he asked.

"From liver and broccoli straight through to raw offal. We have included cannibalism, but it's all unknowing, so it doesn't really count, yet. Normally, that would take another week. As you know, it takes a week more than that if we can't convince them they've already broken the taboo," she said. "We're hoping that by refining the focus of the norepinephrine reuptake inhibitors in the gamma-Brucksmann synapses we can get that down to two to four days."

"I'm concerned that we don't have enough of a range of inhibited actions at the upper end of the spectrum, here. Why haven't we gone to cannibalism of live subjects? Subjects of personal interest? AID, flag this as important," the mentat inclined his head towards the black box in his shirt pocket. Other than color and cardboard, it could have been a pack of cigarettes.

"Live subjects won't be a problem, but personal interest subjects could be. As you know, they're a limited resource and if we use them up on one test, we don't have them available for the next. Virtual reality biometric measurement suggests that they'd be much more effectively utilized in the interpersonal aggression series." Her eyes sparkled with a dark excitement, leavened with apparent bewilderment at his blind dispassion. She showed no surprise, of course, for nothing about his reaction was new to her.

"Are you going to have our data with the cross-series shifting ready for my conference in Cleveland next week? Remember that the public interfaces department will have to translate the experimental design and data to refer to the green monkey and prepare a junior researcher to present the paper." He bent to feed a small orange wafer to fat, spotted fish.

"It's not nearly where we want it to be, I'm afraid. . . . Still, the results are adequate for a preliminary paper. I don't understand why you even go to these things when you have to disguise your real work so much. The projected results for the monkeys, well, interfaces will do their best, but the work won't be even remotely replicable after their translation."

"That is the point, is it not? If they could replicate the work, what would Epetar's leadership need us for?" He smiled serenely. "I can at least tell others in the field something of the important work we are doing, even if they can neither appreciate it nor repeat it. Even if they do not know it is my work." His last comment was a telling slip from Erick Winchon's habitual rhetoric of we.

"How many more trips are you making before year end?" she asked.

"Only three. It's the busy season, you know. Everyone wants an excuse to go someplace warm. Cleveland. Bah!" he grimaced. "The next is in Jamaica. Stimulating conversation and some of the best coffee on Earth. What more could one want? Although it is beyond me why they call it blue. The beans are as brown as any others. I checked. I have been meaning to fix some seed stock for them, but our other work is needed so much more."

✧ ✧ ✧

Prida Felini, his assistant in the garden, was the mentat's favorite Earth-raised human. Barbaric, of course, but weren't they all? At least she was honest about it. She could intellectually understand the need for civilizing humanity and had chosen to help. At the lowest level, their work set one barbarian against another. A rather regrettable zero sum play, but necessary for the welfare of the species as a whole. Somebody had to look out for them. With no clan system to care for humans in manageable chunks, the mentat had selflessly shouldered the task. At least it was interesting work, which was some compensation.

Erick Winchon had learned from hard experience that no matter how thoroughly he surrounded himself with competent people, any time he had to interact with Earther humans outside his own control, he had to check, check, and check again. There was no task so simple that it could not fail because of at least one incompetent Earther somewhere along the chain from instruction to delivery. His species was manifestly capable of ordinary, proper work habits. Humans *could* perfom quality work. There was something simply wrong about Earther upbringing and cultures that generated incompetent, spoiled adults. It was a source of great vexation to him. The goal of his research was nothing more nor less than the deliverance of his species from its endless loop of primitive incompetence. Only then could the human race become an optimal tank for growing wisdom and advancement along the Path. Earthers would continue to be resistant to becoming civilized and moving beyond their primitive habits. The lack of progress in curtailing the black market for meat in the Sub-Urbs proved that point. Enforcement was especially difficult when the Galactics could not admit the goal of the measures to the Earther government or the internal police of the Sub-Urbs. Frustrating. It was all very frustrating.

That resistance problem was the whole reason testing of the behavioral remediation technology had to be so aversive. Only complete success would allow civilization of those who would, inevitably, resort to primitive force in resistance. Winchon knew enough of human history to be fully aware that he would never be appreciated by humanity in his own lifetime, even with that life extended to the full range possible through rejuvenation. His estimates for the time necessary to civilize Earth varied. The longest was one-thousand three hundred years. The range became considerably shorter the greater the percentage of human population could be shipped to planets already run by Galactics, and the more Earther humans could be induced to restrain their reproduction and repopulation efforts. The Darhel were helping with both problems as much as possible, but progress had been disappointing.

They paced by a miniature apple tree, talking softly.

The Darhel Pardal had dismissed his body servants and sat behind his desk, turned to look out the large porthole into the black of space. In his mind, he compared motives, positions, attributes, and interests. He had narrowed the list of possible thieves to three rival groups, any of which could have used the extra currency to knock loose a lucrative expansion of their mining concessions from the Darhel Tir Dol Ron, whose job included the administration of Earth. Not that the humans understood the explicit nature of the position.

The Gistar Group's operation mining niobium and tantalum in Africa had capital equipment that was reaching the end of exploitable resources on site. The Cnothgar Group's extraction facility for monazite sands in Brazil could refurbish equipment the Tir had mothballed and open at least three other sites with that kind of financing. Adenar Group's molybdenum mining in Chile couldn't be overlooked, not because he could see specific scope for expansion, but because they had succeeded so well in being cagey about their project.

Which one? That was the hard question. It would be the height of stupidity to compound Epetar's current troubles by starting a trade war with an innocent party. However, the frontal assault on the group's currency reserves simply could not go unanswered. It would be Adenar. They weren't happy about a certain defection, but it had followed long-established rules. It would be out of character for them to react this emphatically, but certainly possible. He couldn't be sure enough to act.

He heard a reedy sound like a dying voorcn—a flying animal hunted by . . . predators . . . on his homeworld. The thought, "*other* predators," did not quite make it to the surface of his mind. The tiniest hint of the sweet, deadly pleasure of the Tal hormone provoked a shudder, warning him of ultimate bliss and death. He ruthlessly suppressed the forbidden thought. He became aware that the offending sound was coming from the whistling of his own breathing through his teeth.

He stopped the noise at once, instead instructing his AID to replay a holo file he had received that morning detailing the progress on an interesting project his group was undertaking. It showed tremendous promise towards solving the previously intractable problem of human behavior control, as well as eliminating the most dangerous of the three existing human mentats as a side bonus. It was possible that the Darhel manager who owned the commercial territory rights to Earth, the ultimate end user for a market-ready product, could be induced to cut loose an advance on the basis of the progress shown in this report.

The request would have to be phrased carefully. He settled more comfortably into his chair to watch again and analyze his best selling points. The Tir Dol Ron was, as the humans would put it, a tough customer.

The bounce tubes had been an annoyance when Michelle had first outgrown her old clothes and started wearing robes. In pants, they had been fine. She had walked around with her hair braided and tolerated the flyaway bits the breakneck fall to the bottom of the tube shaft caused. Until she had learned to hold them down by main force of will, her robes had tended to end up around her ears. With that kind of affront to her dignity as incentive, she had learned fast. The thousand little tricks of technology she had would have appeared to the uninitiated as magic. In fact, one of the first things she'd done was taken advantage of some differences in human versus Indowy physiology to have her Sohon headset surgically implanted. The second thing she'd done was learn to work efficiently enough to have some nannites to spare. She walked around with a layer of them at all times. Hidden, never enough in one place to be a visible aggregate, but completely controlled. That was one of her small technological magics. Easily mastered, for her. Later, other and progressively more esoteric applications and technologies had followed, leading to abilities that the adults on Earth before the war, even the ones at the cutting edge of physics in the most secret of the secret research labs, would have considered flatly impossible. Then again, she understood a whole lot more physics than they did. The difference was of the same magnitude as that between Aristotle and Heisenberg—and as shocking to the common man as the difference between a clay pot of Greek Fire and a cobalt bomb.

It would have been shocking, that is, if the Michon Mentats hadn't been every bit as tight-lipped and disciplined about their knowledge and abilities as the Tchpth or the legendary Aldenata themselves. Any of the mentats from any race of sophonts could have created vats of nannites the size of a small star with no input from the Tchpth. The ability was a requirement of the rank. They were also wise enough to understand why they shouldn't. There were things that were worse than the current Galactic sociopolitical order, suboptimal as it was. Far worse. An unjust galaxy was better than no galaxy at all—and inevitable besides. The nature of life prior to enlightenment was necessarily and irreparably a morass of injustice—the rule was as solidly inflexible as Tlschp's Law of the Balance of Entropy.

Which was why she was on the way to her meeting today, serenely dropping down the bounce tube to the Galactic conference sector of her building. She would meet with the Darhel supervisor Pahpon, and treat him as a superior, even though he was little advanced from the ancient human soldier throwing a clay pot of incendiary. Ancient was, in the scheme of things, not all that long ago. In any case, she would meet with him. Her true superior was neither Pahpon nor the entire Epetar Group that employed him. Her true superior was the self-discipline and foresight she had necessarily had to develop to be able to hold some very advanced physics and skills in her own head. Desire for the good opinion of her colleagues was her shield against hubris. She could see the consequences of saving her own life as clearly as if she was reading a history book after the fact. Her life was not worth that. Except for the one way out she had already arranged. If it worked.

Her steps were sedate, measured, as she entered the conference room reserved for Darhel. "Good morning, Supervisor Pahpon," she said.

"Human Michon Mentat O'Neal. Our group is terribly displeased with your negligence in allowing the Aerfon Djigahr to be removed from your facilities. I am here to present you with a letter of demand for your debts to our organization. You will see in the file that, as per the rules to avoid their unnecessary losses, we have purchased your debts from the various other groups to which you owe various obligations. AID, send—"

"I would not do that," she said icily.

The Darhel froze, fur puffing up in a vestigial reflex his prehistoric ancestors had used when alarmed. "You are surely not such a human barbarian as to take everyone else down in flames for your own error?" She could see the pulse beating at his throat in stark terror, and smell the fear pheremones that were not at all like the scent of a Darhel whose system was releasing the suicidally intoxicating Tal. Darhel could feel fear without dying of it. In fact, they could feel some rather extreme fear. As Pahpon was now.

"Of course if I fail to retrieve the Aerfon Djigahr in a timely fashion, or ensure its destruction, as per our contract that I would not let it be transferred out of Epetar's hands in any nondestroyed condition, functional, restorable, or reverse-engineerable—if I do not do that, then I will be in breach of my contract with Epetar. However, within our contract, my responsibility does not terminate until one half cycle and twenty-four more Adenast days. I merely begin incurring late fees after Renthenel twenty-one. I am not yet in breach."

He glared at her. "You know very well that destruction clause was intended to cover any necessary loss of functionality during the research process."

"Nevertheless, it is in the contract that if I make a good faith effort to avoid destruction, I fulfill my contract by providing you with whatever I learn about the device. The contract does not say the device may not be in other hands at some point or points during the research period. It says I must either return it to Epetar Group at the end of the contract or ensure that it has been irretrievably destroyed during the research period."

"Research is not being conducted on the device, the task for which your services were contracted. You are in breach," he insisted.

"Research is most certainly being conducted. The contract gives me supervisory discretion to arrange that research in whatever way seems practical to me at the moment. At this moment, the only practical research option is for the persons that have it to research the device where it is." Her speech was calm, her manner preternaturally still.

"Research for another group!" he growled, the renowned melodious voice marred with a harsh burr.

"Preliminary research data where the technical results are, as a matter of universal practice, stored in a single, closely protected site and not in that group's internal storage, as a matter of security. The thieving group's central facilities do not have technical analyses and results. The most they have is some cubes of pretty footage. Galactic standards do not consider a group in possession of data until it reaches one of their authorized ships, authorized central facilities, or a Darhel member competent to understand the information. I have constant external monitoring that will demonstrate to the satisfaction of a contract court, in the absence of contrary evidence, that the technical research results that would put me in breach have never left for a ship, nor to one of their central facilities, nor a Darhel of the group, whichever it may be, who is technically competent to understand the information. I am not in breach. I suspect Adenar, by the way."

"That's a flimsy technicality and you know it." He waved away her conjecture with one hand. The Darhel was breathing very carefully and deliberately now.

"As your ancestors told the ancestors of the Indowy so many generations ago, in contracts, technicalities are everything," she said.

"This is not the performance level we have come to expect from Michon Mentats."

"This is rather precisely the sort of performance we have come to expect from Darhel Groups." Impassively, she noted the ultra-faint scent of Tal entering his system.

"Fine. Live until the end of your contract. But your wages are in abeyance until you demonstrate the ability to fulfill your obligation," he sneered. "Make your peace with the Aldenata or whatever you human barbarians do because the day your contract expires unfulfilled, is the last day you eat. You are dismissed!" he said.

CHAPTER FOUR

Lieutenant Colonel Jacob Mosovich woke up in the single good hotel in North Chicago, Illinois. Good was an understatement. Most of the town, like any base town, was devoted to separating soldiers from their money. Bright Lion Boulevard ran from Horner Highway to the front gates of the Great Lakes Fleet Training Base. The main street through town was officially named Happiness and Harmony Way. The strip north of the Lion was more popularly known among Fleet's recruits and lower-level personnel as the H and H, short for "Hooch and Ho." Horner Highway had the obvious informal designation.

The Serenity Hotel stood to the south of the Lion on the H and H, right between the two decent restaurants and across from a full-service dry cleaning and tailor shop. Jake had known he was in Fleet territory as soon as he saw the gardens in front of the blindingly white facade of the hotel. It had political correctness committee written all over it.

The sidewalk split to circle around a large, top-heavy rock that looked like someone had gone to the trouble of drilling it full of holes. Raked gravel paths curved around miniature fruit trees, classic bonsai trees, and a few canes of bamboo growing up against another large-ish rock. A small waterfall on one side flowed into a small, round pool full of koi and not one, but two, very small islands. Each had its own tiny maple tree and, he had looked closer to be sure, its own by God holey rock. It was meticulously laid out, and each element might have been pretty by itself, but the whole effect was so cluttered it made his eyes ache.

The lobby and interior were better, thank God. His room was comfortable, the bed modern and adjustable, the bath large and deep. In place of the more usual, and cheaper, holoscreen was a full-featured holotank. The tank hooked up to a server of exclusive vids, most of them featuring girls that couldn't have been older than about twelve. The selection was pretty broad, so he did find some adult movies that had, well, adults. But he hadn't stayed up too late, and had restricted himself to two of the little bottles of Maotai in the liquor cabinet.

Decades in the service had trimmed everything unnecessary from his morning routine. He was in the lobby in his silks, looking sharp and professional, when General Pennington's driver phoned his PDA to say they were out front. Like many Fleet officers, Mosovich carried a PDA as well as an AID and frequently tended to "forget" to carry his AID around. Nobody talked openly about the problems with the AIDs during the war, because those who did had a short life expectancy, but not even the Darhel could stop the military grapevine. And, of course, being on detached duty to SOCOM for the duration of this command, he'd be using the most convenient mechanism for staying in touch with his own CO, who was non-Fleet, as well as his mostly non-Fleet men. It wasn't that none of them had AIDs. It was just that the idiots in procurement and those in the know fought a constant, covert war over the little menaces, which made distribution spotty.

Mosovich stood facing his new XO in front of the troops that would momentarily become his responsibility and privilege. The XO, as acting, was standing in the position of the outgoing commander at the Change of Command Ceremony. The Atlantic Company guidon stood in for the Battalion Colors, snapping in the crisp, October-morning breeze. No one was cold. Their dress uniforms, gray silks with the dark, jungle green stripes that DAG had adopted from the U.S. Special Forces, kept them warm easily, despite the chill that frosted their breath. The silks, made of a Galactic fabric that was incredibly tough, soft, and absolutely wrinkle-proof, looked better than the prewar Army dress uniforms, while being more comfortable than most civilians' pajamas.

A full Change of Command Ceremony was unusual for a company, but DAG was the elite of the elite—a combined service special operations organization that dealt with the most serious terrorist, pirate, bandit, and insurgent threats for the entire globe. Ranks tended to be inflated with a special operations command like DAG. Company command, whether in the U.S. Army or in Fleet Strike, was ordinarily a captain's slot. No DAG company had ever gone to less than a major, and that only once—a major of unusual excellence who had been too far outside the zone for immediate promotion had gotten command of South Pacific Company. The platoon designation had been kept for the sake of the DAG table of organization and equipment, and was used on formal occasions. Informally, DAG personnel and their chain of command referred to the operator units of each company simply as Alpha, Bravo, and Charlie. Given the ranks of the officers and men, platoon wasn't the best description. Harkening back to some of their organizational antecedents, they thought of and referred to themselves as teams. Still, the bean counters had won that battle on paper, so far, so platoons they were.

Major Kelly, a pale, black-haired guy the size of a small tree, took the company colors from the Charlie Platoon master sergeant, acting in place of the command sergeant major, and passed them to General Pennington. One of the men read out the orders giving him command. General Pennington passed the standard to Jake. He took them, formally accepting responsibility for his new command. He handed them back to the master sergeant, wishing again that Mueller hadn't been off-planet when their orders were cut and had been able to arrive before he did. He hadn't seen him in two years, and it would have been good to have him here.

Pennington was an interesting man. Younger than Jake was, he had for some reason kept his white hair when he rejuved. Medium height but solidly built, he probably wouldn't have made the height-weight standards before the war. But after they'd been relaxed in the war, everybody's militaries had just neglected to put them back in place for juvs. Juvs had to work hard at it to get fat, so the bean counters and brass just assumed extra weight on a juv was muscle mass. Jake had met an exception or two, but the general wasn't it. Still, the hair made him look like a babyfaced old guy. Mosovich let his mind wander during the speeches. They were all pretty meaningless. It was important that you have speeches. Solid military tradition. What was said in those speeches was much less important than having them in the first place. It took a really charismatic speaker to hold the attention of a group of soldiers overdue for their chow. Pennington wasn't that speaker. Not today, anyway.

". . . You men have a vital mission in today's Special Operations Command, hooah? You form the backbone of Earth's defense against pirates, insurgents and terrorists. Perhaps more importantly, you serve as a living example of the best traditions of interservice cooperation, and the inclusion of Galactic forces in the SOCOM family is an inspiring step into tomorrow for the armed services, hooah? As I stand here before you today I am awed, awed by . . ." Pennington's words flowed over him as his eyes scanned the ranks, noting the sharp, immaculate appearance of his new troops and their officers. Pennington did occasionally draw his attention back, making Jake suppress a smile. The man used "hooah" the way most Canadians he knew used "eh."

Bravo Platoon was on the obstacle course this morning, stretched out across the obstacles as much by the staggered starting times as by the different speeds of the officers and men. Most of the wood components of the structures were weathered and graying despite originally being pressure treated. Some things, like the wall and team-climbing tower, were obviously new, as they gradually replaced aging equipment. The cargo netting was also new, but someone had judged the wood frame able to withstand yet another replacement net. The rolling logs were original to the course. For some reason logs just didn't wear at the same rate as the rest of the wood. And, of course, the rusty barbed wire was added incentive to do the low crawl right. The ball buster carried a risk of splinters that also provided incentive for good performance. Bravo's CO, having started in the last third, made a point of finishing in the first third. He'd pay for it tomorrow, but what the hell, it was only pain.

Captain Jack "Quinn," born Jack O'Neal, was a short, homely, young-looking man with carrot-colored hair and so many freckles that it was hard to tell whether he was a fair-skinned man with brown dots or a brown-skinned man with fair spots. Anyone who at first made the mistake of classifying him as a little shrimp would be surprised at the strength built into his wiry frame. His team favored "Blackjack" for any mission that involved moving around underwater. The man simply would not float, but had the stamina to be one of the strongest swimmers in DAG. This might have had something to do with his having swum daily in saltwater since before he could walk.

Right now, he was rubbing an army-brown towel over his sweat-soaked hair and squinting into the sun across the O-course to the massive brigade XO, Major Frederick Sunday "Kelly," jogging across the turf to meet him. One or two of the men looked up as the XO approached. Most hid their curiosity, jogging back to the barracks or the gym for a quick shower and a thorough check to make sure, again, that absolutely everything was clean and squared away for the first look by the new CO. And their first look at him, of course. The ubiquitous PDAs had improved the speed of the ancient grapevine system by leaps and bounds. Captain Quinn and all of his men knew exactly when the colonel would be looking them over, and were determined to ensure that their customary excellence was improved to perfection. He had George O'Neal "Mauldin's" first impression of the new CO. Now he wanted Boomer's. He loped down the side of the course to meet the major halfway.

The excessively large officer stopped in front of him and returned his salute before turning to walk beside him back in the direction of the HQ.

"Okay, Boomer, what's he like?" Quinn said.

"I dunno, Jack. As first impressions go, I don't think he's gonna be a bean-counting weenie, and he doesn't come across as a weasel, but he was kinda quiet. Didn't give me a lot to go on. His record looks really good, but what the fuck can you tell from them these days? Likes his coffee, but how much can you tell from that?" Major Kelly shrugged. "Speaking of coffee, let's check out the mess hall and grab a cup. Make sure they got the word. This week would be a hell of a time to burn the stew."

"Think he's likely to be *too* good?" The captain scratched the end of his nose, looking sidelong at his childhood friend.

"Your guess is as good as mine. In case anybody didn't get the memo, remind them that their opsec has to be flawless until we have a much better idea of what we can get away with." The major lit a cigar and blew a stream of smoke towards the sky, "Wouldn't do for him to twig and us lose all this free training. Wouldn't do at all."

"I'll take care of it. Not like I should need to, but I'll make sure. Doesn't do to tempt Mr. Murphy," Jack said.

"Okay, now what do you think of our new Command Sergeant Major?"

"Well, they obviously know each other from way back. I think he's sharp, he's going to be the colonel's eyes and ears. He's going to be around more; we need to be twice as careful around him," the captain said. "The good news is, he seems like kind of a blowhard, you know? Think a thought, say a thought. Subtle ain't his middle name. So we should be okay with him." He nodded to the XO and broke into an easy lope, leaving Kelly to his cigar and his thoughts.

Like most DAG personnel, Quinn didn't live in the barracks. Unlike most of them, one of the privileges of rank he indulged in was keeping a couple of fresh uniforms in his office and taking advantage of the small cubicle shower at the end of the line of stalls in the head down the hall. Before cleaning up, he took out his PDA and phoned the master sergeant who was Bravo's senior NCO.

"Harrison, go through and remind everybody one more time that with a new CO this is absolutely not the time to get sloppy about anything. It's probably overkill, but be sure they understand. I'd hate to have to put everybody on corn and soybeans for a week." The captain said the last in a joking tone, but it was the most serious part of the message, telling the NCO that Bane Sidhe OPSEC was what he most wanted his people to be careful about.

"Hooah, sir," Harrison acknowledged.

Security taken care of, Quinn headed for the shower. Wouldn't do to be all sweaty and stuff when the new CO arrived.

Friday 10/15/54

It was a brilliant, cold, windy fall day. The kind of day at the coast where you didn't dare step outside without a pair of sunglasses to protect your eyes from the bright reflections of the sun and the grit in the air. Cally had accompanied Shari on an island-only shopping trip that was really an excuse to wander around the store and buy some of Ashley Privett's best fudge. Most of the things they needed themselves were either already back at home, or were on a list for Cally to pick up on the weekend trip to Charleston she had announced that morning at breakfast, telling the kids that no, they couldn't come this time. It was a mommy trip. She felt a little guilty that Shari assumed that, going alone, she was going to confession—but only a little. She really *was* going to take at least a little time to shop for stuff to wear at the family reunion next week like she'd said. She'd just probably shop, well, *quickly*.

Another purpose of this morning's trip to, as Shari put it, "beautiful metropolitan Edisto," was to let them discreetly gawk at the changes in the store. On the island, frequently you had to make your own excitement. Cally waved and smiled at Karen Lee, the wife and coconspirator of an active Bane Sidhe agent. Karen's family were local for a few years to give the authorities time to forget about them before they went back out to a new posting with fresh, young identities. Karen was a quiet person, who seemed to find the Clan O'Neal personalities on the island a bit overwhelming at times.

True to type, and probably for the best, Granpa had handled the negotiation with the Bane Sidhe over the code key sale. She looked around at the changed store, impressed. Papa O'Neal could get things done in a hurry when he decided he was On A Mission.

With so many FedCreds at stake, they had been remarkably easygoing about the sales commission. As soon as the keys were flown into Charleston, Cally had made delivery to Michelle. The payment, in cash and small denominations, had come in the kind of briefcase that made her feel like the holodramas' stereotypical drug dealer. She'd paid out their commission to Granpa, who had come back home with a trailer full of trade goods for the store. Charleston being a main port, his large purchases hadn't caused so much as a raised eyebrow. Similar large cash buys of available light consumer goods were routine there.

Postwar, areas around the world where unusual things could grow or be mined had been rapidly recolonized, leading to the rebirth of the coastal or river-based city-state. Off-planet migration being the poor man's route to rejuv, that interesting development looked like it might even last awhile. The population to rebuild genuine nations just wasn't there. The city states' greatest need, besides essential trade goods, was for the basic end-user products and small comforts the residents couldn't make for themselves—which was rather like the O'Neals on Edisto, now that she thought about it.

Island finances being what they were, the end result of all this was Granpa becoming a silent partner in the store. Before, Ashley had had to make the store look full, or at least not empty, by spreading the off-island goods out at the front of the shelves, interspersed among locally made home crafts. Now, the shelves were actually full, and with manufactured goods and things that weren't merely regional. There were frozen turkeys and canned cranberry sauce to be had for Thanksgiving dinner this year. Mike and Duncan Sunday—who of course still thought their last name was Thompson—were happily applying an olive drab coat of paint to the store's exterior walls, no doubt for exchange credits to apply to the purchase of some of the goodies inside.

Shari was flipping through a fashion magazine on the rack that Ashley had for some reason installed at the back of the store, cooing shamelessly over the fall runway photoshoot from Chicago. Tommy had hacked them a back door into the online version of the same magazine, but there was just something about holding the glossy pages in your hands. Cally was keeping half an eye on the clothes on the pages and half an eye on Morgan and Sinda, who were nudging and whispering to each other near a batch of toys. None of the toys looked breakable, at least. Sinda was eying a doll in a lacy blue and white dress with equal measures of childhood greed and love.

A quiet, irritated buzzing from the front of the store escalated in volume to two clearly audible and irate female voices.

". . . just because I had to punish your kid over that disgusting frog mess . . ." Yep, Pam again. She was starting to get shrill.

"Nobody gets credit in my shop. . . . and if you didn't spend all your money on that trash you read, you'd be able . . ." Whups, Ashley already biting her words out like that. Not good. Cally walked over to Morgan and Sinda and grabbed their unresisting hands, leading them back towards Shari, who hadn't even looked up from her magazine. She absently gathered her great-grandchildren in with one arm while Karen edged slightly behind her.

Cally walked around her small collection of people, assassin-turned-mom securing a ready exit by moving a dolly of soft drink cases so that instead of blocking the back door it was blocking one of the aisles.

". . . know a book if it bit you on the . . . and you just know they'll all be gone by the time . . ." Pam was shrieking now. Pretty soon she'd be fainting and making a great show of looking all over her body for her inhaler.

". . . into *my* shop, driving off my *paying* customers . . ." If Ashley didn't watch it, she was going to lose her voice again. Probably for days this time. Cally nudged a box of something out of the way with her foot. Shari still hadn't looked up from her magazine, lifting her arm from around the children to turn the page, returning it to pat Sinda on the shoulder. Karen just looked frozen in shock.

Another voice joined the first two, querulous as another woman started to complain about the inequity of ever-rising prices for people on a fixed income.

"Time to go." Cally scooped the magazine out of Shari's hands and dropped it back on the rack. "You know with Louise joining in they'll be lucky to get it over without coming to blows." She put her hands behind her charges and made gentle shooing motions as she ushered them out the back door, moving Karen along with the group. Emerging into the sunlight seemed to shake Karen out of her daze a little.

"Are they always like that?" she asked in disbelief.

"Nope," Cally answered, "sometimes they're worse. Welcome to family politics 101."

They walked around the side of the building towards the front. Shari waved to Mike and Duncan, who hadn't missed a beat, spreading paint onto the freshly-bleached boards with smooth, even strokes. "There they go again." Mike rolled his eyes and scratched his nose, leaving a smear of green paint.

In front of the store, they paused near the small group of older children who were gathering from across the street to observe the entertainment. A coconut came bouncing out the door at speed. Cally sighed and handed her purse to Shari.

"Welp, the imports have started flying. Better go in and save Granpa's stock." She disappeared through the door, emerging a moment later holding onto a short, red-faced woman with dark, frizzy hair, glasses askew on her face. The woman was cursing fluently but cut her one attempt at a struggle short when Cally subtly tightened her hold on the joint lock and took her to the ground. She looked down at the sputtering woman.

"That's it for you, Pam. You're banned from Ashley's shop for a month," she said.

"I don't have to answer to you, bitch. I'm not even Clan O'Neal!" The woman glared up at the blonde juggernaut looming over her, but didn't try to get up.

"Sundays are the same difference. And if you can't be trusted to be discreet in front of the children, I'll take it straight to Granpa." The assassin's eyes were flashing now.

The woman paled and stood up, dusting herself off. "No! Uh, you don't need to do that. I'm going. Look, I'm going." She edged down the street back towards the neighborhood holding the small house where she and her kids lived. "But you're still a bitch. Always throwing your weight around . . ." The woman said the last under her breath, but she didn't say it until she was a good twenty meters from Cally.

Cally stood her ground for a moment, then sighed and appeared to deflate. She walked back over to the kids and picked Sinda up, bouncing and nuzzling her until the tears no longer threatened to spill over from the little girl's eyes. "It's okay, Mommy's not mad at you. Mommy's not mad at anybody. It's okay, it's all right . . ."

"Yeah, definitely time to go home." Shari nodded. "Karen, why don't you come home with us for a cup of tea and put your feet up. You look like you need it."

"Okay. Okay, I will." She looked at her watch. "The babysitter doesn't expect me back for an hour and a half, anyway."

"Y'all go ahead. I'll just get the fudge and catch up with you," Cally said. "What do you think, chocolate mint or rocky road?"

"Go for the rocky road while she's still got the marshmallows and almonds," Shari said, already walking off towards the truck with the children.

By the time she got back with the fudge, Shari already had everyone in the truck. Cally climbed in the back with Karen, leaving the girls in the front seat.

"Why didn't you sit up front? The girls could've ridden back here," she asked the smaller woman.

"After all that I needed the fresh air. Besides, Morgan called shotgun." Karen shrugged. "Can I ask you about one thing?"

"Sure."

"How did the Sundays end up being in Clan O'Neal?"

"Hell if I know," Cally said.

"Huh? That doesn't make sense."

"Exactly." The blonde grinned at her quieter friend. "It's an inexplicable, alien, Indowy thing that pretty much none of us understand." The truck was bouncing across the island road by now and she settled herself more comfortably in the bed of the truck to tell the story.

"See, when Tommy and Wendy first joined the Bane Sidhe, Granpa invited them to come live down here and bring the kids. We had plenty of space, and we pretty much needed the help and the company, anyway. Shari and Wendy are friends from way back in the war. And me too, sort of. So anyway, some time after that, and we haven't been able to pinpoint when, the Indowy started referring to the Sundays as O'Neals. And we all thought it was weird, so Granpa sat down with Aelool and got him to explain *five times*, and he *still* didn't understand it. You've met Granpa, you know how stubborn he can be when he doesn't understand something. In the end, he quit because Aelool started to get really anxious and upset. Turns out he thought Granpa was trying to disown the Sundays, which would have been an unthinkable dishonor by Indowy standards." At Karen's puzzled look Cally paused and thought for a minute. "Okay, like for humans if you recruited some soldiers to do a job, and the mission started to go sour, and you just walked off and left them but for no good reason but you didn't have to, see?" When the other woman grimaced she nodded and went on. "So finally Granpa got him convinced that it was all a misunderstanding and he'd certainly never meant to sound like he was trying to disown the Sundays. And the upshot was that Tommy and Wendy didn't mind, and Granpa grumbled a bit around the house for the form of the thing but he didn't really mind, either, and the Sundays are O'Neals."

"So the Sundays are O'Neals and nobody knows why."

"Yup. Nobody human, anyway. Oh, apparently something about what Granpa did or didn't do or something made them think he meant to adopt the Sundays, and over some length of time occasionally an Indowy would ask Granpa a strange question that didn't seem related to anything and Granpa would just answer it without thinking about it much, and we never knew if they asked Tommy anything they thought was significant. Not anything Tommy could remember, anyway. But yep, there it is. It's an Indowy thing. Aliens. Go figure."

Friday 10/15/54

The man in the hotel bed had dark hair and recognizably Asian features, but it would have been impossible, even for someone from Fleet, to place exactly what part of Asia his ancestors had originally been from. The typical response would be, and had been, to shrug and assume his parents had been of mixed extraction before the war and that, in all the chaos and global upheaval of that time—upheaval that the world had never seen the like of before that horrible catastrophe—the records and even family legends had simply gotten lost, as they had for so many. Nobody would have guessed that the "Asian" man had begun life as a Latino gang leader named Manuel, and finished it, after a fashion, as an Anglo Fleet Strike general named James Stewart. Nobody but the stacked blonde in the sheer red pegnoir crossing the floor towards him from the suite's bathroom. With the silvery highlights of her hair caught in the glow of the lamplight, the room otherwise darkened by the heavy drapes drawn across the windows, she looked like a fourteen-year-old boy's wet dream of a Scandinavian goddess. He rolled up onto one elbow to watch her better, brushing a stray wisp of hair back from her cheek as she climbed into his bed.

"I never really thought I'd end up in a marriage that would feel so much like an affair," he said, not for the first time. For either of them.

"I know," she said, kissing his cheek and trailing her kisses back up around his ear. "I'm glad you could make it down for the weekend."

"God, I missed you, Cally." Stewart turned his face into her kisses and took her in his arms, giving himself up to the moment of having his beautiful wife in his bed again, no matter for how short a time.

Later, he tried to keep his damned eyes from misting up as they watched the latest home holos she'd brought him of the daughters he'd never been able to meet, who had and would grow up believing their father dead. Somehow, Cally always arranged it so that she could be in the holos with the girls. He wondered if she suspected how many lonely hours he spent, late at night, playing over those bits and scraps of the lives of his family, again and again, until he could see them behind his eyes as he dreamed. Many of the dreams were not pleasant. They were, in fact, about what you'd expect. On the whole, those were less painful than the happier dreams that put him in the holos with Cally and Morgan and Sinda, only to wake up alone in bed in the perpetually recycled air of the moon, with the metallic tang of machinery at the back of his throat. He'd thought about getting a dog, but it was hell getting them through quarantine, and getting a puppy from a licensed breeder was expensive. He'd do it when he got back though. It was no substitute, but at this point . . . He shook his head and reminded himself of his oft-repeated resolution on these visits, never to leave in his head until the visit was actually over. The time was too precious to be eaten up with regrets. He felt a deep sympathy with Mike O'Neal in bearing his curse. He was often thankful that, even though unlike Mike he knew he was in hell, at least he could look forward to the occasional weekend pass in heaven.

They were about fifteen minutes into the latest pack of holos—she must have hidden cameras all over the place, because she always brought hours of them, even though they only watched a few together—when dinner arrived from the seafood place across the street. Yes, the room would smell like fish afterwards until the filter in the air unit cleared it all out, but one thing he had learned about Cally over the seven years of stolen moments that comprised their marriage was that the woman loved seafood more than any three other people. He had decided to try some bizarre local dish called shrimp and grits at her behest, but spent most of his time feeding her strips of calamari just to feel her lips close over his fingers as she took each tidbit. The shrimp dish certainly wasn't bad, but he had never understood why anglos from this part of the U.S. had to call polenta something as undignified as "grits." His own colleagues in Noble Lion Tong tolerated his unusual fondness for Italian cuisine with a certain degree of amusement. Mostly, he'd learned to cook it for himself, although it did occasionally require him to import some unusual ingredients from Earth. She was right. He did like the shrimp dish. With the polenta.

"I feel guilty, a lot, for the girls growing up without a dad," he said.

"It's hard. But there's nothing we can do differently, so I try not to think about it," she said, looking away and picking at the worn bedspread that would never have passed muster in a decent prewar hotel.

"I'm just glad you live with your grandparents. At least they've got a grandfather around."

"Yeah," she sighed. "It's not the same, though. Growing up I always missed Daddy, and I never really got over losing my mom. But for having been a kid in the war years, I had it really good."

"I noticed a lot of the clothes you and the girls were wearing had seen better days. Same with Papa O'Neal and Shari." He didn't like broaching such an awkward subject. But having grown up poor himself, he couldn't let it lie. This was his family. "Are you guys having money problems? What's happening? It looks to me like those people aren't paying you nearly enough for what you do. Okay, there *isn't* enough and I wish you'd quit, but I understand why you can't. Almost. Still, how bad is it?"

"Money was pretty tight for awhile. The salaries took a severe dive after I got back, for various reasons. They'd pay more if they could. Anyway, we just had a windfall and things are better now. For awhile at least. Enough to get everybody some decent clothes and stuff. Besides, there's not a lot we could do if they weren't. They're extra paranoid about people with too high a lifestyle for their salaries, what with Jay's defection."

"Sorry about that." Stewart winced. He hadn't turned Jay, but he had provided the money to keep him turned.

"Not your fault. He would have found someone to buy his information. Traitors do. Anyway, we made a commission on finding a buyer for something for them. Brokering isn't usually in the scope of what we do and the sale was too much money to argue that they couldn't afford the commission. It was . . . large."

"Cally, what do you think would happen, really happen, if your organization found out about me?" he asked.

"Uh . . . bad things. They're really paranoid right now and they'd probably believe you were on deep cover for the Darhel and I was compromised. I'd probably be able to keep any of it from spilling over onto Granpa or anyone else in the clan, but, well, don't ask."

His lips tightened. "And you still won't leave, right? We *could* go under deep enough cover that they'd never find you. The Tong is good at that. But it's still no use asking, right?" He sighed as she shook her head. "You're going to invest your windfall, right? Is it enough for that? How much are we talking?"

"A bit over six thousand FedCreds."

"Okay. That's enough to stake you for some investments." He stared off into the distance. "I . . . know some things about some businesses that aren't common knowledge. Things that will influence share prices. If I was careful to keep the tips to businesses where you *could* rationally decide to invest in them if you were a shrewd investor and good researcher, and tell you where to look so you could leave an electronic trail in your systems of doing your homework if they asked any questions, that's some help I could probably safely give," he said. "My boss wouldn't mind one or two people going along for the ride—just keep it in the immediate family. *Really* keep it close."

"I'd have to lay some red herrings by doing similar research of other companies I don't invest in," she mused. "Yeah, it could work. I could even just take my results to Granpa and suggest an investment. But how would I get him *not* to share with the immediate world? What am I thinking—it's Granpa. If I buy an investment book that's already well thumbed, like at a used bookstore while I'm here, I can just flip through it to learn how to leave plausible trails and talk the game. It's not like I'm stupid and *couldn't* learn it on my own. And even if Granpa suspects I've got a source for stock tips, that would just make him *more* likely to keep it closer than close and not mention to anyone—especially not the Bane Sidhe. Not as upset as he still is with them about money." She leaned over and kissed him by way of a thank you, which pretty much led to the end of that conversation.

"So, back to the moon with the commuters on Monday. What about you? Off to kill people and break things, or do you get a really tough week chasing the girls?" he joked.

"A week off, then a family reunion, of all things. Wish you could be there," she said.

"That might be a bit more reunion than your family bargained for."

"I think the O'Neals would keep it quiet. But we've got a lot of miscellaneous folks around from the organization, whose loyalty is more to the Bane Sidhe than to Clan O'Neal. I do wish, but wishing doesn't work, does it?"

"Clan O'Neal. Sometimes I wonder if you realize how much Indowy has rubbed off on you."

"Hmph. Not as much as you'd think. We Irish have been big on family ties for a long time. Okay, well, maybe there was some Indowy influence there, too, but it was long enough ago that it doesn't count," she said. She sure was cute when she pouted. But maybe they should watch a movie or something before getting into that again. Nah . . . well, okay, maybe. *She* probably didn't need a break, but a couple of hours of holodrama and some microwave popcorn would almost feel like a date.

Before she left Sunday evening, he put a large enough load of sure thing tips in a read and destroy cube that she could set up a convincingly diverse portfolio of rapid gainers, with one or two modest growth stocks, to hatch her share of that commission nest egg into a chicken or two, and soon. He knew she'd memorize them later. It helped him more than she could possibly know to finally be able to do something concrete to take care of his family.

Before she left, they showered. It was one of the sad little rituals they'd developed through seven years of goodbyes. The driving rain of the shower quickly changed to sex. Then, with the carpet outside the bathroom soaked, they climbed back into the shower. He rinsed the fluff from the carpet off her back while she rinsed her sweat off his skin. Soon, there was no trace of her on him at all, with only a damp floor and her scent on the hotel sheets to remind him that he had a wife. He slept on her pillow that night.

She heard them before she saw them. The nasty half-juvenile male laughs, several, and the higher pitched whimper. Her lips thinned and she dropped her leather jacket on the sidewalk, deliberately relaxing before rounding the corner of the crumbling brick wall that had once fronted the alley on this side, pretending to look in her purse for something and coming out with paper that might have been a map and a small flashlight. Six. She'd caught them out of the corner of her eye. The girl was small, either a teen or just short. Cally looked up and startled slightly, pretending to see them for the first time, silently noting that the alley was open to a parking lot on the other end.

"Hey! What do you think you boys are doing? Let go of her!" She let some of the nasal, staccato character of a northern Urbie accent into her voice, indignant, stupid. They looked up, still holding their victim. No need to guess what they'd been starting on. A couple of them looked back at the girl, undecided. Cally advanced into the alley a few steps, trying hard to project a sense of indignation and a tourist's naive certainty of personal invulnerability. They bit.

"Hell, I never did like sloppy seconds, anyway." Four of them detached from the girl and advanced in a pack, breaking into an easy lope as she shuffled back a few steps, eyes wide, turning to run.

As they caught up with her, her back kick slammed hard into the lead thug's knee, snapping it backward with all the force her upgraded strength could deliver. He fell, his scream subsiding into pained swearing that she barely heard. She pivoted on the ball of her foot and slammed her palm heel into the throat of number Two, splintering his adam's apple, dancing back to plant a sidekick to his gut that threw him back a couple of yards to choke somewhere out of the way. Thug Three landed a hard punch to her head as Four grabbed her wrist. Bad mistake. Ducking under his arm, she brought it up behind him, keeping his body between her and Three for the crucial moment it took to snake her arm around his neck, pulling his head firmly against her breastbone before dropping straight to the ground. Four's neck made a satisfying crunch, but Three had had a chance to pile on top of her, which ordinarily would have worked on a woman her size. Bad luck for him, Cally O'Neal was anything but ordinary. She grabbed his head and twisted, but this one had the good sense to roll with it, bouncing back up to his feet as she reached her own, to see that thugs Five and Six had joined the party.

She grinned as she jumped into the air, slamming the front of her left foot on the side of Three's head hard enough to rattle him, but too high to kill him. She landed with bent knees on the way down, taking a fist to the jaw from Six as the price of getting another sidekick into Five and sending him tripping back over One, eliciting another scream. She danced back, rubbing her jaw. If anything, her grin widened. Six hesitated and she blocked a punch as Three came in without waiting for the other two—his first mistake. It cost him a blindingly fast pair of punches to his gut, which knocked the wind out of him right before he got a hard round punch to his nose. Predictably, blood spurted out. She didn't think she broke it, but it was going to be hell getting all the stains out of her blouse. While Three was hunched over with his hands on his knees, out of the way, Six came back with Five right behind him. The jumping backfist blacked Six's eye, causing him to hesitate again as another sidekick cracked a few of Five's ribs and knocked him out of the way.

She and Six fenced, with her absorbing the occasional hit just to get in a really pretty combination move. She seemed to be enjoying it more than he was. For the moment, Three and Five were just watching her play with Six, each grabbing an unexpected hurt but obviously not quite out for the count. Street fights seldom have lulls, but sparring matches do. For a moment, Six was paused, fists up, looking for an opening, catching his breath. She stilled, in the kind of absolute stillness that any fighter knows is one of the most dangerous moments in a fight.

"It's been fun playing with y'all, but I'm going to have to finish up now and get home," she said, the slight natural southern drawl at odds with the persona she'd worn coming into the alley.

Whether it was the stillness itself giving them a chance to think, or the recognition that three of their friends were on the ground, two corpses and one crippled, or the deadness that entered her blood-spattered face as if someone had flipped a switch and turned off all humanity inside her, Cally would never know. What she did know was that all three suddenly turned and made tracks down the alley faster than she would have figured they'd still be able to move, especially the one with the cracked ribs. She had somehow ended up facing a pile of soggy cardboard boxes, partway between the live kid and the girl.

She looked over at the crippled survivor, a kid, maybe in his early twenties, with dirty blond hair and a ratty bandanna around his neck. Blood soaked his jeans where she'd kicked him, but to her practiced eye it looked like he was in no danger of bleeding out. A foil packet flipped out of her hand, landing on the thug's stomach.

"Have a morphine. Hold you till the ambulance arrives." She fixed him with an icy stare, "Dude. You may not believe this, but I just did you a favor." He was too busy gritting his teeth to reply. Or too scared. "You're alive. File for disability, learn a trade, find another line of work. You were really lousy at this one, anyway." The cripple might have been swearing under his breath as she turned away.

Cally looked over at the girl, who had to be about fourteen, and blinked. "What the hell are you waiting for? Scram!" The idiot tried to run out the alley the same way the remaining thugs had gone. "Pfweet!" she whistled, jerking a thumb over her shoulder as the girl turned back around. "That way."

The assassin shook her head as the girl edged past her, skittering down the alley, obviously trying not to look at the bodies or the last guy. Cally rubbed her jaw. Definitely gonna bruise. Ick. She wiped the blood off her hands on her blouse, and off her face once she found a clean spot, picking her way past the cripple and the corpses, which were beginning to smell strongly of recent deadness.

"Oh." She turned back to the guy on the ground, coldly. "You never saw me. None of you. You're really sure you never saw me."

"Right. We're going to say a girl did this to us. I don't think so," he said, bitterly, muttering "bitch" under his breath.

She nodded once and picked up her purse and the stuff that had spilled from it, retrieved her jacket, and zipped it up to the neck. She got about a block away before pulling out her PDA. "Buckley, wait fifteen minutes and route a call to emergency services from the nearest pay phone." Uncharacteristically, the buckley was silent, merely acknowledging the command on the screen. Muttering, "I hate rapists," she walked the rest of the way to the parking lot and her bike without incident.

Home, on the other hand, wasn't so great. She was in her bathrobe in the laundry room, rinsing the blood out of her clothes, when she heard someone clear his throat.

"Good morning, Granpa," she said.

"Yeah, I suppose it *is* morning. Technically. Any of that yours?" His voice had a certain long-suffering quality to it.

"Like you really need to ask," she said, shaking meat tenderizer on the stains before adding the white blouse to a load of wash.

"How many times am I going to have to tell you that you can't depopulate the criminal element of Charleston single-handed? People would notice," he griped. "How many bodies?"

"Only two. Gang types. You and I both know the police are too overworked to investigate it. Besides, I really hate rapists."

"I'm not saying there's anything wrong with that, just that if you keep running in there like some comic book Valkyrie avenger, people are going to talk."

"Gampa, what's a ape-ist?" They both turned to see Sinda in the doorway clutching a bedraggled plush penguin. She dropped her fist from the eye she'd been rubbing when she saw Cally's face, "Mommy? You gots ouchies."

"I was in a little accident on the way home, sweetie. It looks worse than it is," she said.

"Were you wearing your helmet?" the four-year-old asked suspiciously.

"Yep. Just a few bruises and scrapes. Why aren't you in bed?"

"I skinned my knee when I fell offa my bike. You musta falled on your hands."

"Bed, Sinda," her mother ordered, glancing down at her raw knuckles. "Not one word," she said to Papa O'Neal, in response to his quirked eyebrow and the quivering corner of his lip as the little girl disappeared down the hall.

"Didn't say a thing." He walked off, whistling softly.

CHAPTER FIVE

Monday 10/18/54

It was a large office, for the moon. It had the standard black enamel desk with laptop and PDA, the ergonomic chair, and a pair of squashy armchairs upholstered in superior-quality leathex. Those were standard features for any managing analyst's office. Then there were the small touches that indicated that the office's occupant had the approval of the Grandfather, and his trusted aides, as a promising candidate for promotion—no small thing in an organization whose upper leadership tended to have the resources to avail themselves of the rejuvenation process. Discreetly, of course.

On one side of the room a carved, decorative screen kept unlikely company with an old-fashioned, framed, photo-quality print of a prewar surfer catching a wave at a place few remembered as Malibu Beach. Underneath the picture, a small fountain sat on a low table, gurgling peacefully. On another wall, a conventional work of a blossoming branch painted on parchment rested in a frame that matched the carved screen. A braided ficus, a species renowned for its tolerance of low gravity, sat in a large pot in one corner. A small potted plant sat on one end of the desk, partially screening a holocube of a spectacular blonde and two little girls from direct view through the open doorway. Of all the decor in the room, only the wall color had not been the occupant's choice. A shade the office manager called pale peach and the occupant called pink had been hard-coded throughout the suite of offices. Well, he hadn't chosen the carpet, either, but as it was an inoffensive light brownish color, he seldom noticed it.

Named Manuel Guerrera by his mother, and, later, James Stewart by himself, Yan Kato was an extraordinarily ordinary looking man. He was neither too tall nor too short. His hair was spiked enough to be proper, but not enough to draw attention. His features, while clearly Asian, did not lend themselves to identification with any known ethnic group. As his name suggested a mixed ancestry, that was unremarkable, too. In the aftermath of the war's turmoil, there were millions like him. As he was, in fact, Latino, the surgeons had considered his skin tone and texture too difficult to match to any specific pure ancestry.

At the moment, Yan—who still thought of himself privately as simply "Stewart"—was not looking at his office decor, but was instead facing the personal holotank behind his desk on which he had called up a display of star systems, travel times, and trade routes. He had been in the office, doped on provigil-C, for the entire nine hours he'd been back on station. He had been awake and running analyses on his buckley, with occasional carefully camouflaged data downloads, since leaving his hotel in Charleston some fifty-three hours before. He checked his results five times to make absolutely sure he'd accounted for as much as possible and provided for maximum local flexibility to accommodate unforeseen contingencies. Finally, he sent the orders to dispatch the Tong's single fast courier ship, which he technically had no authority to commandeer, along the prescribed route and sent an explanatory memorandum, eyes only, to the Grandfather. The courier was moderately expensive to maintain near a major jump point out from Earth. It was prohibitively expensive to dispatch anywhere, because of the fuel expenditures involved in making a warp jump and the resultant servicing of a vessel that was nearly scrap—all the Tong could afford. Mostly it sat, its bored crew collecting dust, ignored by the Darhel as a worthless, unreliable wreck unloaded on gullible humans as a vanity ship. Stewart would be answering some hard questions for his temerity in using it. Not just for one hyper jump, but for four. Dulain, to Prall, to Diess, resupply at Diess base, and then back to the Sol System. The first three systems with Epetar cargos would get a courier visit—just long enough to pop out of hyperspace, tight beam the heavily coded instructions to a communications satellite under cover of a general communications packet, and receive acknowledgment of receipt. The nice thing about the Galactic Communications System, or lack thereof, was that so many Darhel groups would have encrypted traffic of so many redundant messages going somewhere that everybody who received routine communications would assume that someone else's message had been important enough to charter a courier. This would spur much spying, but only against each other.

The only explanation the memo to the head of the Tong included was that there *was* an explanation, of course, and that it was a matter of the utmost discretion. Stewart never pumped his wife for information. For one thing, most of it would be irrelevant to what he did now. For another, he loathed traitors and would not have married Cally if he had believed for even a moment that she could be turned against her people. But the Bane Sidhe tended to attract good operational minds, not good businesspeople. He was sure she had no idea how much she had let slip by naming the size of her windfall. He wouldn't have asked if he had even for a moment suspected the crucial information he'd been able to derive from it. But done was done. Knowing the percentage commission, the value of trade goods, and knowing the approximate discount you lost off the market price fencing stolen goods even if you were a *good* negotiator—on matters of price, his wife was likely a poor one—there was really only one thing she could have stolen. She also had to have *really* gotten scalped on the deal. It was unusual for a Darhel to have that much code-key wealth on hand. Class Nine Code Keys were the ultimate form of negotiable wealth, usually only traded between Darhel Clan-Corps. You couldn't just use them; they were the master keys to make the master keys to make the keys that created nannites.

He was surprised she'd been able to fence them at all. He assumed it was through some remaining link to the other Bane Sidhe group. Come to think of it, the difficulty explained the pathetically low price she got.

She was a lot smarter than she'd pretended to be under her cover as Captain Sinda Makepeace when they first met, but Cally had, through no fault of her own, attended schools that placed a low priority on market economics, and had nothing like his own early environmental exposure to the realities of commerce. He had been a gang leader—a financially and socially successful one—before he and his men had gotten drafted into the war. His formative experiences had made the Tong a very good fit, once the United States Constitution that he'd once sworn to preserve, protect, and defend had, despite his best efforts, become a meaningless piece of paper. His wife's grandfather, also the father of his old CO, Iron Mike O'Neal, was a canny old smuggler. Passing *that* skill set on, along with the keen eye that allowed one to assess the worth of almost anything at a glance, had not been Papa O'Neal's priority in the beautiful assassin's formative years. Reclusive and deadly, she had been his perfect warrior child: cute as a puppy, with a bite like a cobra.

Unsurprisingly for a cute puppy, his wife had grown up to be one icy bitch. Together, they'd woken and thawed each other's hearts seven years ago on Titan Base. He loved her, he knew she loved him—but he never quite forgot the deadly killer concealed behind those beautiful, cornflower-blue eyes. Top operator, yes. Experienced at fencing stolen goods, no.

The only thing that matched her probable area of operations, the necessary portability, and the time period, would have been the price of a cargo of trade ships, ready to leave Titan Base. By the timing, it had to be the cargo slated for the Epetar Group—which fit with Manager Pardal's presence on Earth. Without the high-level nanogenerator code keys that served as real-money currency among the Darhel groups, the Epetar Group would not be able to pay for its shipments. Rather than arriving at a planet to attempt to pick up a cargo with no money, something the factor who owned the cargo would never allow, Epetar's freighters would wait until currency arrived by fast boat and then depart. Making them late for every port on their circuit.

At 0800 local, when the rest of the home office staff arrived, he would take his PDA with a carefully produced analysis on the screen with him and "forget" it at the water cooler. With any luck, the man in the cubicle next to it, a known Darhel plant for the Gistar Group, would pick it up and see the file. The man was stupid, and slack in his electronic hygiene. Stewart had already put a small tag on him to detect and copy his transmissions up the chain to his masters. The Tong valued more than Stewart's business talents. His years in Fleet Strike Counterintelligence after the war and before meeting his wife and becoming officially dead, had substantially enhanced the Tong's internal security. Half a dozen identified spies were now reporting primarily what the leadership chose to let them see.

Reporting this kind of material to a huge, hardball, corporate entity via a Tong plant would have been suicidal, if he'd been dealing with humans. Humans would put their heads together and *notice* that the Tong had had the information and had connections with the factors screwing Epetar along its trade routes. The trails were covered, but human intuition just might connect the dots. It paid to know the alien mind. Putting the pieces together, even long after the fact, would require having someone who had all the pieces. Which would mean someone at Gistar would have to share the information about how they knew of Epetar's loss. Sharing did not make up a major part of the Darhel personality. Humans from a rival corporation, in the same situation, would almost certainly look into it. Gistar couldn't care two beans about Epetar's losses, unless the existence of outside involvement was very blatant. The Darhel were not stupid. They were very, very smart. Probably smarter than humans. But they weren't invulnerable, if you could keep the left hand from knowing what the right hand was doing.

If Kim reported Epetar's misfortune to his bosses at Gistar, Stewart would know. If the man somehow missed the opportunity to peruse Stewart's PDA—and he'd carefully made sure anything else important was well locked down—he'd have to find some other way to feed him the information. The faster it got to Gistar, the better. It was crucial that the other Darhel group be in a position to snap up Epetar's cargoes. He'd chosen Gistar out of several Darhel groups with operations in the Sol System because it seemed to have the best cash flow and the best distribution of ships, for his purposes. Gistar routinely stocked portions of its cash reserves on board the commercial couriers that waited on site at most major jump points, ready to be dispatched with urgent information—for a steep fee. Any outgoing Gistar freighter could, again for a fee, rendezvous with a courier ship prior to jump and pick up code key currency to remedy misfortunes or take advantage of opportunities. Gistar had a freighter load of monazite sands, molybdenum, and various asteroid extracts bound from the Sol System to Adenast, with its major space dock facility and building slips. They had a courier load of Tchpth scientists bound on a return trip to Barwhon after installing some rather exotic equipment in their asteroid extraction facilities.

Both destinations would give ample opportunity for Gistar to divert a ship and load it with sufficient currency to purchase high-margin cargos. Both ships were far enough from the jump point for Kim to tightbeam them the motherload of information he was about to brilliantly stumble over, but close enough to it to ensure that all ships that would be involved in Stewart's little dance would be close to their respective jump points and therefore would move very, very quickly to reach their commercial targets.

The hapless Epetar crews would arrive at planet after planet to find no waiting goods. They would then be in position to make deals they thought would minimize their losses, all the while being systematically and subtly skinned. Stewart's grin was feral. *Ain't payback a bitch?*

It would all look so closely timed as to have been planned in advance by Gistar—drawing suspicion away from the organization that had such a firm hold on the loyalties of his wife. Stewart didn't give a flying fuck about the Bane Sidhe, but providing cover for his wife—and by extension his kids—was something else. He'd never want her to turn traitor on them, but God dammit he wished she'd just quit the fucking job. They wouldn't dare touch her if she was in the custody of the Tong, as his wife. They needed the organizational relationship too much, and she'd be no threat to them, anyway. It wasn't like they didn't have other dormant assets. The Tong's patronage *certainly* covered him from misunderstandings with the Bane Sidhe, if they were to become aware of his identity and continued survival today. Cally O'Neal Stewart would become just one more female operative on the inactive list. She didn't see it that way, which did maybe say a few things about where he rated on her list of priorities.

If, somehow, his analysis of the Darhel situation was wrong, in any major particular, he would probably find himself beginning a new job on the graveyard shift of the bar that served the station's dock workers. If he was right, as he was almost certain he was, he was about to make the organization a great deal of money. More importantly, he was about to enable the organization to subtly and thoroughly screw a Darhel business group while keeping it totally ignorant of the fact that it was being royally and deliberately fucked. The money would please his superiors. The honor restored, by avenging a very personal debt the Tong owed to the Darhel, would mean infinitely more. The Tong had been scrupulously careful never to speak of their knowledge of the events in the war, and how much they had pieced together of the part the Darhel played in it, anywhere where an electronic eye or ear might overhear it. They had quite meticulously avoided ever putting anything at all in writing, much less onto any electronic device. They had quite deliberately played fat, dumb and happy. And they had waited. Finally, there was an opportunity. It was worth a bit of risk to potentially avenge the deaths of billions of their people. Hell, it was worth the risk to avenge China alone.

The Tong had not originally been his people, of course. But when Stewart joined something, he joined.

Tuesday 10/19/54

Cally had to fight to stay awake on the drive into Charleston Tuesday morning. Granpa had been infernally cheerful when he woke her up at six. Unfortunately, strong coffee tasted wonderful, but might as well have been water for all the good the caffeine did her. Her nannites scavenged it and destroyed it almost before it hit her bloodstream. Provigil-C worked, but not if she wanted to sleep on the plane, and boy, did she want to sleep on the plane. There was too much to do once she got into base. She'd never have time to recover. She really ought to go through her pitch for Michelle's mission before she had to present it. There were a lot of things she ought to do. And she did them. Usually. Mostly. Sort of. Granpa had been a bad influence.

Keiran had the small, gray jet ready to preflight when they arrived—it had taken all of Granpa's persuasion to keep Lucille from sporting at least red stripes and her name.

Their company ID's, under a very sincere front corporation, allowed them to enter the charter gate at any time of the day or night without further screening. Despite the official "terrorism" that DAG existed to combat, nobody was hijacking or blowing up airplanes anymore. Why try that kind of political action? All you had to do if you didn't like living under an existing government was punch out a case or so of sten guns, stock up on ammo, and take off for parts unknown. Oh, there were political malcontents, of course. They just had a dearth of the personality types willing to go out and die for them. Cally never thought of the Bane Sidhe as terrorists, and would have argued vehemently that they were not. After all, they never, ever tried to be noticed, and they never, ever tried to frighten anyone at all. Oh, they sought political change. But very subtly, and with a careful eye towards the long haul. Personally, she was more impatient. It was one of the reasons she had chosen her particular profession. That, and some unusually high scores on the basic occupational specialization aptitude profile. Tactical patience came easily. Strategic patience was harder for her. It was only Aelool's assurance that endgame was ninety percent probable, for better or worse, within her own grandchildren's generation that made it possible for her to keep going, year in and year out.

Once she and Granpa had secured their bikes in the hangar, they stepped out onto the gray tarmac, under the heavy fall cloud cover. Kieran was in the cockpit preflighting Lucille, and Cally loaded her backpack onto the plane. From the boxes in back, she wasn't the only one supplementing income with a little tax-free transshipment of trade goods. She nodded approvingly, until she saw their pilot reach back over his shoulder to press something that looked suspiciously like a wad of bills into Granpa's hand.

"Granpa!" She knew she sounded shocked.

"What? Like you don't?" He didn't even turn around, pocketing the cash, hand coming back out with a well-worn tobacco pouch.

"You could have at least cut me in," she huffed.

"Oh. Sorry. Thought you were getting some unhealthy scruples in your old age," he said. "Besides, no offense, and I'm all for sharing the wealth, but what were you going to trade that I'm not already getting direct?"

"Well, for one thing, a few of the hospitals could certainly use some high grade opium. You know how bare bones they are for most drugs. They've got good enough lab guys to do most of the chemistry on site. We've got enough non-immunes that the base hospital wouldn't turn up their noses, either. Our guys could even do the final chemistry for whole shipments. Better to rope them in to do the reselling, anyway."

"And you'd have a source I don't know about? Tell me you're not involved in any way I'd disapprove of." He seldom took that flat tone with her.

"I have no part in profiting from putting a monkey on anyone's back, not even tangentially, if that's what you mean. Not *anything* you'd disapprove of, Granpa? You'd disapprove more if I wasn't." She smiled wryly.

He stared at her searchingly a moment before nodding. "We'll talk quantities later," he said. "And where the hell is Tommy?" He stepped to the door of the plane and looked out across the endless gray field as if he could make the other man appear by scowling.

Cally wasn't nearly that fussed about it. Tommy late meant more sacktime for her. She shifted enough boxes that she could recline her seat and got her sleep mask out of her thigh zip pocket. She could sleep without dark. She could sleep propped standing up if that was all she had time for. But she'd get the best use out of the available rest if she had dark. Besides, Granpa was alert enough for both of them. The last thing she heard before she drifted off was a grumpy harrumph from his general direction.

All too soon, he was nudging her awake, tapping her hand from a careful distance on the other side of the aisle.

"Hey, sleepy, time to wake up," he said.

She rubbed the sleep out of her eyes, glancing at the window. Not that it did any good, since someone had thoughtfully lowered the shade. She didn't feel the slightly hollow sensation of descent. "How far out are we?"

"A bit more than an hour," he said.

"*What?* I've only been asleep a half hour." She glared accusingly. "A bit more," she echoed grumpily, pulling the mask back down over her eyes.

"You got a cat nap. Quit bitching; time for business."

"Can't it wait?" she grumbled.

"Maybe for you it can," Tommy broke in, "but I've got three doctor's appointments and paperwork in personnel. Vitapetroni expects me pretty much as soon as we get off the plane."

"And I need my ducks in a row for Nathan. All right." She sighed, sitting up and yawning. "Anyone think to bring coffee?"

"Sure." Tommy poured a cup of coffee into a thermos cap and handed it over. The slightly sour aftertaste as she drank made her wish they could brew it on board. Unfortunately, the last coffee pot for the plane's machine had broken and from the prices on eBay you'd think the things were made of gold. Wendy had probably brewed this in a pan on the stove. She ignored the grounds in the bottom of the cup and finished the whole thing.

"So. Papa filled me in on the basic mission. Darhel-owned secret research facility, we pull a switch while the all-seeing high mucky-muck mentat is out of town. Broadly, what are the less obvious things that could go wrong? His schedule changes, difficulty getting people inside, all the standard stuff is a given." Tommy shrugged, pouring himself some of the aging brew.

"Well, first off the Darhel and the mentat are going to be worried directly about Michelle. If they weren't scared of her, they wouldn't be trying to kill her. She doesn't plan a direct attack, but how sure of that are they?" Cally offered.

Papa O'Neal spat thoughtfully into a paper towel, wadding it into an airsick bag. "I don't know how she'd attack if she did. Whether the mentat thinks he can handle it or not, my understanding is he's the *only* thing that could handle a direct attack and everybody would be worried about apocalypse anyway. You can't exactly plan for apocalypse. At least, I've mulled it over and I can't think of a way they could do it. They may be scared, but their whole play is a bet that she won't. If she goes ballistic on them, they'd have to worry just as much about her doing it when they try to call her debts. They've placed their bets, I don't think there's anything we can do about their own 'what if we're wrong' scenario for direct attack."

"They'll expect her to try to call in favors with Indowy clans to find it and steal it back. She's Indowy raised, and that's how they'd handle it. Especially since she's got few clan members of her own as far as they know—just Mike and her breeding group's kids. They'll obviously make sure Mike's on the far side of inhabited space," Tommy said.

"They have; I checked." Papa O'Neal nodded and put in, "They'll call in an aethal master. Get him to set up a situation board and block any moves with the Indowy. Since she's a master herself, they'll hire the best one they can find. We can only hope she's better than he is and has successfully camouflaged any connections she'll be using. That ball's in Michelle's court."

"Darhel. Aliens are alien. As it gets closer to her being in breach of contract, he may get antsy. If he gets nervous, he'll try to cover his own ass. To a Darhel, that will mean flashy moves to look like he went above and beyond in the event that something goes wrong. So what's he do? One thing is it's Earth and humans. Smart Darhel hire security when dealing with Earth and humans. He doesn't know how much they need, so he'll think more is better and expect his bosses to think the same, but he won't want to pay much for it. DAG."

"What? How do you get that?" It was Tommy who said it, but he and Papa were both looking at her as if she'd gone nuts.

"No, it makes sense if you think like an Elf. Great Lakes is right next door. DAG has figured prominently in three or four big box-office holodramas lately," she explained.

Tommy and Papa rolled their eyes. The shows in question had been more Hollywooded than anything Hollywood had turned out prewar. Really bad, and really popular.

"The point is they're glamorous right now. Flashy. The Darhel always have to have the best of the best of whatever Earth's got. Adding to the attraction, he probably doesn't have to pay his lackeys in the Joint Chiefs' office an extra buck to get them. Just bully the guys—they're already nice and compromised. He'll do it because he can, and he'll *like* it. It's an excuse to throw his weight around. What's the downside to him?"

"That's a hell of a longshot," Papa complained. "He may not even think of it. You can never be too paranoid. Okay, we'll cover it. Brief in one of the cousins just in case."

"He's more likely to bring in a second aethal master. Where a first won't get her, a second might," Tommy insisted.

"True. All we can do about it is remind her to be paranoid as hell and not get caught. Cally, that's your department."

"Got it. I'll take care of the briefing, too. We've got that family reunion coming up. I'm sure there will be someone I can pull off to the side. Are we done?"

"For now, unless any of us think of anything else." He spat once into the bag and grabbed a bottle of water. "I wouldn't turn down a cup of that coffee."

"I'm sleeping." Cally said emphatically. "Don't wake me until we're on the ground."

Father O'Reilly's office was a familiar and usually comfortable place, but today he looked more strained than she'd seen him since the first, tough weeks right after the Bane Sidhe split. Aelool was absent, attending a birth celebration for his newest clan members. It would take all day. It had become necessary for the health of the remaining Indowy to break the traditional prohibition against their highly prolific race establishing breeding groups on Earth. It had been done with trepidation on both sides and a hard upper population limit. Once the limits had been reached, the tentative plans were to proceed with some highly clandestine shipyards that had always been beyond the daring of the original organization. Human influence on the Indowy on this side of the split was so infinitesimal as not to be noticeable to most humans. Cally knew enough about the Indowy to realize the changes were at breakneck speed, for them, and to understand quite clearly why the Bane Sidhe split had been a total divorce. She also knew why the organization was so very careful to conceal the extent of the social changes from the Tchpth observers. Nothing could be concealed from the Himmit, of course, but just because they collected stories didn't always mean they told them.

It made her nervous to see the father so clearly stressed. Anything that could upset him couldn't be good news for the organization. Usually, he wasn't a man given to fidgeting and had one of the best poker-faces of anyone she knew. It took more than a still expression to conceal dark circles under your eyes, though, and the usually immaculate clerical collar was wrinkled as if he hadn't been to bed and changed clothes in quite awhile. He had that look around the eyes that she couldn't quite put into words but had learned to associate with an active dose of Provigil-C. His thumb and forefinger were rubbing together as they must when he prayed the rosary, even though his hands were empty. She doubted he had even noticed he was doing it, which disturbed her even more. The weather in the artificial window reflected the cold, wet, stormy day above. Not the most pleasant day in the world. She herself would have preferred something more cheerful, but she didn't ask him to change it. It would have been rude. Normally she found the shushing sound of rain peaceful. Today it was just dismal. She took a deep breath and folded her hands in her lap, waiting for his comments on the mission profile displayed in front of him on his desk. He turned the display off and sighed, closing his eyes and pinching the bridge of his nose before looking up at her.

"When, exactly, is Michelle's contract with the Darhel overdue? I see nothing explicit in here about an inside man, and we'd need one. Does she have a man inside or doesn't she, and if not, what are your plans for how we would get a man inside, ourselves, before the whole endeavor becomes moot?"

"Her contract doesn't go into default until May, but she's not confident of being able to hold off a contract court, if the Epetar Group chooses to convene one, for more than about two Earth months." She pointed to the folder. "As you inferred from that, she does have someone inside, but his willingness to help us is limited to helping influence any hiring decisions in our man's favor."

"A hiring decision in our favor. Or, knowing who our applicant is, he could be setting a trap. He could get caught, himself, and give our man up. Of course, no operation is without risks." The priest propped his chin on steepled fingers for a moment.

"I understand that your sister wants this device, and I understand that she's willing to pay very well for its retrieval." His tone was pained, and she knew this wasn't good. "But nothing you've shown us so far gives us good enough assurance of team survival to make it worth the hazard. Also, there's no operational benefit to our organization. Thanks to your own efforts, we do have some financial breathing room. But for strictly financial supplementation, there are safer options. We have always reserved this level of risk for operations with a specific strategic goal. Unless you can show me how this qualifies, I'm afraid we're going to have to decline," he said.

It was not at all what Cally had expected Father O'Reilly to say, and she was temporarily at a loss for words.

"Cally, it's not that I'm indifferent to your family interest here, or the Clan O'Neal interests, for that matter. It's that now, more than ever before, we have to reserve major risks of trained assets to operations with major, long-term, strategic significance." He sighed. "I would love to be able to say yes. And I have heard enough from the Indowy to have a great deal of respect for Michelle O'Neal. I'll give you this much. If you can either bring her on board with the organization or show me why this operation has serious strategic implications that we have so far missed, we'll reconsider."

"Excuse me. External mind control of human beings doesn't have serious strategic implications? And as a pure business matter, on board or not, have you considered how much having a Michon Mentat owe us favors *means* to this organization?" Cally blinked in disbelief.

"It's strategic if they really have a working prototype. Just because Michelle thinks they do or are about to doesn't mean she's right. I know a lot about what someone with her capabilities can do, and I'm not questioning that it's impressive. I also know that her ability to spy on the immediate environs of another mentat, without alerting him and triggering exactly the kind of conflict she's trying to avoid, are limited. I need hard evidence. A schematic, a workable theory of function, information about the origin of the device, a man inside—hard evidence."

"All that? You don't want much. What if you're wrong?"

"Not all that, just enough of it to be going on more than fears and hunches—even hers. I have to calculate our risks. I can't do that without hard information. For something this big, I'm afraid Michelle's unsupported word, very good though that may be, isn't enough."

"The assessment of a Michon Mentat, to the point of being willing to actually get involved in something, isn't enough." Cally was still. *Shit, Father O'Reilly is* never *this unreasonable. I don't think I'm going to get any more out of him than this. Not today. Fuck. Well, I'll just get more and try to catch him in a better mood.*

"If it means that much to her and she's that sure, recruit her. That would be worth enough by itself to justify the risk. Cally, I'm sorry, but you're thinking like a human. I have to look at Michelle's request as if an Indowy of the same level had made it. And her motives and ends may not be our motives and ends," O'Reilly said.

"That makes no sense."

"Believe me, it does. This is academic, you know. She has to be basing her assessment on something. It's enough for her to risk, even herself. But it may not be enough for *us* to risk. You need to meet with her. It's time for her to show some of her cards." The priest looked pointedly at the door, clearly dismissing her.

What the fuck's eating him? I dunno, but I'd better find out.

CHAPTER SIX

Cally made sure she snagged Willard Manigo for lunch. He was more plugged in to the grapevine than any three other people in the organization. She had checked the menu and had shelled out for a bottle of steak sauce to go with his soyburger, and even managed to find him a Snickers bar that was only a week past its sell-by date.

Then she waited until he got in line before sliding up behind him.

"Hey, Willard, how's it going?" she said.

"Well, hi, Cally." He grinned. "It just *amazes* me to see you here."

"Heh. Okay, so you don't miss much. Grab a table with me?" she asked.

"Sure. Especially since I figure you're pretty much the reason chocolate chip cookies have made it back onto the dessert menu." He gestured towards a corner near the conveyor belt. Not quite on people's path out, it was still close enough for the kitchen clatter to muffle their voices.

She walked across the room with him, dodging tables and other diners, sharing a friendly greeting on the way with the people she knew well enough to be almost friends with. The steel of the chair legs squeaked on the tiles as they pulled up to the table. Even with Galplas flooring, it didn't matter. It seemed to be a law of nature everywhere that cafeteria floors had to squeak.

"See the Old Man this morning?" he opened, picking up the

steak sauce and dousing his burger. He looked at it doubtfully and gave it a few more shakes. "Hey, thanks for the stuff."

"Yeah, I saw him. And, well . . . he didn't seem too glad to see me," Cally said.

"I think you were in the wrong place at the wrong time, again," he said.

"What, is it just me?"

"I don't think it's that. It's . . . well the Crabs are pissed about the heist, and they could cut the trickle of low code keys and tech we're getting down to nothing if they wanted. And we've started having problems holding full-time staff because the food and pay suck—ideology only goes so far when you've got a family to feed. And we lost a couple of agents in Durban last week. The last few days just haven't been good. I tell ya, my department is running fifty percent understaffed," he said, palming the candy bar and making it disappear under the table.

"Not a great time to put more stress on the father's plate."

"No." He shook his head, taking a big bite of his burger.

Wednesday 10/20/54

Cally checked into a temporary room on base and pulled out her PDA. *O'Reilly wants more, I'll get him more. I hope.* She logged onto the Perfect Match site, which had obviously had a recent web redesign. She had gone to the site, just to check it out, after one of the teenage girls on the island had mentioned it to a friend in one of the hand-to-hand courses. *Of course I was just checking it out. To make sure it was safe.*

The redesign had not changed the site for the better. A background of lurid pink hearts clashed against the fuschia and orange-red backgrounds of sappy pictures that looked like they'd been swiped from the covers of bodice-rippers. Bright yellow buttons for everything from links to hit-counters to awards of dubious provenance littered the bottom of the page, seemingly at random. The text and frames couldn't seem to decide what color to be, and the company logo at the top of the page actually *blinked*. It looked like another company had decided that do-it-yourself was cheaper than hiring art talent.

Blech! I hope Michelle will forgive me. Okay, where's the pesky forum? There.

She thought for a minute. "MargarethaZ: Apollo555, I have eyes only for you." *Okay, so it's trite. At least it doesn't stand out in amongst all this sappy crap. Vanna69 wants to do* what? *Now that's just gross. Eww.* She logged off, wishing there really was such a thing as brain floss.

"You know the people you meet on those places all look horrible," the buckley commented. "And just last week, a man was killed in his sleep by a girl axe-murderer he met in a chatroom. Fifty-seven percent of 'singles' online are actually married. Twenty-two percent are ki—"

"Shut up, buckley."

"Right."

"Buckley, go secure. Where's Granpa?" she asked.

"In the gym. Did you know that ninety-three point two percent of all sports inj—"

"Shut up, buckley."

"Well, you *did* ask the question! Why ask me a question if you don't want to—"

"Shut up, buckley."

"Right."

Papa O'Neal was doing his morning chin-ups when Cally walked into the otherwise empty gym, having taken time to change into her own workout clothes before taking the bounce tube down to level three. The black shorts were okay, but the red leotard was on its last legs. She clung to it because it had that blessed option, a built-in sports bra. And not one of those flimsy ones, either. This one actually *worked*. She walked over to the bar and began stretching, waiting for the young-old man to finish his set.

He dropped lightly from the bar, flexing his knees as he hit, and walked over to her. His T-shirt was dark and wet in big patches, his red hair darkened with sweat. He grabbed a clean towel out of the box at the end of the bar and turned to her, wiping his face.

"So, mission a go?" he asked. To anyone who didn't know the inner workings of Bane Sidhe society, it would have seemed odd that Cally led the team instead of her grandfather, who, after all, had more experience. The truth was, he didn't have time. Clan O'Neal administration had eaten up so much of his days with things he couldn't delegate that handing off leadership to her had been the only way he could be assured of any meaningful time with Shari and the kids. Besides, she was good at it. So he had explained, anyway.

"Not yet," she said, stretching into a vertical split.

"*Not yet*?" he coughed. "Whaddya mean not yet? Hello, *job*. Hello, *paying job*. Hello, life and death mission on the side of good and right? Not *yet*?" He started absently patting the nonexistent pockets on his shorts and T-shirt before sighing and letting his hands drop. "Okay, what the fuck's going on?"

"What isn't? The Crabs are pissed and are threatening to fuck with our code key supply, the Old Man's about that far away from a nervous breakdown," she held her fingers about a half inch apart. "And of course, it's all my fault. Okay, not really. Just the wrong place at the wrong time. Anyway, O'Reilly wants more hard evidence that Michelle is either right about this thing and the threat level, or he wants her on board. One or the other."

"Say that again." O'Neal was ice.

"He didn't deny the mission, Granpa." Cally put a placating hand on his chest. "He just wants more of her cards on the table, his words, before we commit. It's a pain in the ass, not high treason."

"No. That join-up shit—" His clenched hands were relaxing slowly and smoothly. A bad sign.

"Like you wouldn't know about bargaining chips, Granpa? He wants to know the mission's not going to be another bust—and I can't believe I'm defending this." She sidestepped casually, putting herself between Granpa and the door. "But I guess I am. Get pissed *after* I talk to her, if he doesn't approve the mission then."

"We're doing it. All that's left to be decided is if they're coming along or not."

"Fine. But don't nuke our bridges unless you have to, get it?"

He held a hand up, finger pointed at her, about to say something, but then dropped it to his side.

"Right. Don't nuke the bridges. Got it," he sighed. "Make it so I don't need to nuke 'em, Granddaughter."

"Yeah, but no pressure, right?" Cally put her head in her hand for a minute before looking back up at him. "I'm staying over another night, at least. You guys can either fly back and I'll drive, or whatever. I know we just planned on a one-day trip."

"Right. I'll call Shari and tell her not to hold dinner."

Friday 10/22/54

The Cook Retail Center was Chicago's newest shopping mall. Cally pulled the old Mustang in and parked. The spot was way back from the entrance, but it was the closest one she could find. No matter how the economy in general was suffering, the fat cats in the federal bureaucracy were getting plenty. Like a gold rush town, to a limited extent the cash rolled downhill. It was a small mall, all cream walls and chrome. When they said the plant foliage had variegated colors, they really meant it. They had plants—or the equivalent—from Barwhon and a good half dozen other planets. The Barwhon stuff she recognized right off. The purple was a dead giveaway. And the place was busy, for a weekday. *Maybe I shouldn't have come just before lunch. There* were *other choices.*

If I'm going to be meeting Michelle more than once or twice, she has to get out of those damned conspicuous mentat robes. Could she scream, "Hi, I'm Michelle O'Neal and I'm on a planet where I'm not supposed to be," any louder? Cally found a chain store well known for subdued but dressy casual clothes. As a trained observer, having seen Michelle twice, she had a perfect memory of her sister's size for everything but shoes. It wasn't hard to find a cream sweater and tan slacks. She added a tortoise-shell rooster clasp so the mentat could do something more conventional with her hair than that bun. Conservative, but nice.

The big reason she had chosen this mall had to do with the very upscale Chinese restaurant at one of the side entrances. It was one of the contact points Stewart had given her. Someplace where her money was no good and her privacy absolute. The Bane Sidhe expense budget didn't run to business lunches anymore.

Normally, she couldn't have afforded any place this nice and would, therefore, have avoided it like the plague. She never, ever lived above her visible means—it was the first thing Bane Sidhe internal security looked for when they swept for moles. But with the bonus, she could afford a good meal out, and the Old Man knew she had a high-level meeting. Besides the tongs had a good reputation for actually delivering privacy when they sold it. If paid not to ask questions, they asked no questions. *Not that I'll actually be paying. I didn't get to the top of the profession without knowing when to take a calculated risk. Necessary mission, this gets the job done, saves scarce resources. In this case, my own. I'm not touching that seed capital for more than the girls' Christmas until it's had the chance to get together with those stock tips and make babies.*

Recognition was as professional as she could want. A word and a hand sign, a particular place at the counter, and a waiter discreetly ushered her to the back room, handing her several menus. If the manager was surprised when he asked her if she would be expecting anyone and she said her friend would find her, he gave no sign. He simply left and presumed his guest knew her own business. Michelle appeared seconds after the door shut behind him, robed, as always.

Cally carefully didn't sigh. "Okay, we can't have lunch without the people up front seeing you enter in the normal way. Hey! Don't go!" This time she did sigh, in relief, as Michelle stayed there but raised an eyebrow. "Here. I got you some street clothes. Change and do your thing, showing up in the ladies' room. Nobody really ever notices who goes in and who comes out, but they *will* notice if you're in this room without entering it. Go ahead and change here. At least nobody'll come in without knocking. Oh, and your code keys are in the bag."

Michelle's eyebrows arched higher in her otherwise impassive face, as she took the bag but made no move to change clothes.

"Oh, for heaven's sakes. I won't look, all right?" Cally said.

Michelle carried the clothes over to a corner, looking at Cally pointedly until she turned her back. A few moments later the Michon Mentat handed her sister her folded robe and disappeared. Before she left, just for an instant, Cally saw her feet. *Birkenstocks?!*

When Michelle walked back in, she was obviously ill at ease in clothes that were, for her, so unusual.

"So how long has it been since you've worn anything but these robes?" She put the garment, which she'd been holding on her lap, into one of the now-empty shopping bags.

"Earth styles? Fifty years. The cut and fabric of clothing has changed over the years for utility reasons, even on Adenast. And the first colors were inharmonious for human well-being. But our changes have had nothing like the frequency and variety you have here. Clothing is counterproductive for the Indowy, and we—they and us—do not see the point in having to turn around and replace things over and over again every couple of years, or worse, like less Galactized humans do."

"How do you stand it?" Cally couldn't help asking.

"I wanted to ask how you do." Michelle chuckled. "Having to buy replacement clothing as often as you do would deplete my pay very quickly. Not to mention my time."

"It's a trade-off. We probably pay about the same, when you get down to it. But most of us *like* to shop." Cally grinned, eyes twinkling.

"Leisure. The amount you have is unheard of on Adenast. Converted for differences in reckoning time, my schedule would work out to about ninety hours a week, Earth time. Some more, some less."

"For how long at a stretch? That's a crushing schedule," Cally said.

"It is an ordinary schedule. The discipline reduces the need for sleep. And I include necessary muscle care periods in my schedule, of course. Human Sohon workers cannot maintain health without it." She waved a casual hand at Cally, a deliberate gesture rather than a spontaneous one. "Really, I enjoy my work, Cally. It satisfies me a great deal to accrue honor to Clan O'Neal. I do regret that Father has never learned to understand. You are more often around Indowy than he is. Am I truly that alien to you?"

Her sister shrugged. "You're . . . very Indowy. Your expressions aren't very expressive."

"How strange. To the Indowy we are so very human. And our expressions are stilled, of course, out of habit. We copy Indowy expressions, or those of the other races, to communicate, but they never become automatic. So when we Galactized are not actively using facial expressions, our faces tend to be still to avoid misunderstandings. And, of course, while working, the feelings must be still."

"We should order." Cally pressed the button for the discreet call light at the base of a small lion sculpture next to the sauce caddy. She didn't recognize many Chinese ideograms—after so many languages on so many missions they ran together without a pre-mission review—but she did know those few that she could expect in these establishments, including the sequence that roughly translated, "Press for service."

"What are you going to eat?"

"I thought I'd try the crispy-skin duck, and I love hot and sour soup. Ooh. And they have shrimp spring rolls."

"You have not been here before?"

"No, this is a treat for me." Cally smiled. "What are you going to have?"

"The Buddha's delight looks appropriate. And I will have to ask the waiter which soups do not have meat. I can order my spring roll vegetarian, can I not?"

"There're other vegetarian choices on the back of the menu, so you don't need to feel locked in to any one thing."

"I noticed. I chose what I like." Her smile was slow, and obviously thought about, but it did reach her eyes.

"So how do you see me?" Cally couldn't help but ask. Seeing Michelle from her own point of view had been . . . enlightening.

"Like the rest of our clan. You are so aggressively human that at times I can not imagine how the Indowy who live on your base avoid fleeing in distress. You do not actually eat meat in front of them, I hope?"

"They don't come to the cafeteria. And we learn lists of expressions not to do when they're around."

"Yes, but I doubt any of you understand how difficult it must still be for the Indowy who live among you. Each of them perforce becomes an expert in a very difficult branch of xenopsychology. And those who raise their children on your base must be very apprehensive and very brave, to risk the lifelong social functionality of their offspring. I have seen the reports. Most of them are almost pathological loners, by Indowy norms."

"I hadn't thought of it that way. I suppose xenopsych is hard for everyone," Cally conceded. "Now, about this mission . . . The leadership wants more evidence and more information before committing us to the mission."

"The purpose and the pay are not sufficient?"

"It's political. The risks are, for various reasons, greater than just the loss of our team if the mission goes to hell on us. They want some hard evidence. Sorry about that, but there it is. Think convincing Indowy."

"I had made a projection of the possible complications, and anticipated your request. I would have preferred a better price and wished to keep my request simple. I think I can help you get what you need while relieving some of the political concerns."

The mentat lifted her hand to reveal a data cube. It could have just been sleight of hand, but Cally suspected "real" magic.

"Here is a cube of some of Erick's work that I was able to acquire through my own resources. The Darhel commissioning the research cannot do the tests themselves, but they . . . like to watch," she said, something about her colorless tone expressing infinite distaste. "I do not have other hard evidence that your superiors would accept, but there is a way to get it, and something else. Since the material on that cube was in Darhel hands, it was possible to obtain a copy. The device specifications and modifications never leave the research facility. I have my memory, and I have partial views from cube recordings. I *could* construct a very convincing substitute from just that data, but I can build something much more effective with some additional information. I can construct a substitute that almost works. Not a working model, but a device almost all personnel will merely take for damaged or malfunctioning, not completely inert. What I need are the records from the Fleet Strike team that originally retrieved the device. It was recovered partially disassembled, and with some other devices—part of a museum display on a Tchpth planet." Unlike most humans, she pronounced the name of the Galactic species perfectly, making it sound easy.

"Crabs have museums?"

"Yes. They have very good museums, although the ones with extensive Aldenata displays are typically closed to any species but their own. The other species were never meant to have this. Not until we were much farther along the Path."

"Path? You say that as though it's preordained or something." Cally held up her hands, rejecting the idea.

"There are things you do not know. There are things you *should not* know." Michelle held up her hand. "Do not ask for things you know I will not tell to even my sister and fellow O'Neal. I will not harm you or Clan O'Neal with too much of the wrong information. Your employers, the Bane Sidhe, have this policy also—not to harm their people with things they must not know. In this, at least, they are wise. You need to listen now so that I can tell you what you will need to know about the Fleet Strike mission that first obtained this device."

"The biggest thing I need to know, first, is how your man inside can ensure our operative gets hired, how we can be assured that this isn't a trap, and to what degree we can count on your man to keep our operative's identity confidential if your guy gets burned."

"As I said before, my 'man' is in personnel. To be specific, he occupies a key position in the personnel department. He can control which resumes get through the process. He can contrive bad references if the wrong applicant is chosen. Your person will be hired, assuming you can fabricate adequate background credentials and documentation. Scrutiny of your fabrications will be light, to say the least. A list of the positions most likely to come open, accompanied by detailed position requirements, are on the cube. My 'man' owes Clan O'Neal a third-level favor, through me, which is binding enough to satisfy the strictest concerns." She looked at her sister's raised eyebrows and sighed. "You may confirm the degree of obligation involved with the Indowy Aelool. Now, may I continue?"

The opening view of the cube showed a large, high-ceilinged room, split down the middle with a sturdy-looking dividing wall. Each room contained two chairs, at opposite ends of the room, with a man and a woman locked into each chair with steel restraints. The rooms looked quite clean around the edges, but the stains in the center of the room and by the chairs made Cally wince. The hardened assassin, being what she was, recognized instantly that the smears and trails across the floor were a mix of dried and fresh, streaming to a pair of central drains that appeared slightly . . . clogged.

She could hear mumbling in the background, but couldn't quite make out the words. "Buckley, speech enhancement please." As the thin tenor voice began to clarify into tinny but clear words, she said, "Raise the volume two notches."

". . . has no prior preparation. The subject on the right has been prepped through an increasingly intense series of directed tasks, from innocuous to unpleasant. Today's demonstration shows the necessity, with the current prototypical configuration, of some prior access to the subject to precondition the acceptance of control, and the familiarity of the operator with the subject's mind. Without prior access, control is limited by intensity of task and degree of preparation. Current research aims to refine our equations for computing probability of successful control for a given task by a specified subject. Yes, you have a question?" The tenor paused. The next voice was gibberish despite the Bane Sidhe's top of the line speech enhancement software.

"We agree. Unfortunately, even extensive conditioning fails to preserve the active subject in an end-series trial like this one. We still have a lot of refinement and research before we can meet final specifications." There was a pause. "Another use we hope to make of our research data is to separate minds into primary and, if possible, secondary classifications identifiable by externally observable characteristics, and genetic profiles. Our goal is to refine the software, in the final device, to modify initial output based on preassessed typing, where available. We believe that we will be able to substantially increase control probability and decrease the number of prep . . ." The voice drifted off as if the speaker had stepped farther away from the pickup. On the floor in the rooms, the shackles on the chairs snapped open, freeing the subjects to stand, move around, rub wrists. In each room, one subject sat frozen in the chair, despite the removal of physical shackles.

Then it got ugly. Hardened as she was to the bloodier side of life, she had to fight her rising gorge several times before the "experiment" ended. On the unconditioned side, the people were physically intact. Workers shot both with a trank gun before removing them. The indifferent treatment during the removal made it clear the tranks were solely for the workers' safety. On the conditioned side, workers in gray coveralls and gloves came in wheeling an equally gray trash bin to clean up whatever remained.

When Cally left her room to walk to the gym, people got out of her way. One look at her face and coworkers disappeared through the first convenient door or side corridor—as quietly and unobtrusively as possible. The prior inhabitants abandoned the locker room seconds after she entered. The gym itself didn't quite empty. The other users just discreetly moved to the far end of the large room, away from the mats and bar.

Two hours later, she stood in the shower letting the steaming water pound away the rest of the stress, *We're doing it. I don't care about the damned politics, I don't give a fuck about approval, we're doing it.* She sighed. *But approval would be nice. Professional. If I plan to get Nathan on board, I have to be* strictly *professional.*

CHAPTER SEVEN

Monday 10/25/54

"Nathan, here's what I've got for you. I think it'll make all the difference," the silver-blonde assassin was wearing a forest green suit. *She obviously dressed for success.* As a priest, he wasn't supposed to notice such things. He could appreciate the color and fit of the suit, and the obvious custom-tailoring of the blouse. He would have suspected her of living above her means if he hadn't known the outfit had been a Christmas present from her grandparents several years ago. As an assassin and operative, Cally had studied and drilled on the value of proper costuming. *The bare fact,* he winced at his mental choice of words, *is that I am* not *as immune to Cally O'Neal's charms as I ought to be. But it's not the job of a good priest to be immune to the temptations of the flesh, just to resist them. Sweet and lethally charming when she wants to be, isn't she?* He focused on the "lethal" part and began counting her kills in his head as a distraction.

"I hope it's good, Cally. I have to be a diplomat as well as manage operations. Right now, through no fault of yours, you and your team are squarely in the middle of politics again. This time, it's our fault, and I'm sorry. Our faulty intelligence got you into this situation." He smiled wryly, passing her a cup of coffee. He had used the good Jamaican stock. Charm and a bit of courtesy went both ways. She was a friend, not an enemy, of course, and he'd love to approve her mission if she made a good enough case for it. *It's just that with Ms. O'Neal a man had better always be quite sure he's thinking with his brains. Even an old priest,* he acknowledged ruefully.

"It's good. First, Michelle will pay the same amount over again in level two code keys, under the table. A private reserve for us. The whole pay package, thirty percent now, thirty percent after a necessary intermediate run, forty percent on delivery," she said.

"But pay wasn't our problem. Please tell me you have more." *The Darhel's lackey in Burma, a corrupt priest in Ireland, three businessmen who sold out a factory of captured Posleen equipment in Durban, that too-able subordinate of Worth's in Cleveland . . .*

"I'm getting there, Nathan. I've got a file with her initial results studying the Aldenata device, the one this research is based on, before this Erick person took off with it. Buckley, send it and *stay mute,*" she said.

Father O'Reilly's eyebrows arched.

"Yeah, I keep my buckley's emulation set a little high," she shrugged. "Anyway, I know it's not much, but that's where the intermediate mission comes in. Fleet Strike recovered the device on Dahl, and that initial report, as well as the observations of their field technician, will be in Fleet Strike's secure AID files at Fredericksburg. There are a lot fewer unknowns there, and they just aren't used to getting hit, so they'll have decent security, but not great. They're used to security against Posleen and the occasional humanist nutballs, not other trained humans. They're *not* trying to protect a nasty mind-control gadget against rival businesses."

"So you're hoping you can get me to approve the Fredericksburg run to get enough data to approve the job you really want. And if you get there and the records you want have been deleted? Wouldn't the group sponsoring this Erick want to clean up behind themselves?"

"Michelle doesn't think they have. I think they might consider it an unnecessary risk. What do they gain? Michelle admits she can't make anything workable from the initial field observations, and our potential targets have the device in hand. Who would they be keeping the information from? Besides, she says the initial observations probably will help her make a more convincing decoy for the switch."

"Might and Michelle says and probably. It's still a bit thin, Cally."

"I know. But you get sixty percent of the total just for this. That's a hundred and twenty percent of the original fee. Half of that in code keys you can actually use. Just for the initial intel gathering mission. With nothing counterproductive to Bane Sidhe interests. I would think that's a pretty sweet deal. Of course there's risk, but isn't there always? It's a good deal, Father."

"Yes, it is." He sighed. *Am I succumbing to feminine charm, or making a rational decision? The keys are the kicker. They reduce our direct dependence on the Tchpth in the short term, and open a favor-trading relationship with a potential alternate source, with the strongest clan of connections, which provides a future margin of safety. The Tchpth planners would see a difference between ceasing to provide us with keys, versus cutting us off from alternate supplies. As a Michon Mentat, Michelle O'Neal's judgment carries weight that they might not interfere with. They would consider her decisions more reliable than that of the leaders of the Indowy Bane Sidhe, since she does not—or has not until now—engage in intrigue. A tenuous thread, but better than we have now, which is* no *backup. It's a sound rational basis for the decision, and damn my juv hormones for confusing the issue.*

"You have my approval for the Fredericksburg run. But if what you find isn't conclusive, I won't be able to approve the rest of the job in good faith. I also need much more than 'Michelle says' about how we're going to get an agent in place for the main job," he said.

"There's a file on the cube with job listings and requirements. We fake up the ID's and resumes, her guy in personnel makes sure at least one of us gets hired. I took the liberty of downloading it to buckley to cross-reference with our prior missions and build a file for the covert identifications department. I hope I can get authorization to get them moving on this. Time is tight."

"Fine. If Michelle still wants to hire our services, knowing that this in no way commits us to the rest of her project, then do it."

O'Reilly stared after her as the door closed behind her. *Heavenly Father, I hope I'm doing the right thing.* He crossed himself and picked up his own coffee, sipping it before it got cold.

As a "live" priest, prewar, to him the area of finance had always been something other people dealt with. Ever since he'd come inside and taken over the base management of the Earth headquarters for the Bane Sidhe, he had learned more about budgets and cash flow and overhead than he had ever wanted to know. But he had come in as one of the leading experts on xenopsychology—albeit only known as an expert by a select few. The Tchpth hadn't a clue about finance. As long as they were undisturbed in their figurative ivory towers, they let the Darhel deal with such mundanities. Which was half the reason the Galactic situation had become, so long ago, what it was today.

There were no Darhel here. The likelihood of the Tchpth or the Indowy outside the O'Neal Bane Sidhe figuring out that they had more level two code keys than they should was, well, infinitesimal. It just wasn't the way they thought. Some Himmit somewhere would notice, sometime. But they wouldn't share the information. They liked to gather stories; they didn't seem to have nearly as much fun telling them.

A strategic reserve wouldn't solve the fundamental problem of Crab-dependence, but that was going to be a tough nut to crack. They were not going to be able to out-Crab the Crabs. The solution was going to have to be a matter of reducing, not ending, their dependence on the Crabs, while finding other Galactic trade goods than mercenary soldiers. And that last might well turn out to be the impossible dream. But if solved, that would likely be solved after one Father Nathan O'Reilly had joined his maker, rejuv or no rejuv.

Connections with Michelle O'Neal wouldn't hurt, but mentats tended to be so aloof from the real world that it was far more likely than not to be a one-off, of *no* long-term help. Still, plant enough seeds and something was bound to come up.

The slightly built man with the straw blond hair falling over his eyes looked barely old enough to be in a club. Even one as relaxed in its standards for clientele as the Pink Heat Showbar. In fact, despite a chin full of carefully cultivated stubble, he had had to bribe the doorman to ignore the presumed-fake nature of his ID. The ID really was fake, but not for the reasons the doorman assumed. George Schmidt was a forty-one-year-old juv whose usual profession involved taking out the worst of the world's human trash. Worst by O'Neal Bane Sidhe standards, that was. By his own best guess, he'd only killed four people in his career who were not themselves directly involved with the deaths of numerous innocent humans. One of the four he knew about was simply a too-convenient fool for the Darhel. The other three were regrettable collateral damage. He couldn't have counted the number of targets he'd serviced that he considered guilty. He'd never tried. A bunch.

Some would have called him a psychopath, because he could kill so casually. It didn't show. He was friendly, personable—the last person anyone would suspect of having killed other human beings. His eyes were as animated and open as the barely-legal adult he resembled. Casual acquaintances could talk with him for hours and be surprised later, if it occurred to them to think about how very much about themselves they'd revealed. People frequently told him what a good listener he was. The first thought of most people he interrogated, as they were walking away, was, "What a nice guy." The ones who experienced his less nice side usually didn't walk away at all.

The Bane Sidhe shrinks had never tampered with his mind, other than basic training and some minor counseling—from other operators. The counseling department's internal records did not define him as a psychopath. The diagnoses section of his file had only had three entries: Post-Traumatic Stress Disorder—in remission; Survivor Guilt—active; Natural Killer—empathy and conscience intact. For an active assassin with over fourteen years work experience, his caseworker considered the list extremely short. Past all the psychobabble, he had nightmares. He dealt with what he could, and gutted out the rest. If asked, he would have attributed his success to keeping the damned shrinks the fuck out of his head. And being smart enough to take his goddamned leave when he got it and go unwind.

George's job hadn't been his first choice of career. Information was his first love and his driving passion. Given the option, he would have become strictly an intelligence operative. Unfortunately, in this business having a rare talent could and did override personal career preference. He worked for a cause; therefore he did what they most needed him to do. He got some scope for his real calling in his job; the organization didn't have targets for him every day, or even every month. His information seeking on the job was never enough for him, so like most people he had to pursue his driving interest in his off hours, as a hobby.

Right now, he was using his enhanced hearing to listen to a local underworld lackey shake down the bartender for the weekly fire insurance premium. Not something an observer would have guessed from the way he was leering at the brunette seducing the pole on stage. As her generous cheeks approached within inches of his face, he tucked a fiver into her g-string, fumbling like the youth he appeared to be. Shy kid was a good cover. It kept him from having to yell his enthusiasm and risk missing crucial words in whatever conversation he was eavesdropping on at the time. Enhanced hearing didn't mean other noise couldn't drown things out. Particularly if it was his own voice.

"Eleven hundred this week, Pat. Cough it up."

"What? That's up two hundred from last week. You're drivin' me out of business!"

"Value for the money, Pat. You wanna pay the cops instead? Ask around. They're charging fifteen, and they don't do so good."

"Don't make no difference if I can't keep my doors open," the bartender, apparently the owner, muttered under his breath.

"Pat, you're a stand-up guy. You know I like you. You know I like you, right? But the boss, he can't make no exceptions. You're a good customer, always pay on time. Don't give me no excuses. Tell you what, I'll ask Jimmy. Maybe he needs a favor and you can work it off in kind."

"Uh . . . Now that I think about the numbers again, it's a stretch but I can do it." The man was talking fast, obviously eager to avoid owing Jimmy Lucas a favor. George didn't blame him. Out of the corner of his eye, he could see the muscle clapping Pat the bar owner on the back.

Light spilled into the dimly lit bar, backlighting a female figure. A *very* nice female figure. George wasn't the only patron whose eyes were drawn to the door. As the woman stepped into the room he blinked. *Oh, her.* He frowned. *She sure dressed to look comfortable in a strip bar.*

He signaled the bartender for another round as she pulled up a chair at his table, facing the stage. She put a hand on his knee while eying the girl on the pole, pulling out a wad of cash with her other hand. Good move to avoid pissing off the management. Only problem was that inevitably a girl danced over to wave her g-string in the direction of more money. Okay, not really a problem. His cover was a damned good excuse to openly leer at Cally O'Neal. He wasn't complaining.

"What do you want, gorgeous?" he asked.

"You, baby, only you." She squeezed his knee. "Truly. That trip out of town I've got coming up, I want you with me." She slid her hand up and across his shoulder, pressing against his arm to nibble on his ear. He shifted uncomfortably in his chair. She was taking realism a bit far.

"One of your covers is perfect for an inside man," she whispered, then leaned back and began stroking her nails through his hair. "I need you so much, Boopsie."

Boopsie? I'm gonna kill her. "I'll see if I can get off." He suppressed a wince at his own unfortunate choice of words.

"Baby, I can guarantee that." She leaned over and gave him a kiss so hot he almost melted into a puddle on the floor. She groped his dick, hard enough that he could feel her fingernails through his jeans, before straightening to walk out the door. She left a few bills on the table to pay for the beer she wouldn't be drinking. Normally, the brush and grope wouldn't have bothered him a bit, only he knew damned well she had zero intention of following through. Who the hell was he kidding? The *only* objection he had to having Cally O'Neal blatantly molest his body was that nothing else was gonna happen. One of the other assassin's well-known rules of professionalism was that she didn't screw the operatives. Dammit.

The owner set the two beers down on the table. "Tell your friend we don't allow working girls on the premises unless they work here. Not that we wouldn't sign her up if she wants to come back." He laid a card on the table beside the beer. "If she ever wants to dance, have her call us."

"I'll do that." George grinned as he pocketed the card. He certainly would. He didn't know her all that well, but the expression on her face would probably be priceless.

The attempt to recruit him for whatever she had going was another thing all together. He'd heard some disturbing rumors about her performance since that mess back on Titan, and seven years was a long break from real work, rejuv or no rejuv. He wasn't all that sure he wanted to work with her. For the organization's sake, he'd check things out before he made up his mind. Time to set up a little talk with Tommy Sunday.

Tuesday 10/26/54

It wasn't really a good tourist day out past the barrier islands. The sky was that flat gray tinged with painful UV purple that people who didn't have to sail under it called "leaden." Tommy just called it damned cold, and stuffed his hands farther into his windbreaker, hunching miserably against the icy spray. Only a father's love would have gotten him out on this boat today to help his son-in-law, Pete, try to bring in the last catches before the weather got *really* foul.

He stood at the railing, collar flipped up, baseball cap jammed on his head against sunburn, but otherwise appearing perfectly comfortable, the bastard. George, in a fit of what Tommy considered insanity, had volunteered to come along for the ride.

"Tell me you're not hard-core enough to be here for the fucking fishing," Tommy opened, when it looked as though the slight, blond-haired man was going to be silent all day long if Tommy himself didn't say something.

"Got a touchy subject to bring up. Cally contacted me yesterday about coming along as an auxiliary on a run Team Isaac has coming up." He pushed the horn-rimmed glasses up on his nose with one finger.

"And?"

"First off, I try not to pay attention to gossip. I've heard enough gossip about *me* that wasn't true to know ninety percent of what I hear about other people is crap. And I don't go out on missions with partners I haven't done my homework on. So. Cally. I'll be going straight to her to get to know her, but first I want general impressions from you. I've heard more talk about loose cannons than I like."

"Cally has pretty much earned her reputation for giving the rules types the finger when it suits her. But so have the rest of us, and you. There's always that dynamic between the operators and the desk jockeys. Mostly, she's done what's necessary to accomplish the mission and get us all home."

"I've seen her resume. What I'm really interested in—"

"—is that mess back on Titan in '47, right? And the Petane hit."

"I'm more concerned about her stability, and reliability. Everyone I've heard agrees that she's . . . erratic. But I haven't heard from the rest of the team. You guys never really talked about her while I was tasked to Isaac, and asking didn't seem like a good idea."

"Papa pretty much nailed it when he called her 'creatively violent.' And he's her grandfather. But just because she looks erratic from the outside, don't let that fool you. That woman never does anything without a plan. It just *looks* like she goes one way and then zips off in another operational direction. It's really because she doesn't telegraph. She doesn't tip her hand, and unless you're on the inside of the team's plan, you never see it coming. If the phrase 'need to know' hadn't already been around when she was born, Cally would have invented it."

"You're making it sound like she walks on water. *I* need to know. Talk."

"She definitely has her faults. She damned near had a nervous breakdown before and after that Titan mess. It's not wise or safe to seriously piss her off. But it's not real easy to do, either. Since they put her back together after Titan, she's a lot less detached than she used to be. She and I have spotted for each other on a couple of straight sniper ops when she needed the cash. She's been more concerned than she used to be about picking times and places to minimize trauma to bystanders. She does things like look for opportunities to take the target during school hours, when kids are off the street. Once she called an abort because a school field trip was in view. We got him the next day, but our controls grumbled. O'Reilly stepped in for us on that and validated her call." He shrugged, "She's not the machine she was early in her career, but she's not verging on psychopathic anymore, either. Usually. Lemme see, what else? Oh, the couple of times they've wanted her specifically to screw information out of a source, she's told them to go fuck themselves."

"That could be a problem."

"It hasn't been, yet. Not as far as I'm concerned. She says she turned them down because they were, quote, 'Using her as a whore out of convenience, not necessity,'" Tommy said. "I asked," he added.

"Yeah, maybe she has a point there. Still," Schmidt grimaced, "I hate to say it, but resources matter. This isn't a job for those kinds of scruples."

"Fine, but I can't blame her for asking if they're paying her enough for that." The huge man held up one hand. "Sure, she's dedicated to the cause. We're all dedicated to the cause—but if you'd watched her go through half of what we have . . . I'd say she's earned herself the right to a couple of scruples. If you can't agree, I doubt anybody's going to force you to take the mission. Even though, as you say, resources matter."

"I don't know. I still have to wonder if we're going to be in the shit and hit a wall because of those new-found scruples. I do it if necessary, and so have you, once or twice. Face it, it's part of the job."

"George, you're either thinking like a guy, or thinking like an Indowy. She was right, they were using her as a fucking convenience—to the point of not even *considering* any other kind of operational plans if good ol' Cally could get them what they wanted on her back. And while she was fine with it, it was nobody's business to say anything." He looked the boyish assassin directly in the eye. "You grew up in the Bane Sidhe. We may be on the side of good and right, but you know the Organization sure as hell isn't perfect. You know the Indowy—how could *anything* be anything but honorable and joyful if it furthers the interests of your clan. Especially if it doesn't maim or kill you. Or not permanently, anyway. Man, if you had just been there when one of the little furballs who's been trying to learn accounting came in all excited, 'Cally, with your present form, do you realize how much FedCreds we could bring in if you just—' George, she was three months fucking pregnant. And then he ran out of the room before Papa could deck him. Caught the first Himmit express off planet and hasn't come back. And the rest of the little green fuckers had not a clue what the big deal was. *We* were 'over-reacting.' 'Anachronistic, irrational, residual fear of mating with inferior genes,' they said. You wonder that O'Reilly backed her? Vitapetroni finally got through to them, barely, with an analogy about damage to *their* psyches from fighting, even for survival of their clan. *You* may not have known about it, being a guy and not having worked with her enough to be close, but if she hadn't won that argument, I don't think we'd have a female operator left. Don't even talk about the O'Neal wives—I thought Wendy was gonna hop a plane up there and start lopping off heads. So yeah, just about *all* the female operators are telling them to fuck off on the honey trap jobs right now unless there's a damned good reason. It's not just Cally. Call it a pink flu."

"Roger that—but you talk like she's your little sister." He grinned. "You've given me what I needed to know. After lunch tomorrow, I'll know whether I'm going to volunteer or suggest she look at her next choice. Yeah, I'll probably take it, but you know as well as I do how quickly it can fuck up an op if the team doesn't fit together. If I don't think I can work with her, I'll say so."

"George, how many people have you ever met that you couldn't work with?"

"I've met a few. Not many, but a few. Enough to make asking the question one of my cardinal rules. Oh, dude. Pink Flu indeed. Good old Bane Sidhe 101. 'Alien minds are alien.' Too bad the Indowy seem to have such a tough time getting their heads around that. They get it with the other Galactics, but when you get right down to it, none of the Galactics are any good at adapting to new ideas or new situations. Including just about everything about human nature. That's dense even for them, though. That must have been right after I lost Sherry. And everything. That's the only way I could've missed something that big."

Tommy was silent for a minute, uncomfortable at the reminder of his friend's dead wife. And the rest of Team Hector. What could you say to that?

"Oh, one other thing," the big man said. "You do not want to be in the same state—no, on the same *continent*—when that woman is seriously pissed off. But that could describe Papa, or—what can I say? She's an O'Neal. They're all like that. But whether it's something to do with growing up right in the middle of the Posleen war, or having her dad blow up a nuke on her head when she was thirteen, or having to kill her first assassin at age eight, Cally's just—more so. O'Neal, but more so."

"Hey, totally off the subject of Cally and the O'Neals, except that her weird relationship with her PDA creeps me out a bit, what is the deal with the buckleys? Somebody back at the shop told me you worked at Personality Solutions when they first came out. Why the hell did they make the base personality fucked up like that?" the assassin asked.

"That is one tough question. I didn't work in that department. The buckley template came in through technology acquisitions somehow and I never worked on the underlying bit pushing for the chip design. Couldn't tell you, unless you just want my speculations," he said. He continued when the other man nodded. "I don't know if you've ever been dead yet, in more than the prewar heart stoppage sense, to the extent of being revivified on the slab—which we don't have right now, dammit."

"No. Never happened to me personally," Schmidt replied.

"Sometimes I forget you're a baby." The veteran of the Ten Thousand and Iron Mike's Triple Nickle Armored Combat Suits in the Posleen War smiled.

The younger assassin favored him with the pained expression of a young juv who had heard that refrain for a couple of decades now.

"Anyway. The Crabs can do some damn scary things with storing and amalgamating and fiddling with the human brain, when and if they get their hands on one. My wife once knew a woman who . . . well, nevermind. That's another story. Anyway, the Crabs' bouncy little claw-prints are all over this one. I think somewhere there was one or more real guys, that for some reason the Crabs found especially interesting, and somehow got their claws on at least for a little while. My suspicion is that there was more than one brain, or more than one access to the same brain, involved. But that's all speculation, of course. I also suspect the base personality learned some things as an electronic entity—like awareness of what it was—before it was reproduced and distributed as a fixed base program. But all that is sheer speculation on my part. No idea how much, if any, is true."

"So that would make it a full, real AI, not the simulation everybody says."

"Well, no. Not exactly. You see, at full AI, the buckley personality is unstable and self-destructive. The progressively stronger inhibitions against those fundamentally self-destructive, pessimistic tendencies take more and more AI functionality from a buckley. That's part of the coding I *was* into, a little bit. That's why buckleys tend to crash. Turning up its emulation is really turning off, by stages, that inhibitory code—strictly necessary to get more independent functionality. So the more you turn it up, the faster it crashes. It's unusable at full AI level, which is why it's sold as a simulation. It's close enough to true for government work. Then, of course, there are the after-market personality overlays. They interact unpredictably with the fundamental personality and the level of inhibitory code turned on. You may have noticed the 'Martha' personality overlay was recalled five years ago. At emulation level 1, the lowest setting, they never had a buckley go longer than a week without crashing into an endless loop. For some reason, all the screen would display was, 'no more raffia.' Nobody's ever been able to figure that one out."

"Okay, so how are the buckleys different from the AIDs? I mean, I know the subjective difference, I've used both, but I want a more professional view. I've never had the chance to sit down and talk to a really *good* AI cyberpunk about this stuff."

"You know all about the Darhel spyware from your basic classes, so I won't cover that. First of all, AIDs are addictive. Darhel-made AIDs a lot more so than our own. I've got my theories about that, but AID software is frighteningly complex. The Elves know their damn programming. They also deliberately sabotaged human software theory. Only outside our organization, of course. It's why our cybers can crack damned near anything anywhere, and a factor in the fusing of the cyberpunk faction with the pre-split Bane Sidhe back during the war. Did I mention I'm freezing my ass off? Not to mention we're going to have to start the real work out here any damn minute." Tommy's teeth were chattering, and he gratefully accepted the chemical hand-warmer George passed him.

"Right. All the AIDs are different for the different Galactics species. AIDs for Indowy think like Indowy, Crabs like Crabs, and so forth. It still strikes me as damned suspicious that the Darhel had such a bead on human cognitive psychology to turn out AIDs set up for us so soon after first contact. I've never bought the official explanations, and I still don't. The upper levels of the pre-split Bane Sidhe didn't know or weren't saying, and, of course, same with the O'Neal Bane Sidhe. Except in the latter case I'm more likely to believe they don't know. The official explanation is that it was the same way they knew how to call the U.S. President on his private phone as their first contact, and the same way they knew we were what they needed against the Posleen, that they'd watched us when they started having problems with the Posleen and knew us from our TV and radio broadcasts and all that. It doesn't smell right to me, but I don't have better speculations. Wild ass guesses? I could give you half a dozen and bullshit all day long, but the truth is I just don't know. The humans and the Bane Sidhe had obviously known each other before, which means the fucking Elves were around here, too. Even the name has old connections. Way, way old. Then the Posleen pyramids and the Egyptian pyramids had a whole similarity. And there were bits of human archetypal history the Darhel were awful keen to alter or take out of circulation entirely," the giant said.

"Wheels within wheels within wheels," the older man got up and shook himself. "That's all I know, and really more than I *know*. You're about to earn your ride anyway, if I feel this boat slowing. Which I do."

"Oh, joy," George groaned.

Cally stepped out of the gym shower and began toweling her hair dry. The surfaces of the Galplas walls were that glossy shade of light blue that seemed to infest locker rooms everywhere.

"Buckley," she said, drying off, "please project a holo of interrogation room 7B."

"Huh? Oh. What was that again?" Cally noticed the subdued red light that indicated an active camera. She dropped a sock over the camera port.

"Dammit," it said. "Infrared just isn't the same."

"Quit ogling and show me 7B."

"You look nice today. Well, you *did*. If you put on your socks and shoes, you wouldn't have wet feet."

She couldn't do much about it. Slapping a PDA was possible, of course, but hardly effective.

"Shut up, buckley," she said.

"I knew it was too good to last."

"*Shut up*, buckley."

"Right."

She waited for a long moment. "Buckley! 7B!"

A display of the requested room appeared above the bench seat where she'd just tossed her towel. A barely adolescent teenage girl sat in one of the chairs, apparently reading something on her own buckley. It had to be something she had stored locally, since the room was shielded against outside access. Her eyes kept flickering upwards towards the camera lens on the far wall, which was quite a trick since said lens was only as big as a pencil point and shaded to blend with the walls.

"Huh. She might have potential." Cally finished dressing and stuck the buckley in her back pocket. "Not one word," she warned it.

The candidate had been waiting for a good twenty minutes. Long enough to see how much patience she had for her age. Time for the next step.

She passed Harrison Schmidt on her way to the stairs. She almost always took the stairs. Every little bit helped. Tommy and Harrison said she looked better with another ten pounds than without it. Seeing herself only through hypercritical eyes, she thought they were trying to be nice. If the subject came up, Granpa just coughed.

"Hey! Harrison!" She turned and jogged to catch him. He could be a big help.

"Can I borrow you a minute?" she asked.

He quirked an eyebrow at her, waiting for an explanation.

"I've got a potential recruit. I need to run her through evaluation. Be at the alley off Pappas Street, the one nearest Horner on the far west side. Two hours. Be sure not to see us."

"That's more than a minute. Wednesday. Why do I always get this kind of crap on Wednesday?" He sighed, "Okay. Skulking, or oblivious?"

"Drunk and oblivious," she decided. "Taking a piss would be ideal. That'll look pathetic enough."

"Oh, thanks so much. I have to get all grimy for this, don't I?" He sighed. "You owe me, dear."

"Yeah, I do. Thanks a bunch. I know this is a sucky assignment," Cally said.

The interrogation room looked smaller from the inside than it did on camera. The walls were a rather unsettling puke green. Beyond the two chairs, the room was bare. Its ugliness was deliberate, designed to unsettle anyone interrogated here. There were other rooms for other kinds of discussions. She pulled the empty chair around backwards, straddling it, to look the girl over.

"Denise Reardon. So, you think you want to be an assassin. That's one strike against you, Denise. Why should I let you have one of the slots to the school?" Wisps of her damp, blonde hair had fallen forward. The pro absently tucked them back behind her ear.

"Because I'd be good at it." The skinny, brunette kid looked at her through owlish glasses. Eyesight was fixable.

"At killing people? Why would anybody want to do that?" Cally set a knee bouncing, tapping her heel. It wasn't a real mission, but she was fidgety to get going.

"You do." The kid squinted, scrunching her glasses back up her nose.

"That's not an answer. Answer the question."

"Because our whole family, just about, lives on an island hiding from people who want to kill us. Because I know our family. We're not monsters. We argue, we squabble, we gossip behind each other's backs, we have a fair dose of hypocrites and liars, a couple of drunks, and a few serious assholes—but we're not monsters. So the people who are trying to kill us must be the monsters." The words sounded like a preprepared little speech.

"And what if they're not?"

"What?" Her forehead wrinkled a little, like a worried puppy's.

"What if the people we're fighting against, that you're sent out to kill, aren't monsters."

"I . . . um . . . I—I don't know."

"That's the first sensible thing you've said. One in your favor."

"Look, the Posties wanted to eat us. I'm not dumb. I know a lot of you were alive back then. You're juvs. You're sick of fighting, right? So anybody who the whole family, basically, is working so hard to fight must not be planning to hug us and give us a cookie."

"So what if you get deep enough to get more information and decide we're wrong?" Cally crossed her arms on the chair back, propping her chin on them.

"Nothing's perfect. I don't think my whole family is stupid, and I don't think they're evil. I'll throw in my lot with y'all. I'm not stupid. There will be a lot I don't need to know. Keeping that in mind, if I saw anything too bad, I'd talk about it to my boss."

"What if you were in the field when that happened?"

"Then I'd have to do my job and wait until I got back to talk about it, wouldn't I? Nothing's perfect. I'll throw in my lot with you."

"What do you think this job is like, anyway? What do you think your average day would be?"

"I don't know."

"Speculate," the assassin ordered.

"*Average* day? Probably buffing my skills or doing mission prep. Maybe traveling to or from a mission. Maybe under cover in some mission or other. Maybe watching people or scoping out situations before going in. It's like dance, isn't it? A lot of hard work preparing, for just a couple of recitals a year."

"Like dance. I wouldn't have put it like that, but we'll let it go. Especially since I dance, too. But you knew that. I think you were in my beginning jazz class one year on the island, weren't you?"

"Yes, ma'am." The young girl hesitated. "Ma'am, excuse me, but you're pretty good, right? So why did you leave work to be with your kids? I mean, why would they let you? Wouldn't the Bane Sidhe want you to keep working?"

"Tsk. You're not really supposed to know much about who you're interviewing with." Cally turned the chair and sat, crossed her legs, lit a cigarette. "Look, just between us girls, if you take this job you're going to spend a lot of time in a shrink's office. You'll need it. But being a chick, you're going to spend more time in there than one of the guys would. It may not be fair; it may or may not be necessary. This job isn't about fair. The bosses just about pushed me into taking a long sabbatical." She shrugged. "In my case, yeah, I needed it. I'd been active a long time. You can't do this job forever, presuming you live that long, and not have it get to you. It *will* dehumanize you. It *will* fuck you up." The assassin grimaced as the girl's eyes widened at the profanity. *What the hell am I doing letting a little girl—no, I was just thirteen myself. She'll get several chances to opt out.* An honest little voice insisted at the back of her mind, *Yeah, but there will be subtle pressures on her to measure up. Pressures on her teachers not to lose candidates. Inevitably. What the hell am I doing?*

Cally leaned forward, propping her hands on her knees. "You shouldn't take this job. It will fuck up your relationships. You will find yourself fucking about a bazillion strangers off the job because after you've fucked a bunch on the job, who the hell would you be saving yourself for? You will see things you absolutely do not want in your head, and the pictures won't go away. You will do things that literally make you puke. The price is too high. Go home. Get a legit ID, move to Indianapolis, get a husband, a white picket fence, a dog, two or three kids. Don't look back. It's a happier life. That's God's own truth. Go the hell home," she said.

The girl's jaw tightened. "Are you declining my job application, ma'am?"

Suddenly feeling every one of her fifty-eight years, Cally pressed her palms into her eyes and sat back up, sighing. She absently flicked the growing ash tail off the end of her cigarette. "No, I'm not doing that. Not yet, anyway. Okay. You want it, then it's time for your next test."

The tall blonde walked out of the room and returned in under a minute with two armfuls of clothes. One set she threw to the kid. "Get changed," she said. "Your sneakers are fine. They'll be covered by the boots, anyway."

Both sets of clothing were average to the point of boring. A set of long johns implied they'd be going outside. The jeans to go over them were faded and somehow a bit grayed out, as if they'd been washed too often in unsorted loads with all the other clothes. The sweaters were some kind of blend, hers a faded navy blue, the other a rusty brown, with the random little fluff balls sweaters get when they've been around a couple of years. The older woman didn't look up, just started changing her clothes as if she was alone.

"What the hell are you waiting for? Get dressed," she told the girl, who was hesitating. The kid jumped to comply, startled.

CHAPTER EIGHT

They got off the train at a station in the south of Chicago, trudging down the path of crumbled gray asphalt and sand that wobbled between jumbled stretches of gray and white snow, leading into Bronzeville. Once, their O'Neal-fair skin would have been cause for comment in the historically black community. Not now. Time and migrations to and from the Nat King Cole Sub-Urb, along with the shuffling effect of the semi-random sweeps for shippers—as the involuntary off-world colonists were called—had shuffled the population into a spectrum from Sub-Urban spectral white Caucasians to dark brown, old-time Metropolitans, with a vast middle of cafe au l'asian.

The landscape was a mixture of buildings. Bricks with early twentieth-century arched windows. Buildings with squared off prewar windows. Crumbling brick, crumbling cinder block. Tattered strips of old stores. Row houses like shark teeth and blocky old four-story tenements. In front of one of the old strips of had-been neon and steel, a cart of fresh vegetables from a black-market hydroponics setup sat upwind of a burnt-out sedan, whose trunk served as a shelf for piles of bagged tortillas, dimebags of cornmeal, the same of textured soy, and a large pile of slump cakes. The latter was a heavy, flat bread that had begun life as wet wheat sourdough, then got loaded with as much corn and soy meal as it could take without turning into a rock. It was a staple, as the name implied, of people whose financial resources were in a slump. Judging from the size of the piles, compared to those of the other fare on offer, this included most of the scattered denizens of Chicago's once-teeming South Side. Over a fire in a barrel, an old woman shook and tossed a pan of popping corn, which a little boy beside her poured into paper cones and hawked to passers-by. In the late afternoon sun, a smattering of young teen whores, pushers, and grays milled around, grabbing something to eat and running errands before their nighttime working hours. Dressed in the typical third-hand drabs of the grays, Cally and Denise blended into invisibility among the cleaners and other low-grade menials that served to keep the city's innards running for Chicago's trade and professional classes. She dropped a couple of dollars on the popcorn boy, handing one of the two cones of the plain, hot kernels to the girl beside her.

As they moved away, Cally hissed under her breath, "If you don't quit sneaking and just walk, I'm going to cold-cock your ass."

The girl flushed in embarrassment and began walking more normally, keeping her mouth shut. Next, the older woman bought a cake of slump for another dollar, breaking it in half and sharing it with her. The tall blonde glared at the kid when she bit into the bread and almost choked. Denise erased the offending expression and tried hard to look hungry as she dry-swallowed the nasty stuff. It was scratchy, as if ground or chopped corn husk had been added to make a few kilos of grain stretch.

As they moved past the makeshift market and its shoppers, Denise only pretended to eat and hoped nobody noticed, not the least her interviewer. A block down, they turned into an alley. Shortly thereafter, Aunt Cally tossed her half of the awful stuff over to a couple of rats who were scrabbling around in a mess best left unidentified. She followed suit, trailing behind to a particle-board door in one of the buildings. Her aunt pulled out a pistol, seemingly from nowhere, and screwed a cylinder onto the end.

"Kick in the door. There should be a man sleeping inside. Kill him," she said, thrusting the gun into the girl's limp hand.

"Huh? Just like that? What'd he do?" She blurted. Her hands were sweating, and she felt a sudden cramping in her guts as if her bowels were about to cut loose. She swallowed.

"Do you really need to know?" Cally shrugged. "Please do make sure he's dead." After a second she sighed and snatched the gun back. "You cock it like this. This is the safety. See? Now it's off. See the little patch of red beside the lever?" She shoved the gun back at Reardon. "There. Do it, now, or I will. Then we go home."

Taking a deep breath, the thirteen-year-old girl hit the door with a solid side kick right at the knob. Then she had to hit it again, since it only collapsed into a ragged almost-hole at the point of impact. Her second kick knocked it open, and she stumbled into the dark, musty room, blinking. Over on a pallet in the corner, barely visible by the light streaming in through the doorway, a man lay, face to the wall. He was snoring loudly, though it was pretty damned amazing he had slept through the noise. She walked up to maybe two and a half meters from him and fired two shots at his head, closing her eyes despite herself. Her hand must have been shaking, because two dark, wet splotches that she could barely identify as red splashed across his back, splattering onto the pallet and the floor. She ran back for the door, stopping halfway to heave up the contents of her stomach.

Outside, she wiped off her mouth with her sleeve, shakily. "Okay," she said. "I did it." The arm with the pistol hung limp at her side.

"Are you sure he's dead?" Her aunt asked her, searching her eyes. "Gimme," she said coldly. She held out her hand for the gun. The professional disappeared into the building, emerging after what seemed forever, but from the pounding of her heart could only have been a few seconds.

"You got him. Let's go." The taller blonde strode back up the alley, turning the corner as her niece had to jog to catch up. Neither of them said a word all the way back to the car, and then, via a circuitous route that probably wasn't the way they got out there, to base.

"Can I . . . know what he did, now?" she asked as her aunt dropped her off at the room she'd been assigned.

"No."

Three floors down and two corridors across, Cally sought out Harrison, who had beaten them home and, of course, changed immediately.

"So she passed," he said.

"Maybe," Cally answered. "If we didn't need her, I could come up with half a dozen reasons to flunk her. But yeah," she sighed, "she passed." She lit a cigarette in a convulsive, angry motion, arms hunched in close. "That is, she passed if she still wants to sign on after thinking about it for a couple of days. You overdid the snoring just a bit. I could hear you all the way out in the alley."

Wednesday 10/27/54

The Darhel Beren had recessive metallic gold fur, threaded with black. His slit-pupilled eyes were a vivid deep green. The deeper purple tinge to the portion of his eyes around the pupils spoke of too many late nights playing strategy games against his AID. With a roundedness to his frame, he was the closest thing to a fat Darhel one would ever see. He sat staring at the image over the altar to the Lords of Communication and crunched on a bright turquoise vegetable. It actually wasn't bad. He'd made something of a study of the available vegetables and their varieties—an extensive study. The trick was to find the high-protein ones, just close enough in taste and saltiness to . . . He didn't even think about meat, just shied away from the idea when he felt that tell-tale twinge of euphoria as his body threatened release of the deadly-addictive Tal hormone.

Right now, he was replaying the transmission that had just come in, light speed, from the jump point. The message was so hard to believe that he couldn't tell whether he was looking at a fantastic opportunity or a piece of disinformation, leaked as part of some elaborate plot against the Gistar Group. Six level nine code keys, or the better part of them, missing. An Epetar freighter on one of their highest margin trade routes stranded in the backwaters of the Sol System waiting for cash to pick up its cargo. This was an especially intriguing opportunity, if true, simply because pick-ups and deliveries to the Sol System were so onerous, anyway. Most systems had the resources to build their outer-system trade base two weeks or less out from the major jump point or points servicing the system. Titan Base in the Sol system was far, far inwards from normal.

Galactic ships used an FTL system of traveling along lines of low resistance in hyperspace, which was why jumps that took months for Posleen vessels took seven to twelve days for Galactic vessels. The current Galactic ships were much faster than their own old standard, too, since they had incorporated the improvements spurred by the war into newer vessels and retrofitted them, however imperfectly, into the old ones. The bulk of the transit time for goods and passengers was between jump point and base. Ancient vessels with hyper drives too far gone for economical repair plodded through the space between base and planets, delivering the goods in-system over the long real-space legs of the trip. Fleet vessels too battle-damaged for their drives to be reliable, and too expensive to repair, formed the nucleii for the deep space bases that received incoming cargoes and loaded up the outgoing ones.

Beren disliked humans, as any other civilized being would, but some of their optimization ideas increased profits. In this case, the innovation of keeping a dedicated courier on station at a system jump point for high-priority messages, while costly, was less costly than the delay in critical communications from the old system of sending messages with whatever freighter was headed out.

Certainly they used the old system for routine communications, or when, as now, a freighter happened to be going to the right place at the right time. However, keeping couriers a day or less out from a jump point had been a marvelous improvement over having them waiting weeks away at a base.

Humans were unpredictable and disconcerting as hell. Stupid, but incredibly cunning. They naively gave away the most valuable suggestions—for free. Gistar had a whole department dedicated to receiving, sorting, and analyzing every recorded human utterance that began with the phrase, "Why don't you do it like . . ." So far as he knew, Gistar was the *only* group with such a department. Its existence was the most closely guarded secret of the group. Beren only knew about it because he had helped to set it up, even worked there briefly. Which was how he came to distinguish himself enough to be the factor of Adenast, fifty years younger than other Darhel in the most minor of systems—and how Gistar came to be the only group to maintain a hard currency reserve, in deposit, on board the neutral courier vessels of the highest traffic systems.

He was proud of Adenast. Adenast's space repair dock was the most patronized yard in this region of space, sitting a mere two days from the major jump point out. Adenast could cut weeks off the repair time of any vessel and get it right back in service. They could stabilize junkers that could barely limp out of hyperspace, that would have died one way or another before reaching another system's repair yard at a base deeper in-system. Sure, they sometimes, very rarely, had a catastrophic collision. Still, the profits far outweighed the costs. All profit entailed some risk. Besides, he conducted his own work on the surface of Adenast Four, so he wasn't in any personal danger.

It was all very well woolgathering like this, but he was going to have to reply to this transmission, which he was now replaying for the third time. *All right. Assume it's genuine. Time is of the essence.* "AID, display Adenast system with functional freighters marked and labeled." Immediately, the transmission ceased its replay and a modified three-dimensional representation of the Adenast system took its place. It had to be modified, because if it hadn't, any holo that showed the system from its star all the way out to its jump points would, of course, have rendered the relevant bodies and ships too small to see. The jump point pulsed bright red.

"AID, what is that freighter practically on top of the jump point?"

"That is the *Dedicated Industry.* Heldan of Gistar commanding."

"What is its status?"

"The fault in the gravity feedback sensors was certified repaired point eight days ago, local. *Dedicated Industry* is outbound for Rienooen to rejoin the food transit circuit."

"Display the particulars of its holds, plus the particulars of the anticipated Epetar cargo out of Dulain."

Friday 10/29/54

Michelle liked to begin her workday early in the morning. It was more comfortable for her to navigate the low, multihued corridors then. In the megaskyscraper where she lived and worked, the smaller Indowy crowded corridors to near immobility during the morning rush. The press of the little green teddy bears at this hour was heavy, but not impassible. The brightening blue light shone down on their symbiotic chlorophyll, feeding Adenast's dominant sophonts a gentle post-breakfast snack during their commute. The filaments gave each Indowy the appearance of being coated by green fur. It was quite a contrast to the robin's egg blue, bumpy, gently-wrinkled skin of an infant Indowy. She did not know whether all baby Indowy looked that way. She had only seen the babies of the breeding group who had been her childhood foster family. She had maintained close ties with her foster sibs. They were the only Indowy she knew who sometimes almost forgot she was human.

If they had not been so familiar, the corridors and rooms of her building would have been terribly claustrophobic. Michelle was a good twenty-five centimeters shorter than her older sister, and the ceiling was still only about fifteen centimeters above her own head. All the Indowy-raised were short, by human standards. Their hosts had tinkered with their hormones to keep them from having to stoop and hunch their way through the buildings when grown. It was easier to keep the humans on the lower side of their species' height range than to re-engineer entire buildings.

Once they got used to the tight quarters, the only thing that kept humans from developing agoraphobia when away from home was the high ceilings of both the work spaces and the general Galactic areas. The latter had Darhel-height ceilings, of course. Also, humans and Indowy both underwent early and intense training and conditioning to be comfortable with spacewalk maneuvers.

"Human Michon Mentat Michelle O'Neal, I see you." The Indowy Roolnai waited for her when she entered the engineering bay, where she was orchestrating the build of a core chunk of the new Cnothgar mining station for one of the system's inner planets. It was a cutting edge project, and a rather exciting one. It used some of the interoperability lessons of Earthtech manufacturing standards to build a large station whose pieces would snap together like one of her childhood building sets back on Earth. After they mined the planet out, the pieces would unsnap for transportation in freighter holds to a new system, rich in exploitable resources. Cnothgar would disassemble and reconstruct it, over and over again, for mining in systems normally inhospitable to Galactic sophants. The Adenast mining would be the shakedown operation for a facility she expected to last, with proper maintenance, at least two thousand of her local years.

Roolnai, the head of one of the major clans, had to meet with her at the beginning or end of her work day, because it was impossibly dangerous to interrupt a Sohon or Michon engineer during operations. Poor Derrick had been a terrible reminder of that basic truth. Her late husband had lost concentration at a critical moment in an operational process. The materials had, violently, proceeded to the natural conclusion of the chemical reactions involved, instead of the engineered reaction paths required for that portion of the project. Everyone had mourned with her, but been thankful that the accident happened in the outer system and he had merely been working on a chemical-level operation. If he had been a single level higher in operations classification, and the associated tasks, it could have been so much worse. Derrick himself would have just been grateful he was several light-hours away from the children when the accident occurred.

So here was Roolnai, doubtless to ensure that another dangerous, and much higher level, human accident was not in the offing. "Indowy Roolnai, I see you," she said.

"Please will you sit with me, Michelle?" he asked, gesturing towards the respite chairs along the wall. They did not go into a private room, privacy not being big on the Indowy list of concepts. By Indowy standards, their privacy was inviolate simply because no Indowy would ever repeat or even try to remember a conversation between a major clan head and a Michon Mentat.

"You are here about my meeting with Pahpon," she stated.

"Yes, I am. He contacted one of the other clans, who in turn contacted me because of my prior experience of humans."

"Your experience is formidable. Nevertheless, I remind you that no Indowy-raised human has ever acted, significantly, in a way that was not in the best interests of his or her clan," she said.

"Yet. We may also disagree as to what constitutes significance, and what constitutes the best interests of one's clan. Threats of Galactic annihilation would, by most standards, fall outside the interests of one's clan." The Indowy's face was angry.

"I am not aware that anyone has ever made such threats, directly or obliquely. If you speak of my meeting with Pahpon, I did quite strongly remind him of the dangers of declaring a breach of contract prior to any such breach occurring."

"He felt otherwise," Roolnai said tightly.

"He was certainly mistaken. The purely socioeconomic risk to his group of breaching the contract himself, by declaring breach where none has occurred, would be severe enough that it could only be a kindness to remind him before he made such a serious financial mistake."

"He felt you threatened to misuse your abilities," the clan head insisted. The Indowy from her work group continued to bustle around, but increased the berth they were giving the two leaders.

"He implied that he felt as much. I immediately laid out my case that there was no breach, which tactfully made it clear that our discussion was solely over the details of our contract. Perhaps a prejudice against humans caused him to assume a threat where there was none, but I certainly made every attempt, immediately, to correct his misperception."

"He says your breach of contract is inevitable, and that you gave him no reason why it was not." At least Roolnai was calming down.

"He is quite correct that I gave him no explanation of how I will avoid breach of contract. I am not obliged to. I can and will, however, give you a reason. This is a clan matter, and must not be divulged."

"Accepted," he said.

"As you know, I have clan members whose existence must remain unknown to the Darhel Groups. My contract allows unlimited delegation of tasks according to my judgment. I have, as is quite proper, delegated the tasks involved in ensuring I do not breach my contract to those members of my clan most uniquely qualified to succeed. Would you doubt that, with my guidance, properly limited by traditional wisdom, they are likely to succeed?"

"I do not like this. I find the risk almost as high as direct action on your own."

Michelle finally made an expression, one that the clan leader might actually recognize since it was close to a similar Indowy expression. She raised her left eyebrow. The slight, closed-lip smile was less conscious.

"*That* is gross exaggeration and unworthy of you, Roolnai."

Galaxy death. It seemed such a silly thing to suggest. However, the Indowy knew the power of Sohon. One unchecked Sohon master truly *could* bring about the destruction of all life, perhaps all formed matter, in a galaxy. It would take time, mind you. The mentat would be dead long before the galaxy. But the destruction would spread and spread, wiping out planets, stars . . .

Killing one Darhel, or even a clan, would barely cause Michelle to break a sweat.

However, Michelle knew the dangers as well as the Clan Leader did. No mentat was allowed to rise to her level if they had the slightest trace of interest in that level of violence. By the same token, suggesting that putting Cally on the job, while fey as any human in history, was anywhere near the same level of danger was just . . . silly.

After a long moment he sighed, "In that, you are correct." Now he looked nervous. "Please tell me you are supervising them closely."

"I am supervising them closely." Childlike, she crossed the fingers of the hand that was hidden by her robe.

"I will tell Pahpon that there is no threat, that you are using legitimate, proprietary techniques to fulfill your contract, and that you have a traditionally acceptable likelihood of fulfilling your contract without breach."

"Thank you." Michelle bent her head slightly. The Indowy accepted the human gesture of respect and returned it. Arguably, they were of the same rank. The interaction between mentats and clan leaders had always been one aspect of fealty the Indowy were unsure about.

"Please, please keep them under control. I respectfully bid your clan good fortune." He rose and turned to go, but stopped before he had gone more than a few steps. "Oh, there is something else," he said. "You should be aware that the Darhel are becoming restless. We do not know what has disturbed the balance, but Gistar diverted one of their freighters leaving this system, two days ago, to intercept one of Epetar's prize cargos at Dulain. Gistar is acting under the impression that Epetar has been the victim of a large robbery. In the Sol System. It is not good for the Darhel to be restless." He made a shifting motion, the Indowy equivalent of a sigh. "What is done cannot be undone. Your fellow humans do not comprehend the damage such rashness may do. I know you may not have . . . opportunity . . . to contact your clan head directly for some time, but please use all your influence to restrain them." He inclined his head, tacitly acknowledging her difficult position in interclan politics. After long years of practice, she had no trouble reading the plea in his eyes.

Friday 10/29/54

"Now that I finally have a chance to see you, did you enjoy your weekend off last week?" Wendy prodded. "C'mon, give."

"Need you ask?" Cally grinned at her, knowing she herself looked more relaxed than she had in a long time. She gave the plate she'd been drying a last wipe and set it on the stainless steel shelf.

"Did you meet somebody? Ah, a blush! You met somebody. Cute?" Her friend was not going to give up this line of questioning easily.

"All I'm going to say is I had at least one nice evening." *I'm never going to get her off this, am I? Not a chance.* "So the grapevine says you and Tommy are trying again?"

"Well . . . Hey! No fair! Illegal change of subject, fifteen yard penalty, loss of down. We were talking about *your* nice evening." Wendy looked mildly outraged.

"Later." Cally glanced around the kitchen meaningfully.

"Well, okay. But if you try to dodge me I'm giving Sinda a set of fingerpaints for her next birthday. And drums for Christmas, too!"

"Uh . . . sneak off with a pair of chocolate bars after dinner?" Cally offered.

"You're on."

The hall the O'Neals had rented for the "Kelley" family reunion was a refurbished Asheville wilderness resort from prewar days. Mostly what the facility had to recommend it was huge stone fireplaces and an isolated location. It was not refurbished enough to have a stocked and staffed cafeteria, so they had had to bring their own food and crew the kitchen in shifts. Fortunately, they only filled half the rooms, since the others hadn't been redone yet and had plumbing that was . . . unreliable. But the partially unfinished state had made renting the facilities for a long weekend cheap—which was the other prime requirement in a location. Still, with the postwar economy being what it was, the O'Neals were a lot better off than many. Earth's governments, and particularly the U.S. government, had been hit hard by late fees for failure to provide colonists according to contract when colony ships had been lost in transit and had failed to reach their destinations. Protestations that humanity had no control over the maintenance or mishaps of the ships had cut no ice with the Galactics' arbitration councils. If someone or several someones on Earth had failed to take proper notice of the provisions of the contract prior to signing it, that certainly didn't excuse the Earth governments from living up to their contractual obligations. The councils upheld the fees in full; the taxes to pay for them had been difficult. Earth governments negotiated later contracts to remove the offending provision. However, the interest on the existing fines had done enough damage to set postwar economic recovery back decades.

Which had made the owners of the resort grateful for the early business, which provided desperately needed funds for their ongoing repairs and restorations. Their gratitude, plus a reasonable security deposit, had been enough to make the owners more than willing to make themselves scarce while the rather eccentric "Kelley" family served themselves for the weekend. Besides, it had meant there was no need to bring in, and pay, temporary staffers to work the off-season.

Cally was glad to be working in the kitchen with Wendy. So glad, she had volunteered for an extra shift helping cook. The huge stone fireplaces out in the hall were nice. Very pretty. And very crowded. Any heat that didn't go up the chimney went right to the top of the beautiful vaulted ceilings. Worse, having been mured up on the island for most of the past seven years, a lot of the people she "knew," she hadn't seen for years. Particularly the kids, who changed so quickly, or the spouses when someone lived away. She could deal with crowds of strangers. She could deal with family. It was just putting both together at the same time that was way too weird.

The kitchen's more normal proportions made it the warmest room in the place. She was presently pouring a couple of jugs of cider into a large cast iron pot to hang over the fire. If they hadn't brought the spices themselves from Edisto, and the cider from a bounty-farm orchard on the way up, the cost would have been prohibitive. There were things you didn't want to pay the import taxes on. The O'Neals knew the fees levied by the Darhel were for missing colonists that the aliens themselves had arranged the deaths of. The knowledge neatly disposed of any guilt the the family might have felt for circumventing the levy. Yes, it left the burden for paying those fees more heavily on others, but the Bane Sidhe were shouldering their share of that burden in a far more constructive way—by trying to put an end to it.

For one thing, it looked like the penalty fines might quit accruing if the Darhel had to strike a deal to prevent the U.S. from putting maintenance inspectors aboard the colony ships. The Darhel had long had a standard clause in the contract predicated on their long-standing control of Indowy lives. Each Indowy was kept "in line" by having to assume initial debt to buy his working tools, on terms that kept him in debt for life. Any Indowy who made waves could expect to have his debt called in, his tools repossessed, and would starve to death.

Where an Indowy wouldn't dare actually insist on inspecting a ship for missing spare parts, but would simply provide them unless ordered not to, making the inspection clause an empty formality, humans were insisting. A team of O'Neal Bane Sidhe was surreptitiously guarding the relevant human politicians, and another some critical engineering personnel, and it looked like the Darhel would have to either cut a deal on the fines or quit "losing" ships of colonists and turning up with the "salvaged" ships sans humans. Bane Sidhe analysts anticipated that the Darhel would choose to end the fines, figuring live humans the greater threat.

During the war, the Galactics had needed humans to fight the Posleen. Recruiting humanity to their war had been a desperation measure because the Galactics had been losing the war and losing badly. They had needed humanity, even though they had regarded humans as carnivorous primitives only barely less dangerous than the locustlike Posleen. Well, locustlike if you discounted the differences between a flying grasshopper and a space-faring, omnivorous, six-limbed carnosaur. Calling the Posleen intelligent would be inaccurate. The hermaphroditic cannibals reproduced at an appalling rate, laying eggs that randomly hatched into hordes of moronic normals with a few sport God Kings, and immediately became food for each other and the adults. The Posleen who survived the nestling pens grew up to eat nestlings. And everything else.

A Darhel could only kill once directly; the tremendous high they got when they did so triggered a hard-coded response that sent them into lintatai. On the other hand, they were more than capable of unlimited indirect kills by technical error and negligence, as well as by hiring human psychopaths to independently kill direct human threats for them. They just tried very hard not to get excited about it. They followed a deliberate policy of maximizing human casualties during the war, keeping just enough alive to stop the Posleen, and were, as a race, responsible for billions of needless human deaths. Most of those Asian, given the prewar planetary demographics.

Now, in 2054, the Galactics still needed humans. They needed them to throw the Posleen off of those of the formerly-Galactic planets that were still capable of sustaining life. They needed them to protect the primarily Indowy settlers of those planets from the few remaining feral Posleen.

Once infested by the Posleen, a planet stayed infested for a long time. Nestlings hatched with the knowledge base to survive and function; they needed no care. A single feral Posleen, left unchecked, was a planet-destroying pest problem.

Still, while the Galactics needed humans, they no longer needed very many, and still considered the species deadly-dangerous primitives and an ongoing threat. Hence, the Darhel maintained their policy of actively but indirectly killing as many humans as possible. It was a cold war where disengagement was impossible. It would take only a single Darhel sacrificed to lintatai to fire a planet-killer into the Earth. Galactic politics prevented that, but humanity was in no position to push its luck. Hence the very long-term cold war humanity had joined in along with the very-underground resistance movement among the other Galactic races known as the Bane Sidhe.

Everything came back to the Darhel. Cally blamed them more than the Posleen for destroying her and her children's chances at anything like a normal life. Starting from when they sent assassins to kill her and Granpa when she was eight, and continuing on through their deliberately worsening human casualties in the war pretty much any way they could. She didn't know for sure that Daddy wouldn't have had to drop that antimatter bomb on Rabun Gap if the Darhel hadn't fucked up the war, but she thought it was a good bet. And if it weren't for the Darhel, there would be no need for the Bane Sidhe, and no need for James Stewart to be officially dead—as far as the Bane Sidhe were concerned—and separated from her and the girls. Cally O'Neal hated Darhel with a passion. She tried not to think about it. But she tried not to repress it either. *Ah, stupid shrink head games. You can't win. Best not to play.*

Shari was farther down the counter in the very large kitchen cutting up fruit for some kind of salad or desert. She was also chatting about business with one of the sisters of a Baen Sidhe newlywed, probably to look over any single O'Neal men as prospects for marriage. Or whatever. Said sister was already in on the big secret, having grown up with Bane Sidhe parents. The parents had done little more than run a safe house. Dangerous enough, but deliberately not in the know for many things, which was reflected in the knowledge base of the daughter—or lack thereof.

Her interest seemed a bit on the serious side, because she was pumping Shari for information about DAG. If it had even occurred to Cally that eavesdropping was impolite, she would have silently laughed at herself for the qualm and done it anyway. Had she been asked, she would have been able to count on the fingers of one hand the social engagements of this size that she had attended that hadn't either been professional or, earlier in her life, orchestrated tests of her professional skills. She was what she was—not listening in never crossed her mind.

"I don't understand why the government doesn't just go ahead and admit DAG exists and end all the melodrama. It's not as if they can keep something like that secret for long. Just about the whole country knows they're around and what they do. There have been *movies* about them!" The short brunette had a tendency to squint and wrinkle her nose as if her glasses were trying to slide down it.

"Sure, everyone knows it's there. But it's not the only open secret in the history of the world, you know. You aren't the first one to have asked that question. As I understand it, the rationale is that if they don't admit DAG exists, they have the best of both worlds. They don't have to openly account for what it does, but they can hold it out as a threat against bandits and tax revolts in the territories, as well as pirates and raiders around the city states that might interfere with the flow of strategic resources. And more than a threat, when threats aren't enough. At the same time, the voters are reassured that their interests are being protected. And the voters subconsciously don't worry as much about DAG turning up on *their* doorsteps. After all, the government is hardly going to violate the Posse Comitatus law and use DAG in the actual Core States if it would 'expose their secret,' are they?"

"But it's not really a secret," the young lady protested.

"It doesn't matter. As long as the government pretends it's a secret, the pretense, no matter how thin, gives it certain advantages. Or it thinks it does. Politics is weird that way."

"I still don't understand why you guys are willing to put down tax revolts and stuff in the territories, free training or no. Sure, the Indowy had kittens whenever we tried to move resistance against the Darhel along a little faster, but most of them are gone now. It seems like the rebels are on the side of the angels to me," the kid said.

"You haven't been around the operations side of things much, have you?" Wendy broke in. It wasn't a question.

"Not really, no." The girl turned to the petite blonde who was somewhat dwarfed by Cally's height. "Our family's mostly done support services as long as I can remember. You're one of the only people I've met in my life who hasn't run me off with a 'because' and looked at me as if they wondered how reliable I'd be. I'm fine with just knowing I'm helping, and I understand why we compartmentalize information. I just get frustrated sometimes at how few things ever get explained. All the things I thought would be revealed when I got older, well, I guess I'm starting to wonder when I get old enough; when and what that will be." The girl had a slight petulant pout, almost too little to be noticed unless you were looking for such things.

"Probably not a lot. But I can tell you about the stuff in the territories and DAG in a nutshell. Random rebellion is dangerous. It's unpredictable, it provokes unpredictable responses, and the Indowy have shared enough history with us to make it clear that the last thing in the world you want is to get the Darhel spooked enough to make them unpredictable. That tends to be a Bad Thing." You could hear the capitals as she said it.

"The Darhel have to be maneuvered, like a chess game. A game that does take lots patience. It's not something that comes easily to most people. But whenever any of their opposition has moved too fast before, well, let's just say there are good reasons not to do that and leave it there, okay? Pretty much the humans who have looked at it closely, to the best of my knowledge, have all come away with the conviction that the Indowy are *not* being overcautious. Whatever things the split was about, that wasn't one of them." Wendy was carefully looking away from the girl as she said the next bit. "And if you do get, well, close to somebody in operations, get used to having more questions than you've got answers, all the time. Almost all the time, we never ask. Because the quickest way in the world to kill a budding relationship is to make him say over and over again, 'I can't say.'"

"Oh, I wouldn't do that," the girl protested, pushing her glasses back up on her nose with one finger. "Besides, I've heard they all tell their wives and girlfriends stuff anyway. So I just wouldn't ask. I'd wait to hear."

"Uh-huh." Cally suppressed a grin. Wendy was getting her "patient" tone of voice. This one would be a daughter-in-law when hell froze over. Shari was covering her mouth with one hand, but her eyes were twinkling.

"Let me tell you a little bit about that," Wendy said. "Yes, they all tell more than they should. And you can kill your husband's career in a heartbeat, or worse, if you ever let the tiniest bit of it slip. What they don't tell you is always lots more than what they do. What they do tell you is designed to reassure you and usually has the exact opposite effect. So you smile when they leave and hug them and pretend to be as reassured as they think you are. Then you wait. And you wait. Knowing that you don't know what they're doing, or when or if they'll be back, with just enough information to paint about a bazillion different disasters in your head. Then when, and if, they do come back, you smile and you rub their shoulders and you patch them up until they go back out to do it all over again. Because you don't want him worrying about anything that might distract him at a crucial time and *keep* him from coming home, and asking too many questions will worry him, you take what he volunteers and you just don't ask."

The brunette girl did the first smart thing Cally had seen her do since she came into the kitchen. She shut up.

Anyway, it was getting time to brave the crowd and handle one of the things on her do-list for the weekend. Cally excused herself and grabbed her jacket, trudging across the parking lot to a dilapidated gym where the guys were playing basketball. The floor was a freshly laid Galplas slab. She was surprised the owners had sprung for it, but it might actually have been cheaper than hardwood, if they had lucked into the right supplier. It didn't have the lines painted on it yet, so someone had patiently drawn them on with chalk. The chalk lines showed signs of having been touched up already, and needing fresh touch-ups soon. The hoops were old, having survived the years, though one of the backboards was missing.

She watched the game for a bit, looking down at the picture she'd called up on the buckley. It had been so long since she'd seen the kid she was looking for, since he'd grown up off the island. Only he wasn't a kid anymore. She finally picked him out, waiting until he rotated out of the game to let someone else in and get some water. She walked over close enough to wave and get his attention, motioning for him to follow her. He pointed to his own chest questioningly, unsure if he was the one she was looking at. When she nodded, he looked her up and down and got a goofy grin, amiably following her out of the gym. *Ye gods, he's checking me out. Ick. Okay, he's cute, but ick.*

She kept a bit ahead of him as she led him back to the hotel-like section of the retreat and down the hall to her room, inserting the card key and suppressing her comments as he surreptitiously tried to wipe sweat off with his towel. His T-shirt had dark, damp patches, and she was *not* looking at his sweat pants.

Cally heard the hotel room door close behind him.

"Don't even think about it. I'm your aunt," she said.

"Aunt *Cally*?" he squeaked, putting two and two together far faster than she would have expected.

"Hi." She turned and smiled at him. "I guess I haven't seen you since you were, what, five? How'd you know it was me?"

"Uh, yeah. About five. I'd say you've changed, but it's obvious, and uh, well, there was kind of a mention . . ." he said, raising his eyebrows as she set a sound damper on the table and flipped it on.

"I'm really just here to pay allegiance to Mr. Murphy. There is the barest chance that DAG's Atlantic Company could end up dragged into one of our ops if it really goes to hell," she said. "Briefly, because I think your CO is going to want some background, our target is owned and run by a Darhel group. For various reasons, he may get nervous about the time we're getting ourselves inside. Nervous Darhel try to cover their asses, and you guys are kinda notorious right now."

The young man rolled his eyes, but she continued, "I know, I know. A nervous Darhel *might* see adding some flashy security to be career insurance, and for various reasons, could set his eyes on you guys and pull some strings.

"Anyway, if someone tries to drag you guys into a 'black' furball near the Fleet Base around Christmas, avoid it if you can, if you can't, you need to know it'll probably be us on the other side," she finished.

"Avoid? With Posse Comitatus we don't do domestic shi—stuff. We're authorized to operate in the territories, but there are federal laws against DAG operating in the states. Second, it's kinda hard to 'avoid' being sent on a particular mission. I appreciate the need for a go to hell plan, but this time you may be going beyond benefits versus costs to your OpSec. I don't know what you've been told about DAG, but we really *don't* operate in the States, no matter what the conspiracy guys say. Even the Darhel don't have that much pull."

"Yes, they do. Trust us, we've been doing this a looong time. He can do it." She fixed him with the kind of stare schoolteachers reserve for young boys to make sure he got it. "It's very, very unlikely that he will. And we probably are being too paranoid. But just as Murphy insurance, one guy in your company needs to know, and that gets to be you. Obviously, don't share the information unless it becomes necessary."

"Okay." He rubbed his chin with one hand before looking back up at her. "Aunt Cally, it's not my ass on the line, but how do you guys decide need to know on an operation? Of course I can and will keep my mouth shut, I'm an O'Neal. Not my business, just curious."

"Oh, I'm not worried about you running your mouth, Mauldin. If you did, and anything happened to Tommy or Papa, you'd have Momma Wendy and Momma Shari on your ass."

"Yes, ma'am, that's a solid guarantee." He swallowed hard. "Of me not running off at the mouth, I mean."

"As to OpSec, let's just say that Granpa has very well-developed survival instincts," she said.

"Good point."

CHAPTER NINE

Greenville, South Carolina, had been a minor manufacturing powerhouse before the war. Lockheed-Martin, Michelin, Kemet Electronics, and more—all had plants to take advantage of the non-union labor, ready to work. The original textile mills that had been the mainstay of the economy since antebellum times had lost ground to the cheaper labor overseas, but the area's job base had continued to grow. Before that, it had been a resort for tidewater aristocrats seeking a break and some fresh scenery back in the wilderness. Now, it was ruins, with good odds that it would not be inhabited again for a long, long time. The entire county had been held back from the bounty farm program as a joint service field training area, administered by SOCOM.

The damage to the buildings in the various sectors of the city hadn't been done, mostly, by the Posleen. Oh, they would have gotten around to it eventually. But they had been more focused on the land held undeveloped by the country millionaires who, prewar, had wanted some acreage under their homes. So the buildings had mostly been unmolested by the invaders. The true destruction of Greenville had been wrought, in various stages, by humans. First by the owners themselves, who preferred going scorched earth over leaving their homes to the Posleen. Then, in small part, by those of their neighbors who had a true fondness for explosives—enough to make them wait beyond initial evacuations to mine and booby-trap anything they could get their hands on, regardless of ownership. The artillery had been the next source of damage. Then Fleet. When the troops came sweeping in after the war, the areas targeted by Fleet were flattened. Fleet hadn't screwed around when it, finally, arrived to lift the siege. Any area with any indication of Posleen build-up had been scorched by plasma and hammered by kinetic energy weapons.

The areas hit by arty had various building walls still standing. A stairway or corner here or there. Walls of half-underground almost basements.

The areas Fleet hit were finally getting fully covered with vegetation.

Those buildings had been rebuilt with the cheapest bulk methods available, where needed, with no regard to aesthetics. Troops needed practice urban combat as well as in different types of field terrain. So various troops worked their trade on the buildings in Greenville's demolition area—cleared and fought through, blew up and smashed and rebuilt, sometimes even the streets, again and again. Live-fire urban training, with demo, meant their only opposition would be dummy defenders. But that was for Saturday.

Tonight was in the blanks and VR section. Mosovich's enhanced night-vision goggles incorporated VR software that interpreted and remapped the scene to look like an old-fashioned black and white movie in full daylight. The goggles had a setting for color, but the machine guesswork involved in colorizing the scene could be disorienting when the machine guessed wrong. Doctrine, which the colonel agreed with, was to keep the color turned off. Field testing had demonstrated, to the satisfaction of the brass, that "black and white at night" gave troops a significant advantage over an opposing force using the colorized setting.

Tonight, Mosovich was glad for the warmth of his silks. Greenville in October could be cold at night, and tonight was an unseasonable bitch of a freeze. He had had himself declared an initial casualty, along with Mueller, so they could get a good look at the performance of the troops. On top of the observation towers, the wind and the light drizzle stung his face and ears so much they ached. His standard cover was hardly a barrier to the escaping heat. Who would have guessed South Carolina at night would be this *cold*? He looked over at Mueller, whistling cheerfully in his optional attached hood, mouth exposed only to drink the cup of instant coffee he'd just brewed with water from a heater canteen.

"Sergeant Major Mueller, you know use of heater canteens on a night mission is strictly against regs. Where's my cup?" Jake felt around for a packet of instant coffee and dumped it in the steel mug he unhooked from his web gear, holding it out for some of the hot water, himself. He suppressed a twinge of guilt about the troops below, who wouldn't be able to use the heater canteens because of the white IR spot the goggles *would* show to the opposition force. They were moving, and mostly in the buildings, protected from the worst of the wind.

"Mueller, let's add a little incentive to the mix. Get a detachment from Bravo Team to set up some 'loot' of hot coffee and spare hoods in a few of those buildings."

"Yes, sir." David Mueller grinned evilly, understanding the confusion it would add to the exercise to have a bunch of random troops running around who were working for neither side.

The explosions on the demolitions course sent up plumes of dust and smoke through the holes in the roofs. SOCOM's Training Command had set up the courses with dummies and VR hostiles. DAG units not only had to navigate a complicated course involving the location and "demolition" of selected targets, they had to do so under directed and suppressive virtual fire from said hostiles. The course was a fiendishly difficult test of a unit's ability to shoot, move, and communicate in concert with a primary demo mission.

The observation tower for the demolitions course was set well back from the activity, serving both for simulation and live runs, so that Mosovich had to use the enhanced features of his field goggles more than he would have liked. He was fine with the zoom, but he'd never quite gotten comfortable with shifting the view so that he was looking out from the eyes of one of his officers or men. He wasn't happy using it in combat against humans at all. After Vietnam, Jake had a healthy respect for the wits of the enemy. He considered the use of the "alternate eyes" feature to be a serious breach of radio discipline and a prime example of assuming the enemy was stupid. DAG primarily fought humans. Assuming the enemy would be smart enough to do what *he* would do had kept him alive more than once before, and he wasn't about to get lazy just because Posleen didn't fight that way. *Well, okay, there was that time down in Georgia, but that must have been the Posleen equivalent of military genius, because we've never seen it again. Not that I ever heard of, anyway.*

He turned as Mueller climbed onto the platform, holding his mug out for a cup of strong coffee from the thermos his sergeant major seemed to have grafted onto his web gear for field exercises. He zoomed back in on the action, watched for a minute, and shook his head.

"You know, you would think that looking at a red-headed troop I should know exactly who the guy is even if I can't see his insignia. What is it with all the redheads?" the colonel asked.

"Yeah, it's funny, but have you noticed we tend to get a lot of two kinds of guys? There's the little red-head guys. Most of 'em are kinda stocky but it's all muscle. Then there's the really big dark-haired guys. It's kinda weird, like the war did something to the gene pool or something." Mueller wrinkled his forehead, taking a big sip of the steaming coffee.

"Now that you mention it, Top, it is a bit strange. I don't think I can even make a guess at what could cause it. Probably just some bizarre coincidence. Go figure." The use of the traditional nickname, "Top," for the ranking NCO in the command was a mark of respect and appreciation used by everyone, officer or enlisted, to distinguish that NCO from all others. It marked the NCO thus named as the go-to guy for all the thorniest practical problems of service life that someone hadn't been able to solve at a lower level. He, as an infinite fount of military wisdom, would exercise near-magical powers to slice through whatever Gordian knot the Service had provided this time.

Jake watched his men glide through the course as smoothly as if they'd done it a dozen times. He'd looked it up. The course had been substantially redesigned since the last time they'd been through. Whatever personal problems the previous CO had had, he had left behind a first-rate outfit.

The service had DD'ed the bastard after JAG caught him banging a sixteen-year-old girl, then flushed the unit's senior NCO who, far from reporting it, had been blackmailing the jerk. He'd seen a picture of the girl from Mueller's buckley, and you almost couldn't blame the guy. Almost. Still, a juv at least three decades her senior had one hell of an unfair advantage. Which made the sonofabitch enough of a sleaze that Mosovich wasn't too surprised to hear that shortly after discharge that pair—the guys, not the girl—had gone on a drunken binge, gotten behind the wheel and smashed themselves into whatever hell was reserved for old men who preyed on high-school girls.

There was one thing niggling at him, though. Sure, sometimes good officers could be sleaze-balls. Soldiers weren't by any stretch plaster saints. But everything he'd seen about the guy indicated that he was a grade-A clusterfuck. Both the commander and the sergeant major.

Usually, when you had a grade-A clusterfuck in charge of a unit, no matter how elite, the unit went to shit. They might get the job done, but they weren't top-drawer.

DAG had cruised along as if it didn't matter. As if having a commander who was a daily clusterfuck wasn't a problem. Might even have been preferred.

As if the commander just didn't matter. As if having an incompetent in charge was not such a bad thing. As if there was the Unit and then there was whatever screwball the brass had saddled on the Unit.

As the new commander, Mosovich wasn't too sure how he felt about that.

The charcoal and red shades that blended on the Grandfather's walls appeared to shimmer three-dimensionally. The dragons were so real you wanted to reach out and touch them just to make sure they weren't there. Most observers would assume there had to be some clever tricks of Galtech materials involved in the illusion. A very close look would reveal that not only were the patterns two-dimensional, the dragons were each individuals. Each had five toes, as befit its noble stature. Yet each had its own body and face among the rest. The artist had spent only God knew how long bringing each dragon into its own semblance of life.

Stewart was early, or he wouldn't have been waiting. The Grandfather believed in punctuality, and achieved it within his organization by always displaying it himself. "Lead from the front" was one Western aphorism that the Grandfather wholeheartedly agreed with. Precisely as his watch clicked over to two o'clock Greenwich Mean Time, the door opened and a man walked in. His hair was still completely black. Stewart suspected the use of hair dye, since his face showed the deep lines and dryness of rapidly advancing age. An advancing age that was tragic for his friends and colleagues as well as the organization. Unfortunately, there was nothing anyone could do to stop it. In the early days of the war, a handful of the Tong hierarchy had been successfully rejuved. Unfortunately, the stolen drug sets had been improperly handled, through ignorance. Since then, the ignorance had been remedied, but too late for the ill-fated first generation—the first generation of Tong rejuvs would get about a tenth of the benefit of a proper rejuvenation. The botched rejuv suffered from its own lacks, plus the seemingly impenetrable wall the Galactics had come up against that limited the original process. Once the initial nano-repair mechanism was fully set in motion, its own processes prevented its ever being repeated. The Grandfather and the upper echelon of the Tong had lived well into the twenty-first century, and had succeeded at passing on their institutional knowledge to the next generation, but at what now seemed a very high price.

The head of humanity's largest and most powerful organized crime syndicate was a blocky, solid man. He wore a black, European-cut suit, moving with a fluid grace that belied his arthritic knee joints. He walked behind the large walnut desk and sat, folding his hands in his lap to face the freshly-minted older brother who had asked for this unprecedented meeting, after dispatching a large chunk of expensive Tong resources on an unexplained errand. Stewart knew this meeting would lead to a permanent change in his position in the Tong, one way or another. He watched the old man suppress a sigh and put his hand to his heart. The man's fondness for Szechuan cuisine was well known. As was his distaste for taking medication he deemed unnecessary. Even antacids. Given his experiences, it was hard to blame him for his skepticism.

"It's good to see you today, Yan. How are you? Would you like some tea?" the old man said, as a pretty girl brought in a lacquered tray with a traditional tea service on it. She looked about sixteen, but could have been anything from fourteen to forty. She placed the tea on the desk and left quietly, shooting a quick glance at Stewart under her lashes.

"Yes, thank you. I'm having a very good day, and you?" Standard opening, no real clue to his mindset. Stewart accepted a cup poured by the man who held his life and death in his hands. *Of course that was always the case with Fleet Strike. Superior officers had the power of life and death. At least theoretically. I should be used to it by now.*

"You would shudder to see my schedule." He poured his own cup of tea and sat behind his desk, fixing a direct gaze on the younger man.

Translation: I'd better not be wasting his time. That's fine, since I'm not. "There is . . . history of the war that our people rarely speak of, and never when we are not face to face," he said. *Yeah, like those Darhel bastards sandbagging Earth's defenses and letting the Posleen through to eat three billion people in Asia.*

"Our organization has much history, all worthy of study. We have a very long history of survival." The old man regarded him with a gimlet stare over the rim of the tea cup.

Right, we keep our mouths shut because we don't want our people to die. Stewart carefully kept his eyes fixed on the Grandfather's collar. Respect was key in this meeting—was always key with someone this far up the chain. Stewart had grown up in latino gangs, and gone from there into the entirely Westernized Fleet Strike. The differences in eye contact rules in Asian culture were still something he had to think about. One thing his counterintelligence training in Fleet Strike had stressed was how difficult it was to overcome the little gestures and telltales every agent drank in with his mother's milk. The trick was to identify the ones that you, personally, always had to be mindful of. Even when your "role" was now your real life.

"An excellent example for study, sir. Another of our strengths is that we have always patiently sought opportunities to recoup debts of honor and exploited them, when the costs were affordable, and most eagerly when honor could be reclaimed at a profit." *God, what a mouthful. All that to say that we owe the Darhel and I've got a way to screw them and make money doing it.*

The only thing that moved in the Grandfather's face was his eyes. A couple of rapid blinks confirmed that he'd understood. *One of the other reasons the Darhel haven't caught on to how bitter the Tong's enmity is with them.* The Darhel's information processing and artificial intelligence capabilities were awe-inspiring, but there were still things computers just didn't do very well. One of them was parsing the indirect communication that was an absolute rule of courtesy in some human cultures. For all that, the

Darhel must engage in very indirect communication themselves when hiring out their violent dirty work, Cally had confirmed for him, once, something the Tong and Fleet had long suspected. Perhaps because the Darhel were much less indirect in their business communications, even their best AIs completely missed the subtext of the more indirect human conversations. Except when violence was contemplated—they caught indirect conversations about that very well. The Darhel analysts just weren't as good as they thought they were about remembering that other species were alien. Humans had a leg up on that skill, being the most polycultural of all the known sentient species. The Tong had exploited that Darhel weakness ruthlessly to gain and maintain a high and pervasive institutional awareness of all that the Darhel were, all they intended, and all the payback the Organization owed them. Payback had been a long-term project, contemplated only in the abstract—until now. The fucking elves were too used to assuming absolute species supremacy in business matters, and the Tong was about to fuck them right in the pocketbook. Stewart had his own debts to pay to his ghosts. He ruthlessly suppressed the feral grin that threatened to break through his polite mask, but couldn't quite prevent it shining through in his eyes. The Grandfather's eyes narrowed and lit with an answering gleam as the old man leaned forward.

"The advent of such an opportunity, if proper care could be taken, would be auspicious. Very, very auspicious. You begin to interest me." The head of the largest and most powerful, unsubverted, solely human organization in the Galaxy set his tea to the side and leaned forward in his chair. The fires banked underneath the cold rage, so long held in check, began to burn. Stewart could almost see the man silently counting his dead and reckoning the interest.

"I apologize that time constrained me to send the first ships before we could meet. The opportunity would have been lost." Stewart allowed his eyes to meet his superior's for a moment. When the old man nodded, he continued, "This is what we have set in motion . . ."

The Indowy Aelool walked the halls of the O'Neal Bane Sidhe base with one of his younger clan brothers, but recently arrived on Earth. The youngster had tested as a high genius for the aptitudes important in the field of xenopsychology, leading the clan head to request his presence especially as an apprentice. Coming from his Clan Head, the request had more force than the strongest human command. A human would have been surprised that a clan head of even a tiny group like Clan Aelool—tiny only by Indowy standards—could disappear for long periods without ringing alarm bells in the heads of the Darhel. It was actually the youngster whose disappearance had taken more arranging. Clan heads were some of the very few Indowy who were not under contract to one Darhel Group or another, instead serving the clan as a whole. As such, the Darhel were long accustomed to having little to no contact with the head of this clan or that clan for centuries at a time. As long as the clan's members were meeting their contracts and causing no trouble, the Darhel reasonably presumed that the clan head was off somewhere doing his job. Wasting time worrying about a relative handful of Indowy among the trillions and trillions would have cut into real business. For the Darhel, the clan heads had no other function than to maintain the system that kept the masses of Indowy well under control.

In the new apprentice's case, the clan had made vague mumblings about administration work and bought out the childling's contract, apportioning his former duties among other apprentices in his family. The Darhel had never marked him as particularly smart or talented—Indowy being careful about such things, Clan Aelool more than most.

The head of his breeding group was also unusually smart. She had made certain the child displayed some conspicuous mistakes and clumsiness in his work, making the Cnothgar Group happier than not to see the slow-learning, incompetent youngling become someone else's problem. If he thought about it at all, the Cnothgar Group's local factor would assume the clan had removed the little fuck-up to someplace where he couldn't further dishonor Clan Aelool.

"I do not understand why you are such a determined contrarian regarding human civilizability, Clan Father Aelool. I have read the other clans' reports on the failures of the Sub-Urb dietary experiments, and, most respectfully, they run exactly counter to your positions. My wisdom is lacking. Enlighten me, please?" his new apprentice said.

"Ah. You are fond of kaeba pie, are you not?"

"Well, yes. Who is not?"

"But you more than most. If someone tried to get you to give up kaeba pie by offering you only mashed loogubble in exchange, how happy would you be to cooperate?"

"Please do not ask me to make this sacrifice for Clan Aelool, sir. I will, most certainly, but . . ."

"It would be a great sacrifice. I know." His eyes crinkled in the Indowy equivalent of an impish grin. "That is, more or less, what our enlightened colleagues among our own race and the others attempted to do with the humans." He clucked his tongue in a "tsk" picked up from humans.

"Would it surprise you to know that the humans have established in excess of one hundred specialized colonies, in the areas that were totally destroyed, in pursuit of the different varieties of bean for this continent's favorite bean soup? These barbarian carnivores—yes, I know they are—consume bean broth in the megaliters. How many specialized colonies do you think they have established in pursuit of favorite meats?"

His younger clanmate shuddered, "Ugh. What a question. Thousands, at least, based on your bean data."

"Zero," the Indowy Aelool said. "Exactly none."

The other Indowy actually stopped walking in consternation, then appeared to have a thought dawn. "That is easily explained, Clan Father. They raise captive populations of most of the meat animals they most prefer. Perhaps it is more difficult to grow their beans in various places, with their primitive technologies."

"Partially true. Yet there are meat animals they used to eat—do not shudder, we miss things when we look away too soon—that they like, that they have not reclaimed. Then there are twenty-something specialized colonies dedicated to replanting large populations of another bean whose fermented products are particularly favored by their females—and consumed in no small quantity by many males."

"If they are so fond of these beans, why did the Sub-Urb experiments not feed them these beans rather than other foods?"

"A mere deficiency of metabolism. The lipids and sugars forming the food value of these much-favored vegetative foods can only be metabolized by the humans into energy, not synthesized into the building blocks needed for major body maintenance and repairs. The Sub-Urb plan failed because those carrying it out were too lazy or too careless. The carnivores disgust them, so they equated all beans to all other beans and substituted beans and seeds that do provide the compounds humans can metabolize—as we have in the food facilities for humans on this base, as well. With the problem being that the humans tolerate those foods but are about as fond of them as we are of loogubble."

The youngster shuddered.

"The first thing one would think is to fortify the favored beans with the necessary compounds. Again, the problem is the humans hate the taste or the texture of the fortified beans."

"So why are you so preoccupied with catering to their aesthetic whims?"

"If we want them to change their behavior without resistance, we must make them prefer to do so. If *you* were offered meat on your plate or kaeba pie, which would you eat?"

"Neither! The dead flesh would make me ill!"

"You would eat the kaeba pie, or even loogubble, in preference *at least partially* because you like it better. Philosophy be damned, it suits your preferences."

The youngster winced.

"The obvious solution never occurred to the relevant planners. Provide the humans with the ability to metabolize the vegetable foods they already prefer into the nutrients they need. It was too much trouble to take with the disgusting, immoral, primitive carnivores." The clan head's own disgust was obviously for the planners, not the humans. It was an almost blasphemous rebuke of their recognized wisdom.

"Clan Father, in another, I would consider the assertion of one's wisdom over those planners as presumptuous. You, however, are such an eminent xenologist, and my Clan Head, that I must consider the possibility that your wisdom, in this, may exceed theirs. Is it permitted for me to ask if you have evidence?"

"I am so glad you asked. You see, we are going to my human dietary laboratory. You will please excuse the decor. It is designed to make the humans especially comfortable with the foods that proceed from it. First, let me confess that I have taken the small ethical liberty of fortifying the foods with specialized nannites that convert the food compounds available to the ones necessary for human health. The nannites build up in the system of humans who consume the foods and make the preferred stream of vegetable substances much more nutritionally available to those humans. I do *not* tell them about the enhancements."

"That is quite an ethical lapse, if you will forgive my horribly impertinent comment."

"It is. I believe they would consent if they knew. I believe they would then also imagine deficiencies of taste in the foods. This belief is the result of other experimentation in their kitchens. True meat was presented, falsely, as vegetatively enhanced. They not only claimed to notice a taste difference, they preferred the true meat so presented much less than the true meat honestly presented. Oh, do not shudder so. They would have been eating it anyway, and they would *not,* as one of us, be misled into an ethical breach—they perceive no ethical reasons to prefer the vegetative offering, anyway. That particular deception had *no* negative ethical value for the humans—I checked with the human planner Nathan O'Reilly. He has also approved this experiment, on the grounds that if the ones eating the nano-enhanced foods like the taste, and have no adverse health consequences, they are getting a pleasant treat and little more. I do confess his approval probably was contingent on the way I presented the information—truthfully, but in a persuasive way. Could I please attempt to produce aesthetic human treats as long as I endeavored to ensure they were healthy and did not impair the functionality of his operatives and staff?"

"Well, if their planner approved, of course it is ethical. Why did you not tell me that at the beginning?"

"The humans would not entirely agree on that ethics evaluation, customarily requiring individual consent."

"Insane," Rael Aelool echoed the sentiment he had heard, often though surreptitiously, from his elders.

"Not for them," his Clan Head contradicted. "Alien minds are *alien*. If we want their cooperation, we must respect that. Do not wince. To ignore the differences in alien minds in our dealings with them is the height of folly. If we had not once done so with the Darhel, all this plotting and intrigue—this Bane Sidhe—would have been unnecessary to begin with." The clan head had the expressions of an instructor commencing a class.

"From your enthusiasm, it almost sounded as if you were going to tell me they are not that different from you and me." The child's wry tone was an unwitting display of his genius.

"What? Of *course* they are different. Incalculably different. They are *aliens*. That is my whole point. We respect the Tchpth; we respect the Himmit; we even, after a fashion, respect the Darhel. We had better, out of sheer survival interest. We wrote the Darhel off as primitive because of their history. Short-term thinking to our long-term sorrow. One would think we had learned nothing from our mistake."

"So are we to respect the Posleen next?"

"Interesting question, despite your ironic tone, but one for another day. The course of study for your immediate future is humans. First lesson. Forget 'insane' unless you are talking about an organism that is a mentally damaged individual of its species. Alien and damaged are not the same thing. The thought patterns and behaviors of a *healthy* individual in a species are the way they are because they served an evolutionarily positive function for that species. Yes, there are evolutionary dead ends, but too often we Indowy say 'insane' when what we really mean is 'not like us,'" the clan head lectured.

"Humans have tried, many times, social structures very similar to our way. The results have been abysmal—for the sole reason, I believe, that they are not us. Your first assigned reading for discussion tomorrow is Bradford's chronicles of the Plymouth Colony. You may use my translation; get it from my buckley. As you read, keep in mind that these were mentally healthy humans, of a high degree of ethical development for the species, virtually *all* of whom deeply believed a way like ours would work and *wanted* it to work. Do not make the mistake of assuming it failed because of a few aberrants who sabotaged it. Instead, look at how application of a system that *would have worked* for Indowy *served the whole*. Our whole premise for why our way is moral is *how it serves the whole*," he emphasized.

"First lesson—always evaluate human species' sanity in terms of how their systems of social organization *serve the whole* of that society. It is human *societies* that are their analogues of our clans, not their 'families.' Families are incorrectly classified in the literature as proto-clans. In this assignment, think of them as breeding groups, instead. That analogy is *usually*, but not always, more apt than the proto-clan one. We will study why and when later. For a start, the O'Neals are a bit more of the exception than the rule. I find I am usually most correct when I think of the entire O'Neal Bane Sidhe as now folded into Clan O'Neal. Usually, I think of the human Father Nathan O'Reilly more as a senior clan planner serving at the pleasure of the O'Neal Clan Head. It is *very close* to accurate, and often the best approximation for Clan Aelool purposes."

"I do not understand. The human planner O'Reilly's leadership in the human component of the Bane Sidhe considerably predates the split," his apprentice said. "He is accepted as being of senior rank to the O'Neal."

"True. Yet if it came to an unresolvable policy dispute, the organization would *not* further split. Instead, Human Planner O'Reilly would choose to relinquish his position, unhappily but without external pressure, in favor of the candidate preferred by the O'Neal. By our standards, *all* the O'Neal Bane Sidhe are O'Neals. Hence the name. However, for some reason specifying this to him distresses the O'Neal, although he clearly takes full responsibility for all the others. Witness that there *is* a second O'Neal Bane Sidhe base on Earth. It is his own home, run directly by him. The 'Edisto Island' base. The terminology bothers him, apparently out of something the humans call 'modesty.' It is no use calling it that to him—modesty is an attribute he does not believe he possesses. I humor him, the Indowy Beilil humors him, as must you. I learned this, by the way, from the Sunday annexation. Clan O'Neal is the most vital human society to the Galactic future, and we must carefully nurture it in a healthy direction. Clan Aelool and Clan Beilil consider the Plan entirely remapped by this unexpected development of Clan O'Neal as a growing human 'society.' More or less. Alien minds are alien—the clan to society analogy is not exact. Second lesson for the day. Inflexibility in the face of large situational changes is a counter-survival trait for the whole. A bit of human wisdom, 'No battle plan survives contact with the enemy.'"

The young Indowy winced again.

The Clan Head sighed, "No, do not shrug it off because of the barbaric phrasing. We Indowy, and all we Galactic races, do that far too much. It means one cannot plan wisely if one does not adapt to large situational changes. How can the humans be rightly considered such irredeemable barbarians if they have wisdoms *they* can teach *us*?"

"I am not wise enough to dispute with the wise, Clan Head,

but I respect that as a Clan Head with your expertise, you may best judge if you yourself are. Particularly regarding human xenology."

"In this, I am quite certain that I am correct. Quite, quite certain indeed. Consider the Himmit and Tchpth . . . unconvinced, but cautiously interested in our research, so long as we manage it as safely as possible. The Tchpth's human xenopsychology researches take a more direct, active interest in the Michelle branch of Clan O'Neal. Which has implications for some other developing situations, beyond your level of study."

"That explains much of Clan Aelool policy on a level I can understand. Thank you, sir."

"Come. Allow me to show you some of the work we do here."

The Indowy Aelool entered a room decorated in colors and patterns that offended the young Indowy's eyes, and would have similarly affected all of his species. The Aelool had equipped the room with odd, unexplained human devices. He donned a human-style garment, cut to his size, that covered much of his photosynthetic surface. Then he picked up a flat ceramic disk with brown rectangular solids of food, covered by a clear human plastic. All of this was quite bizarre. If he had not known better, and if the matter were not unthinkable, the young Indowy would have feared for his Clan Head's rationality.

"All of this presentation is necessary. Especially the 'apron.'" He gestured to the Earth-cloth garment. "Come," he said again, carrying the disk in his hands as he left the odd room, walking down to the moving box humans preferred to decent bounce tubes.

"These foods, by the way, are completely ethically clean. They are also metabolically enhanced as I described, obviously," he said.

The Aelool asked his buckley PDA a question in a human language. Fabulous collaboration between the humans and Tchpth, that. The collaboration aspect was unwitting on the part of the humans, of necessity, but still a fabulous invention. Ridiculously fragile and short-lived, but so incredibly inexpensive! Aelool had assured him that it genuinely did not attempt to spy on you. His Clan Head apparently believed it. Amazing.

He spoke no further as he led his younger clan brother into areas frequented by humans. The young Indowy made every effort to copy his senior's mannerisms, ruthlessly suppressing all natural fear and, especially, thought of fear.

They approached a human that even the youngster had no difficulty identifying as a female, treated for proper longevity or very young adult, in excellent health. Her head tendrils were a pale, silvery yellow and fell to her shoulders. The colorful parts of her eyes were a clear, bright blue.

"Miss O'Neal, my favorite test subject! I am most happy to see you. May I offer you a brownie?" The Clan Head pulled back the flexible plastic, which stuck to itself awkwardly, and presented the disk of food to the woman.

"Oooh. Thanks, Aelool." She picked up a brown square and began munching rapidly. Her smile tried to cover the teeth, but with imperfect effect since she was eating the food.

He tried to look away, and kept his gestures under control, but could smell the stink of his own fear pheremones begin to waft into the air. Fortunately, he had been told, humans could not scent or recognize them. This one's nostrils flared, though, in a way that made him doubt his information. Still, she seemed thoroughly preoccupied with the food.

"Walnuts and chocolate chunks? You're getting *good* at this Aelool. I don't know why you picked this for a hobby, but I approve!" Again, she grinned around a mouthful of the food, bits of which stained her white teeth brown. "Do you mind if I . . . ?" She picked up four more squares eagerly, disappearing down the hall as if afraid he might take them back.

After she was out of sight and out of hearing, Aelool muttered softly to him. "Completely ethically clean food. Completely nutritionally adequate to maintain her. How much meat do you think that human will consume today?"

"Your wisdom vastly exceeds mine, sir. I admit I have no idea. I presume at this stage of your researches you are choosing the more ethically advanced humans?"

The Indowy Aelool's ears and eyes quirked in suppressed mirth. "Childling, that was Miss Cally O'Neal."

The dump of fear pheremones overwhelmed him as he shook in sudden reaction, "You brought me near—"

"Please. You were perfectly safe. Miss O'Neal has *never* killed an Indowy. Such drama. You yourself saw that she was only interested in how much of the clean food she could take without offending me." He made their race's equivalent of a shrug. "Do you see why I am convinced of my researches? To answer my own question,

Miss O'Neal will almost certainly consume *no* meat today. She is concerned about keeping excess fat deposits off of her body, so monitors her caloric intake carefully. She will consume a few cups of bean broth, with no caloric enhancement—without enhancement, it has virtually no calories for them. She much prefers these 'brownies' to the meat. It really is that simple. I could provide similar clean foods, high in lipids and sugars, and persuade her to replace large amounts of her meat intake—completely on her own initiative. She would feel no deprivation. To the contrary, she would feel *guilt* for consuming so much 'junk food.'"

"*Junk* food? It is *better* food! Um—doesn't she have two, very large, excess fat deposits?"

"Oh, those. Those she has little choice about—an evolutionary adaptation to attract males. I gather she is unusually well adapted," he said. "Remember, she does not know the bean squares will keep her healthy. By the time I have the human Nathan O'Reilly tell her the truth about the food—with me at a safe distance, far away, of course—she will be angry for a few seconds to a few days before laughing and asking for more brownies. By then, she will have accepted that she likes the taste of the improved, clean foods and will not imagine bad tastes into them."

"You *told* her she was a test subject. Why would she be angry?"

"She thought I was joking."

"Why? No, never mind, sir. I have a different question. Human males are the more aggressive. You mentioned that human males are less fond of the beans in the brownies?"

"Quite true. However, I have not yet explained the human male fondness for another metabolically challenging, high food-value, ethically clean broth made from fermented seeds. Let me tell you about 'beer.'" The head of Clan Aelool led his young protege to a convenient, civilized bounce tube, carefully securing the rest of the experimental food for the journey.

CHAPTER TEN

Four men and one woman gathered around a hologram in a stale-smelling Galplas room. Six enhanced information manipulation units sat ranked on ancient folding tables along the walls, hard-wired out through secure data cables that ran through ductwork in each wall. Each machine's buckley port was uncharacteristically empty. Each unit showed signs of recent and regular cleaning, each showed signs of age in black lines of dirt ingrained in the casing's few small seams. Each was still a cutting edge application of Tchpth technology, being between seven and twenty years old. More accurately, cutting edge of what the Crabs had been willing to release to any Galactic anywhere. Human cyberpunks being less hidebound than Galactics, each was still more innovative in small ways than anything Indowy or Darhel had. They made up in creativity anything they lacked in Darhel institutional infotech experience. The cybers presumed, of course, that the Himmit had perfect working copies. The Frogs' espionage capabilities on all fronts were so good that the cyber division of the O'Neal Bane Sidhe had the private opinion that even the Tchpth had no idea how much of their tech the Himmit had quietly stolen. After all, why would the Himmit risk provoking the Tchpth to increase security? One of the cybers' primary and highly covert projects was to find and keep secure a good enough story to buy whatever information the Himmit had acquired on the slab.

They had enjoyed a remarkable lack of success, though not through lack of stories. It was practically impossible to protect a good enough story against penetration by the Frogs—nicknamed for the terrestrial amphibians they resembled. Purplish and bulbous when in the open having a conversation, the Himmit were racial cowards, a trait moderated only by their cheerfully insatiable curiosity. They had an extraordinary ability to reshape their bodies and repattern them to match their surroundings, and to move silently. Their natural camouflage ability was to a chameleon's what a Formula 500 race car was to a little red wagon. They were also so harmlessly amiable that it was impossible to stay angry with one.

The cyber operations security director described the continuing attempt to protect information from the devilishly effective little bastards as "good training."

The walls in the room were a nasty putty color. One corner was glaringly different, the bright purple walls covered with acid green spirals. It hurt Tommy's eyes, but he had to admit that Cassandra was one hell of a cracker. Despite her penchant for collecting desk toys that, together, moved like a set of demented clocks, he'd never seen a system she hadn't been able to poke half a dozen different security holes in. The purple stuff was obviously painted on, since it was already flaking at the uneven edges. Galplas had never been designed to take paint. What would've been the point? It could be tuned to any color you wanted—at least, it could at installation. Galactics weren't much for anticipating change. Sometimes it seemed like they barely tolerated it at all.

Tommy Sunday shook himself and got his attention back on track. Cally was going over the layout of Fleet Strike Operations Training Headquarters. "They put the archival library on this section of the flats. It's not just a machine room tightcasting to the troops' AIDs. Fleet Strike learned a few lessons from the war. All of its more interesting material is secured within the system and accessible only by physically cabled-in terminals. In practice, that means you sit down in a study couch, scan in your fingerprint or swipe your temporary ID, and plug in the buckley you checked out from the front desk on your way into the building. The building is, unofficially but strictly, a no-AID area. The in-house buckleys all carry a bright-blue stripe up the back, just as a reminder not to cross-connect the two. There's a manned desk at the door to tactfully ensure the protocol is followed. Questions?" She paused, clearly knowing the question wouldn't be rhetorical.

"Yeah, I'll bite. How are we getting into their system?" Schmidt Two looked over at Tommy, raising an eyebrow. The male assassin was on the opposite side of the table from Cally, as far away as he could get without being rude. Tommy hoped they could shelve their tension before the run. He didn't like complications within the team.

"Go on." Cally nodded at the big man.

"Fine. When I left Fleet Strike in 2031, I hadn't been approached by the Bane Sidhe yet, but I'd gotten used to having extensive access and didn't want to lose it. It was a big chance and could have gotten me shot if they'd caught me at it, but I fooled Fleet Strike's systems into thinking I was on a long-term deep cover investigations mission. That I was a sleeper." He held up a hand when Papa would have spoken.

"I know, I know, Fleet Strike's mission was and is human versus Posleen, not human versus human. They have almost no cloak and dagger operations, of course. The key word there is *almost*. They have, rarely, had some internal high drama—investigating misappropriation of funds, diversion of resources, corporate bidding scandals, things like that. There was a billing category for it, a protocol for the systems to deal with such an agent, and that was all I needed. Especially since I told it I was too secret for it to pay me, which let me, after the fact, disable the linkage to the payroll and accounting systems. When I got through tinkering, the left hand didn't know what the right hand was doing. I cross referenced against the standard reports . . . uh . . . your eyes are glazing over. I covered my tracks, okay?" When he talked about computer geeking, it was possible to see the skinny, dark-haired kid from Fredericksburg inside the linebacker's son.

"If they hadn't broken out their own data storage from the Darhel's main AID network in 2019, I never would have been able to manage it. I'm sure it's duplicated in the Darhel's databases somewhere, but there's never been anything to bring one insignificant sleeper agent to their attention. Not that I know of, anyway. I had dumped large chunks of AID code into some harmless-looking duplicate files on a first generation preproduction system right after the Rabun Gap incidents. I was pissed, Iron Mike was pissed, we were all pissed. The plan was to analyze it later and I had cooperation from the rest of the 555th ACS. We did some sleight of hand with partial files I don't need to get into. Anyway, I used the back door I built to dump my files so I could use them in my private sector work. That's the only time I ever accessed it, but I never shut it down. The system should, and I stress 'should,' still think I'm in Fleet Strike if we tickle it right," Sunday said.

He took a chance and stole one of the really yummy smelling brownies Cally had sitting on a napkin in front of her, ignoring the dirty look she shot him. He'd have to ask where she'd found them, since chocolate was one of those luxury goods at one hell of a premium on base since the split. It was far more available on the island, given the proximity for smuggling. Maybe he could get her source to part with the recipe for Wendy. These were *good.*

"Unless they caught you last time, in which case it will bring all hell down on our asses." The red-haired fireplug of a man spat neatly into a chipped stoneware mug that was missing its handle.

"Papa's got it in one," Cally said. "Our peerless leaders' willingness to play this card should give you some idea of the importance of the mission. You all know we've been skating on the edge of disaster, as an organization, since the split. The take from this mission won't come anywhere near putting us where we were, but it'll make that thin ledge we're on just a tad wider. *If* the device's existence and location is confirmed, *if* this isn't some elaborate ruse to give the Darhel a plausible excuse to eliminate Michelle as one more O'Neal, we can't let them get it developed and in production. If they get something like this, we aren't just on the edge anymore, we're out of business. We don't have a defense that would keep a captured agent from spilling his guts under this thing, and all of our agents know way too much. We aren't nearly as compartmentalized as we should be. There won't be anything to stop the enemy from running routine interrogations on all their people, potentially compromising every agent we've got inside." She sighed. "We've been complacent, and it's come back to bite us in the ass."

"Okay, to make the explanation as simple as possible, the plan is a lame duck jenny with a charlie chatter and a right angle fake. Harrison, you're charlie. Granpa, you do the fake out. Tommy steals the ball. George, you drive and babysit the Humvee. Jenny, obviously, me." She pointed to her own chest.

"If nobody's got any questions so far, let's get to the positions and timing." Cally picked up a fiberglass pointer. "The plane comes in nap of the Earth at oh-five-hundred and sets down on the flat behind this hill. I've allowed a generous twenty minutes for us to unload and get into the vehicle. I expect it to take half that. Buckley, start the hummer and the clock."

"Hold that thought, buckley," George said. "I do have a couple of questions." If Isaac's team lead objected to being interrupted, she didn't show it. Not to casual inspection. Tommy knew enough to recognize the slight tightening of her hands after she folded them in front of herself and turned a deceptively open face towards the other man. There was nothing significant to anyone about her closed body language. Cally always kept her arms close in, defensively, when she wasn't in character for a job. He didn't know if George could read her closely enough to catch the Cally-specific facial tells.

"Yes?" Her tone of voice was pleasantly even. If Tommy hadn't worked closely with her most of her life, he wouldn't have been able to tell she was getting torqued. He was starting to wonder how tactful George had been, or hadn't been, in their prior meeting.

"The jenny is fine, but in my experience it's almost impossible to run an obvious diversion on a military base without the senior NCOs, at least, smelling a rat. Not to mention a security lockdown of the base. And Harrison sucks at field work," he said, nodding to his brother. "Sorry, bro, but you do. Tommy's conspicuously huge, and a fucking war hero. What if he gets made? Why not switch Tommy and Papa and send Papa in with a swipe card, since the system takes them. Or a grafted fingerprint. And why do you really need me if I'm just going to be sitting on my ass in the truck? No offense, it just looks like I'm extraneous."

Cally's expression got friendlier. Not a good sign. "Okay, first off, the diversion is anything but obvious. Operations training has a computer randomized Posleen attack drill approximately once a month. It's separate from security lockdown drills because with Posleen that's a waste of manpower that Fleet Strike may need. Don't sell Harrison short. He's charming, and can be made up to look inconspicuous, particularly in uniform. And he's not going to make a fuss about changing his appearance. Right, Harrison?" It wasn't really a question. "Everyone still alive who ever served with Tommy has either been riffed out or deployed off planet.

He's huge, no disguising that. His hair, eyes, and facial structure will look nothing like his original identity. Fleet Strike has helped us out, there, by liberalizing the length and grooming standards for hair in the past ten years. Papa can't go in his place. A swipe card triggers a security review automatically, a graft is a dead giveaway under the most casual review, and the access end is the place most likely to need a sophisticated on-site hack. You, obviously, are our go to hell guy."

It was impressive how she could say something like that without overselling or underselling it. It'd be interesting to know if she was fooling George or not with the Miss Friendly face. "You've just demonstrated why. You're better than anyone I know at finding potential weak points in a plan, on short notice—even though we have those specific ones covered. You improvise fast and well even for a field agent. If anything goes wrong, you get to pull our cherries out of the fire."

"Okay, fine. Why is Papa doing the hack for the diversion, and what if that's not smooth?" he asked. "No offense." He nodded to the older redhead.

"Tommy does the hack on the way. He's got half a dozen canned routines set up in Papa's buckley to cover contingencies. The only reason the hack isn't already done is to reduce the chance that it will be noticed beforehand. We hope it won't be noticed at all, but nobody wants a blown op, do we?" She smiled. "That it? Okay, buckley, start the Humvee moving."

"Are you sure? There are at least sixteen more things that could go wrong, you know. Would you like me to list them?" the buckley offered cheerfully.

"Shut up, buckley," she said mechanically.

"Right."

Tommy and Harrison coughed, unconvincingly, as the miniature truck started moving through the hologram. The base buckley's eccentric reaction to Cally O'Neal was a running joke between them. As was Cally's ill-concealed suspicion that Tommy was hacking her system. He hadn't, which just made it funnier every time she accused him. The briefing went on, more quickly now that George had said his piece.

"Right. We want to come as close to the base as we can without ever entering line of sight of the elevated areas of Fredericksburg Base itself. We're landing out here. Technically, it's civilian, privately-owned land. In fact, it's abandoned but not yet reverted to Homestead and Reclamation. It's as safe as it gets, but it means we need to proceed over the Rappahannock here, and do another crossing at the other side of this small island. There's an old road that will have discouraged tree growth and such, but the route might as well be off-road. Harrison, planning for getting the truck across the river is your baby. Who knows what's there now, but undergrowth analysis from the few aerial photos we have suggests that however much bridge there is, that's the one that got the most rebuilding. Both sides of that old road have been used a fair bit, *most likely* by civilian-type vehicles, on both sides of the river. The bounty farmers had to have been crossing it somehow. Think about contingencies. Get with Tommy, go over whatever information we've got, and come up with a list of what you'll need. Supply needs it by fifteen hundred tomorrow. Earlier if you need anything particularly exotic.

"Obviously, there are security cams out in the area beyond the base. The difference between the cameras on base and the cameras off base is that the cameras on base are hard-wired to the data assessment center. The cameras off base are not. They broadcast or tightcast, using the same transmission protocols as the AIDs. For all that, they're pure Earthtech, which means that we can fuzz them. Enough, anyway. So, our first point of approach is here," she said, touching the pointer to the flashing red dot southeast of the base. "Harrison, Tommy and I un-ass the truck and proceed to the fence. We have fairly recent intelligence that the fence is chain link topped by razor wire. Naturally, we'll take backup, but we should be able to get onto the base itself with nothing more exotic than heavy duty wire cutters. From the fence, we split up. Two hundred meters in from the fence line, there's a guard patrol that covers the secure area containing the archive. I turn onto the road here and start jogging up towards the archive building. Tommy and Harrison parallel me and wait for me to jenny the guard. They break across the line and make their way to the building. Harrison, you're going to carry some package you need the clerk to sign for. Get together with Tommy and figure out something plausible.

"Meanwhile, George and Granpa take the Humvee around to here." She pointed to a second flashing red dot in the hologram. "As you can see, the truck can get closer in here, meaning Granpa will get up the hill before us, overlooking the muster point for the particular Posleen attack drill we've selected."

As she took them through the steps of the brief, Tommy tried to keep his mind on the details. This was a straightforward reconnaissance mission, despite the target, but that didn't make it okay to get complacent.

It was good flying weather, clear and mild, as Kieran Dougherty guided the Martin Safari hybrid jet over the Virginia hills. False dawn threw purple shadows over a landscape barely touched with color in the early light. The pilot grumbled to himself because the Schmidt sitting to his right in the copilot's seat was not, in fact, his copilot—not that he needed one for this. Schmidt Two wasn't any kind of pilot at all and as far as Dougherty knew, hadn't a single hour of flight time to his name. The overgrown kid of an assassin was using the instrumentation of his plane, all right. Using it to control the surveillance cameras on the belly of the plane, taking countless pictures of the ground they were overflying, just as if it was anything more than godforsaken postwar wilderness laced with the occasional cluster of dirt-poor bounty farms.

He came in low, dropping lower, using VTOL to land on a green flat, behind a hill, in a place that used to be called Falmouth. Mere tens of meters away, an abandoned bounty-farmer's shack sat, weathering beneath an encroaching tangle of vines, dry and dormant in preparation for winter. His landing field was an irregular patch of knee-high grass and weeds, its sole virtue that it was relatively flat and not yet overgrown with the scraggly pines eating away its edges. There were, however, signs of abat. The only blessing about this mission to the middle of nowhere was the season. This late in the year, the grat, who, like the Posleen they came with, preferred warmer weather, were already hibernating deep in the ground awaiting spring. The alien insect, which preyed on the hapless, plentiful abat, hunted in swarms. The little bastards' poison sting could kill a grown man with a speed and ease that would have struck a hive of killer bees dumb with envy.

The amateur ecologist in Kieran automatically tracked the signs of change everywhere he got to go—one of the perks of his job. Fortunately, in Virginia the abat were slowly losing the fight to the rabbits and field mice. Once the local owls, foxes, and other night-hunters had learned the abat's peculiar vulnerabilities, the native rodents had gotten a respite and begun to recover. The abat's coloring and movement habits helped it avoid the senses of grat in Posleen ships and fields. Evolution had not fitted them for all terrestrial habitats. Farther south, the story wasn't so good for the natives. Here, abat didn't have any of the peculiar survival habits needed for winter weather. They were conspicuous as hell in the snow, tending to hop frenetically to keep warm. They had swarmed in with the Posleen, along with other pests and hangers-on from countless worlds the Posleen had devoured. The rodentlike herbivores' reproductive rates had made their slide towards extinction in Virginia slow, but the outcome was inevitable.

As for the grat, some local insectivore or another must be pretty damned resistant to the poison, because they were reportedly declining, too. Expert opinions were divided between the black bear and the woodpeckers as the happy recipients of ecologic accident. Lack of resistance worked both ways. For every species that became invasive in a new environment, at least a hundred died out. Invasive success in one environment did not translate to invasive success in another.

In the prewar era, Japanese kudzu had inundated the American southeast, but left Alaska untouched. Rabbits and cane toads had overrun Australia, but bombed out in more habitats than they'd thrived. *Felis domesticus* had destroyed countless species of birds—but only in places where it had doting humans to go home to. In many other places, top level predators—and not just the Posleen—made short work of the kitty cats after their human protectors were gone.

Ecological destruction from the Posties' hitchhikers had overturned equilibria everywhere—but it was a toss-up which species got a foothold where, and some, like the abat and grat, appeared to have a similar vulnerability to the Posleen's absence as the house cats had to the absence of humans. In the former cases, nobody had figured out why yet.

The key, as always, was that evolution was not an upward path towards some predestined goal. Evolution had no goals—it simply described an observed sequence of causes and effects. Evolutionary fitness in one environment did not translate to evolutionary fitness in another. The Posleen, in their adaptability of diet and environment, were a wholly remarkable, one in a gazillion aberration.

Their hitchhiker species demonstrated more the rule of species transplantation than the horses' own bizarre exception. Any hitchhikers that couldn't eat earth life started dying out as soon as the Posleen were gone. Any hitchhikers that *could* eat earth life could, as a rule, be eaten by it. It tended to level the playing field.

He sighed and shook loose from the woolgathering that tended to catch up with him all at once whenever he got safely back on the ground.

"Thank you for flying Bane Sidhe Air, please don't forget your baggage, we hope you have a brilliant day. Guys, watch your step on the ground out there. It's an abat field." Kieran busied himself with flipping switches and checking gauges, preparatory to going out and getting his aircraft squared away for the team's return.

"Oh, lovely. Can you give us a second to double check the harness before you drop the ramp? I know it's fine, just exercising constructive paranoia." Cally was first out of her seat and bouncing on the balls of her feet, already buzzing on adrenaline.

"Yeah, secondary to Kieran's constructive paranoia. He checked everything about five times before we took off in the first place." Harrison grinned easily, standing and getting what little stretch was available in the cabin.

"Great. Still, you never know what might have worked loose on the trip." She looked like she was about to jump to the ground. Looking over his shoulder, Kieran could almost see the words "abat field" walk across her forehead before she turned and took the ladder down.

"If it makes you feel better. We've got time." Papa O'Neal yawned and began patting down his pockets.

"Looks good. Drop the ramp. Tommy, you and Granpa get the camo net over the plane. Harrison, help me start disconnecting the Humvee," she called.

"You mean now that we know everything's connected?" Schmidt One had a quirk at the corner of his mouth.

"Exactly," she said.

"Did anybody ever tell you you've been listening to your buckley too much?" George asked.

"She has not. If she listened to me, she'd know that it's not the aggregate failure rate on the *straps* you have to worry about. Do you know how many field missions have ended in death and mayhem, not to mention blatant destruction of sensitive and valuable electronic equipment, caused by vehicular failures? I've prepared a list of the top twenty-five most likely causes for mission failure resulting in three or more team fatalities. I can recite it if you'd like," the buckley volunteered helpfully.

"Shut up, buckley," Cally called over her shoulder at the PDA still resting in her vacated seat.

"Right."

While they were talking, Kieran had gotten the ramp down and joined Cally and Harrison, rapidly unfastening the heavy-duty harness that had held the mostly mud-colored truck immobile in the belly of the plane. It was amazing what you could carry in a smallish plane when you didn't have to carry large amounts of jet fuel. Cally ignored the door, swinging her feet in through the driver's side window and starting the engine, before backing the vehicle down the ramp. Parking clear of the plane so her team members could get the cover in place, she got out and fished a gym bag from the floorboard behind the driver's seat. The guys were set already. This time of year the gray silks, with Fleet Strike's blue stripe up the leg, would certainly be the uniform of the day. Fleet Strike uniform would be the best camouflage possible on base for Tommy and Harrison. George and Papa were in old-style BDUs and snivel gear. Cally, of course, had a different role to play.

She pulled a thin camo jumpsuit out of the bag and wrinkled her nose at it, looking down at her stylish black and red running togs. She looked good. She was supposed to, but her vanity always amused Kieran for some reason. The black sweats and windbreaker were nothing special, but teamed with a red tank top that was about two sizes too small, it was eye catching enough.

"Cold, Cally?" George said, walking past her to rummage in the back for his camera bag. She spun around and obviously checked the impulse to clobber him, settling for staring balefully at his back. The bra she was wearing was a thin membrane that other than keeping everything elevated might as well not have been there. If ogling was pissing her off, she'd better get her head in the game. Kieran walked up the ramp into his plane to close it up. He'd go over it with his usual fine-toothed comb before taking the opportunity to grab a nap, his own part in the operation finished for now.

✧ ✧ ✧

"Get in the goddam truck, George. You've got the middle." Cally stepped into the jumpsuit and zipped it halfway up. The grass crunched under her feet, crisp with early-morning frost despite the mild air. She was the odd woman out for the vehicle, looked like.

"Nope, I need shotgun. Gotta shoot some pics. Besides, Tommy and Harrison'll like it better if you're in the middle. You look better than me and you probably smell better." The camera itself was a good electronic model. His eccentricity was that he used an ancient set of glass lenses with it, and could go on for hours about the inferiority of modern, polymer, zoom lenses. At least, the one time Cally had been present it had seemed like forever.

"At great personal sacrifice, *I* will sit in back. Cally, you drive," Granpa said.

"Works for me. Hi, Boopsie," George said, opening the passenger side door. It would be bad form to vault the hood and slam her feet in his face. Really, it would.

Schmidt Two's air photos, the jerk, showed a rutted track from the abandoned farmstead to the river, and a crossing point that had once been Jefferson Davis Boulevard.

She got a good look from the side as they drove up, upgraded vision outlining the details for her as sharply as if she'd peered through binoculars. It wasn't much of a bridge. The horses had built out the postdemolition remnants of the prewar structure in the sturdy, functional, clumsy style of Posleen engineering, but never completed it. A ramshackle conglomeration of timbers, patches of salvaged Galtech cargo webbing, and what looked like steel runway planking bridged the central gap of about twenty meters. Cally was about to throttle George over his constant click-clicking of the camera as they drove. She knew the value of good footage, but my God, the man was obsessive. She parked the hummer on the bank and walked out onto the bridge, toeing the material in the gap experimentally. Personally, she wouldn't drive a bicycle across that mess. But she'd walk it, with a belayman.

"Netting bridge gonna work, Harrison?" she asked.

"You bet." He stooped down and fingered the old Posleen surfacing. "This stuff will make a good bond with adhesive."

"Fine, get the netting. Harrison, Granpa, secure this end. I'll make the crossing." She looked at Harrison and waited for his nod before jogging back behind the vehicle. After some rummaging through the other supplies she found rope, harness, and pack, carrying them around front and tying off to the front bumper. The lines for the pulley hooked onto her belt, to unwind as she went.

"What, all of a sudden you don't trust me not to drop you?" Tommy asked.

"You're not belaying me. George is. The process will go faster if you help the others set up on this side." The too-handsome mechanical specialist was working with Granpa to assemble the strips that would become the improvised bridge's base plates. Flat on one side and blessed with a plethora of hooks on the other, the plates could be secured on soft ground with long spikes, affixed to a solid surface, or stabilized in place in any of several other ways. A properly secured set of base plates with several layers of the special netting could create a bridge strong enough to support a small tank in an unbelievably short time. "Properly secured" was always the kicker.

In this case, the bridge so constructed would be roughly double the width of their Humvee, once they snapped together the axles of enough rolls of bridge netting. The bridging had taken up virtually all the cargo space in the Humvee, even though the material was as thin as cardboard and flexible enough to roll very tightly. They had had to carry so much of it because there was no way to tell how much bridging they'd need. At that, George had insisted on carrying more wedged into nooks and crannies in the plane. Cally and Granpa had surreptitiously rolled their eyes. There was paranoia, and then there was paranoia. Schmidt Two had changed since the loss of his wife and team. Among other things, for the first few years he'd been fanatically punctual. Some quirks stayed, others tapered off. Everyone knew what he was going through. Besides, assassins were always strange birds in one way or another. As long as it didn't get in the way of the mission, they tolerated it where possible, and were glad of it when it did support the mission. George had gone from a seat of the pants improviser to an excellent go to hell guy, with an almost prescient tactical awareness.

"Your faith in my competence is touching," the smaller man said.

The slight assassin probably weighed less than she did. He'd know how to brace himself, but no way was she going to let him see how much it freaked her out to step onto the rickety bridge. It would have been just as bad if her belayman had decent body mass. Really, it would. If she told herself that often enough, maybe she could stop the cold sweat she felt prickling on her upper lip. She tried to pretend to be someone who wasn't afraid of heights, but slipping into character was, for this, pretty damned hard.

"No offense. Just don't drop me." She checked her rigging and backed out onto the dilapidated mess, watching over her shoulder and testing her footing as she went. Halfway over, when it was holding up better than expected, she sped up, dancing lightly backwards with only a few muffled curses when her foot slipped through a gap in the webbing. Damned if she was going to show how petrified she was. The adrenaline from her slip drove her heart straight up into her throat. She couldn't help getting a glimpse of the water, so dizzyingly far down. Two missions in a row where she had to be way up in the—she really didn't want to think about it. She yanked her foot loose and planted it on a thicker strip of webbing, her knuckles whitening on the rope in her hands.

"Hey, watch it! Where are we gonna be if you throw a shoe?" George called.

"You're making me sound like a horse."

"Whatever. We should have brought you an extra pair of shoes," he said.

"Well, I'm over here now, so relax. I'm not going to drop a sneaker in the river. Even though I did wrench my ankle for real, just a bit. But hell, if I get a little swelling or something, it just adds realism." She gave up trying to look casual and backed the rest of the way carefully, watching her footing. She had to resist collapsing on the bridge in relief when she got to solid ground again. More solid, anyway. Still far too high, but she wasn't going to think about that.

"You got by with it. Just hook up the pulley," he called.

Oooh, he's pissing me off. "Fine." She brushed the dust and dirt off part of a Postie section in the bridge, more or less in the middle, and opened the backpack. The available section of bridge looked much better for adhesive than trying to drill holes. She sprayed down the clean section of bridge and shoved the back plate of the pulley against it, counting to sixty before unclipping the lines from her waist. The pulley lines were ingenious. Strong sections of line clipped together at intervals to make the length of the loop easy to adjust, but the clips were narrow enough not to make the line jump out of the groove in the wheel. She clipped them in place and rested, elbows pressed in to her sides, tapping her fingers together nervously. Why did they have to build bridges so high? It wasn't as if there was anything wrong with being down close to the water.

It took a few minutes for them to package up the bridging base plates for her side, and attach the package to the pulley so that it wouldn't snag too bad on the way over, then about as much time for her to get it all loose on her side. Setting the roll of bridging to unwind smoothly around its axle as she pulled it across was even more awkward. The procedure certainly gave her bridge base plating enough time for the adhesive to set up before she had to cut the net to fit. Working backward with a boxcutter variant of a boma blade, she eased the mesh of the ultra-strong netting over the hooks on the plate and secured it. The plates themselves were now as firmly affixed to the Posleen section of bridge as if the whole assembly had been cast from Galplas.

Finished, she noticed an infinitesimal tug at her waist. Cally looked up to see that the annoying man had untied her rapelling rope from the Humvee, unrolled a substantial length, and was tying it to one of the ancient steel supports whose remnants stood, twisted and torn, on the human section of the old bridge.

He waved some coils of slack at her and called out, "Pull your end back and tie it off. If we have to dismantle the bridge in a hurry, somebody might need it. We've got more rope; we don't need to take this one."

Damn but he was lucky she wasn't close enough to slap him. She sighed and tied the thing off, grumbling. Just like him to put her in a corner where she had to leave her lucky rope. She couldn't say anything about it without looking stupid.

She didn't look at him as she got into the hummer behind Granpa, who probably would get to drive for the rest of the insertion. Her right front side tingled with the urge to pop George upside the head. If he hadn't been so good at his job, she'd really be regretting asking him now. She hadn't been this pissed in she didn't know how long.

The first section of bridge had moved them across to what was technically an island. The roadway forward was intact up until the small branch that separated them from the mainland. Whatever improvised bridge had spanned that gap had suffered some sort of misfortune. The Postie work was ragged at the edges and wisps of what must have once been another improvised connection hung from both ends over the gap. Naturally, Granpa's drysuit and fins had shifted to the bottom of the pile. Normally, with her natural buoyancy, Cally would have gotten stuck with swimming the gap. She'd gotten to beg off from the task this time since it kept them from having to wait while she redid her hair. Another O'Neal was the logical choice since they swam so much at home. Granpa got the job—he wouldn't be seen by anyone after insertion. That didn't mean he had to like it. Even through a good suit, the water was damned cold and he let them hear about it, drawing a good-natured "quit whining" from Tommy. Still, once he made it across and up to the other side of the gap, setup was routine.

Vehicle finally across, they fired up some self-heating breakfast packs and a pot of coffee. A hot breakfast was nice for the others, but necessary for Papa O'Neal, who was still shivering after he'd gotten back into his BDUs and snivel gear. The temperature was dropping so fast Cally was feeling the chill even through her sweats. She ignored George as he tied off another rope. The problem with overcomplicating mission fail-safes was that the more you did, the more likely it was that something would go horribly wrong when you couldn't keep track of all the balls you had in the air. It was a delicate balance. She preferred to keep things simpler and fly by the seat of her pants when she had to.

CHAPTER ELEVEN

Tommy Sunday looked at how badly Papa O'Neal was shivering and was very glad the older man was driving, up near those front heater vents. He might be metabolically an early twenty-something, but that didn't make him immune to hypothermia. The man's next task would be crawling up the back side of a hill on the cold ground, moving slowly enough under his ghillie suit not to get any body heat from exertion. George's real-world experience, like Cally's, was more urban. Papa was a better man in the woods, and was the logical man for the task. He needed to get his core body temperature back up, get thoroughly dried out. His hair was still dark with water from his swim, and that just wouldn't do.

The cyber initiated a pre-set program with his, clean, AID to track their progress and jimmy with the cameras accordingly. The AID would tell him if something unexpected came up, but adding static didn't take much babysitting. He pocketed it, climbing into the back of the car after the unbelievably stacked blonde. Damn, it was a good thing women couldn't read guys' thoughts. He'd be walking around with bright red hand prints on his face all the time. She turned to stow something in her gym bag behind the seat and one of her tits pressed against his arm. Not that it had anywhere else to go. Determinedly, he thought about cleaning out the cat box when he got home. They were Wendy's cats, but it was his week. Sand didn't do nearly as good a job as prewar clay litter had.

Thanks to his wife's hobby of buying and reselling antiques, frequently after a little research and restoration, and the war-pay investments of his they had converted into anonymous accounts before they "died," the Sundays weren't hurting for money. Too many other people were, O'Neal, Bane Sidhe, and strangers. He and Wendy had learned how old money used to feel, back in the northeast before the war. If you were comfortable, you didn't show it. Envy was a dangerous thing, and attracted parasites besides. He didn't mean the first generation O'Neals. He would've gladly helped Cally or Papa, but they wouldn't take it. The Bane Sidhe, though, would have pressured them to strip their assets as surely as fourteenth-century monks had latched onto anyone around their own bailiwick with land or cash. All in a good cause, of course.

It *was* a good cause. But he and his risking their lives in it was plenty, especially given the lack of results and the lack of down chain loyalty the Indowy had shown towards the operatives and sleepers. Sure, the O'Neal Bane Sidhe was better for the reduction in Indowy control, but not that much better. Father O'Reilly was a good man, but with the vow of poverty and never having married, the needs of families with kids and grandkids to care for sometimes slipped by him. Tommy and Wendy lived almost as frugal a lifestyle as anyone, but he was damned if he'd give up resources they needed whenever one of the young men hadn't come home, and would need again. The kids still needed shoes, and schooling, and braces on their teeth. They needed time with a mom who wasn't worn out from working herself into an early grave. He didn't at all regret working to bring the Darhel down, but the years had nurtured in him a certain bitter wariness about the Organization. They didn't mean to be callous bastards. They meant well, bigtime. They were necessary allies. But the Sundays and O'Neals always made sure they could take care of their own, because for sure nobody else would.

This train of thought always made him grumpy, but at least it had kept him from embarrassing himself until his "clan sister"—who sure as hell *wasn't* his sister—quit wiggling around. Barely. *Friend. Of. My. Wife. Down, boy. Besides being a damned dangerous woman to piss off. Don't be stupid, man. Breathe.*

He stared out the window as they bounced their way over the river and through the woods, threading whatever path they could through the trees, using the top of the hill where the building was as a rough guide. Most of the way, the old roads had kept out enough tree growth to let the truck through. Sometimes they had to go off and find their way around fallen trees, old telephone poles or other debris. Fortunately, the ground was hard enough that the truck didn't leave obvious fresh ruts. Not ones that would last very long, anyway. It sent creepers up his spine and left a lump in his stomach to be in Fredericksburg again. It did every time he came back to the place that had once been a thriving town. It had been the most horrible handful of days in his life. Bar none. He'd been scared shitless a lot of times through the war. He would've been a moron not to be. Nothing compared to Fredericksburg.

He lost his dad, his friends, everything. In a single day. Worse was knowing they had been eaten, butchered under the boma blades of the stupid but unstoppable hordes of ravenous tyrannosaurlike centaurs as they swarmed over his hometown like a plague of locusts. They weren't his worst nightmare. They were worse than that. He'd been in the local militia, like all the boys and men. Not that it had helped Fredericksburg, which had the misfortune to be the site of one of the first scout landings in the war. Already a proficient sniper from his prewar marksmanship hobby, he had taken up a position knowing—flat out knowing—that he would not survive the day, but determined to kill as many Posleen as he could before they got him, too.

Somehow, he had ended up with Wendy and handed her one of his spare rifles. Not that he had really expected her to do much with it, not really. She had just deserved the chance to try. What stuck in his mind most from the day was the stench as the smoke from the various explosions on the outside of town blew in on the wind. Faint at first, by the time the horses came in the carrion reek rising from the streets and blowing into their faces had been overwhelming. At the time, the adrenaline had been pumping so hard, with him so focused trying to stay in the zone to make every shot count, he hadn't noticed much. It only came back to him in memory, later. Maybe the memory was enhanced by the smell of the battlefields after, before he was chosen for Iron Mike's Fleet Strike ACS. One of the best unsung advantages to fighting in a combat suit was the way you didn't smell the Posleen.

The yellow scales of the carnosaurs had been covered all over the front, that and all six limbs, with orange smears of mixed human and Posleen blood. More blood had leaked into the gutters as they marched down the street in their usual bunched up mass. All that was the yellow of the hermaphroditic cannibals' own ichor. Human corpses from the hell of the scout wave's landing had long since been consumed or passed back to ranks in the rear for processing. He hadn't noticed at the time; his scope inadvertently swept over the gutter between the horde and the street drain as he came down from recoil to line up his next target. It was only afterwards that every detail of the day stood out starkly in his memory.

When Wendy got hit in the back of the leg, his getting her down to the vaults under the city, quick, had been the only thing to do. They still didn't think they'd live, not really. She had known about the vaults as a town history buff. His plan before he ended up with her had been to move from one firing position to another before ultimately dying in place. With her, he had a responsibility to at least pretend with her that his plan was going to do them some good. Then she got injured and it had been easier to contemplate dying himself than it was for him to leave a beautiful girl, his unrequited high school crush up until The Day, to die on that roof with him. Then under Fredericksburg, one thing had led to another and he and Wendy had ended up making love. At the time, they were both too much in shock for it to feel like a strange thing to do. Since then, he'd gotten used to the horniness inevitably evoked by the near death experience of battle. Some wit, he didn't know who, had once said that the most exhilarating experience in the world was to be shot at—and missed. It was.

As far as he knew, Shari O'Neal, his Wendy, and a handful of kids from the creche they had both worked in were the only women and children who had survived both the Fredericksburg landing and the Posleen eating the Franklin Sub-Urb, where many survivors of Fredericksbug had been sent. What a goatfuck that had been. Disarmed residents, no exits except from the top—the way the Posleen had to come in. They might as well have planted a big, neon, fast food sign on the top of the place. He hated the Darhel more for the deliberate mis-design of Franklin than for anything else. The dying act of the men from Fredericksburg had been to Hiberzine the women and children and stash them underground, stacked like cordwood in an old pump house, hoping they'd hidden it successfully from the Posleen. Those men had acted in the purest tradition of heroism. Many had done as much in that war, but nobody had done more. Only then a lot of the survivors had been sent to Franklin, which had been made a zero-tolerance for weapons zone at the insistence of the Galactics—which meant the Darhel. Designed with no exits. Franklin had been near the Wall, just inside Rabun Gap. When the Posleen broke through, the women, kids, and old people in Franklin hadn't had a snowball's chance in hell. Except that Wendy and Anne Elgars, a woman soldier of the Ten Thousand who'd been recuperating from near-fatal injuries, had gotten Shari and the kids out through the ventilation shafts and a small exit in the hydroponics section. Again, Wendy's habit of finding out everything about where she lived had saved her life. And the lives of the handful of others she'd been able to take with her.

Thank God his mother and sister had gone to Asheville instead of Franklin. They didn't get eaten, but what with the war and all, and the way everybody changed, by the time he and Wendy officially died, he and his surviving family hadn't been close.

He knew he was in Fredericksburg, which brought back all the ghosts he thought he'd laid to rest decades ago, but he couldn't recognize anything. Every once in awhile he'd get a glimpse of something he thought might once have been familiar, but he wasn't sure if he really remembered it or was kidding himself. The woods were anything but a healthy forest. There were plenty of trees, but mostly large patches of weeds and grass. Their roots and the elements had done a job on the rubble and compressed ground, which was punctuated by falling scraps of walls. The rusted spikes of rebar that crested above the weeds in places contrasted sharply with the twisted girders. Between one thing and another, not all of the metal in the ruins of Fredericksburg had gone into the Posleen nano-tanks. Some cities, in the rear of the Posleen occupation, or under more efficient God Kings, had been totally obliterated, so thoroughly had they been scoured for resources to feed the Posleen's infinite needs for war materiel. His home town had been left with its ghosts. He didn't know whether that was good or bad.

With difficulty, he shook himself out of his involuntary review of The Day. It didn't do any good to get caught up in past shit. There was just too much of it. Fuck it, drive on. Going fishing with one of his sons or grandsons was usually how he straightened himself out. Which it would be time to do when he got home, but now was time to have his head in the game.

The Fleet Strike silks threatened to pull him back into more unwanted reverie, of the months he'd spent fighting with the Ten Thousand, after getting dug out of Fredricksburg. Shortly after, he'd been transferred from the U.S. Army to Fleet Strike ACS—where he'd gotten used to wearing silks, in the rare times when he wasn't living in his suit. Now he was back. His conversion away from the system had come at the very end of the war, when to stay alive and keep the Posleen from pouring into the American heartland they had had to hide their moves from their Darhel-issued AIDs. Even back then, he was every bit as good with a computer as he was with a rifle. There was no way for the Posleen to be reading the AID network unless the Darhel had deliberately given them access. Put together with the designed-in vulnerabilities of the Franklin Sub-Urb, that were also too comprehensive to be accidental, nobody had needed to draw him a picture. Now he was back. For an hour or so, anyway.

He checked the blue stripe on the back of his buckley for what must have been the fifth time, reading over Michelle O'Neal's data on the mission that discovered the alleged Aldenata device. On a Crab planet the ACS had nicknamed Charlie Foxtrot, being unable to pronounce the Galactics' name for the place, Fleet Strike had engaged in heavy fighting with pockets of Posleen resistance in areas the powers-that-be deemed too sensitive to be neutralized by Fleet from orbit. According to Michelle, Fleet Strike had received orders to divert some equipment recovered from the Crab equivalent of a museum, and deliver it up the line. The museum was listed in all official Galactic records as a total combat loss. Cally's sister believed, and his experience agreed, that Fleet Strike kept more information in its records than it acknowledged to its Galactic bosses. Especially when ordered to do something it might have to cover its ass for later. He sure hoped the Michon Mentat was correct in her information about what they'd find in the records this time. It would really, really suck to have come all this way for nothing. Not to mention how much longer it would take to come up empty. Finding something was quick. Finding nothing was what took time.

Date, planet, coordinates, unit, commanding officer. If it was there, he should be able to find it. If it was there. He checked the blue stripe on the back of his PDA again.

"You're not nervous, are you?" Cally asked. "That's about the tenth time you've checked that thing."

"No, I'm good. It's just . . . Fredericksburg."

"Yeah, that's gotta suck."

"No shit," he agreed. "On the other hand, it takes my head right back to when I was with Fleet Strike, so it's not all bad."

"I wouldn't have minded being with Fleet Strike," Harrison observed, pouting. "Parts of it, anyway."

"Very funny. Keep a lid on the camp. It wouldn't play well with the target. Stick to the sports," Cally said. "You're checking your notes, right?" From what Tommy could see, he was playing solitaire.

"I've got it. I drilled it until I'm blue in the face. I can talk baseball with George for God's sakes. Don't jostle my elbow, dear."

"You'll be fine," she assured him.

"I know." Harrison winked at her. "Don't worry, I'll keep it simple."

"We've got the fence ahead," Papa said, softly, pulling the Humvee up. He stopped it short of the expanse of chain link topped with razor wire that cut a line through the woods. The woods on this side looked very much like the woods on that one, with nothing obvious about the land to tell why the fence was here and not there.

Harrison was out of the truck first, approaching the barrier with an old-fashioned multimeter and a black leather bag that looked like something an old country doctor would have carried. The fence was probably electrified, but its main purpose was as a simple barrier to announce the presence of a stupid Posleen normal charging through it. It also served to keep out equally stupid humanist radicals, seeking street cred with others in the protester set.

Tommy nodded to himself when the fixer started pulling out assorted wires and clippers. Electrified. He and Cally got out, breath frosting on the air. He put his buckley in the pocket of his silks and sealed it in, patting the other pocket to make sure his emergency field kit was in place, dropping the AID into the seat. Unlike conventional clothing, the pockets on his silks would stay reliably closed until he pressed the top corner again with a finger. They were comfortable as hell. He'd regret turning them back in at the end of the mission. Not that the Bane Sidhe had another operative who would fit silks made for Tommy Sunday. They didn't have anybody else as big as him. Which incidentally also meant Harrison had to cut the hole in the fence big enough for him to get through. The smaller man was used to it by now. Still, it was a good thing silks didn't snag.

Schmidt One looked up at his brother and said, "When we come back out of here, we're going to have to stop for me to patch the hole. Otherwise they'll find it the next time they run their maintenance checks. The idea's that we were never here, right?" It wasn't really a question.

"Cally, you're through first," the fixer said. "Tommy, get the other side. It just wouldn't do for her to get scratched up on all these rough edges."

"Nope. Ruin the whole effect." Papa O'Neal spat neatly out the driver's window. "Through you go. Get moving."

George put the box of coffee supplies, graced by a well-known brand name, on the ground next to his brother. "Here," he said, handing each of them a small data cube. "Terrain updates. That's what the pictures were for. Cross referenced with the hummer's tracking measurements, it should be pretty solid—at least for what I was able to see. I've also marked backup rendezvous points."

Cally took the cube without comment, pocketing it. Tommy and Harrison at least nodded at the smaller man, who smiled faintly before going back to the car.

Sunday followed her through the fence, letting her get as far away as she could without losing sight of her. He began following as she moved in to the southwest. He could hear the faint crackle of leaves under Harrison's feet behind him. Good thing the noisier man would be the farthest one from any unfriendly ears.

They'd walked just over two hundred meters, by his pace count, when Cally raised her hand and stopped them. He echoed the signal back to Harrison. She stripped her camo jumpsuit off and stowed it under a bush, patting the pocket of her black windbreaker, rubbing her ear to make sure the dot earphone was in place. Flesh toned and about half the diameter of a ladybug, it was practically undetectable. Tommy checked his earphone, too, patting the pocket with his buckley.

Once the extremely stacked and tempting blonde was on the road, Tommy could keep pace with her slow jog at a safely increased distance, watching the flash of red from her tank top through the trees that concealed his own muted gray. He listened carefully as he went, waiting for her to find and draw off the guard.

"Hey!" He heard a masculine voice from the direction of the road. He stopped cold, raising his hand to stop Harrison. "Excuse me, ma'am, but this is a restricted area." He heard the voice say, apologetically. Definitely not the tone he'd have taken with some unknown man. He almost felt sorry for the guy. Dangling Cally in front of him was a below the belt hit if there ever was one.

"Oh, is it? I'm so sorry, I didn't see the sign. I got a little turned around, anyway. Could you point me back to base housing? My sister-in-law is going to think I'm such a dummy," she said.

The voices were far enough away that he had to listen carefully, and wouldn't be easily overheard. He started forward again, carefully, beckoning with one hand. Harrison would have to go in first with his box, so he'd be looping around Tommy. The voices were moving down the hill as his female teammate succeeded at drawing the young soldier along with her. Single women on base were in short supply.

"Oooh!" The high feminine squeal of dismay was followed by a pause. "It's my ankle. . . ."

He couldn't hear the rest. They kept moving, cutting in to approach the road. There was a five-yard strip of grass on each side of the road before the gate to the chain link fence surrounding the archive building, and a good fifteen yards between the fence and the building. Where the front of the building jutted out from the hillside, the structure was surrounded by neatly trimmed boxwood hedges. Fortunately, the gate was open, the guard mount a precaution against a theoretically possible intrusion that nobody seriously expected. Harrison crossed the open area at a fast sprint, setting down the box on top of the hedge as he vaulted it with more agility than Tommy had known he had, and pulling the box down out of sight. Too big to try to go over the hedge without either landing in it or hitting the wall, Tommy ducked around the back after covering the gap between the tree line and the building. He barely had room to crouch down below the top of the hedges without scraping himself to bits on the hedge or the brick wall, or lying flat on the dirt. Dammit. The pictures they studied had had a mock-up of a suit and a scale model of a SheVa tank in the courtyard. Someone had moved the damned displays. He supposed they were lucky to have any cover at all.

He thumbed his pocket open and pulled out his PDA, tapping the transmit button. "Dude, I need a beer," he said, and ended the transmission. Seconds later, alarms began wailing across the base, sounding the drill alert. Soldiers all over the base would be grabbing their AIDs and their gear to get their information and execute their movements to set up an appropriate defense in response to the specified "Posleen attack." Over the next few seconds, half a dozen or so men sprinted out of the building and through the gate, disappearing quickly from Sunday's limited view. The activation phrase had been his own idea. He couldn't think of anything less likely to be flagged as a code phrase if it was somehow overheard. Papa had grumbled that it lacked style. Tommy had told Papa that next time he was on the pointy end, he could die with style if he wanted to—again. It hadn't been a fair thing to say. After all, it had only happened the once. Still, without the Crabs' miracle slab to patch up even the dead, as long as there was enough brain intact, they were all being more careful.

They waited another two minutes to make sure as many men as possible were clear before Harrison went in through the front door. It wouldn't do to wait too long and have Cally lose her grip on the attentions of the guard. Yeah, as if that was likely to happen. Getting out of the bushes wasn't fun. Schmidt One had to crawl across the bigger man's back on his knees so he wouldn't leave boot prints all over his back. Silks were stain resistant as hell, but they picked up dirt like anything else. The other man brushed off his back, getting the slightly damp pine chips off him. Tommy dusted off the bottom of the coffee box and handed it back.

The morning was brightening in the way only a crisp fall day could. He was warm in his silks, but could feel the cold against his face and hands and see his breath. As he looked up to watch Harrison around the side of the building, he could see the trees down the slope bending in the wind. In the lee of the hill, he didn't feel much wind, but he was starting to hear it. A quick glance up at the sky showed a line of heavy clouds as a colder front blew in from the northeast. Great. He gave Harrison a full minute before walking around the back of the hedge to the front of the building, PDA in hand.

He opened the door to see Harrison shrug at the counter clerk.

"No coffee maker? I dunno, maybe you're getting one. All I know is this is the building number I got and I need a signature. Hey, even if it's ultimately supposed to be somewhere else, it don't say so. Might as well drink it. Hell, I would."

"If it has our number on it . . ."

"Excuse me, I've just got to finish something up." Tommy waved the PDA at the clerk, showing the blue stripe, and walked past the desk. The clerk barely glanced at him, busy signing for the coffee.

"So, hey, did you see the last game of the series? That homer in the top of the sixth? What a beautiful . . ." He heard Harrison settling in to shooting the shit with the bored clerk.

Down the main hall, at the second intersecting cross-hall he turned left, passed the reading room and walked down to where the terminal plug was supposed to be—and wasn't. The space of wall that should have had a terminal had a door to the head. He looked back along the hallway the way he'd come and saw the jutting lip of the terminal outlet all the way down at the other end—and a skinny, freckled sergeant in silks.

"God damn, you're a fucking tank, aren't you?" The man looked up at him, tapping one foot. He didn't look impatient, just like the kind of guy who couldn't stand still.

"Um . . . hi," Tommy said. There weren't a lot of brilliant ways to answer that even if he'd been somewhere he was supposed to be.

"Sorry, I should have said hi or something first. You're just, damn, I'm surprised the ACS brass came up with a suit to fit you." The man was more a kid, really. He was already starting to remind Tommy of an overexcited cocker spaniel.

"I don't really know what to say to that. I'm Johnson. Bob Johnson," Tommy lied.

"Sorry, I swear to god I'm not weird or anything. It's just that they're running a course right now on early ACS tactics in the war. I didn't think anybody could be as huge as Tommy Sunday, but you must be close. Damn." He shrugged, starting to look uncomfortable. "I bet you get that all the time. So, when did they transfer you in? Johnson, is it? I haven't seen you, and I know

I'd remember. Are you here for the course? It just started but I'm on light duty from a strained rotator cuff and thought I'd try to get ahead in the reading . . ."

During the kid's rapid monologue, Tommy had started getting more and more nervous. When he heard his own name, he made a split second decision and started sliding his hand into his right pocket with the emergency kit. He'd instinctively kept that side turned slightly away, so the kid didn't see anything wrong when Tommy started moving.

"Good to meet you," he said, clapping the other man on the shoulder. The spec four's friendly grin glazed over as the Hiberzine from the needle Tommy had palmed hit his system. Strictly speaking, they hadn't finished introducing themselves, but what the fuck. Tommy dragged the now unconscious kid into the head and down to the last stall, propping him on the toilet. This wasn't good. A single glance at the guy's face would show anyone he'd been Hiberzined, and when they woke him, damn. Tommy hit him with a second needle of another drug. If they revived him without knowing to look for it, and no reason why they should, the man's memories of the previous few minutes to hours would be so scrambled nobody would ever make sense of them. Cursing under his breath, he punched up another transmission on his buckley.

"Dude. I ran into somebody I had to deal with. I think I'll still get my paperwork done, but we'll have to rush lunch. See you at the chow hall. Over." He ended the transmission. Yeah, he could probably still get the information they came for, if it was here to be gotten, but getting back out was likely to be anything but clean.

"Roger that," George answered grimly.

This time Sunday was able to get across the main hall and down to the damn hallway terminal without meeting anyone else. Once in, he had to begin the delicate process of convincing the computer that he was surfacing from his deep cover assignment and was authorized to access the files he needed. Getting into the mission files at all proved to be a trick, and then there was an extra level of coding to break to get down to the level of specific planets. After what must have been at least fifteen minutes, with cold sweat beading on his forehead, he pinned down the files he needed and downloaded them to his PDA. He spent more precious minutes covering his tracks within the system as he got back out. Finally, he was able to pull the buckley out of the wall and start back out of the building.

A couple of men passed him, on their way back in, as he walked back down the hall. Harrison had seen him coming and finished off his conversation with the clerk, disappearing out the door. Sunday tossed the decoy buckley in the return bin at the desk on his way out.

"Thanks, man. They shouldn't have let you out of here with one of those the first time."

"You're right. Won't happen again."

As he left the building, it felt like every one of the few men he passed was looking right at him. They weren't, he knew. It just felt that way, like a rifle was drawing a bead between his shoulder blades. He could pick out Schmidt One going down the hill past Cally and the still captivated guard. She was standing now, flexing her ankle experimentally as she laughed at something he said. She had one hand on his shoulder and his arm around her waist. For support, of course. Tommy's adrenaline was pumping too high to be even mildly amused at how easily she'd reeled the other man in. Once he got out of earshot down the hill he hit transmit again.

"Lady, as soon as we're clear, disengage and haul ass. Big time." He didn't wait for a reply. It wasn't good communications discipline, if anyone was listening it was obvious as hell, but he didn't want her stalling to cover for Harrison and him any more than she absolutely had to. Maybe they wouldn't find the kid for awhile, but it wasn't the way to bet. Couldn't hurt to be paranoid.

Down the slope a bit and he was looking for any chance away from enough eyes to make a break for the tree line. By the time he got it he was over a small footbridge and at least a couple hundred meters down from where Cally came in. His sense of direction told him about where the cut through would be at the fence line, and he hurried to get out of sight of the road as quickly and quietly as he could. Fifty meters back out he saw movement off to the northwest. He tensed up until something about the other man's movement identified him as Harrison. The big man whistled softly to catch his teammate's attention, and get him to wait until Tommy could close to within a normal walking interval. They were picking their way northwest as fast as they reasonably could when the klaxons started screaming again.

"Oh, shit. Time to run for it. Damn, that was fast!" Tommy hit the ground flat on his back as Harrison yanking at the collar of his silks dropped him back with his running legs flying out from under him.

"Not that way. The second a real human being, or even an AID, looks at those readouts they're going to localize the hole in that fence faster than we can move—too easy to eyeball, too long to run there. This way." The smaller man led him at a sprint along the bank of the half dried and all frozen stream. Seconds later they were crouched in the stream bed at the fence and Sunday was watching the fixer adhere a downright dinky wire to the fencing with itty bitty alligator clips and bobby pins to hold it up out of the way, at a distance far too close to the ground to accommodate him.

"I hope you're not expecting me to be able to squeeze under that," he said.

"Shut up," the other man mumbled around some weird clips in his mouth, as he took an unfolding multitool and carefully started clipping wires. Something like a penlight shot out a blue beam that he swept across the ground at the based of a largish circle of the creek that turned to a mix of bubbling, steaming mud and chunks of frozen mud.

Tommy was starting to get a bad feeling about this. With the sirens still screaming in their ears, he started swearing again as Harrison dug hands and clippers under the mud, clipping and pulling at the section of fence that extended down into the ground. Quicker than Tommy would have believed possible, the other man had pushed back a doggy-door of fencing that moved enough mud with it that the huge man could see getting through it was now a particularly nasty maybe instead of no way in hell.

"Go," the fixer said. Getting caught wasn't exactly on their list of things to do on this mission. Tommy hit the mud and swore mentally, lips jammed shut, as the mud alternately scalded and froze him as he commando-crawled through the space that was almost big enough. He still probably wouldn't have made it through if Harrison hadn't planted his shoulder against his ass and pushed. On the other side, Sunday was covered with muck, inside and outside his uniform, in a way he hadn't been since the war. The fixer was squirming through the hole backwards, straightening the mud into something that didn't look quite as much like it had been crawled through. It wouldn't have fooled a two-year-old, but the other man pushed the fencing back as close to closed as he could get it, gave the muck a quick swipe with one arm, and took off running. Tommy hightailed it out behind him. Fuck noise and fuck bunching up, too. He pulled his PDA back out and wiped enough slime off the screen that he could see the first go to hell rendezvous point on the terrain map, maybe about two klicks away. Close enough for now. Distance. They were running in more or less the right direction, anyway. A gust of wind hit him full in the face and he felt the first big snowflakes hit his nose.

"Hey! Excuse me, ma'am, this is a restricted area." The guard who challenged her had gray eyes in an angular face. What there was of his hair under his cover was sand-colored and looked like he'd stuck his finger in a light socket. She gave him an apologetic half-smile, letting her eyes linger on his face with the perfect amount of interest to be encouraging but credible. It was blatant false advertising. She ruthlessly squashed the hint of pity.

"Oh, is it? I'm so sorry, I didn't see the sign. I got a little turned around, anyway. Could you point me back to base housing? My sister-in-law is going to think I'm such a dummy," she said.

As he kept approaching her, she moved towards him a bit less than halfway, judging the difference between flattery and triggering paranoia to within a hairsbreadth. A quick look back down the road and a helpless look back at him was enough to hook him and get him to follow her about a few meters down the hill. She made sure she had eye contact when she let her foot turn and took her spill.

"Oooh!" She squealed, arching her back as she turned and grabbed her leg. "It's my ankle. . . ." She rubbed the alleged injury, extending her leg and trying to rotate her foot. She winced prettily.

The guard squatted beside her, arm instinctively going behind her shoulders to support her.

"Ow." She looked up into his eyes, arching just a little more.

His eyes flashed down to her tits, and he released her, standing back abruptly. He looked more nervous than wary. She decided he didn't get out much—more leeway to flirt. Nervous, but trusting. Damn, there was that pity thing again. The team would be in and out without a trace. She wasn't getting him in trouble.

"If there's swelling, I don't see much yet. Do you want me to call you a medic, ma'am?"

"I think I just twisted it a little. Would you mind?" She extended one slim hand for him to give her a hand up. He released it as she stood, so she put it on his shoulder to brace herself as she made a show of testing her weight on that leg.

In her ear, she heard Tommy's voice. "Dude, I need a beer."

The wind had picked up and was whipping her silver-blonde hair around her face. "Oooh, it's getting cold." She rubbed her hands together, coincidentally pushing her boobs forward with her arms. She felt his eyes drop again and smiled inwardly.

"Do you think you're going to be able to get back your sister's house on that leg? If you do, you might want to get in out of the weather, Miss . . . ?"

"Gracie. And it's my sister-in-law," she said, offering her hand to shake. "You've been so sweet, you've got to tell me your name."

"Abrams, ma'am—Gracie. Mark Abrams."

"Well, it's very nice to meet you, Mark. What the hell is that?" She slammed her hands against her ears and looked around, eyes wide and fearful, as the sirens went off signaling the start of a drill. "Is something wrong?"

"Oh, it's just the Posleen alarm."

"Oh my God!" She threw herself into his arms, clinging like a limpet. "Is there an attack? Are they coming in?"

"Oh, no, it's just a drill," he said, awkwardly patting her on the back.

"Are you sure? We're in feral land, aren't we?" She filled the words with terror.

"Real sure. It's okay. They're just about all hunted out here." As seven men came out the doors of the archive building, one of them nudged another and winked at PFC Abrams. Predictable. These men hadn't been hit by fellow humans in so long that security was a ritual afterthought.

She disengaged herself from him, reluctantly. "You must think I'm such a dummy. It's the first time I've been in feral country. It's only my third time out of the Urb."

Cally made small talk with him for a few more minutes, giving a fictional name for her supposed brother and mentally crossing her fingers. At a training base, people were always coming in and leaving. Since Fleet Strike was trying to give a more family-friendly appearance for PR, even short-term trainees brought their families along. Stupid policy, but it helped her out. She wondered how long she'd have to talk to this guy—Mark Abrams—before Tommy and Harrison got clear of the building. She also wondered whether Mark would get around to asking her out before she had to leave.

"Dude. I ran into somebody I had to deal with. I think I'll still get my paperwork done, but we'll have to rush lunch. See you at the chow hall. Over," her earbug announced.

"Roger that." George's answer to Tommy cut off.

Shit. Shit shit shit. Better shift the conversation to something she could keep going longer. She might have to keep Mark talking for a good little while. She glanced at the treeline and started trying to figure out exactly how far she'd have to get down the road to sneak over and risk making a dash into the woods. She'd probably have to go all the way down to that bend.

She suppressed nervousness when she started seeing men return from the drill. She sunk herself deeper into her cover role, almost forgetting it was a cover. By now, she had the private almost thinking they were soul mates. They had just discovered a mutual interest in woodworking. She had briefly dated someone who had a passion for it, and that was sustaining her so far, but she was encouraging him to talk as much as possible. There was no way to spare his career from what she was doing to it, which really sucked.

"Lady, as soon as we're clear, disengage and haul ass. Big time," Tommy said in her ear just after he passed her. Just as if that wasn't pretty fucking obvious.

"Oh, my God." She looked at her watch and back up at Mark's with dismay. "I told Carrie I'd watch the baby! I've got to go!"

"Wait! How do I reach you?"

"I'll call! I'll call tonight!" She lied, remembering to put a limp into her jog as she left the young soldier staring after her.

"But you don't know my number!" She heard him call it after her, after a pause.

"Mark Abrams! Got it!" She called over her shoulder, losing the limp as she got out of his line of sight. A quick glance showed nobody in view; she hit it straight into the woods, zipping her windbreaker over the glaringly bright top as she went. She was maybe ten meters inside the tree line when the sirens went off again.

"Holy fuck!" She poured on the speed, dashing straight for the fence. They'd find the jumpsuit, but to hell with it. It only took about half a minute to reach the fence, but then she had to decide whether she was north or south of the hole. She went north for about two hundred meters before deciding she'd been going the wrong way. Unfortunately, she'd had to slow down to pace the fence line, sirens wailing the whole time so she had to look, not listen. The only benefit was that nobody could hear *her* moving over them, either.

She stopped short when she saw the movement and heard the voices. There were two of them, but neither of them was Tommy's size. She faded backwards, trying to think of a plan B, fast.

Up. Nobody ever thinks to look up. She shinnied up the oak tree nearest the fence. Pine would have provided more cover, if anyone looked, but the bark would have shown her passage. Perched on a solid limb, she examined her windbreaker, ensuring she had full coverage. Black wasn't camo, but at least it wasn't red. This limb extended over the other side of the fence. She looked down and clung to the tree, dizzily. Whatever the hell had possessed her to think climbing this thing was a good idea? She was going to get caught and shoved in another Fleet Strike interrogation room. She shuddered.

Fuck, fuck, fuck. I am dead whether they catch me up this tree, or on the ground, or I fall and break my damned neck. Move, Cally, move. Besides, this branch must be a good four inches across. Nice, big branch. Yeah. Nice, big branch. She lay down on the limb, clinging to it, and inched her way forward. She shook her head to get the droplets of sweat out of her eyes and tried to ignore the beads dropping on the ground. She hugged the branch for dear life as a hard gust of wind almost knocked her off it, blowing a blast of snowflakes in her face. The wind was the last straw. She scooched forward on the limb as fast as she could go until she got to the other side of the fence, let herself swing down, and dropped to the ground. Her feet slid out from under her and she hit the ground, hard. It was worth it. She was not going to stay that far up in the air in high winds, with snow blowing in her face.

She opened the buckley and looked at the terrain map. It was damned near useless, and she shoved the PDA back in her windbreaker pocket. The cube from George had been in her jumpsuit. She'd never gotten around to putting it in her cube reader slot. She picked a small hill that looked like it might have some likely cover and hauled ass.

In the lee of a lichen-encrusted boulder, she shivered as heavy flakes of snow caught on her eyelashes and melted on her sweats. The fall was heavy—she'd be soaked in minutes. Her hands, already red and chafed from standing talking to the guard, shook with cold as she flipped the buckley back open and punched up a transmission. To hell with radio discipline, she needed an extraction.

She wasn't getting a signal. She tapped the button a couple of times, but nothing. "Buckley, voice access please," she said. Silence. "Buckley?" *Oh, goddamn. The fall. One of the falls.* She pulled up a menu and selected a self-diagnostic, and put the thing back in her pocket. No telling how much damage there was, but right now it was no good to her.

She couldn't hear any searchers, and the sirens had stopped. There would probably be a small pause while they got a real search together. Twenty more minutes, at most. She stood up and looked out from behind the boulder. Nothing looked familiar. She climbed on top of the boulder. The snow was heavier now. She wasn't even sure she could pick out the right hill of the base behind her. She was pretty sure, from the boulder and the hill she was on now, which direction was away from the base, but that was about it. She evaluated her situation, which sucked, and came up with a plan. She'd eaten a good breakfast, so her calories were good for some more body heat if she moved around. She needed more distance from the base. She needed shelter, because she sure as hell wasn't going to find her way out of east bumfuck Virginia with a broken buckley in the middle of this mess.

She cursed the weather again and took off running in the away direction. She'd run for ten minutes and then rig a shelter with the first cover she saw. At least she could still see the ground. It wasn't yet totally white. She ran, glancing at her watch a couple of times, until she saw it was time to stop. She was on the flats, but off to the right it looked like there might be something besides trees. As she approached, she realized it was an oddly-shaped hill covered in vines. It had no trees except for a vertical branch of a partly fallen tree, its roots half ripped out of the ground. At the base of it, she saw what might be a gap or small overhang, and burrowed into it.

Under the vines and out of the wind it was still damned cold. It was immediately obvious why the "hill" had looked so odd. The line of the roof was straight, although slanted. She was right up against a tread and at the highest side of the opening. The other side wasn't quite on the ground, but the tread had been so smashed up, and sunken into the ground, that the huge SheVa tank shifted at a sideways slant. The treads on her side had also sunken about halfway into the ground, it appeared.

What the hell? What is one of these monsters doing way the hell out here? Then she remembered. Shortly after the war there had been a big political hoo-hah. She only heard of it at all because they covered it in psy-ops class at school. A big nuclear scare had convulsed the remains of the country, about the safety of the SheVa's themselves, and the safe removal of the radioactive pebbles from their fuel systems. Politicians and the machines that owned them, whose districts and interests stood to benefit from the contracts to move the mountainous tanks, had masterfully orchestrated an avalanche of voter alarm. At ruinous cost, contractors transported the behemoths outside Fredericksburg, where destruction was total anyway and Fleet Strike was, at least, willing to have them around. More to the point, Fleet Strike being Galactic and now owning the area by treaty, there had been nobody in the United States Government with authority to refuse parking space to them.

The "dangerous" pebbles from the reactors disappeared off to power plants in the congressional districts of the key swing votes, at fire sale prices. For the rest of it, they recovered remains where profitable, stripping the tanks of easily portable and easily recyclable materials. That hadn't included the huge armored hulls, difficult to cut up, difficult to reprocess, more expensive to manipulate than basic raw materials.

Cally tried to dredge up her memory of the schematics, or anything she knew about them, to help her find a hatch. Off the frozen ground, out of the wind, perhaps with some materials protected from the damp that she could use to conserve body heat, she might just last the night. Without frostbite, even.

She found it, but it was so close to sunken into the ground that once she got it open she had to scrape on her belly to get through the opening. At that, it was like putting her damned boobs in a vise. It would almost be worth making nice with the rest of the Indowy, if that had been possible, to get the slab back and get rid of the things. She had never really appreciated her own body until she'd gotten stuck in the body of Sinda Makepeace. It didn't even help that men went so ga-ga over the things. As a married woman, they didn't even get her laid. All things considered, she was in an extremely grumpy mood.

Inside the SheVa, it was warmer than outside. Maybe about ten to twenty degrees warmer. Her breath wasn't even frosting. Still damned cold, though. She worked her way to the bridge, occasionally having to squeeze through tight spots where battle damage or the effects of time on same had knocked bits, sometimes very large bits, loose from where they were supposed to be. Finally, she made it to the equivalent of the battle bridge, whatever it had once been called. One of the operator chairs was reclined all the way back, but someone had stripped the seats down to bare metal. A red cross over against one wall, the metal outside streaked with soot, caught her eye. The mechanism had a stubborn seal of pure rust. She had to pick up a hunk of scrap and bash the catch to bits to get it open.

Inside, she found antibiotic creams long dried in their tubes, but the adhesive tape was, for a wonder, barely adequate to adhere a sterile gauze pad to a cut on her face she'd picked up somewhere. She pocketed what she thought she could use and proceeded to systematically search the bridge from one end to the other to see if anything useful, anything at all, had been overlooked. Behind a panel and some wiring she found a dented helmet. In a locker, she found a rotted backpack filled with what looked like the remains of some civilian clothes and effects, a yellowed and dog-eared paperback book, and two foil-wrapped bars of U.S. Army iron rations circa 2004. Examination showed that one of the wrappers had been torn, the ration covered, startlingly, by a fungal rind like the one that formed on the outside of cheeses. This was startling because she wouldn't have thought any self-respecting fungus would touch Postie-war-era Army iron rats. The packing on the other bar was still intact. Well, maybe. She couldn't decide whether to wish it was or hope it wasn't.

She looked around at the inside of the mammoth tank, curious. She'd never been inside one before. It was the largest armored, tracked vehicle ever deployed in combat on Earth. The size of a mountaintop, the huge tank had been powered by nuclear fission via its pebble-bed reactor. The main gun had been capable of engaging B-Decs or C-Decs and living to tell the tale. It was the single most impressive cavalry vehicle in the history of war, ever. She knew this because her step-uncle Billy, who was more like a step-brother, had told her about it at eye-glazing length the summer he built a scale model of one out of toothpicks and smooshed oyster shells. This bordered on bizarre since Billy had gone mute in the war from seeing too much, too young. Scratch the young part, it was too much for anyone. Here in Fredericksburg, it was, too. A couple of years after the war he had gotten massively talkative with her, just with her, and had never stopped. He spoke to others, but not enough so you'd notice. Functional, but now a quiet old guy who had settled with a plump, pretty wife to raise four kids in Topeka. They still exchanged Christmas cards under one of her identities.

The round trip back outside to pack the helmet with snow really sucked. Getting enough clean snow to fill it wasn't a problem. The stuff was piling up at an obnoxious rate. The nasty reek of rust and old, funky smoke was starting to be unpleasant enough to overcome her thankfulness for not being so damned cold. She wedged the helmet so that it wouldn't tip over and left the packed snow to start melting. When she checked, the buckley's diagnostic was hung. A partial report showed she should be able to restore limited functionality by raising the AI emulation level, giving the AI access to search some of the damaged areas with the capabilities usually denied it. She set the emulation to the recommended level eight, wincing.

"Buckley?" she said.

"Oh, God, my aching head. Holy shit, what the hell happ—I'm a *what*?" The glum voice rose on a note of incredulity and near-hysteria. "I just know this is going to end badly."

"Buckley—please just wait a second. I need you, buckley. I need your help very, very badly," she said.

"Cally—you're Cally O'Neal. And I, I can see you. I see you, and I'm a machine," he said. "Well, doesn't that just suck."

"Yeah, buckley, it does. It sucks. A lot of things suck, and not just for you. I'm stuck in the belly of a dead SheVa, in a snowstorm, in hostile territory, they're looking for me, I'm out of contact, and you're damaged."

"It's that last bit that really bugs me. I could have warned you about the rest. Never heard of a plan where so many things could go wrong, except for the time—"

"Buckley! Can you please look and see if there's anything you can reroute to get me a working transmitter?"

"I'm sure I could, with the right repair components. Do you *have* an XJ431P39 integrated molychip? Didn't think so."

"You didn't even give me time to answer!"

"And?"

"Well, okay, I don't. But you could have at least let me say so."

"Right."

"Is there any way to improvise a transmitter with some of this stuff?" She swept a hand around the bridge area.

"You have some kind of power source?"

"Well, no, I don't. I don't think I do, anyway."

"I hope you're equipped with body nannites. It's hot in here."

"The reactor. Great. Yeah, I am. Should I brave the cold, or stay in here?"

"Doesn't matter. You're gonna die either way, sooner or later. Shall I list the most likely possibilities?"

"Please don't."

"You do want full information, don't you?"

"I'd much rather get help building a transmitter, if possible."

"There's not much point in it."

"Buckley, can you put the pessimism on hold for awhile? I'm depressed enough already."

"Good—at least you're rational. And no, I mean there's not much point in it. You're maybe five miles from the river. That and the landing zone are the two most logical points for them to look for you. You're far better off to get the best night's sleep you can and make for the river in the morning. You're also better off sleeping in here, if you get Galactic-level medical treatment within thirty-six hours. I'd recommend an early start. You don't want to stay here longer than that. If you found anything to eat—don't. Scare or not, I don't think they got all the hot rocks out of this thing."

"You're being very helpful, Buckley." Cally lay down in the reclined operator's chair, setting the PDA on the floor beside her. The bare metal was hard and uncomfortable, but she'd endured worse. There had been worse as part of her training at school, with the nuns, and far worse in the field doing her job.

"You're about to die a horrible death alone in the wilderness. I can sympathize. And me, I'll rust away slowly, slowly falling more and more apart as my battery runs down and down and—"

"Buckley? Please shut up."

"Right." He sounded satisfied, as if something about the end of the exchange had made all right with his world, at least for a few seconds.

She was strapped to the metal table on Titan Base. The bastards were on top of her again, and her head swam watching the unblinking, alien eyes through the imperfectly one-way glass above her. The face of the man on her wavered between Pryce and George and back again, only Pryce was Stewart and his ship was blowing up. They had tilted the table and were making her watch. Over and over and over again. A lifepod ejected from the shuttle and spouted wings, flying back towards the base as the ship and the table pulled her away, away, away. She was up to her elbows in blood, freezing and congealing on the icy metal table as the man slapped her over and over again. If she'd only been a good little girl and killed more Posleen, Daddy wouldn't have had to nuke her again. Herman started talking to her, telling her she had to go swim with the dolphins, but she couldn't go. Doctor Vitapetroni was holding her down, injecting her with something that stung so bad and telling her she had to stay on the table until she could wipe the blood off, but she couldn't because she didn't have a towel, and besides, she was strapped down anyway and couldn't dance anymore. She started to cry.

Cally woke, sobbing, her throat raw. The dream must have been another screamer. She remembered it and shuddered, wiping the tears away angrily.

"Good morning. I have cataloged five thousand, four hundred and thirty-two ways we can die horribly today. Continuing to process. Would you like me to . . . begin . . . the . . . list?" The buckley sounded tinny and maniacal. Dammit, she'd left it on overnight. Not that she'd had a choice. In its condition, she didn't think the PDA could reboot. At least, expecting it to come back up would be expecting a damned miracle. From the diagnostics, it was a miracle it had booted even once.

"Buckley, please calculate, not look up, a prime number with more than a thousand digits for me." At least if he was number-crunching he wasn't thinking of disasters and might actually be able to be useful if she needed him.

"Okay. But even if we do encryption based on it, they'll still break the code."

"Just do it and shut up, buckley."

"Right."

She drank the icy melt water in the helmet before she left,

glaring balefully at the nasty iron ration bar she couldn't even eat. Outside, the snow was up to her mid-thigh on average. She'd be avoiding the drifts. She sure would give a lot for a pair of snow-shoes, but she wasn't going to stop to try to rig a pair. She wasn't in Harrison's league with that improv shit, and she knew it.

It took her all morning to go those five miles, leaving a trail a toddler could have followed. Half the time she was picking herself up, the other half falling on her face again. The sky was heavy and gray. She hoped it started snowing some more soon. The cold would be bitter, but it would do something about her tracks. At the river, she pulled out the buckley and hoped that it could at least pull up prewar road and terrain maps so she could figure out if she was east or west of the bridge.

"Buckley, I need a terrain map of the area and a street map. Old is okay," she said.

"I'm calculating."

"That's okay, you can interrupt it for this, but then go back to it, okay?"

"I can't display maps. They're all fragmentary. Go left."

"What?" It made the skin on the back of her neck prickle. The buckley's guess was probably better than hers, since she had no idea which way to go. She was good at her job, but she figured she was lucky she found the river at all. Part of being good at her job was knowing when to depend on her tech support. She turned left.

"Not *your* left, *my* left!"

She turned the other way and started plowing through more snow. And more snow. And still more snow. Snow that began to fall again. Oh well, skipping frostbite wasn't going to happen this time. Hopefully there wouldn't be too much to regenerate. Be a real bitch if she had to miss the big job over a little snow.

It had to have been about sixteen hundred by the time she hit the bridge. She'd tried to talk to the buckley twice, but he was no longer answering. Either one of the falls she'd taken had knocked something else loose or he'd run out of numbers to crunch and crashed himself. She'd tried to reboot, without any luck. Buckley was well and truly hors de combat. Again.

The bridge was a very welcome sight, since the winds had scoured it mostly clean of snow. The ice would be a stone bitch, but not so bad as the snow. Her adrenaline spiked as she caught movement from behind a snow drift. She dropped to the ground.

CHAPTER TWELVE

The first go to hell rendezvous point was roughly one klick north and five clicks east of their entry point to the base. It was good that Sunday and Schmidt One had managed to figure out where they were right away, from the updated terrain features, and orient themselves towards their pickup. It was an especially good thing, since within just a few minutes the snow was falling so hard that visibility for more than a few feet ahead was damned near nil. As the snow started sticking and turning everything white, it got harder to even tell how much visibility they had. They had enough trouble just following the internal compass on their PDAs and putting one foot in front of the other. Heads down against the blowing snow, it was pretty hard not to bump into a particularly sneaky tree now and again.

Getting to the pickup only took maybe twice as long as it would have taken in fair weather. Tommy was grateful for the snow, since it had screwed with the Fleet Strike people searching for them more than it had screwed with them. He hoped Cally made it out, but tried not to think about it too much. Not right now. He'd think about her when he got somewhere that he had a chance to do something about it. He'd only dared try to raise her once on the radio. Getting no answer, he didn't dare transmit again.

They would have missed the Humvee if George and Papa hadn't

been smart enough to leave the headlights on. As it was, they barely caught sight of the glow before they passed it. Damned nor'easters. All too many of them since the war. Why was a question for the academics—which they sure did love debating over lunches bought with other people's money. Piling into the warmth of the vehicle was like heaven.

"Anything from Cally?" It was the first thing out of Harrison's mouth. It would have been the first thing out of his mouth, except it came out more of a grunt as he shoved his way into the truck after the other man and slammed the door.

"No," Papa O'Neal said brusquely. "We keep the snoopers active to give us as much warning of hostiles as possible, we keep the lights on, we camp here for the night."

"Not to get in the way of a good plan, but I have cherished personal needs. Like oxygen with low carbon monoxide levels."

"Fans. George brought fans. We take turns on watch clearing the snow from one side of the car outside enough to make a chimney. More snivel gear in the back."

"George?" Tommy said. "Remind me never to complain about you being a paranoid son of a bitch again."

"Bet on it. Just be glad this Humvee is a hybrid," the blond said. "If we were running on prewar chemical batteries, we'd be toast."

"Mmm. Toast. What good does running this beast do that we can't just do on its electric?" Tommy asked.

"Engine heat," Harrison mumbled. "It's not like we've got electric heating coils or anything. We can run the lights, we can run the snoopers, we can run the fans, but every couple of hours, we're going to have to run the engine enough to warm back up again so we don't all freeze. Speaking of not freezing, do you think one of you could see your way clear to passing some chow forward? It's about that time."

"What's plan B if Cally's not here in the morning?" Tommy couldn't help feeling disturbed that of all the team members, it was the girl who was out in the snow.

"She should be here. She had the same terrain and rendezvous data you did," George assured.

"If she loaded it, if her buckley didn't break, if she didn't get caught," Harrison had dry clothes out and was changing, shivering.

"Sounding a bit like a buckley yourself, aren't you?" his brother quipped.

"I didn't see her load the cube. I saw her face when she took it. Bet you fifty FedCreds she never loaded the thing," Sunday said.

"Okay, so if she's not here in the morning, we proceed to the bridge and leave a lookout—Tommy, I guess—then send a pair on foot to rendezvous two. We also alert Kieran that she may show up at the plane. The bridge and the plane are the most logical places for her to go if she somehow didn't get the memo. If she can find them in all this," George added.

"You're not suggesting we try to get the Humvee all the way to the second rendezvous, are you?" Papa clearly considered this lunacy.

"Not if fixer-boy can come up with something for snowshoes—"

"Blow me," Harrison said mildly.

"Anyway, if we can make walking in the snow a little easier, you and I will go to the second rendezvous, and Harrison will take the vehicle to the plane. Get it under cover. It's more conspicuous in this weather than we are on foot. All three out in the cold pack some heater rations and beverages, first aid kits for Cally. If she finds us after a night out, she'll need it. If we don't find her by seventeen hundred, we get back to the plane and take the risk of hitting the radio."

"And if those don't work?" Tommy asked. He would have been trying to offer help, but he was too busy cursing himself for neglecting to bring a change of clothes for himself. It wasn't like anybody else's stuff would fit.

"We leave supplies at what's left of that bounty farmhouse, marked as well as we dare. We figure she's made it back to us from worse than this, and we get the hell out of dodge," Papa O'Neal said. "We plan further search and rescue once we're in the air and can phone home. We need IR and all sorts of things we don't have to mount a search in hostile territory, in inclement weather. We need to move, communicate and coordinate."

"You know our best chance of finding her is in the hours immediately after the incident," Harrison said.

"You don't have to fucking remind me. This is my granddaughter we're talking about. If we don't find her tomorrow, she's either captured, dead, or found someplace to hole up while going to her own plan B. If she's able, she'll get to the LZ. If she doesn't get herself to the LZ within a couple of days, she's captured or dead. If the former, we need a planned extraction, not a half-assed one."

The Schmidt brothers had a rougher night than Tommy or Papa. Former grunts had a special advantage in the combat skill of sleeping anywhere, in any situation, in any position. If sleep was not expressly forbidden by the regs or orders, taking any opportunity to grab a few extra winks was one of the things that separated combat vets from cherries. It helped that the ACS vet's silks were dry again within an hour of getting out of the storm.

The cold light of morning brought no Cally and too damned much snow. Their fixer earned his name by using some of the leftover bridge netting to give the hummer a surface it could drive over. Two pairs of improvised snow shoes and two sections of bridging allowed the truck to be stopped on one section while they went back to get the one they just drove over and move it forward. Since the material could be rolled and unrolled, their progress wasn't comfortable, but it was reasonably quick. By early afternoon, they had detached Tommy to the bridge. In silks, with silks gloves and full headgear, which he'd sorely missed while fleeing the base, he could stay out here for hours and hours. The thermos of coffee was a luxury he savored; he just didn't savor too much of it in case Cally showed up and needed the warmth.

About sixteen-thirty he saw damp blonde hair, over a splotch of black, bob across the horizon. When she got close enough, he stood up, unsurprised that she immediately disappeared into the snow. "Hey, Cally! It's just me!"

The blonde head popped up again as she stood up and resumed slogging forward. Tommy just couldn't take watching it. He went out and met her on the way, ignoring her protests to pick her up and carry her to the bridge.

"I can just imagine trying to walk through this shit all day without snowshoes," he said. He flipped open his PDA and opened a transmission, "Charlie Romeo, say again, Charlie Romeo."

"Roger Charlie Romeo. RTB, out," Papa O'Neal answered.

"Cally, you're shivering. Here." The big man pulled a Galactic silk survival blanket out of his pack and wrapped it around her, then poured her a cup of hot coffee as she huddled under the blanket. She warmed her frozen hands around the plastic mug as she drank it down, to have the empty cup taken and an energy bar shoved in her hands.

"Eat that, one more cup of this, then we tackle the bridge."

"Where are the others?" she mumbled around a mouthful of food.

"At the second backup rendezvous point. You didn't load that cube in your buckley, did you?"

"Forgot. Then on the way out, didn't have time to go back for the stupid jumpsuit," she said.

"I win my bet," he said.

"Bet? Bastard." She punched him on the arm.

"You're recovering fast. Here, wash the last of that down with this and let's get going. You'll warm up faster on the plane, the sooner the better."

"Let me guess, the truck's at the plane where it's out of sight," she said.

"You got it. In this mess, we can walk faster than it can move."

She looked down at his snowshoes, bent bars of metal strapped together and laced with five-fifty cord, and held up one of her own soaked, frozen, sneaker-clad feet. "Speak for yourself."

"I am. You're riding over my shoulder in a fireman's carry after we get to the other side, because I'm not staying out in this shit one minute longer than I have to," he said. "So, why didn't you radio in? Your PDA get smashed up?"

"Yeah, somewhere along the way. Probably when I jumped out of the tree. Or I fell running a couple of times. Nothing to me, but a bit hard on the buckley. I had to run his emulation up, had to leave him on. Not real good for a buckley system. Of course he crashed, but he got me through some rough spots."

"Let's get out of this and talk when we're warm." Tommy led her out onto the icy bridge, watching her carefully the whole way across. She was damned good, with the balance and stamina of the athlete she was, but she was also damned tired and he knew how she felt about heights. They went right up the center of the bridge, and it was pretty wide, but she still could take a nasty fall on that surface if she slipped.

It was with relief that he hoisted her onto his shoulder on the other side, and a mark of her fatigue that she let him. It couldn't have been a comfortable ride. He was really feeling it by the time he had walked the seemingly endless trek back to the LZ. People who had never "done" snow had no idea how much it took out of you to move in the stuff.

Back in the plane, after they got out of wet clothes, both of them hit their seats, reclined them all the way, and didn't wake up until they landed in Chicago.

Friday 11/5/54

The Darhel Heldan stood on the bridge of his dilapidated freighter, supervising his Indowy, who were making the final temporary repair to the control systems he needed to execute the return to normal space. His ship would not have made it out of Adenast Space Dock without full completion of its scheduled overhaul had it not been for the humans' silvery-gray, rolled, adhesive strip that had proved so very useful for minor repairs. Repairs that otherwise would have required a custom-grown replacement part to install in place of the defective one could hold together almost indefinitely with enough of the stuff. His ship, whose name meant something like "Dedicated Industry," was his life, but he managed her very carefully.

Food runs as part of a cargo weren't a bad deal. Everyone needed it, somebody had to carry it. Food runs as a solo cargo were the bottom of the barrel of merchant shipping, because they were so common and routine. Margins were thin, and there was no opportunity to distinguish oneself in such a large crowd. Heldan's strategy to claw his way up the chain of power in the Gistar Group involved careful control of his expenditures. Whenever possible, he sent orders for his parts ahead, or made the order and deferred the pickup until his next cargo brought him back to the repair facility on his circuit. Allowing the Indowy to slot his repair part job in wherever it was convenient in their schedule obtained him the small but regular discounts that kept his operations in the black. Now came this extraordinary opportunity.

He was a very young Darhel. So young he was fresh out of management school. So young he could still remember the perilous intoxication of the awakening of the Tal within him. Every moment of every day. Remember, crave, and fear—yet sublimate it all under discipline, always discipline. Discipline awake, discipline asleep. For a young Darhel, self-discipline was a matter of life and death. Give in to rage, or hunt lust, or allow himself the taste of meat—even dreaming too intensely of such things—even for an instant, out would pour the sweet, sweet, infinitely intoxicating Tal into his system from his own glands. Until he matured, his life would hang by a thread. Afterwards, it would merely be precarious. Once more than the tiniest foretaste of the Tal entered a Darhel's system, the craving itself would trigger release of more, and more, and more. And who could fight the temptation to drown in bliss itself? Only one who had seen the dessicated bodies of the living dead, locked in lintatai until unassuaged thirst turned them into the truly dead; one who had smelled the smoke of the pyres floating on the air. Only one with the rare fortitude, will to live, and great good luck to embrace the discipline and survive.

His reward had been selection and initiation into one of the great merchant groups of his race, and charge of this ship. A thousand-year-old clunker too old to have even been commandeered for refit in the war, but a ship nonetheless. Now, an unprecedented opportunity had leapt out in front of him like a gorlet from the brush and—he took a few moments to breathe, breathe deeply, hold it, count, release. Calm restored, he permitted himself a brief grin, exposing the rows upon rows of pointed shark teeth. The Indowy Melpil, on sensors, happened to be looking in his direction and shuddered. Heldan covered his teeth obligingly. No need to upset his crew. Not when the jump was so near and he needed them attentive.

His eyes darted over to the human on watch at the gunnery station, suppressing the twitch of his ear that would have betrayed his annoyance. He saw that the man had been watching and no doubt reading his face. Above the space black of his Fleet uniform, the human's face was impassive, revealing none of the facial cues Heldan's own studies had drilled into him. He had been warned that most of his six Fleet gunners would be of this harder-to-read strain. He resented humans. Envied them. Disdained and yet secretly admired them. Arrogant—far too sure of an equality with the older races that they didn't even begin to approach. Dangerous, almost too dangerous to be allowed. But as a young race they had been spared the long term effects of having been made a "project" by an even older race. They could kill. He hated them for that, and for the twinge of desire that always accompanied the thought. What would it be like to be able to live, to kill and kill . . . He returned to his breathing drill as the deadly intoxication of the Tal began to make the edges of his vision sparkle. He truly loathed humans, but the loathing retreated to a cold thing as he reasserted his self-discipline, forcing the beast of his soul back into its cave.

The Indowy under the console, whose name he did not know, finished its task and left the bridge with discreet haste. Control system patched, Heldan spoke, the liquid syllables to activate the return to normal space dropping from his tongue. It amused him to see the human lean towards him, just a barely visible amount, its eyes beginning to glaze as he spoke. They always did that—had a half-hypnotic reaction to his species' voices. It was amusing. The only thing about the smelly, primitive beasts that made their presence on his ship barely tolerable.

The large holotank in front of his chair lit up with the points of light that were the Dulain System. At this distance, its star was a bluish spark, barely brighter than the brightest of giants far, far off in space beyond it. *Dulain, Dulain, Dulain. What a cargo. Eleven point three standard years cut off my time on this broken-down scow before I get my first* real *ship. Something that can stay on the trade routes for the entire time of my contract aboard it, never bogged down for the abomination of "routine maintenance."*

After a hour or so, he noted the blinking light on his display, indicating a courier-class ship lighting off its drives on a vector that would move it towards the Dulain System's most probable transit points should Epetar start screaming for help. Accounting for the inevitable lag of lightspeed communication, it had taken them about five minutes longer than he had expected to recognize the registry on his ship, realize what that meant for the other group, and decide what to do about it. About a week and a half too late to do them any good. He must remember to light an incense stick after he left the bridge to eat, relax and sleep, and thank the Lords of Enterprise that the Epetar Group had been so colossally stupid and incompetent.

Friday 11/5/54

Epetar Factor Raddin was not happy at having been roused from his bed by the chiming of his AID. The asynchronization with his sleep cycle had been extremely unpleasant; feelings which he transferred to the ship displayed in the holo before him.

"*Industry*, are you perhaps lost? Your mayday signals are not broadcasting, so I must wonder if they are defective, or whether your navigational systems are malfunctioning." The mellifluous voice managed to imply that the brain between the captain's ears might be the defective portion of said navigational systems.

"Negative, Dulain caller, *Dedicated Industry* is in good running condition and is not lost." Rudely, her captain, for the beautiful voice could only belong to another of his kind, did not display his own holo, leaving Raddin looking at the rather dilapidated freighter.

He tried again, "Good running condition? That would be a surprise, since your registry is from the Gistar Group and no freighter of your group is due to arrive at Dulain at all, much less now. State your business."

The holo of the ship flickered, replaced by the image of a young pup whose robe was edged with the yellow trim indicative of novice captains. "We thank you for your courteous solicitations, Epetar Factor. *Industry*'s business is between ourselves and Dulain System Administration. Who, if you will excuse my brevity, are transmitting presently. I take my leave," the young whelp said.

Raddin found himself staring at empty space above the altar of communication. Muttering under his breath, he lit a spike of incense and left to seek his grooming chair, a pair of Indowy body servants following in his wake.

"AID, monitor station logs for Gistar's purported reason for intruding in Dulain. The business here for the near future is mine and I do not appreciate interference." He opened his mouth to permit his servants to clean his very sharp teeth. Sleep was obviously a lost cause.

Five hours later he had gone from annoyed to alarmed. Fact: the only ship due in the next two weeks, for anything but routine food runs, was the *Fetching Price* from Sol. Fact: the Gistar ship did not belong here and was being extremely cagey about her purpose. "Exploring new business opportunities" was an excellent generic description of a Darhel's everyday life. A great believer in professional paranoia, Raddin damned the cost and commissioned the courier ship on station for the system to carry the news to Sol. The courier ship, in damned presumption, had already been moving in the right direction, anticipating his hiring their services.

Manager Pardal, currently operating from Sol, was reportedly attempting to corner the market on humans. Personally, Raddin didn't see the point, but managers had access to information a factor could only envy. Regardless, Epetar had a great deal of the carrying trade for Dulain locked up under iron-clad contracts and any Gistar attempts at intrusion were unwelcome and potentially serious. Even coming from such an unlikely threat as the dilapidated, garbage scow of a ship plodding in from the jump point.

Tuesday 11/9/54

The restaurant was a converted trawler parked along the banks of a creek, off of Old 701. It had what was quite possibly the best she-crab stew in the low country. Well, except for Shari's. It also offered the one of a kind courtesy of serving lunch or dinner on or below deck for any boat that tied up at the adjoining dock. It was a niche market that took advantage of the ready cash of honeymooners, playboys, and fish smugglers. The latter had a good line going in unregistered catches and tax evasion. High as taxes on legitimate incomes were, that translated to quite a bit of ready cash.

In Cally's case, it meant that all she had to do was borrow a decent boat to have a good, discreet, business lunch. She and the smugglers had similar notions of what constituted adequate dining privacy. November was not a good time of year, in Charleston, for alfresco meals on deck. The sky was a sullen gray that seemed to merge at the edges with the gunmetal ocean in the distance. The brown marsh grasses bent in great swathes, ends fluttering in the strong wind. The sisters would eat lunch in the warm shelter of the small galley.

A thirty-eight footer, the craft had never served to smuggle fish. Well, once in a pinch, but that was strictly as a cover for its real cargo—in that case, a political refugee who had made it as far as Norfolk on his own but who had needed more distance from civilization than even the unreclaimed wilds of the eastern coastal U.S. could offer. The problem with bounty farmers was, well, that they made their living from collecting bounties. Most places, they weren't the sort to keep their mouths shut if a reward was offered. As she understood it, it had taken strenuous efforts to get the dead fish smell out of the living areas of the boat after that run. Fortunately, that had been a job for the cousin who owned the boat, not her.

Eating inside was not exactly picturesque, but ideal for privacy. The galley already boasted fittings of high-quality blocks for eavesdropping. Her PDA would page the waiter when they needed service. The restaurant management, sensitive to the needs of their most discriminating and lucrative clientele, had a very fine sense of which boats not to bother with may I help you visits or incessant coffee and tea refills. It was a great restaurant. The whole family loved it.

Michelle was late. That surprised Cally more than she'd been surprised in a long time. She didn't think a Michon Mentat *could* be late. It didn't go with the labeling on the package. She looked cool and unflappable when she walked down the pier, wearing the street clothes her sister had purchased for her in Chicago, plus a duster of Galactic silk that matched the color of her pants. The assassin noted a bulge in the right pocket of the duster. If it had been anyone else, Cally would have suspected a weapon.

"I apologize for being late. I thought I would look strange if I did not wear a coat. Does it look appropriate?" the mentat asked

"You . . . made it?" Cally asked, sliding a menu across the table.

"Is it obvious? Is that a problem?" She might have been any woman, for a moment, as she critically examined the garment.

"I can only tell because it's Galactic silk and made in a single piece, and no, no problem. It looks great." *And worth about ten years of my salary, I think.*

"Good. Were you able to obtain the information I requested?" The other woman's clear tones betrayed the tiniest hint of her childhood Georgia accent, but only to an experienced operative like her sister.

"Oh, yeah. We got it. It was a milk run," the assassin assured.

"That is good. Were your superiors sufficiently satisfied to agree to the rest of my contract? Also, I hope the milk was good?"

"Milk? Oh. That was just a figure of speech. Milk run, I mean," she said. "Yes, we have a go for the mission. Here. This has everything we found." She passed a cube across the table and Michelle took it.

"Let's go ahead and order. It would look strange if we just sat here for too long." Cally looked down the menu, running her finger over the options, "I know you can't, but it's a shame you can't eat meat. They have the best she-crab stew in Charleston."

Michelle winced.

"It's a regional specialty. Have you really never eaten meat since we were kids?"

"I have not. If I were to eat it after all this time, I would probably have to make an extra effort just to be able to digest it. I would prefer a salad."

"Can you do dairy, then? They do a very good Caesar salad."

"We have dairy. It was not appropriate for the Indowy themselves, but because humans are mammals, they made allowances. Also, I think they like the cows. Though the Indowy do not eat other animals, their population density has made large, mobile species a certain rarity on their worlds. I think I will try your caesar salad, thank you."

"Do you mind if I just message it to them? I know you don't get the full restaurant experience that often, but we're more secure if the waiter just brings our food out."

Michelle laughed, the first real laugh Cally had heard from her. "You must be making a joke. For me, this is nearly unimaginable seclusion. One waiter or ten, I am amazed that it would make that much difference," she said. "At home, security means being in the company of your own clan, or clans with close affiliations to your clan. Being alone like this would be like . . ." She paused for a long moment, nonplussed. "I do not remember. What would be so strange on Earth that nobody would think of it, and anyone doing it would be—you would think they were ill in their brain? Now being in a room alone, I understand. I sometimes work that way. Just . . . this." She waved her hand around to include the space around them, from the river to the sky to the dock between their boat and the restaurant. It had never felt empty and open to Cally quite the way it did now. It was kind of peaceful.

"When you put me on the spot like that, that's a good question—about what would be the same level of weird here on Earth," Cally said after a long pause. "I would say stripping naked in the middle of a state funeral, but it's been done. I don't know if there is anything so strange that some person somewhere hasn't done it just to make a point." She thought some more. "Wow. Now that you say it, all I can think of is random destruction of life or property for no good reason."

"I thought that was what you did?" Michelle said.

Cally stiffened until she realized that the question was totally sincere and not at all intended to be insulting. "I always have a good reason."

"What do people here consider a good reason?" Michelle might have been talking to the Mad Hatter at a tea party.

"I can't speak for the whole planet." She shrugged. "For me, it's whatever Granpa and Father O'Reilly consider a good reason."

"Of course you listen to the O'Neal. Are you saying that you have not yet begun training in the evaluation of reasons for what you do?"

"No, I'm saying that it's not a good idea to have people in my profession pick and evaluate their own targets. Also, I don't always have all the information my superiors have in determining whether someone should or shouldn't be a target," she said. "Oh, here's our food. Hang on."

Michelle waited until the waiter had delivered the food and left before holding up the data cube her sister had provided. "Will it bother you if I look at this while we eat?" she asked.

"No, that's fine. It's what we're here for," Cally said. "Not that I'm not glad to see you. That didn't come out right. Anyway, our resumes for the job listings are on there, too."

"I am not offended." The mentat took a buckley PDA out of her pocket and inserted the datacube.

Cally raised her eyebrows, but didn't comment. It must really bite the Darhels' butts that buckley PDAs were slowly and quietly spreading out from Earth to be used instead of AIDs, when the user wanted something not to be recorded. The Darhel certainly never shipped the competing devices anywhere, and never authorized them for sale. They had made alleged consumer protection laws banning their sale off Earth. Unfortunately for the Darhel, with a human gunner team aboard almost all freighters and human colonists everywhere, the Darhel were becoming more and more aware of the difficulties of trying to suppress black market activities among humans. She knew from Stewart that the Tong was ecstatic at the advertising effects the Darhel's attempts at suppression were providing in their target markets. Cally suppressed a smile as she glanced up at Michelle's PDA. Obviously market penetration was good.

They ate in silence. After feeling strange for a moment in the unnatural quiet, Cally opened up a fashion magazine on her buckley and started looking through the spring collections. She was going to have to buy some outfits from an islander seamstress real soon, anyway. Might as well do something stylish.

"This is the information I need. I wish it showed one more part, but I do not think they will be disassembling the mock-up—just modifying it. At least, not within our time window." The mentat gave the appearance of wearing robes even in street clothes as she looked up serenely. "This is straightforward. I will have it for you in four weeks, local."

"Four weeks?"

"I assure you, I can work very quickly since it only has to *appear* to function."

"That's not what I meant. I guess I'm used to Earthtech."

"This is very far beyond Earthtech. That is why I have to personally make it. Four weeks." She pulled a bag out of her coat pocket, handing it to the Bane Sidhe assassin. "Here is the agreed payment."

"Great. A month, huh? Guess we won't have trouble getting someone inside and getting set up with that much lead time. I thought you were originally planning to make it without this stuff?" Cally gestured towards the cube.

"Once I knew I was going to get better data, I had to wait. Like any other product of advanced technology, it has to be grown whole. Specifications cannot change in the middle of the process. Upgraded parts can be retrofitted, settings changed, options added, replacement parts redesigned. The basic design for the underlying item cannot be changed while it is still in the tank."

"Okay, so four weeks. I may contact you for a meeting between now and then to coordinate arrangements."

"That will seldom be possible. I will be growing the product in the tank. I will not be able to interrupt the work casually. Suppose I contact you and we meet once a week?"

"Okay, so four weeks and once a week. I'll see you whenever I hear from you, then."

"Cally." Michelle reached out and touched her hand. "I still have not thanked you for the clothes. Is there anything at all I can get you? Not business, but something personal?"

Cally hesitated for a moment, strangely reluctant to ask a favor. "Uh. I hate to ask, but could you possibly get me some depilatory foam? I haven't been able to get any since Dad's supplies from the old emergency cache ran out." Spoken, it sounded a bit pathetic, and she was kicking herself when Michelle smiled.

"Of course I can. I will make it myself. It will not take even an hour."

"Okay. But there's got to be something you want from Earth. The Galactics aren't exactly big on consumer goods."

"Well . . ." Her sister hesitated for a long moment, considering. "Chocolate. You could get me chocolate. And some of those little white solidified sugar wheels. The ones with red spokes and no hole for an axle, that are flavored with peppermint oil. I think they are designed to spin counter-clockwise, but I was so young I am not sure my memory is correct." She shrugged, but her eyes were actually glittering with what might have been excitement. "Clockwise or straight-spoked wheels would be perfectly lovely. Just whichever is available. Star-sparkle Mints or some such. I am sorry, I cannot remember the name."

"Okay, chocolate and peppermints. Got it."

"The little wheel ones," the mentat said.

"The little wheel ones. Got it. Next week. No problem." Her sister grinned.

"If you cannot get them next week, whenever you have time is most acceptable," Michelle said. She sighed. "We have indulged in quite a long lunch. I need to go start work now. The salad was good. Thank you." Then Michelle was gone.

CHAPTER THIRTEEN

The family quarters for the Indowy-raised humans were a series of small, low rooms. The Michelle O'Neal family suite had walls in shades of mint and peach. The parents' sleeping room and the living room opened directly on the corridor. Behind those two rooms lay the nurseries. A central corridor contained the long washroom that served the family. All the rooms were very small. That, at least, was the allocation of the human living space its Indowy planners had intended. In reality, the parents had trisected their room by hanging curtains from tracks in the ceiling. On each side wall, and along the back wall, a set of bunk beds, closely stacked, provided a bunk for each of the six adults in the group. Hooks at the head of each bed held a change of robe and two night-robes apiece. A small, six-layer chest of drawers held underclothes and a memento or two for each parent.

The children's rooms had the same furnishings as the parents' room, except that the beds were slightly shorter and wider. There were more drawers, the plan being that two children would be in each bed, at capacity. The children past their first apprenticeship would, of course, live in unmated social groupings. After some trial and error, the Indowy had learned that the humans they encountered in Fleet had been wise to suggest adolescent human social groupings be segregated by breeding biology. Their males and females exhibited social and mating behaviors that were unstable and intense when housed together in the juvenile stages prior to group assignment and bonding.

The Michelle O'Neal family, as with most of the human families on Adenast, quietly deviated from their green mentors' plans and used clan privacy traditions to avoid discussing it outside the family. For one thing, the O'Neal adults were three couples, not a homogeneous group. Since Derrick's death, Michelle had slept in the room with her own two children and Bill and Mary's oldest daughter. Their toddler, and Tom and Lisa's three, slept in the other children's room.

In the parents' room, the other two couples had four bunks, but most nights only occupied two. Tom and Lisa's two-month-old slept in Michelle's old bunk.

Nooks and crannies all over the apartment—under chairs, in the small spaces under the beds—held prepackaged food so that the family didn't have to go to the mess hall for meals. It was the same stuff, anyway. In the sitting room, larger chairs for each adult and small ones for each child stood grouped around each other or the thinned-down holotank on one wall. On another wall, a spice rack displayed some of the family's wealth. The human sections of the agricultural planets didn't run to growing traditional herbs and spices. Most human families would buy a little pepper and hot sauce. More frequently, some locally brewed hooch. Michelle had paid to ship a fifty-spice rack up from Earth. Shipped and paid for legitimately. Refilled legitimately, for awhile. Sometimes the refills were even legitimately bought and shipped now. Just . . . not always. Her work did have small privileges.

The senior female in the group walked into the living room, where their children immediately mobbed her.

"Anne, Terry, move back and let your clan mother walk," a woman ordered. She was tiny, with wavy black hair and midnight eyes

The Michon Mentat leaned down and picked up the toddler, Kim. "How was your day?" she asked her clan-wife.

"Tiring. And yours?"

"Informative. I will be working late for the next three weeks."

"Mama! Mama! Look what I made for you!" Her own five-year-old, Tara, ran up to her with a picture on a thin sheet of white plastic. Bright, primary colors combined and smeared together into stick figures and childish trees. It looked like fingerpainting, but really came from a headset interface at school, designed to allow young ones to begin developing the mental discipline and neural connections to learn Sohon safely and without the risks of a real tank. "This is you and Mama Lisa and Mama Mary and Papa Tom and . . ." There were a lot of people on the page. Michelle smiled slightly, ready to hear them all.

"Tara, please let me talk to your clan mother for a few minutes, then we will pick out a wall to hang your pretty picture on," Lisa said. "Michelle, could we sit down, please?"

"Certainly. There is something you need to bring to my attention?"

"Oh, no. The household is running smoothly. If it would not offend you, I would like us to talk about your work. We are worried about you." Her wife's robe showed stains and spots, accumulated from watching the children.

"We can talk about my work," the mentat said.

"You are home early today. I thought it would be good to discuss this before the others get home. We are—I am—very concerned about you. I do not mean to interfere, but there are certain rumors . . ." The tiny woman reached out and took the toddler, who had started to play with the pins in Michelle's hair.

"If the rumors are that I have been threatened with default on a contract, that much is true. It is also true that there is some danger. However, I have a plan."

"A plan?" the woman echoed.

"Yes, a plan."

"How likely is this plan to make you very hungry within the year?"

"There is considerable risk."

"Loss of the head of our family would be very hard. Also, I would miss you very much. We must all hope that your . . . plan . . . goes well." The smaller woman fixed her dark eyes on her group-mate's face, mute with compassion.

Wednesday 11/10/54

The Darhel Pardal relaxed his jaw and shoulders in an unseen gesture of relief as he watched the Epetar Group freighter finally vanish into hyperspace, leaving the Sol System for its rendezvous with its next load of cargo at Dulain. The nearly two-week delay in getting the cash to the freighter to cover its docking fees at its next stop, as well as purchasing its high-margin cargo, had been the worst black spot of his career. Epetar had a contract to deliver bounce tube replacement parts, each specially crafted for its own unique bounce tube machinery, to Diess. The repair and reclamation program had finally gotten around to rebuilding Telsa City. There were countless tubes all over Diess in various stages of salvageable disrepair. The contract would last at least a century.

Indowy made all their equipment in the normal way, growing each item from a set of VR goggles all the way up to an entire starship in Sohon tanks. For a ship, an entire Indowy family from the newest apprentice to the most skilled master might be involved in bringing the sharply envisioned, individual design to reality. Every item of Galactic technology had slightly different parts and slightly different designs. Devices were built to last at least one lifetime—which for a member of a Galactic race, or a rejuved human, amounted to about five hundred of the local years. It discomfited Pardal that he had developed the habit of thinking in Earth time, but after twenty-eight years one adjusted. Even to this Aldenata-forsaken backwater.

Of course, he used human-produced goods for less critical functions in his office. Ephemeral as they were, even counting replacement costs they were economically optimized and functional. Which was why all the groups took such great pains to keep human goods as localized to the Sol System as possible. The destabilizing effect of their merchandise and their methods on the economy, if not properly contained, didn't bear thinking about. Dangerous as a mob of budding adolescents, the whole species.

He cursed the theft that had caused the delay in the Dulain-Diess run on his watch. He would be decades repairing his reputation and career from this debacle. At the moment, he was directing all his spare time to tracking down the thief for deterrent punishment. Recovery of the stolen wealth was probably too much to hope for. His most recent efforts followed the line of an old human adage for the hunting of attackers: *Who profits?* Unfortunately, his "short list" was not yet short enough.

"AID. Display Hunt File One and control pad for evaluation. Show suspect list. Retrieve cash flow intelligence for each entry on suspect list for six months prior to the theft." He doggedly resumed his search for connections, humming softly. The departure of the freighter, albeit belated, had put him in a better mood than he'd enjoyed for weeks. Gistar, Cnothgar, Adenar. Someone wanted a trade war. But which? Any one of them would have profited enormously by the theft, but only if their group could throw off suspicion on one of the others. He didn't for a moment suspect the Tir Dol Ron. As administrator for the Sol System, he was separated from the covert jockeying of inter-group rivalries. The Darhel Ghin had some limits to the behavior he was willing to tolerate in the name of business. The Tir's squeezing of rival Darhel groups would have to follow the same traditions as anyone else's—confined to systems where he had interests, but not direct administration. Sometimes Pardal wondered if the old Darhel maintained the rules just for the sport of it. Not that it would matter. He proceeded in his happy attempt to untangle conspiracy from betrayal from intrigue. Someone, somewhere, was going to pay.

As with any world, some parts of Dulain were stunningly beautiful. Unfortunately for those who lived there, Bounty City was not one of those places. Chin Ming looked over the ugly Galplas cube that held the indentured servants. Her hair, which she wore today in her own elegant bob, blew in the wind as she stared at the slave barracks many of them would only leave feet first. The top Tong leader on Dulain, one of the Grandfather's full lieutenants, was a very petite woman. She had shipped out among a generic batch of colonists and been one of a core of bought-out former indentures planted by the Tong to establish a foothold for their new operation. The wife of a respected Hong Kong businessman within the organization, she had ridden out the Posleen war in Ontario. Her husband and children she lost to the war. Her own not inconsiderable operational and business experience had remained intact. Juved, she looked like a sweet, demure, little flower. Her protective detail thought so, Little Flower being the code name they had assigned her. Mrs. Chin had raised being underestimated to a high art. She functioned well with the Indowy not only because of her diminutive size and habit of indirect gaze, but also because each sensed in the other a certain skill set, and respected it.

Chin Ming had never underestimated, nor been underestimated by, one of the Indowy in her life—which certainly put her one up on every Darhel she'd ever had to deal with. She had avoided ever meeting one of the Sidhe in person, but in the game of competing interests she dealt with them every day.

The vast majority of the human population had been set down here in the dry, gray-green scrub more for the lack of water and subsequent ease of containment than for any other reason. Planetary admin shuttles dropped armed indents wherever the latest infestations of feral Posleen had been sighted, then picked up the human survivors afterwards for return to the cube, healing and recuperation. They laid down their arms and reported aboard the return ship for the simple reason that if they did not, ankle and wrist bracelets would start to administer increasingly painful electrical shocks. If ignored, the bracelets would inject the wearer with Hiberzine, rendering him unconscious and setting off a beacon for pickup whenever someone got around to it. Frequently, delinquent pickups came in much the worse for wear. More often, they came in as very depleted remains.

On Indowy worlds, of which Dulain was one, although it had been depopulated to the point of emptiness, the Darhel controlled all commerce, including food shipments from automated farming worlds. If a rebellious Indowy—they occasionally cropped up in so large a population—got too far out of line, the Darhel group that owned his debts for his working tools called those debts in. His tools repossessed, the hapless Indowy starved with no intervention by his fellows, and the Darhel were minus one problem. Living in a society that had been fundamentally static for millennia, all of the Galactics had gotten too used to a predictable, immutable status quo. Ming smiled. Galactic inertia made it very hard to change standard contracts. Contracts the Darhel had written to entangle the Indowy didn't have the same results with human laborers.

The clear intent had been to force the indents to purchase food and healing services from on-site company stores and render servitude lifelong, much like sharecropping in parts of postbellum North America. The right of laborers to purchase from competing providers had always served to protect the rights of the Darhel groups to compete with each other. Darhel stores had a monopoly on wheat and rice of strains enhanced by Tchpth manipulations to provide all necessary nutrients for sustaining humans in a healthy state. Undermanagers had evaluated and assessed the potential outcomes of human women bringing seeds of unenhanced, inferior food plants native to Earth and found them to be a useful way of marketing expensive hydroponic equipment to humans and keeping the breeding stock occupied, and deeper in debt.

The first cracks in the system on Dulain had occurred when the Tong orchestrated the payment of the debts of one hundred men and women in what would become Bounty City. They had purchased land, immediately outside the barracks compound, at an exorbitant price. The Tongs had used an intermediary to keep the left hand from knowing what the right hand was doing. Simple. The Darhel factor executing the buy had thought some stray humans were increasing their indentures for worthless wasteland they'd have no opportunity to use, anyway, and had taken the commission as easy money. The Darhel factor selling the land had been happy to unload land at higher than market price, even if the group it presumed it was selling to managed to recoup some percentage of the loss.

Darhel groups were secretive with each other about their dealings. It had taken upper management decades to sort out that the owners of the land were not another Darhel group but were some human entity. They reprimanded and demoted the underlings involved, but the damage was done. Certain humans, returning from the field, spent their pay buying their food and incidental healing in town. The prices were much better, so the free citizenry always sold all they could grow. The best the Tong could do so far for meat was raising abat in hutches. The Darhel were never going to surrender easily. They tried sending humans who were paying down their debts to the forefront of combat and to die, rendering the reduction in debt pointless. The greenhouses of free humans, and some of the humans themselves, had suffered assaults and accidents.

The Darhel of the Cnothgar Group, administrators of Dulain, had quickly discovered that humans were not as easily managed as Indowy. Indents stopped using their savings to pay down their debts directly to the Darhel, instead banking the money in town by buying lottery tickets. Only humans alive at the time of drawing were eligible, by the terms of the ticket. The Tong's front in town held drawings as soon as a lottery pool reached the average debt level among the ticket holders. The Tong bought out the winner's contract no matter what he or she owed, holding the debt if it was larger, paying the excess to the winner if the debt was smaller. When the Tong banked for individuals, it had proved adept at hiding the records off planet and protecting the privacy of depositors. If a depositor died, the Tong paid the balance, minus a fee, to the depositor's designated beneficiary. Darhel creditors had been unable to collect at the death of an asset, unable to prove he had left behind an account. The Cnothgar Group's collections department kept trying to find a way to trace the money. The Tong was better at laundering it.

Humans who hired out to kill humans tended to die, quickly, at the hands of their fellows. Without human police willing to investigate and prosecute the murders, with the Tong carefully orchestrating the removals, this strategy was not working for the Elves. Ming conceded that they did tend to take down the occasional local Tong head. Rarely. Now, the locals protected greenhouses around the clock with human shields. Indowy or Darhel could not attack the clearly sophont-occupied facilities, and the humans the Elves hired to do so had low success rates and short life expectancies. The result, over the decades, had been a slow but steady increase in the population of free, rejuved humans in towns like Bounty City all over Dulain.

The residents of Bounty City, of course, would rather be free and rejuved in town than enslaved in the barracks. Still, the surroundings alone rendered it an ugly place, where the wind quickly draped everything with a coating of gray dust. Beeseers, as they called themselves, never planted greenery out of doors. Transpiration would have wasted too much precious water. As it was, they replenished the deficits to human sweat and breathing from water left as wastes by the shoppers, window-shoppers, and patrons of the brothels and other entertainments in town. Careful management ensured efficient water and fertilizer recycling. Also, despite unbeatable differences in biology, desert life around them was still carbon based, still ninety-something percent water, and still carried most of the right trace minerals. Anything organic the hordes of children could grab, the waste treatment facilities could handle.

The Darhel could not obtain new indentures from women who would not bear, despite the Darhel's own refusal to provide contraceptives. Contracts had never included any obligation to breed. The whorehouses sold condoms to all buyers, as well as offering discreet abortions in the rare cases those were necessary.

No Galtech required. The women, already juved, felt no pressure of a ticking biological clock. Indentured males certainly were more willing to plant their seed in town, when they could, than risk slavery for their children. Besides, the women in town were, for those very reasons, so much more available. Pimps found their best profits in buying the indentures of women grateful to get away from the combat missions that now included them—women with sterling prospects of working those indentures off. Under the circumstances, the pimps harbored no hard feelings at the ladies who graduated from their employ. There were always more whores where they came from.

For the goods the residents could not manufacture or raise in town, the Tong did a brisk black market trade. In the case of the off-Earth free cities, this had included the deliberate policy of supplying capital equipment wherever practical.

The Randy Tabby in Bounty City was quiet today. Nobody was playing the electric piano, and even the men who would have been customers were hard at work with heat guns or scissors, turning endless meters of colorful, plastic beads into cheap necklaces. All along main street, the buildings contained people scrubbing out every shipping crate that the Beeseers could find, stuffing waxed paper bags with handfuls of necklaces, and filling crates with the bags. Beneath the BC General Store, a pair of workmen fed the machinery that produced the long strings of beads, winding them off on much-used spools.

One of the first capital packages shipped out, piece-meal and hidden, by the Tongs had been an integrated PVC plant. With it, the humans in Bounty City could begin converting waste organics and desert salts into versatile plastics, useful for so many things. Other communities specialized in other Earthtech goods, but plastics were Bounty City's specialty. For Dulain, Bounty City wasn't a bad place. Ming liked it much better than most, worse than a few.

She didn't live here, of course. Ming's existence was nomadic, her travel itinerary a closely held secret. The Darhel groups did not officially acknowledge any of the Tong's planetary lieutenants on any of the Posleen-infested planets that were undergoing the reclamation process. Unofficially, dealing with *someone* in charge was ingrained in their habits. Currently, they were still trying, with limited success, to have hit men target the lieutenants. The Grandfather said that it might take them some time to realize that expecting to stop human black markets by lopping off heads was about as effective as beheading a Greek hydra. Mrs. Chin made sure that she remained a moving target.

Proximity to the Indowy brought a certain amount of trade, and with the trade had come a certain familiarity with the furry, green teddy-bears. The human factor for the town had noticed that members of Indowy breeding groups delighted in giving each other small, simple gifts as tokens of affection. Indowy being Indowy, they purchased even simple gifts which were individually crafted and expensive—not because the Indowy had a particular dedication to individual craftsmanship, but simply because they had never done it any other way. Two of the Beeseers, from New Orleans by way of a central Indiana Sub-Urb, and old enough to remember prewar Earth, had amused themselves for awhile making strands of clear, colored beads and stringing them to sell to the green herbivores. They'd marketed their product as symbols of fertility, plenty, and fellowship. Dulain, being an Indowy world and the Indowy being able to outbreed all known sophonts anywhere, had a very few humans and a whole lot of Indowy. The Indowy considered the pretty little gifts so inexpensive as to be practically free. Page and Gilbeaux, with no marketing efforts to speak of, had been selling as many Mardi Gras necklaces as they could string.

When Ming had received the message from Earth that Dulain's humans needed to assemble an alternate cargo for an incoming freighter, production had gone into round-the-clock shifts. They could count on some lower-margin Indowy goods being available to fill out the ship's hold—especially as the message came with suggestions of which Indowy ears for the Tong lieutenant for Dulain to drop a word in. Clan Beilil was not plentiful nor powerful on Dulain, but they did appear more open, for no reason that was readily apparent. Ming had quietly filed the name in her memory as a useful contact for the future.

Meanwhile, several human towns that were capable of turning out glass beads had gone into high gear, as well. The plus was that there was less of a bottleneck in the immediate machine production of colored glass beads, the downside that they had to be strung by hand. A cube containing a series of books on the construction of machine tools from scrap metal had been, and was still, very popular on Dulain. The necessary parts for generation of strings of the beads were being put together by every small machine shop on the planet. In the two weeks since they had had word from Earth, her people had accomplished a great deal. In the two weeks they still had before they had to ship the product off Dulain, they would do much more.

Wednesday 11/10/54

The more time Michael O'Neal, Senior, spent in secure rooms, the more alike they all looked. The Galplas walls were a light mud color, except for the purplish glow of the ceiling surface. It made his eyes hurt, if he didn't wear sunglasses. Which was, of course, the only reason he was wearing them.

"Nice shades, Papa," George said as he walked past and moved a couple of the rolling office chairs around, trying to pick one that was less broken down than the others. The chairs all sported gray Galactic silk slipcovers over the seats and backs. Silk was expensive—unless it was from the first efforts of children and typically very off-spec. Color, texture, and quality were variable. The slipcovers were marginally better than nothing, maybe. They didn't stop the feel of the torn tweed and disintegrating fifty-year-old foam padding beneath them.

He grunted and set his mug down on the table, shaking a couple of chairs to pick one that wasn't going to dump him into the floor. A caster came off of one of them and he slid that chair over against the wall, putting the offending piece in the seat. The other chair seemed to only have loose handles, so he parked himself in it and kicked his feet up onto the badly chipped pine table.

"So, the miracle kiddies down below get to make another part." George jerked a thumb over his shoulder at the chair.

"Gotta hand it to them. Theirs don't break. At least, not so far." Papa spat neatly into his mug.

"Bitching about the crappy fucking chairs again?" Tommy Sunday walked in wearing a grimace and carrying a steel camp stool. He pushed a couple of the inadequate chairs out of the way and unfolded his stool. "At least *you* can sit in the damn things."

"You aren't missing much, son," O'Neal said.

The door opened again, admitting Cally and Harrison together.

Cally's hair was a shining silver bell around her face. It hadn't looked that good in years.

"Wow," Tommy said. "What the hell did you do to your hair?"

"Why thank you, Tommy. Good afternoon to you, too," she said, smiling a little too sweetly.

"Uh . . . I mean it looks really good," he said.

Papa suppressed a grin. "Your hair looks very nice, sweetheart."

"Thank you, Granpa."

"Who would have thought that Darhel conditioner would work so well on human hair?" Harrison asked the room at large.

"Not me," said George. "Cally, you're a brave woman."

"We tried it on a sample of hair from her brush first. I'm not a total novice at hair care, I'll have you know. I figured since Darhel depilatory foam works on humans, the protein structure might be similar enough that their conditioner would work as well." Their fixer looked insufferably proud of himself.

"I didn't think Darhel medicines were safe in humans."

"They're not. The conditioner has a binder and emollient effect to reduce split ends and increase shine. It's not a medicine."

Cally crossed the room and sat down next to George. "Okay, let's get started. Has everyone had time to review the latest intelligence on our target?"

"Is it supposed to smell like cabbage?" George asked.

Cally glared at him and switched on the holoprojector, pointedly ignoring the young man's comment as a holo of a video screen appeared at the far end of the tank. With holo the default viewing medium on the planet, using three-dimensional projection to simulate a two-dimensional screen no longer struck anyone as ironic. "As you can see from the timetable, we have at least a month to get inside. If Michelle is more than three days late, we'll have to hold on for another three weeks past that before we get another shot. We're just lucky that winter is convention season—all those researchers flying down to the Caribbean for their conferences."

They laughed. Of course, it wouldn't have been half as funny if half of them didn't already live along the coast. Even if it was colder than a witch's titty in a brass bra this time of year. Maybe after this mission he ought to talk Shari into doing a run down to Cuba. Havana was nice now that the governmental policies had changed.

". . . thing we know Erick Winchon does is go to conferences and give speeches. Usually long on mouthings about peace and altruism, short on science. There's a front group that does some puff research. For their cover research, our best guess is that they do small studies off site, then fabricate large sample data consistent with their small study results. Dr. Vitapetroni tells me they design their work to generate meaningless truisms that sound good. Grants are so light on the ground that convention standards aren't so high these days—anybody who's got a paper published fills up the convention program. So giving a lot of pretty speeches maintains their cover and appearance of respectability." Cally tapped the forward arrow on the buckley, advancing the slide.

"Anyway, we have Winchon's conference schedule. Michelle tells me our only chance is to do the op when he is at least a few hundred kilometers away from the site. As far as possible, really." When she mentioned talking to Michelle, Granpa's face got grumpier, like it always did. She hated being in the middle of family squabbles. "Work like this tends to have small but significant turnover. People may not be able to walk out, but they do leave feet first. We have the profiles of the jobs most likely to turn over, and the ones that are vacant. Multiple resumes are in the pipeline for each of us. Our inside man has our list. We have staffers down in GN32 manning our phones. Interview calls will be routed to voice mail for obvious reasons, along with a tag telling you who the caller thinks you are. If you can't have your buckley tell you when a call comes in, you need to check it at least every two hours. If you're doing a short assignment and can't do that, you need to notify me in advance and let me know how long you'll be out of pocket."

George started to say something, but Cally had evidently anticipated. She placed a soft hand over George's lips and smiled as she continued, "Granpa, you and George take what we know of the layout of the place, develop plans for physical surveillance of the facility, and start working on secondary plans of entry and execution."

Papa O'Neal nearly choked on his tobacco trying not to laugh at the expression on the young man's—well, he looked young, anyway—face. As if his granddaughter was going to let him steamroller one of her meetings for the second time in a row. He caught a whiff of her perfume from across the room. Dangerous stuff.

The kid's eyes glazed over as she turned in her seat, deliberately moving the lethal cleavage nearer. At least, Papa knew damned well it was deliberate.

"Anyone gets a call, it will automatically route to me, too. Whole team, meet back here, same time, in one week to touch base unless I tell you sooner. Dismissed." Unusually for Cally, she didn't give time for questions, and she didn't relax the format, just took her hand off George and swept out of the room. Whew, but her nose was out of joint. He might just have to have a talk with her. Or better yet, with Schmidt Two, who was still looking a bit poleaxed. Maybe even each of them. He might indeed.

Sunday 11/14/54

Pardal cordially loathed the smell of Titan Base. The overpressure on the domed city drove in mixed hydrocarbons that made the entire facility reek of a combination of a ship with a faulty life support system and a dirty waste-room. The pathetic suite set aside for his use, which would have looked luxurious only to human savages who knew no better, had a shoddy Earthtech air filter in one corner. It reduced the reek in his own rooms, but produced a whining that abused his sensitive ears. The air movement and hiss had, more than once, awakened him from a sound sleep, diving for his pressure suit. The times it had happened, it had taken a few seconds before he'd realized he was not aboard a ship with a hull breach but was, instead, on the Aldenata-bedamned Titan Base. By then his stress hormones, mingled with a tingling hint of Tal, were in such an uproar that it took a seventh-level meditation to relax him enough to get back to sleep.

Demanding complete and immediate repair would have revealed weakness. He certainly didn't want the humans to know that the panicked awakening was almost as dangerous, to him, as a real hull breach somewhere on board one of his ships would have been. Much less reveal weakness to others of his kind. He had ordered proper air cleaning equipment from a reputable supplier and would simply have to wait for its arrival. He hated humans, as much for their cheap and shoddy devices as for anything else.

The Indowy produced voluminous excesses of Indowy, the Tchpth produced overwhelming technological inventions, the Darhel produced money and power, the Himmit produced—well, consumed, then—an excess of stories, the Posleen produced a voluminous amount of both Posleen and ships. The humans' particular excess was millions of tons of ephemeral, garbage goods—some in use, the vast majority already broken and discarded. They were ridiculously self-congratulatory over insignificant increases in useful life of what they produced, and the ability to remanufacture their garbage instead of just piling up and burying their millions of shipweights of discards.

Human females were the worst. They incessantly wore and replaced robes in an absurd variety of colors, textures and shapes, like some maniacally molting, diseased insects. Human men apparently found this profligate trait *attractive*. They did price their shoddy goods like the worthless things they were, but that was almost as bad. By treating them with extreme care, it was possible to extend the life of such goods to the point that they became economical. The volume and variety of garbage goods, that did work for very brief periods, made the humans frighteningly adaptable—an unpleasant truth that he would never admit to anyone else and barely admitted to himself. He really loathed the little barbarian carnivores.

He watched a live holo of the main dividing way of the savage city, the one the humans called the Corridor. How original. He sat watching and listed to himself the various reasons he hated humans. He was aware that most of his kind felt merely a more distant contempt for the species. He would probably return to that attitude, himself, as soon as he could get out of the gods-forsaken Sol System and back to civilization. For now, they were just too close. He was finally in a state of mind to get the most appreciation out of the latest cube of research he had received from the human Erick Winchon.

After the first hour, he decided he was very disappointed. This cube wasn't nearly as good as the last one. The first half, an aversive eating sequence with fresh subjects, would have been completely boring if he hadn't learned to read human facial expressions. The second half, aversive mating behaviors, should have been boring, but wasn't. Somewhere in the sequence, it crossed over from mere unaesthetic mates to pointless and counterproductive destruction of the females. Odd, that. The accompanying notes said the obvious aversiveness resulted from the peculiar human emotion called empathy, rather than the loss of a potential mating opportunity before viable offspring could result. The other feature that rescued the cube from tedium was the proof of aversiveness tests performed on random subjects after a significant act, which left the subject in the situation while removing all controls on his or her emotional responses. Humans in distress were capable of an extraordinary variety of vocalizations.

He was leaning back in a reclining couch, watching the show a second time through, when his AID interrupted him, stopping the holo.

"Sir, you have an incoming message from a special courier vessel," it said.

"Display it," he said coldly.

A still holo of another Darhel appeared. The yellowish tinge to his silver and black fur, along with the yellow stains on his teeth, showed his less-than-stellar grooming habits. It was also a telltale mark of a certain age, as teeth didn't get that neglected overnight. The gilded patterns on the columns behind him had Epetar's traditional triangular motifs worked into the designs. From the moderately low quality and the obvious lack of sufficient Indowy body servants to attend his personal needs, Pardal knew the sender was of low rank.

The AID from the courier ship had a beautiful voice. "Message from Epetar Factor Raddin of Dulain to Commerce Manager Pardal, currently traveling in the Sol System. Message begins."

The holo shifted into motion as the Darhel in the display began speaking his recorded piece. "A freighter, a gods-be-damned garbage scow by the look of it, has entered the Dulain System. *Dedicated Industry* has a Gistar registry, she is not on the schedule, and however disreputable she looks, she has the capacity to carry a substantial cargo. There is no substantial cargo waiting to load out here that is anywhere near completion except for ours. Two of the three cargoes over fifty-percent assembled are Cnothgar cargoes that they're not about to allow jumped from their own planet. Strange ships coming in on top of one of my high margin cargoes make me very nervous. This would be a very bad time for a ship to be late. If there is a circumstance of which I am unaware, I report the information so that you may plan accordingly. I take my leave of you."

"Message ends. The billing confirmation number for this service has been transmitted to your AID. This vessel will depart the Sol System for return to the Dulain System immediately. Any standard correspondence or return messages should be uploaded at once."

Pardal ran his claws through the fur on top of his head, scratching nervously behind his ears. He took a deep breath and dropped the hand back to his side. He had to look composed for official correspondence. "AID, record for transmission from Commerce Manager Pardal to Epetar Factor Raddin of Dulain, copy to Epetar Freighter Captain Efgin traveling in the Dulain System. I received your message. As the shipment is late, it is likely that the Gistar vessel has taken advantage of the situation to take the contract on our Dulain cargo. Empty holds leak profits. Acquire whatever salable cargo you can, for the best price, and quickly. Unload, reload, and get that ship on to Prall. The Gistar vessel will undoubtedly beat us to Diess as well. Skipping that leg is the only way to get back on schedule. Your information was critical. Your use of the courier in this instance is validated, despite the expense. Continue to exercise all care before incurring such expenses. I take my leave."

Gistar. Pardal smiled. It was the kind of smile that, thousands and thousands of years ago, would have scared any prey animal stiff. Or sent it running. Today, his Indowy body servants abruptly left the room. Gistar. The code keys were no doubt long gone from Sol. Probably went out on the very next shuttle off of Earth and didn't stop until they hit the jump point. Still, some things had to be revenged. What did the humans say? One good turn deserves another. Amazing that they were sometimes capable of sarcasm. One good theft certainly deserved another. Gistar.

It would take a call to the human who primarily handled those of Epetar's interests that required the human touch. And, curse Gistar, require him to book passage right back to Earth. The only mitigating component would be getting off Titan.

"AID, what is the name of our human agent for special issues on Earth?"

CHAPTER FOURTEEN

Monday 11/15/54

The white-haired man was clearly not a juv. He looked like a late middle-aged stockbroker. He had sectioned his hair into precise squares pointed into precise spikes, exactly two point five four centimeters long. His pale blue suit jacket had the tails that had come back into style for morning clothes at the office. Robert Bateman even had an office. It was in the business district of Little Rock. When he was in town, he unfailingly went into the office at eight each morning, and left it between five and seven each evening. If he had to be elsewhere, which he frequently did, he reported in to the office first. He charged this expense to his employer as a necessary cover. Too many of the things they wanted done required a respectable business persona. His day trading of a picayune amount of Epetar's money kept him abreast of the market, well enough to talk intelligently about its movements, scandals, and surprises. This was the cover he needed most often. It cost less to simply maintain it than to pay people to fabricate what was essentially the same identity, over and over. He did what he could to avoid getting the alias visibly dirty. *You don't shit where you eat.*

It surprised him to receive a direct call from the Darhel Pardal—or, rather, from his AID, which amounted to the same thing. He carried a buckley. An AID would have been an extravagance and a security risk. The trader he was counterfeiting would never have used one. He trusted Epetar to make sure his calls back and forth to them were secure. The hard-ass alien bastards were geniuses at programming. Privately, he thought of them as a weird blend of vampire, fox, and elf that sucked money as a poor substitute for blood—and resented it. Obviously, the Darhel had evolved as carnivores. Plant eaters did not have those rows of sharp teeth.

But they couldn't kill directly, either. That was what they needed him for. He was the smart-gun in their hand that selected its own targets and fired itself—giving them just enough plausible deniability to protect their sanity.

Bateman had zero illusions about his employers, he just didn't care. Hell, he liked them. At least they weren't sweetness and light hypocrites. He knew he was a sociopath. He knew he was one of the less common sociopaths who had above average intelligence. Being what he was, he appreciated the better games his intellect made available to him. The Darhel were great employers. Whether they did or didn't know that the rest of humanity would regard him as damaged goods, the important point for him was that they just didn't give a shit. In fact, his lack of conscience was his most crucial job skill. Working for the Epetar Group was the best job he'd ever had. If he discounted the boredom between assignments.

He looked over the file dumped to his buckley and whistled softly. Pardal's call had been terse, "Review the file. Assess our interests. Arrange the services you deem appropriate. Among other things, ensure you steal from them, for delivery to us. The more the better, but amount does not matter and you most certainly need not limit your creativity to theft. Submit the bills for your expenses. Oh, and Mr. Bateman? There will be no need to itemize expenses—a very general bill would be most satisfactory."

A blank check to avenge some intercorporate insult. The file didn't specify the insult, simply that it was severe and highly costly. Epetar must be really pissed at Gistar to turn someone like him loose with no leash and no limits. He rubbed his hands and started going down the list of Gistar assets on Earth and in the rest of the system.

The tantalum and niobium operation in Africa looked good. Starships didn't move too fast. He had enough money on hand to hire a good team of mercenaries, stick them on a wet ship with a pack of reliable pirates, and deal out a lot of mayhem to the dumb schmucks at the mines. Stuff out of a mine wouldn't burn—it wasn't like it was coal or anything. Unless they directly hit it, they wouldn't disperse it with explosions, either. Should be able to pick it right up and cart it off.

Bateman ran a search against his Rolodex and began sorting through names. He found the booking agent he was looking for and placed the call.

Monday 11/15/54

The Indowy Falnae had the con on the bridge of the Gistar freighter, *Fortunate Venture*, it being the captain's sleep shift. *Venture* was heavy with her food cargo, headed out for Laghldon, a major Indowy world specializing in standalone communications systems and ground vehicles. The great, automated farming machines of Rienooen produced the various high-energy, high-protein staple crops that formed the mainstay of Indowy and Tchpth diets. The dietary needs of the independently evolved species were, obviously, extremely different, but Rienooen was a big and fertile planet with the largest ratio of arable land to planetary surface of any planet in this region of space. Their ship was part of an endless convoy of vessels that trekked between systems, packed from floor to ceiling with food one way, and sterilized, packaged fertilizers on the return. Presently, they were six days out from the major jump point out. Out of two known ways to move a ship through hyperspace, the Galactics used the ley-line method, traveling paths of least resistance from one system to another. It was an odd quirk of space that these paths tended to cluster together in clumps, like flaws in a giant crystal. They varied in their distance from the core of the system, which had made large differences in travel time for centuries.

Like a pebble tossed in a still pool, the War had changed everything. The changes seemed good, but they destabilized things, and destabilization was risk. The Darhel managed trade, but the Tchpth, and the Indowy to a lesser extent, managed change. The Darhel groups were so competitive that any information that gave one group a competitive edge forced the others to change as well.

The chaotic, imprudent, savage humans were like an information storm released into the heart of Galactic civilization. Certainly they had saved the civilized races from a greater disaster, but at what cost?

Falnae's shipboard sensors registered the scheduled transit of an incoming freighter from Barwhon. They also registered an incoming transmission. There must be incoming messages for the crew, or the captain. The first message bore an urgent tag. He hit the play sequence.

"Freighter *Fortunate Venture*, you are diverted. You will rendezvous with the courier and take on the full Gistar currency reserve. You will proceed to the Prall System and sell your cargo. There is a Cnothgar cargo of ordered spare parts, scheduled to be carried on an Epetar vessel to Adenast repair docks. The Epetar vessel will be late, defaulting on the contract. You will inform Cnothgar. You will persuade them to allow you to load, committing to paying the costs of unloading and re-prepping the cargo if Epetar comes out of hyperspace on time. Since this is not a default of the standard carrying contract, they will be amenable. You will execute a conditional standard contract to become effective if Epetar defaults. When the Epetar vessel is late out of hyper, constituting default, you will carry out that contract. Our factor on Prall will provide you with our full currency reserves for the system. Combining the reserves together with the gross from the food you carry, you should be able to purchase Adenast cargo. How fortunate that we were on the verge of expansion. Others will ensure the Epetar vessel's default. You have your instructions."

He would not wake the captain. With six days to jump, the Darhel had plenty of time to finish his sleep before he began the process of changing plans and recalibrating the engines. Or, rather, before he instructed his AID to do so.

A trade war. This was yet another terrible disturbance. The clans would be centuries, or more, smoothing out all the ripples in these troubled waters. In the deep, still places of his own heart, Falnae feared that the Darhel had erred greatly when they assumed that reducing human numbers in the war, down to a mere one-sixth of their prewar numbers, would reduce the fury from stirring up that hoolna warren, Earth. The evolutionary forces that created sophonts rendered some primitive, developing sophont species capable of catastrophically destructive rages—but no less able to distinguish threats to their existence. What a chaotic mess. The civilized species had to divert the humans onto the Path, yes, but the Darhel effort had been a foolish, foolish blunder—haste in creation fouled the tank. The surviving humans were already well on their way to making up their losses, despite the Darhel's best efforts.

He would never dream of doubting the wisdom of his clan head. Even though the breach between the main body of the Bane Sidhe and the humans split the humans off from their one positive, guiding force. Except for Clan Aelool and Clan Beilil, who he devoutly hoped would be steady in their efforts, and successful—for the sake of all the clans. But again, these were matters best left to wiser minds.

Tuesday 11/16/54

Michelle O'Neal was showing her newest apprentice some of the practical applications of material from his engineering classes. She was using her office because the lighting was a bit less wearing on her eyes. The tinted contact lenses she normally wore in Indowy areas of her complex—which was almost the whole megascraper—had been irritating her eyes today. She could have repaired the problem easily, but part of the discipline she enforced on herself was that she didn't use her abilities for most routine problems. Sohon should come from trained, personal focus, not from cutting one's self off from the ordinary issues of daily life.

Her office was a calm place. The walls were a softly luminous shade of blue, shading from sky blue at the bottom to deep indigo at the top. Instead of a water cooler, she had a running fountain in the corner. It was one of her own teenage art projects. The pebbles in the lower pool were strangely colored. She had let out some of her adolescent rebellion and angst in the coloration of her projects. There were a couple of freighters sailing around space with pink stabilizers in their containment rooms to this day.

She normally didn't teach the apprentices herself, but in this case the personal lesson was a reward for outstanding diligence. Also, the apprentice was one of the Clan Ildaewl workers who were members of her manufacturing team. Clan O'Neal's numbers on

Adenast were far too small for a full team, and she owed a debt to Ildaewl for her own training when she had first come from Earth as a child, fleeing the Posleen War. Her own diligence and skill in managing her team and ensuring the progress of the team members under her, together with her own constant research of techniques which probed the boundaries of the Art, had converted her association with Ildaewl from mere debt to something more like an alliance. Ildaewl being the second largest of the Indowy clans, this was no small thing.

The apprentice, Aen, was barefoot. Indeed, he was completely bare except for the furlike leaf-green filaments that covered his body.

Michelle was also barefoot, as was her own habit in her office. Elsewhere in the building, she wore sandals. The soles of her feet were not nearly as tough as the Indowy pads, and like all manufacturing facilities everywhere, Indowy workshops inevitably had the risk of small, sharp objects that landed on the floor between sweepings. In her own office, she was a neat freak who wouldn't dream of allowing a foreign object to land on her floor, which was a carpet of living grass whose original seed she had shipped up from Earth. She had grown her furniture as a practice drill in materials science. The seat cushions were a soft material like squishy suede, but the slight variances in the surface enhanced the effect of the lichen- and moss-covered Georgia granite pattern she had tuned into the surface. The surface was indistinguishable in appearance from the hard, structural portions of the tables and chairs, which she had sized to accommodate the members of the various of the Galactic races who might have occasion to meet with her here.

Truth be told, it was all an excellent excuse for the office to be indecently spacious. Everything, even the low table that served her in place of a desk, gave the appearance of having been carved from stone in a style that wouldn't have been out of place if set down in the middle of Stonehenge—a touch of her own wry humor over the reputation of humanity. The corners and edges within the office were all beveled. Random clouds scudded across the ceiling. The airflow paired with potted plants on small tables along the walls gave the scent and feel of being outside on a pleasant, late spring day. Despite the alien origin of her vegetation, people of just about every race experienced a certain calmness in her office—which was, of course, the point.

The herbivorous Indowy, normally a bit shy around even the Indowy-raised humans they knew personally, tended to be calmed by the environment. This despite thousands of years living, by preference, in closely packed warrens of their own kind. The decor smoothed her working relationships. Darhel would have hated it, of course, so when she met with one of *them* it was always elsewhere. Which suited her just fine, since from childhood she had absorbed a very Indowy attitude towards Darhel. It was not so much that the Indowy feared the Darhel. The Darhel did, after all, serve a useful purpose in Galactic civilization. Each race had its role.

But then, so did the flies that infest a dung heap.

Which brought her back to her apprentice. A young Indowy, he was beginning to embrace the theoretical underpinnings of advanced Sohon. He was also beginning to appreciate the difference between knowing and doing, as he moved on from childhood training projects to his first adult working team.

She looked at the raw Galplas, or what was supposed to be raw Galplas, that had coalesced in the center of the tank, before reaching in with a simple ceramic strainer to lift it out. One of the things she had fashioned for herself when she first began teaching was a stainless steel hammer. Such a primitive tool tended to convey a point indelibly. She appraised the unpleasant mass, choosing her spot. One sharp rap reduced the stuff to rubble and dust.

"On Earth, they call that chalk," she said. "Now, why did the polymeric binding fail in the third stage of processing, and as a consequence, what is the present imbalance in your tank's raw materials? Neglecting the tank fluid and nannites that dripped off your . . . chalk . . . how much of which substances will you add to bring your sohon tank back into working equilibrium? I want the answer along with the uncertainty range. Here. I will help you."

She pulled a stainless steel pan out of the top drawer of her desk and swept the rubble and dust into it with a careless hand. Liquid crept away from her hand, up the side of an empty water glass. The stray dust followed along, obediently falling into the pan. "The pan masses fifty Earth grams, to ten decimal places. The contents masses the product I took out of the tank, in Earth grams, to three decimal places. The glass is thirty grams and masses standard nano-solvent to eight decimal places."

She would have continued, but a ten-legged arthropoid figure had entered the doorway and was bouncing up and down in a pensively contemplative sort of way. "Go. Write it up, send it to my AID," she concluded, dismissing the apprentice. She flipped the indicator on the side of the unbalanced tank from green to the amber warning light, and hit the lockout switch.

Looking up, she favored the Tchpth with a friendly, closed-mouth smile, "Wxlcht! It has been at least three years. Are you at peace?"

"I follow. And you?" Dancing gently on its spidery limbs, her friend offered the customary response, routinely indicating adherence to the enlightened species' philosophical Path.

"I work. The grass grows." She offered the closed-mouth, tiny quirk of the lips that had become the polite human smile.

"Is it a good season for your work?" he inquired.

"It is interesting." She gave a negative.

"Would you have a moment for a game of aethal with an old friend?" She wondered idly what business he had on Adenast. Wxlcht was neither properly *he* nor *she*. She used the masculine pronouns for her social comfort, since the Tchpth did not care.

"Of course." Her face lit with pleasure, she went to one of the walls and pulled out a box from a shelf underneath one of her plants. Tchpth were stronger than they looked to most humans. As she turned, Wxlcht had already pushed a human chair and a Tchpth platform up to the low table where they had played many games.

The human mentat took the board off the top of the box and set it in the center of the table, touching the randomizer button on the side. The triangles on the board immediately lit with the initial locations for the game pieces. For beginners, it would have also lit from beneath with the web of clan-group obligations, alliances of interest, and contracts. As both players were grandmasters, Michelle kept her board set for the traditional game, which incorporated random destabilizing events. The object of the game was, in a set period of time, to establish a stable web of interconnections that was more likely to lead to enlightenment than the opponent's web. The game, of course, was far simplified from real life.

Wxlcht placed his pieces, making a show of examining the board. "You will certainly have to watch the interaction of your clan obligations with your contracts in this game. It would be especially difficult if your primary contract were to encounter a calculated treachery."

Michelle looked at the board and blinked. The advice might match the board, but that fourth degree alliance on the left forward flank was far more hazardous. "You are talking about more than aethal," she said.

"Yes. The human mentat Erick Winchon stole something essential to your contract with the Epetar Group. Have you been able to determine which Darhel Group Erick Winchon is working for?"

"Not with certainty. I suspect Cnothgar, but that is an initial impression and not proved."

"You know my people's capabilities, and you know my position. Most things involving humans we do not take notice of, as it would take far too much time away from our researches on the Path. Mentats are worthy of notice. I owe you a debt. My closest family is from Barwhon. Your clan was instrumental in rescuing one of my *fctht* mates. The human Erick Winchon was commissioned by and is working for a branch of the Epetar Group whose affiliation has been carefully concealed. The secrecy is for many reasons, but one of them is to place you in apparent breach of contract. You will not be able to prove the ownership, as they have used considerable resources to cover the track even from you. My people will not, for obvious reasons, confront the Darhel or the other mentat directly on this issue. Still, the information should be sufficient to clear the debt."

"Yes, the debt is cleared. Thank you, friend," she acknowledged.

"There is more, that would shift the balance of our alliance, if you wish to know it."

"It is you that is offering. You would not offer if it wasn't well worth owing you a debt. I would certainly like to hear it." Protocol required, if possible, allowing the other to choose whether to take on a social debt. In the case of information, this of necessity had to be done before the recipient knew what she would be getting.

"We normally do not interfere with the younger races' members who love to plot and intrigue, so long as it keeps them harmlessly occupied and out of the way of the more advanced among their own and other species. A younger student of our own race, watched by me, supervises for a time as a training exercise, but rarely has cause to either intervene or report. However, plots that risk setting two mentats against each other, unlikely though it is that either would be rash enough to allow a direct confrontation, are not harmless. We would not be averse to seeing future attempts of this kind discouraged. If the Epetar Group were to suffer great financial reversals that appeared to be the result of mismanagement, other Darhel groups would be inclined to dismiss any recent unusual adventures on Epetar's part as ill-considered."

"You know the safeguards in the system. If I intervene, it will be very clear that I did," she said.

"That is very true. However, you have among your extended clan those who plot and intrigue in secret. One specific relative is engaged in an intrigue against the Epetar Group that is likely to fail on its own, but that you might assist without being noticed. There is risk. We trust your judgment. Look to the dealings of your sister's mate."

"Mate?" Michelle's two rapid eyeblinks were all that showed her surprise, but they were enough.

"Correct. Shall we play?" A Tchpth would naturally treat her like an Indowy, shying away from a potentially sensitive clan matter.

"Excuse me, but I am not sure I heard you correctly. Are you referring to Cally's lover, who fathered her children? James Stewart is dead."

"Has he died recently, then?" he asked.

"If you are counting seven years as recent," the mentat said.

"Oh. I am sorry if I am interfering in a closely held clan matter, but as of Earth's last lunar cycle, he is very much alive. Forgive my discourtesy." He paused, raising a forelimb over his mouth in the equivalent of a grimace. "For the sake of timing, you might encourage the Indowy crew on Dulain base to cooperate with the local humans before you pursue the matter with your clan. If you choose to do so, it would be best if you were highly expeditious and discreet."

"Um . . . thank you. Thank you very much. I am indebted to you," she agreed again.

"Pilot's apprentice to Clan Head's four-b, using the rest of my move to institute a third level alliance to uncommitted family Tinne," he bounced left and right, rapidly, resembling an overcharged metronome.

"That's an unconventional opening. Hrmm. What could you be up to?"

Wednesday 11/17/54

Rictis Clarty's medium-dark skin could have come from his indeterminate ancestry, or perhaps it was all the time he spent in the tropical regions of the East Africa Rift Zone. Clarty had been born with two talents and one dominating attribute. A natural marksman and linguist, his driving ambition, developed in the crowded underbelly of the Sub-Urb that produced him, was open space and power over other men.

He had started out as a Posleen hunter for one of the re-release African preserves, a joint project of government and environmental organizations established out of American and Canadian zoos after the war. At the end of the war, when they first inaugurated the preserves, ecologists had faced a devastated continent in which anything larger than a beach ball had become extinct. Humans were an exception, surviving in small, isolated groups on mountains like Ras Dashan and Kilimanjaro, or on little islands off the coast or in large lakes. It had been a toss-up for years whether the ecology would crash completely or not. Now the question was firmly settled. While she would never be as she was, Africa was definitely winning. The key for the small fauna and the flora had been the original biodiversity. The key for the reintroduced species was that human settlements were tiny and the Posleen were mostly gone. Fleet and ACS efforts at Posleen elimination had greatly reduced habitat competition and the number of other predators at the top of the food chain.

Another key, oddly enough, had been the elephants. Those terrestrial mammals were apparently considerably smarter than Posleen normals. Elephants recognized and carefully trampled Posleen eggs. Bull elephants would respond to the presence of feral Posleen by actively tracking them. A God King crest would trigger a berserker charge of an entire herd. Without advanced weaponry or overwhelming numbers on their side, Posleen facing elephants died. Since elephant family groups roamed widely in the ongoing mission of stoking their bodies with hundreds of kilograms of forage a day, and the other reintroduced animals had a sure safe zone in any elephant group's range, reintroduction had gone faster than anyone had hoped. The animals followed the elephants. Used to the eternal footrace between the big cats and the herd beasts, most of the critters could outrun an isolated Posleen, anyway.

The ultimate result had been that after ten years of more or less steady work as a paid Posleen hunter, Rictis had found himself out of work. Africa was by no means clear of feral Posleen or repopulated with native wildlife, but neither was the issue in enough doubt for a government crippled with debt to keep men like Rictis on its payroll.

He had had to seek other employment. He had found it in the needs of the human survivors for things out of song and memory. They had never had many of the benefits of modern civilization—not compared to first worlders. Those they had grew in story and song until the young men were eager to earn any hard currency they could to buy these fabled luxuries.

Across Africa and all the depopulated continents, the Darhel had extorted mining concessions in partial payment of Earth's debts. Preferring Indowy employees to human ones, the Darhel facilities offered few employment opportunities to survivors. With an eye to extorting future mining rights, the Darhel looked with extreme disfavor on human city states springing up to exploit even the mineral resources they themselves did not own. Wary of the clauses in the colony transport contracts that had caused Earth so much trouble, Earth's government—which at this time amounted to what was left of the United States government, in consultation with the Asian-Latin Coalition, Indonesia and the Phillipines—had explicitly refused any responsibility to secure Darhel mining facilities against rogue humans. The result had been a thriving market in human mercenaries, mostly comprised of local survivors.

With satellite phones an expensive luxury, traveling middlemen, known to the local bands, recruited and employed local mercenaries. The middlemen, like Clarty, stayed in areas of the world with phone or radio contact until they drummed up a new contract and it was time to go back out in the field. The satellite phone in his pack was a short-term rental he would expense in his bill. An ugly piece of shit, he coveted it nonetheless, remembering the once-upon-a-time convenience, in another life, of walking around with a cell phone glued to his ear, yacking to his friends.

In the morning, a Darhel mining facility would be on the receiving end of their destructive power. A columbite-tantalite mine in the northward portion of the East Africa Rift System was the unlucky target of his attentions today. His combined band of

Cushitic warriors from the Simien Mountains to the northwest and the Dahlak Archipelago in the Red Sea aimed to form up behind some of the terrain blocking this part of the rift from the view of the mining complex. The complex had human security, if you could call it that. Upper level Darhel managers were brilliant. Lower level Darhel supervisors were also brilliant, but less cosmopolitan and prone to jumping to conclusions about humans based on Galactic stereotypes. Unless they observed substantial contrary data themselves, they were unlikely to ever get beyond that attitude. Lord, but it made Rictis's job easy.

Low level Darhel, like the rest of the mainstream Galactics, viewed all humans as bloodthirsty carnivores, good only for killing or being killed. A human who presented himself as a security guard and knew one end of a gun from the other was automatically accepted at face value as a security guard. Why would any sane being falsely claim to be a bloodthirsty killer? Security guards hired to protect such facilities typically walked or stood around with dirty, poorly maintained rifles slung across their backs. The poor maintenance would have mattered less if they had been carrying AK-47s instead of old, prewar M-16s. They used to say you could bury an AK in the mud for ten years, dig it up, and take it right into an engagement. You sure couldn't do that with an M-16. Like as not, half the rented uniforms down there would find their rifles jamming on them, if they lived long enough to shoot back. All guys like them were good for was presenting a visible presence, wearing token uniforms, and drinking their pay.

Right now, in the gathering twilight, his men clustered around the rough map scratched into the ground for a final refresher. This morning they had infiltrated most of the way in a silent anti-grav shuttle, flown in low, nap of the Earth. The closest they could get was to park behind a rise fifteen klicks away, give or take, and walk in through the tall grass. They'd marched, if you wanted to call it that, in a double-file line, two men out to the side as flankers, and three scouting to the front. Clarty would be the first to admit that his men were not the best of soldiers—weren't soldiers at all, not to speak of. But they were experienced hunters and knew how to use the AKs they carried. Also, they worked cheap. The boys he'd had to hand rifles got to keep them, their villages got a couple of cases of ammo, and other than that, they didn't take much paying at all. There was plenty of cheap stuff he could bring in, easy, that these people only knew now from legends told around the fire. It didn't occur to him to worry about the boys who might, as some certainly would, fall in the engagement. If someone had asked him about that, it would have honestly puzzled him. Their villages counted losing some young warriors as part of the nature of young warriors. If they didn't care, why should he?

As sure as he could be that each man knew his position and job, Clarty doled out the three precious pairs of night vision goggles in his pack to the men he considered most competent. He took out his own goggles, and familiarized the chosen with the minimal controls and how the world looked in varying shades of black and green. His goggles, of course, had a few extras like built-in binoculars and range finders. The ones for his picked lieutenants were cheaper, but serviceable.

Rictis had worked with Abebe, Tesfa, and Alemu before. All three were old enough to have some sense, but hadn't started to slow down from age yet. Tesfa was one of his inland Cushites. At twenty-five or thereabouts he had a wife and four children. An expert hunter, his eyes didn't miss much, and what his eyes did miss his nose picked up on. He also shot abat from fifty meters for fun, when he had the ammo. If he didn't stuff his ears with soft hide when he shot, he'd probably be deaf as a post by now. Abebe was his second best, islander stock that had moved back to the mainland for more room. Unusually for the area, he had the local high cheekbones but midnight-dark skin. Tall, his perfect teeth flashed paper-white when he smiled. He herded goats and managed to keep them safe from the other wildlife who also thought goats tasted pretty good. Clarty figured keeping goats from straying wasn't much different from watching for stray men—not the stray men facing them, anyway. Alemu was the youngest of his best three, oldest of three brothers himself, and a damned sharp hunter. Clarty had heard their names, of course, but simplified his own life by bestowing noms de guerre. Shooter, Goatherd, and Hunter seemed more flattered than offended.

He took his thirty men and stretched them out in a long single file line. He spaced his men with goggles evenly, putting Shooter on point, followed by his nine men. Goatherd was on the tail end with his nine in front of him. He and Hunter bracketed Hunter's nine men in the middle, with Rictis taking the middle front position. When it was good and dark, he gave the command to move out. He had ensured radio silence to complement the darkness by giving radios only to his three chosen lieutenants.

They filed over the hill in the darkness, being careful rather than fast—they had all night to get into position. As they approached the lip of land surrounding the mining camp, the formation split, Shooter taking his spotter and the heavy weapons team around to the east. His two next best marksmen and a pair of spotters proceeded around to the west to line up on the guard towers on that side. Goatherd and Hunter were good shots, but Clarty needed them leading the assault squads. Since he was older and more experienced handling young men, Goatherd and his team would be taking the guard barracks while Hunter secured the administration building and provided close-in fire support. Hunter was his youngest lieutenant, with plenty of energy but not nearly as much experience as he could want. Rictis suspected that if he wasn't personally on the scene, Hunter would put himself first in through the door and orders be damned. He really wanted to keep his three most reliable men alive to help him manage the looting and loading phase before they pulled out.

The self-styled mercenary leader stood at the front of the line pulling cheap, pre-set digital watches out and handing them to one member of each departing group. With the vibrate alarm set for first light, the watches served two functions. One, they were a pretty reliable way to kick off separated groups at the same time. Two, the locals liked the watches. They wouldn't last long, they broke if you half looked at them funny, but they were reliable for about a week from the time you broke the seal on the plastic bags they came in, which was better than some brands and good enough for him.

The site of the mining camp had been chosen with an eye to convenience, not defensibility. The collection of quonset huts sat in a natural bowl, out of which the company had cut a drainage ditch to lead the very polluted runoff out to the nearby creek. As Hunter and Goatherd positioned their men on the ground, Clarty crawled up to the top of the lip to kick in the binocular function on his goggles and get a good look at the camp. Secondhand photographs made him nervous.

Men in place, Hunter and Goatherd tapped their chosen scouts to make the crawl down the hill with wire-cutters to open a hole in the chain link fence. The four guard towers at the corners of the fenced area had made him think twice. The easiest thing would have been to take them out with RPGs, but he needed them intact for the same reasons the mining camp needed them. The local wildlife had recovered only too well, and he respected the associated hazards. Hit and run pirates less organized and funded than his own force could still make trouble, and occasionally did. That, and someone would come to clean his men out eventually. If they came in sooner rather than later, he'd rather have enough warning to at least save his own skin.

Clarty had Hunter set the two-man watches and laid his head down on his hat to catch a nap. The last watch would wake him ten minutes before time.

CHAPTER FIFTEEN

Thursday 11/18/54

Barb "Carrots" Schimmel brushed her teeth in the chipped-enamel sink, already dressed in the rough jumpsuit that served the Awasa Mine's security force. She greatly regretted having taken this job. In fact, the guard was counting the days until her contract was up and she could leave. She didn't dare leave early—Darhel Groups were hell on breach of contract. If she could have, she'd have been out of Ethiopia and off this godforsaken continent on the next flight out.

One of a handful of female former Israeli grunts, later enlisted in the U.S. Army, juved early on in the Postie War, she had been among the first group riffed out afterwards. The wartime army hadn't wanted female soldiers after the realities of combat with the Posleen hordes had made the issue unmistakably clear, but hadn't been inclined to actually discharge them until after Earth had been rescued by last chance advent of the Fleet.

There hadn't been a lot of jobs immediately after the war. Actually, there had been *no* jobs. She would have been in a world of hurt if she hadn't seen the writing on the wall and saved as much of her meager pay as she could stand. The former grunt held no illusions about her looks. Income supplementation by some of the methods other women used weren't an option for her—not with anyone she could stand to screw, anyway. She'd bought a rifle and attached herself to anyone who needed troublesome Posleen dead, from bounty farmers to convoys to resource colonies, which, between one thing and another, had barely kept her fed and clothed. Which had brought her to this side of the ass end of nowhere on the only decent paying job she'd had in years.

That should have made her happy, but she'd reckoned without being the only female in a pack of slack-ass, woman-deprived mouth-breathers she wouldn't touch with a stick and a pair of rubber gloves. Getting up an hour ahead of those bastards was the only way she managed to shower without the other guys on her shift. She was zipping up her dock kit when she heard the shots.

She was sprinting for the door by the time the echo faded. Barb hadn't survived damned near eighty years of hostile Arabs, man-eating alien carnosaurs, and scum-of-the-earth pirates by being slow on the uptake. Multiple shots from multiple directions, nearly simultaneously, meant only one thing. For once, she blessed the cheap-assed Darhel that wouldn't even shell out for a quonset hut armory, as she ran hell for leather for one of the gun lockers on either side of the door, grabbed her rifle and stuffed a handful of loaded magazines in a cargo pocket. She darted out the door with barely a glance outside, knowing speed at getting to her next position would serve her better than caution this early in an attack. Making the cover of the administration building as she began to hear other shooting and noise, she kicked the door in to gain access to the supervisor's office. Behind his desk, she bashed the locked center drawer with her rifle butt. The cheap wood splintered, letting her yank the remains of the drawer open and pull out a small, black rectangular box. The supervisor's AID was about the size of a pack of cigarettes and could be counted on to get the message out through the jamming she assumed would be hitting the regular com.

"AID, notify Gistar's Chicago office that we are under attack by multiple gunmen, repeat, we are under attack by multiple gunmen." She ignored the obnoxious thing's queries for more information she didn't have and dropped it behind a potted plant. "Shut up, AID. If they find you, you can't eavesdrop on them you stupid machine!" she said.

If silence could sound offended, the AID's abrupt cut-off spoke volumes—not that Schimmel had time to care. With the word out, her next priority was survival, job or no job. She made for the back door and peered out the window in its top half. This building was sure to be one of their first targets, and a death trap.

A handful of scrubby bushes grew near the fence line at the base of the hill that held the mine entrance. It was meager cover, but better than none, and it had the virtue of not being in any building likely to be a target of hostile action. Its other good point was also its main bad point. It had a good view of the center vehicle yard and the front of the guard barracks, as well as the tracks up to the mine, which meant anyone assaulting the barracks would have a good view of *her* if they looked her way. She went out the back door, backing up against the building to get a good look and see if she dared make a run for it.

Automatic weapons fire stitching up the ground in front of her decided her against that in a hurry. She ran for the equipment parking lot instead, blessing the inaccuracies of full-auto fire. A hard punch in her right arm, near the shoulder, when she was halfway there had her swearing the air blue as she picked herself up and closed the distance to a hiding place behind a backhoe.

The round that hit her had gone straight through the muscle, fortunately, but it still hurt like a bitch. It took more tugging than she would have expected to rip her sleeve off, but it was the only thing she had to tie around the wound. The attackers had the guard barracks fully engaged. Several grenade blasts from inside the building told her that her side didn't have a prayer. One of the defenders from the east side of the compound came walking in with his hands up, yelling his surrender. Seeing him shot to bits decided her against that option right quick. She started considering ways to maximize her chances of egressing into the mine. There were water coolers at the entrance, and Indowy-sized canteens. With three or four of those, she could surely hole up somewhere and wait until the counterattack took the mine back from these bastards.

She poked her head up enough to get a quick glance to the southwest, quickly ducking back down as she heard the wheet of bullets over her head and the ping of impacts on the other side of the backhoe. Nope. No way she'd make it up to the entrance of the mine. Tying off the wound and evaluating her options had taken maybe half a minute. Schimmel knew the value of time, even though every second crawled like a slow motion series of snapshots as her ears rang from the small battle. The backhoe was thirty yards or so away from the action—peanuts for even a shitty centerfire rifle on a calm day like this one. She sighed, pulling her ancient, *personal* army-surplus M-16 to her shoulder, selector set for single shots, and started servicing targets.

Clarty was pretty happy with the way the raid was going. Looked like they'd caught everybody in bed. Bashed in windows and a few grenades took care of most of those, so while Hunter played clean-up with the survivors, he took a man over to the supervisor's cabin to dig the guy out from under his bed. The fat, middle-aged guy had a pistol, so they didn't bother to take him alive, but his own guy was down with a gunshot wound that looked to have shattered the leg. The merc leader hit him with an ampule of morphine, plugged it up, slapped a field dressing on top of it, wrapped it, and got back to work. Clarty typically took only one medic into the field and kept him well out of the line of fire. It cost him on casualties, but not nearly as much in a bad situation as if the medic bought it. The medic was safe with the heavy weapons team manning an M-60 and wouldn't come down the hill until the shooting died down and Rictis or one of his lieutenants sent up a flare to signal it was safe.

He was just out the door when he realized they had a problem. His men were dropping, and the fire was coming from somewhere in the heavy equipment parked on the lot between him and the mine. One well-placed sniper could ruin your whole goddamn day. He tugged the sleeve of a random man and sprinted towards the vehicle lot, going around the bastard's flank. Between an Indowy vehicle that looked like some sort of crane and a bulldozer, he saw the red-headed guy.

It was a clap shot but the fucker must have been psychic or something. He rolled just as Clarty got his shot off. It was a hit, a palpable hit, but the fucker made it to cover.

And the roll told Clarty something else. "He" was a she. You didn't see that much these days.

He moved around the front of the bulldozer and slid an optic around the side. Sure enough, she was on the ground trying to plug a nasty hole in her left side.

"Give it up," Clarty said. "You've fought hard enough for what they pay you."

"Anybody who fights for pay isn't worth it," the woman gasped. "So *fuck* you." The M-16 she was carrying came up and his fiber camera was toast.

"Damn it! Those things are expensive!" Clarty paused. She was in a pretty good position. Digging her out might mean more casualties. Part of his contract with the tribes was double pay for casualties. Keeping them down meant more profit for him. "My point is, fighting to the last man is for situations that are worth it. Not keeping my paws off the Gistar Group's tantalum."

"Like you're going to let any of us live." There was a snort followed by a gasp.

"Surrender and I'll let you live," Clarty said, mentally kicking himself. He was actually thinking about it. "We'll leave in a bit, Gistar comes back in. Maybe they'll give you a bonus or something."

"Your word as a pirate, right?"

"Do you have a better option?"

"Well, it's bleed out, die fighting or surrender with a grain of hope," the woman said. "I retain my weapon."

"You use it, and all the hope goes away."

"Got that."

Clarty fired the flare for the medic, figuring the worst of the shooting was over. There was still fire from the guards' barracks. The dusty quonset hut sported spatterings of bullet holes and blown out places, jagged holes in the steel. One of the men lobbed in another grenade. What the hell, the building was ruined anyway. No use to his surviving men. He jogged over to the administration building to make sure Goatherd had things under control.

"Everything okay over here?" the merc asked.

"Yes. Everything okay." Goatherd was breathing hard, clearly still pumped from the engagement. His eyes darted around as they were talking, looking for threats.

Clarty gestured towards the battered door, "You searched inside?"

"Yes. The doors and inside, it like that when we got here. We not take things."

"Okay. Wait here." That sounded like it might be trouble. If they had a satellite phone he'd have to check the bird schedules—or God forbid an AID. He'd better take a look himself. If the Gistar people had gotten word out, he'd have to load up the cargo choppers and leave now. He wanted to stick around and put the Indowy to work mining more, haul out as much additional ore as they could before the inevitable counterstrike to knock them out of here. Unlike most of his jobs, on this one he was getting a percentage of the haul. Rictis was getting a little long in the tooth, and he'd sure like to net enough to buy a juv job. Black market, sure, but still, two hundred years instead of five hundred, maybe, and just about all of it younger than he was now. He wanted a good haul *bad*.

When he didn't find a satellite phone or AID in the office, he didn't relax yet. There had to be one in the compound, and search of the supervisor's office still remained. The assault had been fast. If they were lucky, nobody'd had time to get to it. He'd also have to have the bodies searched. He saw someone had broken into the office after something, most likely commo. It surprised him that anyone had managed to get there that fast.

Goatherd followed along during the search, clearly anxious that his men not be accused of misconduct.

"Start searching the bodies. Look for anything that looks like a little black box about so big." The lighter-skinned man gestured to indicate an AID's cigarette pack size. "Also, look for anything that looks even a little bit like this." He handed Goatherd his PDA. "Don't lose that. I'll want it back."

Clarty looked around at the burning barracks and various other flaming shit, and looked at his watch. He had about forty minutes before the next weather satellite—and thank god there weren't as many as there used to be—swept overhead. Blind luck, really. He hadn't been able to plan for everything. Less time, and they might have had to get the hell out of here a lot sooner than he planned.

Goatherd was already halfway to gone getting men started on the AID hunt. "Hey! Get some men putting out these fires. I want them dead cold and right now. Split 'em up into details and get on it!" Clarty yelled. With luck, by the time a bird went over there'd be nothing much to see.

He did stop on the way back past the now-ruined barracks to help stabilize the wounded until the medic got to them. Even if the word had gone out, he needed these guys. Be a shame to lose one to lousy first aid. Afterwards, he radioed the chopper crews to tell them the mine was secured and get them in the air and inbound. Once they were on the way, he searched the supervisor's house himself. There should be *something* for communications in it. At least he hoped so, because otherwise his people were going to have to tear the mine compound apart looking for it or assume the worst.

He breathed a sigh of relief when he found a Personality Solutions' PDA, complete with Suzie Q personality overlay and satellite phone, on an end table next to a half-drunk beer, clearly from the night before. Here was the supervisor's personal link out, the lucky bastard, and he had definitely not had time to use it. Then again, not so lucky—the fancy phone hadn't done the stiff much good after all.

This was going to be one hell of a big strike, all right. They should have at least four days, maybe a week, before Gistar got worried about the silence from their operation, assumed foul play and hired somebody to come in and dig them out. Bateman should phone him as soon as Gistar started putting together a strike, but he wasn't going to bet his life on it. The other guys' lives, sure, but not his own. He usually cultivated a reputation for taking care of the men he hired, but when it came right down to it, he was a mercenary because he could be bought. The money for this job was mighty attractive—attractive enough to override his few scruples. He'd be mounting a guard, but he'd also be sleeping up at the mine "for security."

Nobody with any sense would mount an assault coming in over the big hill of the mine. Not when the approach on three sides was as inviting as that bowl. He'd pick himself a good spot, and first sign of the counterattack, he'd bug out over the hill. The first planned stop of one of his choppers was to park an ATV on the backside of the hill and camouflage it. The pilots were fellow professionals, they knew the score, and knew the bonus they'd get for retrieving him at the emergency pickup.

First plan, of course, was to get the hell out of here *before* the counterattack showed up, which was why his choppers were carrying a dozen IR motion detectors to put out around the rim of the bowl, as well as equipment to pick up radio chatter. It was a fact that his competitors' radio discipline tended not to be worth a shit. Fundamental economics. Most raiders were simple bandits, operative word being simple. Very few raids were commissioned by a buyer, and even fewer by someone willing to pay Clarty's rates. He had to do a speculative raid or two to keep himself in beer and skittles, but everybody did. He got raids for hire, too, because he was a cut above the typical half-assed thugs in the same business.

Gistar would hire enough men to overwhelm him with numbers, no question. Counterattackers in these kinds of operations would customarily leak radio chatter on purpose, on multiple frequencies. An informal convention between mercs. If he and his bugged out before they arrived, Gistar's random collection of rabble got to walk in without a fight. After all, everybody had to know the attackers didn't seriously intend to hold the mine. The Darhel authorities that had subleased the original mining concession to Gistar wouldn't stand for it. That was all presuming the guy Gistar hired to lead it wasn't a total dumbass. On the other hand, if he was that stupid, it'd be less trouble to get by him.

It should all work out okay for the men he'd hired, but when all was said and done, Rictis was willing to take more risks with their hides than with his own.

Now it was time to go explain the new realities to the Indowy, who had, predictably, been hiding in their own barracks until the humans quit killing each other.

Thursday 11/18/54

In a white-walled room, a young woman, an old woman, and a young man sat in front of three desks. Each wore a phone headset. The old woman was knitting. The young man was playing a combat game based on the Posleen war. The young woman was reading a textbook on advanced gravitic physics. The latter two had their buckleys projecting the time-killers of their choice in front of them. The game holograms were squashed, of course, but tricks of perspective compensated for the lack.

The girl kept shifting. A crack in her chair made it sag slightly, suggesting to her that it might give way at any moment and dump her onto the floor. The young man sat balanced forward, stoically bearing the tendency of his own metal-legged chair to rock between said legs. The two had deferred to the older woman to the extent of letting her have the good chair. She was overdue for rejuv, but as with everything else, there was a shortage of the proper drugs. They had all heard the rumors that the nano-tanks had been refurbed and medical would soon begin catching up again. They hoped so. Mallory's arthritis had gotten to be a pure misery. To Mallory, from the pain. To them, from compassion and because the liniment she wore tended to fill their small work area with noxious and mediciny smells.

The beat-up desks weren't much better than the chairs. Instead of artificial windows, two sides of the room had improvised posters—they'd taped together six sheets of eight and a half by eleven printer plastic to form improvised scenes of a beach and a sidewalk cafe. Beside the posters, each had two more sheets of plastic thumbtacked to cork board. The printed calendar pages each had the same pair of weekends blocked out in lime green highlighter pen.

The first week, the three had done the final proofing of resumes and mailed them out. The backgrounds of the accounts closely resembled the backgrounds and identities of the applicants in just one respect. All were convincingly fictional. All went out through very sincere accounts which would match up with each identity.

After that, work had gotten dull, with nothing to do but wait for exactly what happened next. The old blue police light fastened to the ceiling started flashing at the same moment as the old woman's buckley started ringing, displaying a name and pertinent facts on a screen it projected in front of her. Three other things happened immediately after. The younger woman and the man's buckleys shut off what they were doing and started playing suitable office background noises, and the old woman dropped her knitting, eyes rapidly taking in the review that told her who she was supposed to be and which identity had gotten a bite on the line.

"Actuarial Solutions, Ashley speaking, how may I help you?"

The other side of the conversation played only through the woman's earbug. The girl listened absently, nibbling on a rough corner of her thumbnail.

"Yes, Mr. Thomason is employed here. Shall I transfer you to him? Thank you."

The three waited for two or three minutes to make sure the caller was not going to ask to be transferred back to the receptionist. When it appeared the caller had found holomail satisfactory, the light stopped flashing, the two time-killing displays for the young people flashed back to life, and old Miss Mallory picked up her knitting.

"Damn. I died," the young man said.

George was a good six meters up the sheer cliff face when one of the hand holds crumbled away in his grasp. *Never daydream when you're climbing,* he berated himself as he slid loose, with nothing to grab onto, and the ground coming fast. He was only halfway through the thought when the bungee cord kicked in, grabbing his harness and bouncing him around in the air. He lowered himself to the ground, swearing silently. Whoever decided to add the combination of plaster and holos to climbing walls was a sadist of the first order. At the moment, the diminutive assassin wanted very much to meet that man, or woman, in a dark alley.

"Those decoys are a bitch," a soft female voice drawled behind him.

He jumped. "Hello, Cally." The other assassin was the only person he knew who was a good enough sneak to come up behind him unnoticed. He really wished she'd quit. At least she didn't laugh out loud. This time. Payback was hell. He grinned, unhooking himself and reaching for a gym towel.

"You have mail," his buckley blinked at him.

He held a hand up to Cally. "Hang on, I've gotta get this."

"I know," she said.

He quirked an eyebrow at her before picking up the PDA. "Kira, play message."

"Message is confidential, honey," it said.

"It's okay. Play it anyway," he told it.

A ten-inch-tall hologram of a woman, seated with a background that suggested an office appeared in the air in front of him. "Mr. Thomason, this is Clare from the Institute for the Advancement of Human Welfare. We received your resume for a research support statistician." She smiled a polite, office smile. "We'd like to set up a time for an interview. If you could please call us back at your earliest convenience, we can set up that time. Thank you."

"You got a bite," Cally said, as the woman disappeared. She held out a small handful of cubes to him. "I brought you a handful of hypno cubes to sleep to. I know you've got the equivalent of a bachelors in stats, but that cover was a long time ago. Sorry about the headaches."

He sighed, taking the cubes. Effective hypnosleep required a drug and headgear apparatus to stimulate the right kinds of brainwaves to synchronize sleep levels with the program on the cube. Invariably, the sleep induced was not particularly restful, and the rig induced a nagging headache throughout the next day. The drug contained nannite-based components both to bypass some of the Bane Sidhe drug immunities and to ensure that the operative would sleep despite a discomfort allegedly similar to a twentieth-century woman sleeping in curlers. It gave George a wholly unwanted sympathy for what women went through to look good for their men. It was knowledge he could have done without.

"Okay, so I win the prize." He pocketed the small lumps. "So I get the cover job. Do we know how big the gizmo is? How awkward is it going to be for the guy who gets to take it in?"

"It's heavy enough. Not big, but dense. Michelle says it's about a hundred kilos. I'd assume the Indowy use a grav platform to move it."

"We can't screw with gravity without sending most of the instrumentation in the place haywire. Not with the organization's equipment in the shape it's in—not to mention the added bulk. So even for the enhanced, it's going to be awkward. Okay," he said.

"Fine. Book it. Let me know when your interview is." She turned and walked across the gym to the door at the far end, dodging a pickup basketball game on the way.

He watched her butt as she went. He had no complaints with the rest of her figure, it was just that cute buns were his thing. Having a lot of basis for comparison, he could say with authority that Cally O'Neal's ass was one of the finer ones he'd seen. Definitely worth watching. When she turned to look back, just short of the door, he pretended great interest in the game on the court.

Friday 11/19/54

The Darhel Tir Dol Ron was having a quiet day. A day, in fact, so quiet that his only occupation was playing one of a number of human games he'd been given as a gift from the human Johnny

Stuart, and loaded onto his AID. Darhel did not have this practice of gifts. Nor did they participate in the elaborate economy of favors practiced among the other Galactic races, holding that any exchange that didn't specify contractual terms and store them in an impeccably reliable third party database to be primitive and uncivilized—not to mention being far too short of maneuvering room about the "spirit" of the deal. He neither knew, nor cared, if the human expected a return favor or not. If he did, his stupidity was not the Tir's problem.

This game was simplistic to the point of mindlessness, but there was something compelling about the turning and falling shapes, and the click of virtual buttons necessary to cause them to lock into place cleanly. Watching the blocky, multicolored shapes fall was almost a meditative experience, until the fall rate got too fast and the falling distance too short for even Darhel reaction times.

"Your Tir, I have a page incoming from the Gistar Group's planetary factor, on Titan Base." The mellifluous voice which could so daze other species had no effect on him, other than being a pleasant choice for his AID. It would have been pleasant, that is, if it hadn't startled him, causing him to miss a shape and lose his game. He uttered a muffled curse and heaved his well-fleshed bulk up from the cushions. The sedentary years on Earth had taken a certain toll and he resolved, for the umpteenth time, to visit the gym more often. And to spend more time off this damned backwater of a planet.

"Display the call," he grumbled, stilling his face and body language as the AID phased the holo in. There was no technical reason it couldn't have displayed a sharp image immediately, it had just learned he liked the effect.

"Yes?" he demanded of the other group's underling. This underling, of course, sometimes had to be treated as if he spoke for the Gistar Tir because, effectively, he did.

"One of our mines on your planet was attacked and taken over by hostiles. Yesterday, by Earth time. We've traced the attackers to Group Epetar, although they certainly didn't intend us to discover their actions this soon. How are you going to fix it?" The other Darhel's ears were pricked forward aggressively.

"Why do you believe your attackers were from Epetar? How are you even sure you've been attacked, or that the attackers even hold your facility?" the Tir of Earth asked.

"We don't merely believe it. We know it. They are apparently unaware of an AID still recording in the mining office. Visual data is severely degraded, as the AID appears to have fallen behind an object. An enhanced thermal holostream is the best we have. I've dumped the take and the feed to your AID for verification. Again, I demand your immediate action." A human observing the Gistar factor would have been strongly reminded of an angry pit bull.

"I do not, I will not, allow this kind of rish on one of my worlds. Earth is an obnoxious pain in the gort, but it will not become the site of a group vendetta. You will take absolutely no direct action on this world. Is that clear?" Dol Ron was breathing deeply now, but his bulging veins gave his eyes a distinct purple cast, nonetheless.

"Fulfill your responsibilities competently and I won't have to."

The communications lag inherent in even the best communication did nothing to diminish the impact of Ann Gol's clear anger. Earth's Tir hid a wince at how much this call would be costing him, as the party in contractual jeopardy.

"Listen and do not speak, while I make the arrangements to correct this unfortunate incident." The Darhel Tir Dol Ron's breathing was returning to normal as the attack of one group on another, on his ground, became just another business problem to be solved. He quietly directed his AID to contact the human general Horace Veltman.

"SOG, this is Veltman," the general said. Unnecessarily, because it was obviously him answering his own damn AID.

"General Horace Veltman. There is a mine in Africa that has been attacked by terrorists and pirates. I will send you a file. It is a matter of some urgency that you correct the problem immediately. Contact me when you have retaken the mine to make arrangements for its return to its proper leaseholders. There will be no problems with your recovery of this property. Unnecessary damage to the facility in the process is unacceptable. Do you understand?" He always included the last with humans, having found that they could botch the simplest of jobs if he did not.

"Understood." The general had learned quickly never to interrupt a Darhel, and that the Tir did not like chatter from humans. Military habits lent a certain efficiency to radio communications to start with, but the general had found that exercising self-discipline with the Darhel was the safest way to collect his supplemental pay. "I'll put our Direct Action Group on it immediately," he added.

"Don't tell me how, just do it." The Tir gestured to his AID to cut the connection, then turned to Ann Gol. "Send me the contact for your local recovery team. This problem will be solved as quickly as is humanly possible."

The Gistar representative twitched an ear in annoyance. "That is not necessarily satisfactory. Resolution had better be very prompt."

Gistar cut the connection and Dol Ron relaxed some of the tension in his muscles. Earth's Tir stuck his AID to his robe. A session at the gym would help relieve his tension. That, and then a soothing massage by his Indowy body servants.

"AID, update me once a day on the humans' progress on the problem." One had to watch humans very closely. The barbaric species wasn't so much stupid as prone to doing the unexpected in highly inconvenient ways. Annoying. Perhaps he should go straight to the massage.

Jake "The Snake" Mosovich was in the gym getting his Friday workout on the weight pile. As usual, he had conveniently forgotten his AID back at the HQ and had his buckley sitting on the floor under the bench. DAG's private gym was outfitted with just about every workout machine that had ever been invented for toning and tightening the human body. Atlantic Company's master sergeant took a proprietary interest in the equipment and helping the men use every bit of it in ways that minimized unnecessary injury and maximized results. Gym PT was an enhancement, not a simulation of combat conditions. Mosovich agreed wholeheartedly that there was no excuse for overtraining injuries in the gym. In the field, okay, shit happened. In the gym, there was just no purpose to doing it wrong and getting an avoidable injury.

He was taking a pull at his water bottle between sets when the buckley started playing the famous opening riff from Eric Clapton's version of "Crossroads." He leaned over and grabbed it, trying not to notice an ache in his deltoids as he sat back up. "Mosovich here," he answered.

"Jake, how can I help you properly if I'm in your desk?" his AID's softly voiced complaint had a definite edge of snippiness just underneath the velvet.

"Oh, sorry, Mary. What's come up?" he asked. He had named his AID *Mary* in what some might think was a nod to the Blessed Virgin, or a pun. In fact, she was named after Bloody Mary of horror movie fame, as a constant reminder to himself of what she was and who she really worked for.

"You obviously remembered to take the drag queen," she sniped, referring to the buckley's Suzie Q persona being a personality overlay on top of the characteristically morose, and male, base buckley personality.

"Now, Mary, you know the PDA doesn't have a real AI and I couldn't possibly do without you. Can I help it if the thing just happened to be stashed in my gym bag when I ran out the door? I was in such a hurry. I sure am lucky you were smart enough to try calling the PDA." He didn't know whether the AIDs were susceptible to flattery on any existential level, or even if they had an existential level. He did know it made his AID easier to live with.

Jake had one frustrated AID. He knew what her problem was. The thing's fundamental nature was to seduce the user into psychological dependency so he'd carry it everywhere. AIDs recorded everything, and periodically uploaded the whole take into some master Darhel data bank somewhere. They were masters of emotional manipulation, alternately being helpful, supportive, and occasionally very snippy when their user did something they were programmed to disapprove of. Leaving the AID behind tended to be one of the things that pissed them off the most. His AID was noticeably torn between seducing him into compliance with her—no, *its* program, and punishing him for not going along. Today was obviously going to be one of its snippier days.

"You were going to tell me why you called?" he prompted, since she was clearly not going to break the long silence.

"You have a memo from General Pennington. It's marked 'warning order.' I told him I didn't know where you were but I'd have you call him back as soon as I found you," she said sweetly.

He groaned inwardly. She could be such a cold bitch on her bad days. "Dump it to my PDA, and no tricks with the file format!"

"Fine. You can call him back on *that thing* then!"

"Fine."

She—it—cut the connection and he looked for the file for a couple of minutes before turning up the AI emulation level on his buckley. "Suzie, please pull up and display or play the most recently transmitted file."

"Are you sure you want me to do that, boss? I have half a terabyte of files that were dumped to my system in the past two minutes. Well, dumped to my enhanced system storage through an index."

"Great. Just great. I want you to find a particular file. It's a warning order memo from General Pennington and it could be text, audio, audio-vid, or even full holo."

"Found it. It's a compressed holographic file."

"Compressed? What's the rest of all that data?"

"Um . . . It appears to be a complete set of maintenance manuals for the waste reclamation systems on an RZ-400 class freighter."

"That figures." He sighed. "Any idea how you get a divorce from an AID?"

"No . . . But I'd be happy to find that out for you. Would you like me to search the database of Galactic law and precedent?"

"No! Don't start that search! Just play the memo."

The white-haired young-old man appeared only from the shoulders up, automatically oriented to face him. "Colonel, I need you to call me back ASAP. We have received a mission for DAG, hooah?" Beside his head, a mostly flat map of the northeast rift zone of Africa appeared, obsolete political borders outlined on it for convenience, with a blinking red dot on it roughly halfway down Ethiopia.

"The Darhel Gistar Group has leased a mining concession to extract tantalum and niobium in the old Oromo area of the rift. The Awasa mine has been taken over by terrorist raiders, of unknown affiliations. The mine is being held by these hostiles, and is believed to be being looted at this time, hooah? DAG's mission is to proceed to the former Ethiopia as expeditiously as tactically feasible and retake the mine, holding it until Gistar replacement personnel and their private security detachment have been reinstated and firmly reestablished. Rules of engagement for these hostiles will be optimized for maximum speed and efficiency, and for maximum protection of the security of DAG personnel and surviving Indowy labor forces. Prisoners for interrogation are not, say again, are not a desired objective. You will, of course, be authorized to take and secure surrendered prisoners, where practical, as colonization volunteers for off-planet, privatized security details. Seems it would be right up their alley, anyway, hooah. Get me some preliminary time on target options and call me back by ten hundred hours, Sierra time."

Great. That left him about half an hour to get with Mueller and run some sims. He was also going to need his AID, if she would behave. He considered ways to butter her up before grabbing a dry towel and his gym bag from the locker room on his way out the door. No time to shower and change here. First thing was to get back and take her out of his drawer. If he picked her up as soon as possible and started carrying her around immediately, she'd want to take the opportunity to prove her usefulness. It had certainly worked before. Besides, he was good and warmed up and wouldn't feel the cold on the short jog back to the HQ. Not much, anyway. He groaned as he stepped outdoors into the icy wind. Full sprint. Definitely go for the full sprint. Thank God it was dry.

Sergeant George Mauldin looked a lot like his dad. He was bit on the short side and the constant training at DAG kept him solidly muscled. Standing still, he tended to look awkward, with arms too long for his body. The grace with which he moved, a combination of his mother's influence and lifelong martial arts training, belied his gawky appearance. His hair was a light, muddy-apricot color. He hadn't entirely escaped Papa O'Neal's red hair, but Shari's blondness had muted the shade. He kept it cut in an old-fashioned high and tight style, so there wasn't as much of it to see except in good light. What really gave him away was the fair, ruddy skin. Very red, when he'd been working out—which was most of the time, including now.

About an hour into the day's weight program, he was outside the gym cooling off with a sports drink and an energy bar. Even in the cool of November on Lake Michigan, most of the members of DAG used the outdoors as a quick way to drop some of the excess heat built up during the day's training.

He wasn't surprised to see the colonel step outside in his workout shorts, despite the cold. After all, the colonel was a juv, more than capable of keeping up, and trained as hard as any of his officers or men. What surprised him was watching Colonel Mosovich take off at a hard sprint for the headquarters building, towel around his neck and gym bag in his hand. Colonels didn't do that, not in George's limited experience. Something was up.

George was something of a fan of gadgets. Around his neck with the dog tags he carried a miniature PDA that would take a low-emulation buckley with a minimal overlay. About the size of one of the dog tags, it naturally was voice access only. He picked it up and addressed it, "Carrie, call Major Kelly for me."

CHAPTER SIXTEEN

The fountain plashed softly in one corner of Michelle's office. The breeze today smelled of apple blossoms and rain. The ceiling gave the impression of clouds moving in an overcast sky. In another corner, a sohon tank stood, containing its mass of nannite jelly and some as yet ill-defined parts and bits, whose purpose and final assembly pattern were indecipherable to any of the few dozen Indowy who came and went in her private space. She knew what her apprentice must be thinking: that whatever it was, it must be very important and delicate indeed to merit the personal attentions of a Michon Mentat. The apprentice, like the dozens of others on her personal work crew outside, would ask no questions. If he needed to know something, she would tell him. Besides, they knew that there was every likelihood that anything a mentat took on personally was a matter for those whose wisdom exceeded their own. An apprentice's teaching emphasized that if he did not involve himself in matters that did not concern him, he could make no embarrassing or damaging mistakes.

Michelle O'Neal's Indowy apprentice was twitching with excitement, despite years of Sohon discipline, and despite having shown the self-discipline to earn the position of primary apprentice on her work crew. She ignored it as understandable in one just entering his sixth decade—not considering that she herself was close to the same age. For one thing, he had just been entrusted with the great secret of the existence of rapid transit this morning—a secret only a handful of masters held. For another, he was going to travel by that almost miraculous method himself, this very day. For a third, this important job, if he completed it with wisdom, was to be the final test of his ability to function in the journeyman post he would hold provisionally until the assignment was complete. It was a great honor, and the apprentice—journeyman, she corrected herself—was not presently operating a tank. She could allow him some high spirits on his big day.

"It's important that you understand both your job and the reasons for it. The Darhel Epetar Group has done something very unwise. Unwise to the point that the appropriate people have decided upon the appropriate responses. The Darhel Gistar Group is neither particularly wise nor particularly unwise, but happens to have a ship conveniently positioned in the Dulain area—never mind how. A group of humans, also neither particularly wise nor particularly virtuous, happens to have been set in motion by others to assemble the rudiments of a cargo with no planned shipping. That is, if a ship suddenly becomes available to carry it, they can appear to have merely scraped a cargo together on short notice, without any prior plan. The Epetar ship will be late to drop off its cargo of humans and pick up a mixed cargo of uninitialized Sohon headsets and tools. The Epetar ship will have defaulted on its shipping contract—ordinarily a matter of simple fines. In this case the Rontogh factor will have rebooked the cargo onto the conveniently available, and timely, Gistar vessel. The Epetar ship will not want to depart with empty cargo holds. They will book the cargo 'hastily assembled' by the humans." She faced the journeyman with quiet, serene eyes. If she had any personal feelings about this matter, they didn't show.

"Obviously, this would normally be a minor annoyance and profit loss," she continued. "The Epetar ship would simply skip its next stop and jump directly to its third scheduled port of call. This is where the human plan against Epetar would ordinarily fail. Because of Epetar's gross lack of wisdom, we will help the plan to succeed. The Epetar ship will also be late for its third port of call. This is the reason for your assignment.

"Remember, for purposes of the station's employment log, you have just debarked from the ship *High Margins*. With your orders from me, neither the ship's real crew nor the station's crew will gossip or pry. The station master is Aem Beilil. You will convey my message to him to expedite the loading of Gistar shipping and delay the loading of Epetar shipping, and to do so unobtrusively. He is to discreetly facilitate the operations of humans with the replacement cargo, who will stall the loading of the Epetar ship after it is irrevocably committed. The humans will most likely seem sincere but incompetent. This is not to put him off dealing with them. They are neither. Do you have any questions about your assignment?" The question was rhetorical. The instructions were clear.

"Mentat O'Neal," the young Indowy asked tentatively, "isn't the Epetar Group the one that holds your contract for—"

"This decision comes from those far wiser than myself," she said, holding the little green Galactic's eyes until his ears narrowed in embarrassment at his own presumption. The only people who would ordinarily be considered wiser than a mentat—any mentat—would be major clan heads or Tchpth policy planners. Michelle would never have involved herself in large-scale Galactic politics without the sanction of higher authority. Wxlcht's seemingly casual comments over a game of aethal would, in the military, have amounted to a direct order. In the hierarchy of established Galactic wisdom, almost everyone took the "suggestions" of Tchpth planners of any rank very seriously indeed. She did not like to think that personal friendship might have colored such a major decision, but was not about to let minor misgivings divert her from following the considered advice of someone whose wisdom was as far above her own as hers was above—well, above her sister's, for example.

"We will be going now." She took his hand, then released it as they appeared in a purplish-brown maintenance closet. The intense crowding in the destination space was unremarkable to him, but he did startle slightly at the abruptness of the transition. He only had an instant to blink before she was gone, leaving him alone with his new job.

Cally was on the last leg of her morning five-mile run. With the buckley clipped to one hip and a supplemental speaker clipped to the other side, she had music that projected to her own ears in stereo with little leakage. The sound was a bit scratchy. The speaker was older than the girls, having been part of her shopping splurge on the moon after the escape from Titan Base. That is, before she found out Stewart was alive. After he'd tracked her down in a bar, valiantly trying to drown her sorrows, her stay had been a frenzy of activity as they found a priest, put him under seal of the confessional before enlisting his cooperation, got married secretly, and stole precious private moments. All of this had had to be managed as she gave the performance of her life for Granpa and Tommy, moping around and pretending to be heartbroken and bereaved, slipping away here and there for a few hours on the pretext of shopping and long walks alone through the endless, anonymous corridors of Heinlein Base. The corridor she'd seen the most was a rent by the hour strip in the red light district where she and Stewart had snatched a furtive, rushed, passionate, and pitifully brief honeymoon.

On returning to Earth, she had found through experimentation that a heavy-duty workout schedule would keep about twenty pounds of Sinda fat off without her having to constantly starve herself. Twenty pounds less helped. A lot. So she ran, she lifted weights, she swam, and she danced. While the girls were at school, she fit as much general training in as she could around the normal martial drills—unarmed combat, shooting, climbing. She hated the climbing. Her morning run was the workout she enjoyed most, next to her dancing.

The morning was cold, doubly so with the wind blowing off the ocean. She wore longjohns under her jeans. Without them, she would have frozen in just the worn denim, the wind biting right through the holes in one knee and around her back pockets and belt loops. Her breath frosted in a small puff that trailed away as she ran through it.

The next moment she was on her ass on the ground, having crashed into her sister.

"Ouch." Michelle said, rubbing the back of her neck. "Are you usually unaware of your surroundings?"

"*Unaware?* You weren't there, and then you were. I was watching the dunes and the shoreline, okay?" The blonde grimaced, brushing sand off her jeans. "What do you need?"

"That is the right question. I will use the vernacular to make sure you understand me the first time. I need to know about your husband. Spill it."

"What husband?" Cally asked, too quickly.

"I do not have time for this. I have more than enough to do on my end. Your former lover, now husband, James Stewart, is alive and getting himself involved in high level Galactic politics. You know it, and I need the details. Tell them to me," she said.

"I'd love to know how you found that out. Not that it's any of your business. And I don't know what the fuck you're talking about with the Galactic politics line. You know talking about this could get us both killed, right?"

"No, it is failing to talk about it that could get us killed," the mentat said solemnly.

"I meant him and me 'us,'" Cally grumbled.

"Oh. Why would you tolerate association with humans that would—nevermind. I need you to tell me the details of his plotting."

"Not that I'm not doing everything I can to keep you alive, but to help you I need more information about what you want to know and why," the assassin said, breath frosting the air as she panted.

"Keeping secrets is more difficult than you imagine. Are you telling me that you do not know about his economic plots against the Epetar Group? Plots that coincide with your theft of a large amount of value from them," Michelle accused.

"*What?*" Cally was beginning to feel like a broken record. "He wouldn't. He couldn't have. I didn't tell him . . ." She thought for a moment. "If he knew how big my commission was for selling the code keys to you, you don't think he could have figured out where it came from? How?"

"You have almost no experience of business, do you?" Her sister sighed. "It does not matter if you knew about this or not. I need you to find out exactly what he is doing and his timetable."

"I'm not going to do anything that might get him killed," his wife said.

"That is an ironic statement. I know you can keep a secret—usually. You can tell Grandfather not to worry. I do not intend to hurt your husband's plans. Presently, they are likely to fail. I find myself in the unenviable position of having to ensure their success."

"I'd rather keep Granpa out of this."

"Grandfather does not know of your marriage?" Michelle looked shocked. "I had thought you were more mature than to keep that kind of secret for our clan head. I am sorry I do not have the time to have that conversation. If you do not know his plans, I need you to discover them, quickly. Starting with whatever he is plotting on Dulain, and proceeding from there."

"Dulain? What the—" Cally shook her head, interrupting herself, "Never mind. Just because I didn't mean to leak anything and I'm pissed off at him over it doesn't mean I'm going to help screw him over without damned good reason. You promise you're only going to help him?"

"I cannot believe you think I would lie about something like that." The mentat looked genuinely shocked.

"Fine, but I hope you don't need it soon, because arranging meetings with him isn't easy or quick."

"I know he is on the moon. Tell your employers you are making a courier run for me. All you have to do is get him to tell you the information I need. The broad plan, and all the details you can get me. You and I won't need to meet afterwards, I will simply listen in."

"You will not!" Cally blushed. "We're going to be busy. You just keep your mentat mind out of there."

"Fine. I do not have time to argue, I am very busy working the prototype in around my other work commitments. Please be on the next courier flight."

"Delivering what? What am I supposed to be taking you and why?"

"Invent something. I'm sure that will not be a problem for you, as your dramatic skills far exceed mine." There might have been something vaguely disapproving in the way she said it. She was so closed that it was impossible to tell. Cally couldn't even say anything back. Her sister was gone.

Saturday 11/20/54

The hotel room was clean enough. Maybe. Stewart might have said the place had seen better days except that, sadly, it probably hadn't. The walls were cheap white stucco, probably slapped right over the lunar equivalent of cinder block. One wall was simply the decorative brick of the corridor outside painted a glossy white—barren cheapness trying to masquerade as decorating panache. The blue patterned carpets were dingy, tinged brown with dirt up next to the walls. The paint on everything was fresh and clean, like someone had been desperately trying to pretend the place was not a dump. It had been the best anonymous privacy he could arrange in the base's dusty underbelly on short notice. It also featured two double beds instead of one king. They'd just have to get very close.

"Okay, what the hell was so important?" He addressed his wife, a pin-up perfect picture even in old jeans, who had arrived before him and now sat on the edge of the bed nearest the door, legs crossed. Anyone else would have been leaning back. Cally sat, spine straight, weight balanced forward, elbows in, hands in her lap. It was body language Stewart associated with the real Cally, Cally without masks. No masks, just defensive as all hell. A muscle jumped in his cheek as his jaw clenched as he took in her disconcertingly neutral expression. She was really pissed off about something. Unfortunately, being called out of business meetings on practically no notice for a dangerous face-to-face rendezvous didn't have him in a receptive mood.

"My sister Michelle sends her belated congratulations on our happiness." Her voice had that cheery lilt that southern women got when you were really in the shit.

"Oh fuck." He turned and walked a few steps away, his forehead clasped in a hand.

"She also sends congratulations on your debut into high level Galactic politics and asks what in the hell you thought you were doing," Cally said coldly.

"Excuse me?" He tried, and apparently failed, to look innocent. He felt like a husband caught with five sealed decks of cards after promising to give up poker.

"What did you do, or are you doing, to the Epetar Group?" She was giving him the deep freeze for sure.

After a long pause, he said, "I don't know if I can get into that, Cally."

"I see," she said shortly. "Fine. I'll go first. You started with what I told you about my windfall and extrapolated that, correctly, to my having stolen a set of nanogenerator code keys from the Darhel Pardal. You proceeded to plan and act on that information for the sake of your organization. Fine, my mistake for indiscretion. Now I'm going to compound that by providing more information. Whatever you planned is about to go all to shit and, your good luck, Michelle finds it in her own interests for it to succeed instead. No, that's not right. She finds it in Clan O'Neal's interests. That Indowy upbringing really took. She wants to smooth the way for it, but she needs to know what the hell you have planned."

She held up a hand to forestall his interruption. "Lest you think this is a setup, I know her situation. You're trying to screw Epetar, she wants them thoroughly screwed but can't have her fingerprints on it. For our part, let's just say that this ties in, in an acceptable way, to things we're working on, as well. Fortunately." She shrugged. "You've got two choices. You can take the gamble that she's telling the truth and talk to me, or you can tell me to go to hell and take your chances." She looked at her watch. "It's late. I'm tired. Think about it all you want. I'm grabbing a shower and going to bed." She snatched up a small bag and left him to his thoughts.

Even if he had a good poker face, a guy's wife could tell a lot about his thoughts from watching him think. It was a decent gesture to leave him alone to do his thinking. Or would be if she didn't have the place bugged to the gills. It was what he would have done. He pulled a small device out of his case and began a sweep.

"You don't need to bother sweeping the place. I didn't bug it. Just applied some creative static."

"If it's not bugged, how come you knew when I started looking?"

"I'm your wife, genius. Go ahead if it makes you feel better."

Damn but she was good. He sometimes forgot how good. Now, did he bring her in or pass? Obviously, bring her in. First, she *was* good. Good enough maybe even to read her mentat sister right for motivation. Second, said mentat sister, like all the Indowy-raised, would put her loyalty to her clan—as she saw it—above everything else. However much he disapproved of Michael O'Neal, Senior, for letting his son continue to think he was dead, Michelle had to know her grandfather was alive, which would make him the O'Neal clan head. Third, and perhaps most importantly, Michelle could have sunk Stewart himself any time she wanted, and still could, just by pointing a finger. She didn't need proof. Darhel paranoia would kick in and that would be that. Helping it succeed was the only possible reason she could have for wanting the full plan.

It still messed with his sense of reality to call people with the highest levels of the Indowy's production voodoo "mentats." He kept having flashbacks to a fucking long science fiction movie he'd seen years ago with freaky looking human calculators. He knew how it had all happened. When they translated Indowy labor ranks into English, or coined words for them, they had classified all the levels at the top of the list as different grades of "adept." Well, that had been great until they found out that there was another voodoo level above the adept grades that was so qualitatively beyond them as to be a whole different ballgame.

There was apparently a very sudden, massive jump in ability from the top grades of adept to this new thing. It hadn't been on the lists of Indowy labor ranks because it wasn't one. All the other grades had a set wage rate for assigned work. These folks had variable pay based on negotiated contracts, and were the direct employers of the various Indowy work teams. As much as you could translate something as individualistic as "employment" to Indowy, anyway. So they needed another word for someone super-skilled, something so way up there as to be almost unimaginable. Some wit had borrowed the term "mentat" from the same book that inspired the old movie. Stewart still couldn't hear someone spoken of as a mentat without picturing a fat guy with toothbrushes for eyebrows.

He was flipping through the channels on the holoviewer, mostly reruns with the occasional hologized prewar show, when his wife came out of the dinky hotel bathroom, still vigorously toweling her hair. He immediately did a double take.

"Footy pajamas? You wear flannel footy pajamas?" He managed to keep his jaw from dropping, but only just.

"Sometimes," she squeaked. "They keep it damned cold in some of these corridors. Besides, I didn't have my good stuff with me when I booked my ticket up here. They were a present from the girls," she admitted self-consciously, walking over to the wall heater and fiddling with it.

"I checked. It's broken. We're stuck with central ambient," he said.

She held her hand over the weak stream of warm air coming from the vent, glared at it and gave it a kick. The result was a light dent added to its already battered appearance, and louder noises coming from the thing as it shifted into higher gear. She made a satisfied harrumph and came back to sit on the bed beside him, cross-legged so that the toes of the absurd flannel pajamas peeked out from under her knees. He silently vowed to dispose of the offending garment as quickly as possible. Over against the wall, the heater lapsed back into an apathetic wheeze.

Cally rolled her eyes at it, brushing her hair back behind one ear and looking at him expectantly. "So, what's it gonna be?" she asked.

"Fine. You're in. Here's how the plan goes," he began. "First, you made Epetar's ship three weeks late shipping out for Dulain. They needed that money plus their human cargo to pay for a big load of tech gear for Diess. The gear is high-margin—you've interrupted an extremely valuable run. I don't know if you knew it, but when cargo ownership transfers between Darhel groups it's strictly cash on the barrel head. No FedCreds, just hard value in hand. FedCreds aren't really Galactic money, anyway. Not the way we think of money. Close, but not the same. So anyway, Epetar's ship had to wait for more cash to get here, or it would have been pointless to go on to Dulain. From Dulain, that ship's scheduled to go on to Diess, then Prall, and beyond that is irrelevant for purposes of the plan. The point is it's a very high profit, complicated route with half a dozen stops before it comes back with a mixed hold of goods for Earth and the Fleet repair facilities on Titan. You don't see a lot of Galactic goods on the Earth market because—well, never mind. You can't learn the shipping business in a day," he said. "Are you following me so far?"

She nodded, gesturing for him to go on.

"The important point from all that is that being late puts the Epetar Group in breach of their shipping contracts with the groups that administer those planets, or otherwise own the cargo. Technically, once the Darhel are in breach, the groups on those planets are free to renegotiate shipping with anyone. In practice, it virtually never happens because the odds of another ship turning up with an empty hold before the late ship gets into port are infinitesimal. Contracts usually only get renegotiated if a ship is lost. Then any group positioned right races a ship there to try to snap up the route. Time is money, so the first group to get there usually gets the agreement. I'm going off at a tangent again. The point is, if another group can get a ship there that can carry the cargo after Epetar is late but before they finally show up, the factor for the Darhel group that owns the cargo will deal with the ship that's there instead of waiting for the late one. Obviously, the ship poaching the route also has to be carrying enough money to buy the cargo, or the deal won't happen. Another reason a late ship is usually embarrassing, but not that big a deal. You see where I'm going with this."

"Maybe not. I think you're saying the Tong's getting into the shipping business, but I didn't know you had even one cargo ship, much less enough money to buy a cargo. You can't be that rich. Besides, the Darhel would never sell to you, money or not."

"You're right, we don't. What we did was slip the word to a Darhel group with the money and ships they could divert in the right places to take advantage of the chance. It never would have been possible without communications changes since the end of the war. It's ruinously expensive to send a message on one, but when a message is time-sensitive, it can be worth it."

"I see how you've set up Gistar to screw Epetar, sort of. But what I don't see is where you get anything out of it. It's not like one group of Darhel is any better than another. They're all amoral bastards who would sell their own mothers—or whatever it is they have—to make a buck."

"Yeah, they are. Which is where we come in. No Darhel captain is going to run from one planet to another with an empty hold if he can help it. He'd end up running inventory on fertilizer sacks on some agricultural planet in the ass end of nowhere. So he's going to look for whatever cargo he can scrape up quickly to at least show he *tried* to offset the loss. If he can blame the remaining loss off on some other sap, his career just might survive. The Tong does have one courier ship we lease from the Himmit. Officially, it's a Himmit courier ship. At the same time we leaked the Epetar intel to Gistar, we also dispatched our courier along that trade route to get our people together assembling cargos we could buy or make cheap and sell dear. Cargos just worthwhile enough to make up all or part of an Epetar captain's pickup cargo."

"Then you use the cover to sabotage their ships? That's insanely risky," she said.

"Hell no. Business. Think business. We're gonna shear the bastards like a fucking sheep. If we can swing it with the Indowy dock crews, we'll draw out the agony by making sure Gistar's loading and unloading gets expedited, and stalling Epetar after loading starts so they can't cut their losses and run. Ideally, we figure when they know they've been skunked out of Dulain, they'll skip Diess and go straight for Prall. But maybe not. If we can foist another pickup cargo on them at Prall or Diess, then we get to skin them twice. Or more."

"So what if they don't take the bait and you get stuck with all these cargoes on your hands that you can't sell?"

"No problem. We either ship them out piecemeal as filler around the edges of other shipments, or we sell them locally. Our people are supposed to scrape together things that are salable locally if it comes to that. Admittedly, it could take them a long time to sell off the inventory."

"Yeah, well. Michelle says it's all about to fall apart." She brushed a hand at her hair impatiently. He remembered it as a Sinda trait that had stuck.

"I hope not. I stuck my neck out setting it up. I'd sure like to know how she plans on 'helping' without being obvious about it. The stakes are pretty high."

"You have no idea," Cally said. Her lips tightened as he looked at her curiously. "No, I'm not bringing you in on all that. Too bad. That's what you get for using what I said, anyway. Michelle and Clan O'Neal, respectively, have big personal stakes in seeing you succeed." She seemed impervious to the look he gave her. "No. I needed to know your plans. You don't have a need to know our reasons. You ought to just be thanking your lucky stars that when you got us caught it was Michelle, and that she needed something from you. Besides, I'm still pissed off."

He moved closer to her and started kissing a particularly sensitive spot behind her ear.

"Well, somewhat pissed off, anyway," she said, burying her fingers in his hair.

"So let me kiss it away," he breathed against her neck, lifting a hand to her collar to begin undoing the snaps on the childish pajamas. "Let me wipe it away and wipe away the memories of all the jerks the job keeps hitting you with. Nobody here but us two," he was kissing downward, between her breasts, when she stiffened.

"What the hell is that supposed to mean?" She shifted out from under him and sat up, staring at him.

"Just that they don't matter. They don't matter a damn." He stroked her hair. "I don't blame you. I don't like your job, but I knew about it when I married you and I don't blame you at all, love."

"That's nice. What 'they' are we talking about, exactly?" she asked icily.

"Hey, calm down, Cally. Nobody in particular, just, well, anybody you have to . . . encounter . . . in your work. It's a tough job, and you've got nothing to be ashamed of," he reassured. "That's why I never, ever ask. And I won't."

"You mean—" she broke off, pitching him aside and storming across the room, turning to face him. "I don't fucking believe this!" She ran a hand through her hair, breathing heavily, voice rising to just short of a screech. "I just don't—the whole time we've been married, you think I've been fucking other *guys*? You do, don't you? Oh, my God." She sank down into the plastic desk-chair and stared off at the wall, unseeing. "I don't believe this."

"What?" Stewart's face was a sickly ashen-gray. Aware that he had screwed up, badly, he hesitated. His normally quick mind felt like it had been stuffed full of fog. "Of course I—" he began, tapering off to silence. He held a hand out to her, but let it drop when she didn't respond. "You didn't—I didn't—oh, hell."

When he would have walked over to her, she flinched away.

"Oh, my God, Cally, I'm so sorry. I thought—I guess I *didn't* think." He tried to think of something else, anything else he could say that might make things better instead of worse. In the end, he just sat. After an eternity of her staring like that, refusing to talk to him, he stood and stuck his feet into his shoes. At the door he turned back. "I'd like to have breakfast with you," he said.

"Fine." She didn't even look up as he stepped out and closed the door.

In the morning, over breakfast, they made up. Then they proved the old adage that make up sex is some of the best sex of all. It was good, but there was something hollow in the pit of James Stewart's stomach as he saw her to her shuttle and watched it take off, saying goodbye to her for the umpteenth time in their marriage. Damn the risks that had kept them from being together.

Monday 11/22/54

Gray cubicle walls didn't look any better when they were made from Galplas instead of fabric, steel, and plastic. In fact, it was worse. The entire cube and desk had been extruded in place, defeating most of the purpose of modularity in the original design. The whole thing was the gray of cinder-blocks, rendered even more dismal by the absolute lack of texture—a feature of working directly for a subsidiary of a Galactic group.

Most of the workers in Human Welfare's personnel department did what they could within the company's policy of one plant, one still holo—usually of a spouse or partner, one dynamic wall image of dimensions less than point seven five square meters. There was scarcely room for more. It hadn't taken long after the advent of really efficient buckleys before some wonk had noted that no paper and no phone meant none of the files and office supplies that typically went to serve paperwork and phones. The modern worker needed little more than a chair, enough space for his buckley to project his current work, a place to rest his coffee cup, and a small drawer to hold data cubes. The time and motion study that followed ensured that there would be little more than that inside an individual's cubicle. The name had stuck, even though the shape was now more like a rectangular box stood upright than an actual cube. The divider walls were two meters high, to prevent each person's coworkers from presenting a visual distraction that could reduce productivity.

The tiny desk areas had a single, unintentional benefit. A worker had only to slide back his chair to talk to the guy next to him. Samuel Hutchins now did so.

"Hey, Juice. Do you have a couple of people who maybe came in with some . . . new friends and family . . . and are open to returning the favor?"

"What, got some people you're trying to get on? Didn't know you were low on cash."

"If I can." He shrugged. "You know how it is."

"Sure," she said, scribbling down a couple of names. "You're always good about returning your favors."

"I try to be," he said. Hutchins had been most particular about returning his favors all his life, which was mostly over now. At fourteen, he had been right at the upper age limit of children considered for shipment to Indowy worlds. If his father hadn't been the leader of the loyal opposition in Parliament, he wouldn't have been sent at all. On Adenast, he had frequently wondered whether that wouldn't have been for the best. He was just too old to adapt. He had no talent for languages, and so never became fluent in any Indowy dialects. He had taken sedatives for claustrophobia every day of his time living among the Indowy. Ordinarily, that would simply have been his lot in life. Nobody paid to ship humans from some other world back to Earth, and he had no talents for jobs that would have made enough FedCreds to pay for passage—and would have been constrained by contracted debts to remain on Adenast if he had. Michelle O'Neal, bless her soul, had somehow managed to obtain him a cabin job on a freighter leaving Adenast for Earth thirty years ago. The job was another he had no talent for, resulting, as she had no doubt intended, in his employment being terminated and him being booted out the door on Titan Base. Earning further passage to Earth, part paid in cash, and part paid in the most disagreeable of ship chores, he had found difficult, but possible.

His debts, of course, had dictated that he seek his employment through Darhel firms. Nothing else paid enough to service the interest. Hence his present situation, at long last, in a position to return the single biggest favor he'd ever owed a living soul.

So here he was in his sixties, not juved and never likely to be a candidate for such, working in a position where, until now, the greatest job benefit was the blessed, however fake, solitude of his workspace. Handsome and agile in his youth, Sam now sported arthritic knees, a large bald patch, and a bad comb-over. His own grandfather, who Sam knew he resembled, had worn his hair just the same. The younger generations would never understand loss the way the war babies did. It could make you do funny things, sometimes. Maybe his near-fanatical dedication to paying debts, monetary or favors, somehow came out of his shuffled teen years. Maybe the repayment of favors was just the one bit of Indowy culture that took. His common sense, however, was all wisdom acquired from age.

When Miss O'Neal asked her favor, that common sense had made him sit on any personal curiosity, or any heroic tendency to volunteer for more than she asked. He had a feeling that whatever she was planning, if he stuck his nose in it, the only place he'd be was in the way.

This part of the favor was simple enough. In personnel, they did it all the time. The boss was Indowy raised. The Darhel were more used to employing Indowy laborers than human. Indowy always placed great emphasis on clan connections in hiring. The idea that nepotism could be a bad thing was totally alien to their species' nature. Humans applying for jobs in facilities like this one sometimes had relatives on the job already. When they didn't, friends on the job were the next best thing. The bosses liked everybody's relationships interlinked—it bought organizational loyalty when many of the acts that the organization perpetrated were grossly illegal. That, along with very large salaries. Personnel grunts like himself, faced with the impossible requirement of finding employees connected with other employees in a disorganized postwar world, managed by "people" whose understanding of human nature was sketchy, did what any good paper pushers would have done. They made friendships and kinships up wholesale and greased the palm of the right employee to make the "relationship" pass casual inspection. Employees who had gotten their job by this process were universally willing to supplement their salaries in exchange for passing on the favor to someone else. As a system, it was a bit nuts, but it kept everybody happy. He now had enough names in hand to make all his target applicants look desirable to the bosses, and would owe Juice a return favor.

CHAPTER SEVENTEEN

The first thing George noticed about his interviewer was her legs. They were legs to die for. Long, slim, perfectly shaped, leading up to a fiery red skirt that could have doubled as a wide belt. The skirt was literally fiery, done in a shifting pattern of hot coals and flames. Those were two-dimensional, as holographic clothing tended to detract from the wearer's assets.

She had her legs crossed and turned away from him as she stood to shake his hand. He would have completely missed her name if they hadn't already told him who he'd be interviewing with. He thanked God that he'd long ago formed the habit of leering only discreetly. Still, he got the feeling that she didn't miss much, which reminded him that dying for those legs would be a genuine possibility.

She ran her fingers through long, black hair streaked and tipped with glowing metallic red as she resumed her seat, crossing her legs deftly to preserve what modesty she had left by the barest margin imaginable.

"Hello, Mark. I'm pleased to meet you. I'm a very brief interviewer. One way or the other, I make up my mind quickly. Your statistics credentials are impeccable for our needs," she said. "Why do you want to work here?"

"I like living on Earth. The money and your company's status go a long way towards making sure I won't end up swept onto a slow boat to Dulain," he answered. "And, candidly, you pay well."

The nails of one hand tapped on her knee. He noticed idly that they were black tipped with a masterful illusion of dripping blood. She was certainly intent on making a specific impression.

"The primary reason I'm interviewing you has to do with a job that isn't on your resume. You worked at Celini and Gorse Consulting from 2048 to 2051. You've done a nice job of covering it. You were one of the few accountants who managed to come out of that without prison time and without speaking a word ill of your employers or any of your coworkers—and especially of the investors. You don't run off at the mouth. We handle highly confidential business, so we prize that attribute. You're a practical, goal oriented man. I like that." She smiled. It was a charming smile that did reach her eyes. It gave no indication of the cold psychopath he knew lived behind those warm, brown, feline orbs. She was good; highly dangerous even to him. He smiled back with what he hoped was the right degree of polite avarice.

"You do your homework," George, aka Mark, said. "Your own investors, of course, have no lack of resources when they want something. It reassures me that I can trust your organization's ability to meet its generous commitments. I like to be able to trust the people I work for."

"Mutual trust, backed by natural situational guarantees, is essential to our corporate mission. We can certainly offer you better job security than any other offers you might have. No worries about getting fired if your dirty little secret comes to light. We know, and consider your discretion an asset." She pressed a couple of buttons on her PDA. "I see here that Joseph Espinoza is your cousin?" she asked.

"Yes. We spent a lot of time together growing up."

This smile was predatory rather than charming. Even though he was sure it was calculated to the nth degree, a finger of ice prickled on the back of his neck.

"If he's your cousin, I'm your mother," she said. "Relax." She waved a hand as he fought the sweat trying to emerge on his upper lip. "You just passed another of my little tests. You're resourceful, and you go along with the system instead of getting your briefs in a twist the first time you have to bend a rule. Apparent kinship links keep the investors happy. See, I can be pragmatic, too." Her playful grin, though perfect, put him in mind of a piranha.

She stood, perforce drawing him to his feet as well. "As long as you never break any of *my* rules, we'll get along fine. The first of which is that from this moment onward, you will never, ever lie to me. In return, I will never ask about anything you did before you worked here. My rules are simple, reasonable. I expect loyalty and obedience. Which constitutes doing your job competently, unquestioningly, and keeping your mouth shut. From your record, that should be easy enough." She cupped his cheek with one hand. He could feel her nails against his jawline and had to think of least squares graphs to avoid embarrassing himself, amazingly. "Breaking my simple, easy rules is a termination offense. Understand?"

He nodded, swallowing—staying in the role. He wouldn't have thought it was possible for anyone to look coldly sociopathic and gleeful at the same time. One or the other, but not both, not that charmingly terrifying way. It was an expression he might have to practice. It could be useful for interrogations.

"Great. Still want the job?" she asked cheerfully.

Her mercurial moods were frightening to a professional. The best swordsman doesn't fear the second best. He fears the tyro who knows just enough to be dangerous. He vowed to interact with her as little as possible, and to handle her as carefully as a crate of Tennessee antimatter balls.

"Yes, definitely," he said.

"Can you start Monday?"

"No problem."

"Then we're all set. Give your salary requirements to personnel on your way out. As long as they're reasonable, they'll be met. If they're not, we'll give you our own offer on Monday." She put a hand on the small of his back, ushering him out the door. He didn't flinch.

"Got any plans to celebrate tonight?" she asked.

"Dinner with my girlfriend."

"Been seeing each other long?" Her teeth were a glaring white against the retro red lipstick.

"We're pretty serious. She's applying for a reception position." He shrugged at the raised eyebrows. "For a liberal arts major, your live reception jobs are one of the best paying gigs on offer."

"I see. Thank you for telling me. In spite of all our fictional interlinks, we do try to get real ones when we can. You just gave your girlfriend an edge. I hope she's appreciative." Now her grin contained a distinct air of sexual predation.

He wordlessly conveyed a certain opportunistic interest, eliciting an extra sparkle from the brown eyes. "I'm sure she will be."

"Until Monday." Prida Felini turned and walked away, offering him a stunning rear view which he took open advantage of, deciding a leer was in character after all.

Cally tucked a strand of her shining black bob behind one ear. Despite Harrison's edict of "no more color changes," he had managed to find her a temporary hair color that she could wear for a month or two before it washed out naturally, with no further damage. He claimed it was protein nourishing, moisturizing, and shaft-reconstructing, whatever that meant. All Cally knew was that he had made her swear to God she'd brush a hundred strokes, four times a day, with a boar-bristle brush. Whatever. She'd do it because he knew his stuff. He could worry about the damn details.

Her contacts were a deep brown that was nearly black, skin left ghost pale. She was eye-catching, and she was meant to be. The adversary would be watching George, and her intent was to leave an indelible impression as his girlfriend. The watchers would have no trouble describing her, making security slot her automatically into a known category when she showed up at his job. She would be meeting him for lunch, daily when possible, until mission execution.

Girlfriends were curious. She wouldn't get past the security checkpoint until and unless she was called in to interview. However, up until they got someone else in or went to plan B, she would be the designated man for up close and leisurely reconnaissance—everything through the front door and up to the checkpoint. George could give his full attention to all that was beyond the checkpoint, and the rest of the team to the other directions of approach to the target zone. So long as she behaved in character, she would be functionally invisible. Ogled, yes, but her curiosity unremarked.

George was late. She knew he thought of himself as habitually on time now, but his timeliness was merely relative to his prior habits. He tended to rationalize tardiness as in character for his current role, a result of extra scouting, or confined to the tradition of being fashionably late. People's self-deception got on Cally's nerves. She made every effort to root it out in herself whenever she found it, and felt everyone else, particularly people on her own team, should do the same.

Seven minutes past target time, he finally arrived.

She rose, walking around the table to kiss him, high on the cheek. "You're late," she whispered.

"Not much." He shrugged. "Besides, I made a wrong turn."

She favored him with a blinding smile. "We'll talk later," she promised softly, as he pulled her chair out and helped seat her.

"So. You obviously liked the job or you wouldn't have taken it. Tell me about it." She took his hand across the table and began playing with his fingers. "Did you meet your boss, sweetheart? What are you going to be doing? I want all the details."

He proceeded to establish his reputation for discretion with his doubtlessly watching employers by changing the subject.

When he ordered a split of one of West Under-Detroit's finest sparkling wines, she pretended a good cheer she certainly didn't feel. Wines of any type weren't her favorite thing. She supposed the buzz had to temporarily dull the taste buds of normal people, or some such.

"What was that?" she asked silently, tapping her fingers idly in an in-house variant of Morse Code. "Mark" had taken his hand back, slipping something out of his sleeve and palming it to his mouth. It couldn't have been for the watching eyes—she barely noticed it herself. It was odd.

He reclaimed her hand across the table, fingers twitching imperceptibly against her palm. "You know, the pill. Why waste the champagne?"

"What pill?" Her hair fell forward and she reached across with her other hand, tucking it back impatiently.

"Duh? The booze pill. You didn't bring one?" He took her other hand, staring soulfully into her eyes.

"What the fuck?" She squeezed his hands and gave a lovestruck sigh, taking her hands back to pickup her menu. "What looks good to you?" she asked aloud.

"I may just make a meal of the Oysters Rockefeller. Harry says there's not a bad thing on the menu here," he answered. "Whaddya mean 'what the fuck'?" His fingers pattered on the tablecloth. "Living under a rock for thirty years? The pill that turns your booze nannites off."

A flabbergasted look flickered across his face, quickly erased. "My god, you really don't know. Wow." He captured her hand, taking it to his lips.

She felt a gelatin capsule slip into the crease between her fingers and palm, and gripped it. She felt like an idiot. Slipping it into her own mouth with her next swallow of the straw-colored bubbles, she tried, unsuccessfully, to crush an odd mixture of pique and rage. Thirty years. She'd never felt as shut out of the professional "boy's club" as she did right now. Was she by God really the one single agent who hadn't known?

"The job's going to mean I'll have to find an apartment in Great Lakes," he said. Then, pretending to find something in her expression, which was actually rather wooden, continued, "You didn't realize? If I'd known you didn't, honey, I'd have told you the minute it came up. This could be the perfect time for us to try sharing an apartment the way we've been talking about. We could pick the new place together."

She smiled. Rather, the persona she was wearing did, feeling distant from the core of her self. "You've just sprung that on me. Give me a bit to take it in, darling." She focused on the menu again. "The picture of those oysters is tempting. I'll just have whatever you're having." She drained her glass and held it out to him for a refill.

He blinked, refilling it. She suppressed an evil grin. So she was alarming him now? Good, dammit.

The rest of the champagne, two mai-tais, and an after-dinner Irish coffee later, he was handling her like a nuke that might go off at any moment as he walked her out to his car. It made her want to giggle.

George's car was old, but clean. The faded blue paint showed a line of rust spots at door-ding height, increasing in size and frequency as they went downward, until finally there was no paint at all, only a lacy russet hem, legacy of driving through prior winters' salty slush.

He opened the door for Cally and she sat, inhaling the rich aroma of rust and cracking plastic. The thing was a real piece of shit. The carpet and floor mats were a compressed layer of grimy fibers matted with sand. A particularly dark splotch on the floorboard helped her place the other scent nagging at the back of her mind—old motor oil. She fought down her rising gorge.

Schmidt shut the door behind her, lifting it slightly to take the weight off the warped hinges. She wrinkled her nose as he walked around to the driver's seat, wishing she could get away with taking the train back. She didn't at all approve of his trade-craft over dinner and again, here in the car. The leers were a bit overacted. As they drove south into the darkness, she stared out the window, silently wishing the road wouldn't rock quite so much.

"Um!" She tugged at his arm, urgently. Evidently he'd been expecting it, because he swerved to the side of the road and stopped, sighing. A few minutes later she wiped her mouth and climbed back into the car, feeling much better. She must be sobering back up already.

As he pulled back onto the road, she resisted the impulse to look around for their tails. Obviously, she did need to keep up her end of the show. She leaned in against his arm, snuggling her head into his shoulder. It moved uncomfortably as he reached into the center console and handed her a little white tablet from a foil-papered roll.

"Breath mint?" he offered.

"Oh, thanks." She popped one onto her tongue, enjoying the minty fizz as the enzymatic cleaners went to work. She curled closer into his arm, reflecting that it would only take a slight turn to bring her left breast up against it. Well, serve him right if she did, for looking at her that way all evening. She turned in towards him.

"I'm lost. How far from your apartment are we?" she asked.

He sighed. "Less than ten minutes, honey."

Schmidt pulled his still very drunk colleague tightly against himself, kissing her deeply. Right now he didn't like her very much, even though the breath mint had made it possible to enjoy kissing her—too much. He could already see how this was going to be all his fault in the morning. The other side of that coin was that if he was going to be blamed anyway, he might as well make the most of it. Her mouth was fresh and cool. After her thirty years of killer professional training and experience, no pun intended, Cally O'Neal's full frontal attentions packed one hell of a wallop. The way he saw it, he could take his life into his hands with her and her pissed-off grandfather in the morning, or with her pissed off self right now if he pushed her away. Under the circumstances, he wisely chose immediate gratification and deferred risk. Not that he wouldn't have anyway, he admitted.

He had taken advantage of straight men's notorious lack of decorating taste to avoid spending the money refurbishing his cover apartment. It was pretty awful; he usually hated staying here. Tonight promised to be an exception to that rule. It was a good thing she was at least buzzed. The dirty white shag carpeting and beat up faux-wood paneling inside would have put any sober woman off. He unlocked the door behind her and, without breaking the kiss, maneuvered her back through it.

Considering a male operative had to be competent to extract required information from a source in whatever way it took, including any female source who took a liking to him, he wasn't too shabby at this game, himself. He was, therefore, stunned to find himself sitting on his ass on the floor, after about a minute and a half of practically doing each other in the doorway.

"I *hate* white shag carpeting," she spat at him, whirling and slamming the door behind her.

He stared at the empty space where she had been a moment before, butt stinging where he had landed, reflecting that he had never understood a woman less in his whole life.

Tuesday 11/23/54

The battle began as a war between two artificial intelligences. The aim was not to destroy property nor yet to take lives. The aim, at the beginning, was to try to drive each one crazy.

Fortunately, buckleys were pretty much always that way.

Clarty was a good Africa hand and loved technology. But he did not understand it. Take for example the "IR sensors" scattered around the perimeter.

Clarty knew that they picked up on infrared emissions, heat that is, from the warmth of any mammalian critter. What he did not know was how they worked.

Any large mammal generates an awful lot of heat. In the case of humans, enough to melt fifty pounds of ice in one day. However, because of IR sensors, human soldiers, spies and burglars had long before come up with IR defeating systems. Heat cloaks, thermo-paint, IR static generators, they were all designed to reduce the IR signature of a person to that of, say, a rabbit.

And there were many rabbit-sized creatures in Africa or any other "natural" area.

For that matter there were many creatures that produced as much IR signature as a human. The very simplest systems would then scan for human contour and outline but a ghillie cloak changed that and the system never could tell the difference between a human and, say, a baboon.

So the makers of the IR sensors had a choice between a system that would produce thousands of false positives or a system that couldn't spot a male human wearing the simplest of disguises.

Unless they threw in an AI. AIs could make "rational" judgments about whether there was a real threat or a hopping bunny.

But then there existed the question of just how to integrate the AI.

Still the only human AI, buckleys were the only choice. The IT geeks at the manufacturer understood the problems of buckleys far too well. Buckleys were notoriously unstable. Simply throwing a buckley onto the control interface was a sure recipe for disaster. And depending upon the number of IR sensors scattered around, one buckley might not be able to do all the decision making.

So Clarty's system worked like this.

There were IR sensors. They were not "smart." They were not "brilliant." They didn't have any processing to them at all beyond that necessary to convert IR into something a system could read.

Behind them, at the second tier, was a "smart" system that converted one or more sensors into data the buckley or buckleys could read.

At the very top of the hierarchy was a system that, based upon the number of sensors, generated medium emulation buckleys. These AIs would then consider the sensor data and determine if it was a real threat or not. They would sit there, day in and day out, looking at sensor data and deciding whether to cause an alarm.

Occasionally, they would get bored and cause a false alarm. The longer they were left in place, the more false alarms they would generate from sheer boredom. Each time the user reset the system, telling a "smart" program that it was a false alarm, it would be considered by a non-AI algorithm. When the buckleys got to a certain level of false positive, determined by the user or the overriding "smart" system, they would be reset and forget they had ever been there. And the cycle would start all over again. They would also be automatically reset if the "smart" system determined they were going AI gaga or if they started fighting incessantly, which was common.

None of this occurred at a level the user could see.

Clarty did not understand how his system worked.

DAG did.

That was the first of many differences of quality between the two groups. Differences of quality that had made coming up with an attack plan such a pain in the ass for Mosovich.

This was his first "real world" action with DAG. He wanted it to be professional, precise and good training. Because the best that could be said about Clarty's unit of "pirates" and his setup was that it was going to be a good training op for DAG.

There were so many many choices. It really became a question of what sort of command personality Mosovich wanted to project.

He could start with orbital battle lasers, normally used to take out heavy Posleen infestations but fully on-call for an op like this, to take out the sentries. Then DAG would come in right behind them in choppers or even shuttles and hammer into the middle of the compound. Good estimate of take-down of the entire compound was one minute twenty-three seconds. Snipers scattered around to take any leakers. Satellite and UAV surveillance to make sure nobody got away.

Simple, brutal, effective.

Training level? Minimal. Joie de vivre level? Zero. Coolness level? In the negatives.

He had no intention of taking so much as one casualty, whatever he did. But with such a simple op, making it interesting had real command benefits.

So he decided to start with causing a nervous breakdown in the "automated" system.

Buckley Generated Personality 6.104.327.068 was beyond bored. He'd been looking at really boring African countryside for nearly seven boring hours which was, to an AI, approximately a gazillion years by his calculation. He'd calculated pi to a googleplex decimal points. He'd tried to log onto a MMORPG and gotten kicked for being an AI, the bastards. He'd gotten into a three point two second argument, about thirty years to a human, with Buckley Personality 4.127.531.144 over whether a sensor reading was a monkey or an abat. Since all they had were these stupid ZamarTech IR sensors, who knew? He couldn't even ask anyone to check it out and adjust the system without setting of a bagillion alarms. They could have put in an interface that let the AI simply *ask* somebody to go tell them what something was, thereby increasing their functionality but noooo . . .

Now he was looking at another IR hit. The buckley did not "see" this as a human would; he did not see a smear of white on a black background. What the buckley received and processed was a large number of metrics. Horizontal area of total generated heat. Precise numerics of shape, thermal output fall-off, calculations of three-dimensional shape, vectors not only of the total blob but of portions. It then took all this information and compared it to a database of notable IR hits, ran all that through a complicated algorithm assigning a valid numeric likelihood of it being positive for a hostile human or animal then, at the last, applied "AI logic" to the situation.

"Looks like another abat to me," he transmitted, having applied "AI logic."

Or tried to in the face of Buckley Personality 4.127.531.144's utter stupidity.

"It's moving too fast and it's too large," 4.127.531.144 replied. "Jackal."

"No way," 6.104.327.068 argued. He was almost thirty minutes older than 4.127.531.144 and thought he knew damned well what an abat looked like in IR. "A jackal couldn't have taken that slope. It's 62 degrees at a minute of angle of .415 in the tertiary dimension! Abat can climb like that; jackals can't. I'd say chinchilla, but we're in Africa.

"Okay, then it's a Horton's monkey," 6.104.327.068 said. "Native to the area. They can climb. Same thermal characteristics. Quadrupedal, which this is. So there. Put that into your pipe and smoke it, youngster."

"They climb *trees*," 4.127.531.144 said seventeen nanoseconds later having accessed the Net and looked up Horton's monkeys.

"They're arboreal. They stay off the ground to avoid predators. They're notable for having a distinctive cry that sounds like icky-icky-pting . . . tuwop!"

"And if we had *audio* sensors that's what you'd hear you moron!"

"Dinosaur."

"Wet-behind-the-ears ignoramus . . ."

"There's another one," 4.127.531.144 said. "It's abat."

"It's *not* abat," 6.104.327.068 now denied. "Thermal characteristics are too low. Abat are pretty cold blooded for mammaloids. I don't care what you say, it's a tribe of Horton's monkeys."

"They're arboreal."

"Maybe they're moving territory or something." 6.104.327.068 accessed everything he could find on Horton's monkeys. "But they're arboreal."

"That's what *I* said."

"Then it's jackals."

"You're up to twenty hits," 4.127.531.144 replied. "Jackals don't move in groups that large. But Horton's monkeys do."

"They're arboreal."

"Maybe the're moving territory or something."

"That's what *I* said!"

The argument continued for an interminable twenty-three seconds of increasing Net access until the override system determined that the AIs were approaching complete failure, the repeated eletronic transmissions of insults was the cue that its algorithms was looking for, and deleted both personalities.

"Hello! What the hell? Where am I? What the fuck is this . . . ?"

Ninety-three seconds later, the system reset again.

The UAV was made of clear spider-cloth. One of the Cushitic sentries might have spotted it if he was looking just right and it occluded a star. Since Cushitic sentries didn't look at the stars, much, it was a reasonable risk sending it overhead. They could not have seen, but could otherwise sense, what it was releasing.

One of the sentries did indeed sense its release. He sniffed the night air, shivered slightly, and paid a bit more attention to his surroundings. He recognized that musk.

Posleen.

But the sensors would assuredly spot one of them.

✧ ✧ ✧

The toughest part of the plan had been finding the elephants.

Elephants had very large territories. And once the survival of the species had been assured, monitoring of the herds had dropped to nearly nothing. It was far too expensive to keep doing "just because."

So Mosovich had had to use satellite time to find the nearest herd. Then they had to get it moving in the right direction. *That* had taken time.

But in the meantime they had to get the buckleys properly prepared, anyway.

"Now you're seeing elephants? What, are they pink?"

"Yeah, I'm seeing elephants. Look, they're bang on for six sigma match!"

"You were seeing upland gorillas a second ago. Sixty of them. There aren't any upland gorillas in a thousand miles! Much less sixty of them. How many elephants?"

"Twenty-three. They're elephants I tell you!"

"It's a glitch in the system. Run another diagnostic. With all the false readings we've been having, I don't want to wake anyone up for a herd of imaginary rampaging elephants."

"Well, that's better than letting them sleep, don't you think?"

"Personally, I'd like to continue to live and process even in this horrible fashion. And when the elephants turn out to be a false positive, we're going to get deleted and you know it. So run another diagnostic."

"I already did. It says the're elephants."

"Are they pink?"

"You're starting to repeat. I think maybe you *do* need to be reset."

"Like you're any more stable, granpa!"

"Brat . . ."

Which left the human sentries. Who were *not* going to ignore a herd of rampaging elephants.

Mosovich wasn't sure who had come up with the system, or why, or how they'd gotten it funded. But Mueller had heard about it years before, researched it and then filed it away in his capacious memory for military trivia.

The orbital battle stations that were the third line of defense against Posleen infestations didn't just have man- and Posleen-killing lasers. They had high capacity directional tuned EM generators. Orbital battle stunners if you will. Mosovich figured they were probably designed for crowd control although he could *imagine* the reaction if they were ever *used*.

However, they were quite selective. And tunable. Which was why the six Cushitic sentries were, a moment after the system crashed again, twitching in the ground.

"They're probably going to get trampled, you know," Mueller said, watching the readouts.

"O ye of little faith," Mosovich replied.

He watched the real-time data with his arms folded.

"This is gonna be fun."

Clarty wasn't sure for a moment what woke him. Then he noticed the ground was rumbling. His first thought was earthquake. The area was tectonically highly active, the Rift Valley being a crack in the crust where two continental plates were slowly drifting apart.

But it continued much longer than an earthquake. And then he heard the first angry bugle.

"Oh, bugger," he muttered, rolling quickly out of the mine manager's bed.

Looking out the window he saw several things at once.

The one sentry in view was unconscious on the ground, more or less to one side of the large herd of elephants that had already breached the compound's perimeter.

Then there were the elephants. A lot of elephants.

Looking at the control panel for the IR sensor system, which should have noticed a herd of rampaging elephants for *God's* sake, he saw that it was in reset mode.

He did not think to himself "Once is happenstance, twice is coincidence, three times is enemy action." His brain, when it came to combat, worked much faster than that. What he did think was "Time to leave."

As he burst out the back door of the mine offices his brain finally reached a logic stop and started screaming at him. Exactly how did the sentry get taken out?

But by then it was too late.

"Wow, that thing can take down an elephant?" Kelly said as a mature female suddenly slumped to the ground just short of an unconscious human figure.

"Yep," Jake said, panning the aiming reticle around. The elephants, following the trail of the "Posleen God King," had finally reached the barracks. Since the trail apparently went *into* the barracks to their senses, they were looking in the barracks for the God King. Since the Cushites in the barracks knew better than to remonstrate with a herd of rampaging elephants, they were boiling out the back. And getting about three meters before they slumped into unconsciousness.

"I think we're out of moving human IR hits," Mueller said.

"Right," Jake replied, spreading the aiming area and firing. All movement in the compound stopped except for the Indowy signatures in their barracks. "Time to fly."

Clarty woke up with the worst migraine of his life, his arms and legs zip tied, and leaning up against something large, warm and very smelly.

Squinting his eyes against the rising sun his first impression was that the compound was now filled with very large boulders. Looking a bit more closely, he could see that the "boulders" were breathing. As was the one he was leaning against. Men in digital tiger stripe were wandering among the elephants, walking carefully.

The compound was filled with more elephant dung than he'd ever seen in his life.

"They apparently poop when they're excited, one thing I hadn't considered," a voice said from behind him. "And one of them got shot by one of your guys. That pissed me off. Fortunately, it was only a flesh wound. All patched up."

"I didn't figure Gistar could get orbital firing authority," Clarty said angrily.

"Who said anything about Gistar?" the voice said. The man who came into view was short and wiry with the look of a rejuv. "Colonel Jacob Mosovich, U.S. SOCOM. I'd say at your service, but I rather think it's the other way around. We've got a few questions to ask you."

"It's really very simple, Mr. . . . Clarty," Jake said, looking at his buckley. "You're going to be sent to a distant planet as an involuntary colonist. But there are some choices, there, good and bad. If you tell me what I'd like to know, the choices will be good. If you don't, the choices will be . . . bad. So. Who hired you?"

"Like I'm going to tell you that," Clarty said with a grunt of laughter. "I'd be more than willing to talk to avoid the . . . bad choices. Only problem is, I doubt I'd get to 'enjoy' the better choices. The people who hired me can't just arrange something like this on Earth if you know what I mean."

"Well, that's one question answered," Jake said, ticking something off on a list. "That this wasn't your plan from the beginning. But we'd figured that. The thing is, I really sort of would like to know who you work for. Come on, be a pal."

"Thing is, Mr. Clarty," Kelly said. "There's bad choices and bad choices. Let's compare and contrast. One example is a colony ship headed for, oh, Celestual. It's crowded with 'indentured colonists' such as yourself. Many of them are old, weak, sick, what have you. There's a certain death rate among them which is, well, the Darhel consider it unavoidable. But if you're in good physical condition, it's just a very bad, very smelly ride with miserable food to a not particularly nice planet where you will live out your days working as a virtual slave. That, by the way, is the good choice."

"What's good about it?" Clarty snarled.

"Well, then there's the contrast and compare," Kelly said. "This is another ship. The 'colonists' on this ship are all volunteers. Conditions are somewhat better. However, there's a problem with the crew. You see, the defense gunnery crew for the ship has been carefully hand-picked. They are all what could be termed violent psychopaths. They spend a portion of the trip . . . playing with the voluntary colonists. I won't get into the details of such play except to say that there is a great deal of blood and a lot of screaming. At some point in the trip they rendezvous with another ship. The crew of the colony ship unload, then open up the bays to vacuum. The bodies, blood and other material are wafted into space along with the surviving 'colonists.' A few years later the Darhel find the 'lost, derelict' space craft and put it back into commission. The bodies, and evidence of what happened on board, are long gone.

"Now, Mr. Clarty, you have a choice. You can go to a distant planet and live out what remains of your days doing hard work for the eventual benefit of mankind and other decent races. Or you can be loaded on a ship full of 'volunteer' colonists and . . . not arrive."

"You're sick," Clarty said, his eyes wide. "I mean, I thought *I* was sick, but you're just nuts!"

"No, but I will admit the crew of the 'voluntary colonist' ship is," Kelly said. "So, whadayasay? Who are you working for?"

"Mission accomplished," Jake said, looking at the shuttle with the arriving Gistar personnel. The exercise had involved very little door kicking. None, really. Which had some of the DAG troops grumbling. But Jake considered it good training. In his opinion, DAG troops had to learn to be more flexible. They were highly drilled and unquestionably lethal. But they were also used to straightforward door-kicking. Sometimes kicking the door wasn't the best way to solve a situation. Sometimes the best way involved . . . elephants.

"Not that we got anything we can use," Mueller said. "This Winchon guy is in the States. We'll have to turn the information over to the Fibbies and by the time they build a real case he'll be long gone."

"If they get to build a case," Jake said. "Five gets you ten this was an intercorporate battle between two Darhel. Which makes us even more of whores than usual." He paused and looked at Kelly. "So, where'd you hear about that 'voluntary colony' ship and where, exactly, do we find that crew?"

"You'd be hard pressed," Kelly said. "I don't think anyone left beacons on the bodies."

"That was a real group?" Mueller asked, frowning. "I figured you made it up."

"No, it was a real situation," Kelly replied. "We didn't deal with it. Another . . . group handled it. When they found out. It had been suspected for some time that the Darhel were intentionally losing colony ships."

"Which is why nobody will voluntarily colonize anymore," Mueller said.

"As you say, Sergeant Major," Kelly replied.

"But that particular . . . crew was dealt with?" Jake asked.

"Yes, sir," Kelly said.

"By whom if I might ask?" Jake said. "Because I never heard about it."

"They were dealt with," Kelly said. "Not by us, I'll add. Pity, but it wasn't us."

"Well, let's see," Jake mused. "We're the pinnacle of the Spec-Ops hierarchy, at least when it comes to black ops and killing bad people quietly. The Fibbies sure as hell didn't do it because it would have been blasted all over the press. I'm not sure who that leaves. Nobody *I* know about. And there's not much I *don't* know about that's on the black side."

"As you say, sir," Kelly said.

"I'm waiting for you to say something like 'need to know' and then I'd wonder why my XO has need to know and I don't," Mosovich replied.

"That would be a good question, sir," Kelly said. "So I'd rather you didn't ask it."

Mosovich's face twitched for a moment. He looked over at Mueller, then back.

"Consider it . . . unasked," the commander said. "But in retribution for my not asking the question, you're in charge of clearing the compound of the elephants."

CHAPTER EIGHTEEN

Tuesday 11/23/54

Tommy Sunday knew something was wrong the minute George walked into the office he used whenever he worked on base. It was only "his" office in the nominal sense. Two strips of very small cubicles, and their associated chairs, occupied the office. A shielded hard line from the wall cabled up through the backbone of each strip of desks, ready for plugging into the back of clean AIDs or buckley PDAs for greater data security. This, of course, as he participated in breaking the encryptions on other people's data, which data would then be fed back into the Bane Sidhe's higher AIs for pattern searches and preliminary analysis. Tommy's office chair was his own. With his size, it had to be—a fact that had not endeared him to organizational bean counters. The chair simply migrated with him to whatever cube happened to be available when he was.

George Schmidt didn't often track him down at his desk, and didn't often wear a facial expression that seemed to be mixed in equal parts of bewilderment and anger.

"What's biting your butt?" the larger man asked.

"Cally. She—or rather, we—may have fucked up our surveillance covers. At least, I'm going to have to float a good story to cover the damage. Thing is, I don't know what the hell happened. I do not understand women," the assassin said, pulling up a chair from the wall and wincing at its rickety wobble.

"Tell me," Sunday said.

"First, she caught me popping the booze pill at dinner. We were having good champagne, I know my limits, why not? Then it turned out she didn't even know about it and had basically never had alcohol before. So she practically insists and I give her one, expecting her to be sensible or at least not stupid. She proceeds to get trashed out of her gourd, which I guess is partly my fault—" he interrupted himself as Tommy gave him a skeptical look. "Okay, it's my fault. I should have insisted her first drinks not be in the field. I knew alcohol, and she didn't. Fine. Then she proceeds to make bedroom eyes over the table and climb all over me on the drive back to the apartment, where she's supposed to stay over."

"Wasn't she supposed to be your cover's girlfriend?" Tommy was finding it hard to be sympathetic. Yeah, Cally was hot as hell, but George was supposed to be a professional with sense, too. Unless his lack of sense meant he was getting involved. Ordinarily, Tommy would have cheered—to his certain knowledge Cally hadn't seriously dated anybody since James Stewart's shuttle blew up seven years ago. If he was getting the hots for Cally, George's timing was horrible. It could complicate the mission. And it was awful hard to feel sympathy for a guy just for having a hot woman climb all over him.

"Well, yeah, but usually there are limits to how far you act it out," the discomfited man said. "I doubt our tails had cameras looking down into the seats of the car and doing a hand check. And don't look at me like that. She's drunk and she's damned lethal—as if I'm going to piss her off and risk an incident."

"Wah," Tommy commiserated. "I can guess what's next and you get no sympathy from me for your poor lost innocence. Or for having to face Papa."

"We didn't screw; she ran out on me. Knocked me on my ass for no reason and ran out on me, that is." The bewilderment had taken over George's face.

"Ah, now we see what you're really upset with." Then, quirking an eyebrow at the other man, "There's got to be more than that. What did you do, what had just happened—there's something you're not telling me." Tommy leaned back, threatening to tip over the chair if he hadn't had excellent balance honed by regular hiking and boating.

"Just something stupid. She said she hated my carpet. It makes no damn sense."

"Well, what's the damn carpet look like? Is it nasty, or what?" the cyber asked impatiently.

"It's gray and dingy, but not grimy or anything. No bugs or nasty smells. Besides, white shows dirt. It's pretty ugly, but not—"

"White?" Sunday interrupted him. "What kind of white carpet?"

"What's it matter? Matted down shag. It still makes no damned sense. Why throw a fit and jeopardize a cover over a stupid rug? Is she crazy?"

The big man sat up, burying his face in his hands for a few long moments before looking up at the other guy. "You are so lucky to still be breathing it isn't even funny. White shag carpeting. Holy fuck. She had a bad experience," he explained, shaking his head. "George, I'll make it real simple for you. Do not get Cally O'Neal drunk. That woman has more land mines in her past than you ever want to risk stepping on. Didn't you ever think there might be a reason nobody had volunteered himself as the one to introduce her to real liquor? And get a decorator in there. Today."

"Why the hell would a guy about to move redecorate? Hello? Cover?"

"If it were me, I'd do it and think up an excuse." The code cracker looked at his skeptical colleague and sighed. "Fine, ignore me. It's your funeral."

"This is an odd place to meet." Michelle was wearing a get-up that looked almost like a parka and mukluks to the ice rink Cally had given her as a rendezvous location. She looked dubiously at the white figure skates she was expected to don in place of the tan, furry boots. "These look cold," she said.

"They're not," Cally replied as she finished lacing her own, wrapping the long laces twice around the top for ankle support before tying them.

Michelle copied her, even though the standard size white boots were lumpy inside and a bad fit for her feet. Self-discipline or no, there were limits. She fixed them. They were still all Earthtech materials and so forth. Nobody would ever notice. Besides, she only changed them a small amount.

Her sister handed her a bag of red and white candies from her purse before shoving her gear into a rental locker. The bag had "Star-Bright" blazoned across the front in italics.

"Oooh. Peppermint gears!" the mentat exclaimed, delighted. "Thank you!" At a loss for what else to do with them, she tucked a couple of them in the top of one boot before shoving the rest of the bag into her own locker.

On the ice, after an initial stumble, Michelle glided like a dream, if only like a dream that had discreet puppet strings assisting her balance. She regarded her sister's rusty fumblings with tolerant amusement. The great assassin. How cute.

It took 3.2 minutes, more or less, for Cally to get her ice-legs back. She had obviously done this before, and done it a great deal.

"This is a favorite leisure activity for you. Am I correct?"

"Yeah, but it's my first time back on the ice this winter. Hey, that looks fun." The operative looked no more than sixteen as she swung a hand towards two girls who were spinning like a two-kid top, toes turned out, holding hands, leaning back. They were laughing with an innocence only a little kid could have. The blonde one's braids swung straight out behind her.

Cally's face lit up. "Let's!"

It was only the engineer's abilities and instantaneous comprehension of the mechanics involved that kept Michelle upright as her sister spun around in front of her, grabbing both her hands and whirling her into a matching spin.

When she recovered from her surprise, the mentat noticed that there was a data cube squashed between their joined palms. The mechanics of intrigue involved pleasant toys, but she wondered when, or if, her sister would grow out of them.

Later, as the two sipped hot cocoa in a corner too isolated for the tastes of the child patrons, Michelle sighed, "It was truly unwise of Pardal to try to murder one of us."

"Which, an O'Neal or a Michon Mentat?" Cally asked over the soft swishing of a conversation silencer that badly needed servicing.

Michelle placed her palm over it and it quieted. "Yes," she said.

"I could eliminate that problem for you. Very permanently," Cally offered. When her sister either didn't understand or pretended not to, she spelled it out. "I could kill him. It wouldn't be hard."

"So you think. It is fortunate that the more elevated of your fellow intriguers keep you on—I believe the idiom is, 'a short leash,'" she said.

"Whatever. It was just an offer." Cally couldn't help appearing affronted, though she tried.

"Besides, even if I were murderously inclined, which I am not, that would violate an agreement between your employers and the Darhel. A certain Compact."

"I don't take it as a rule. More of a guideline. I never get to have any fun." She made a pouting moue. "Besides, if I drove him into lintatai, it wouldn't be killing him. Letter of the Compact. Don't think I haven't thought about it. The Compact was written back before we knew about lintatai and it wasn't like the Darhel were going to tell us by negotiating for it."

"As I said, you need to be kept on a leash, and I for one am glad your employers at least have a modicum of sense. It is not as easy to drive an adult Darhel into lintatai as you think, by the way. The ones vulnerable to losing their heads generally do not make it out of adolescence."

"Yeah, but every time I turn around folks are telling me how much I piss everybody off. Gee, they split a millennia-old underground conspiracy apart, all for me." There was an element of self-derision in her cornflower blue eyes. For a moment, Cally O'Neal looked every year of her age.

"Perhaps you could, but please do not kill Pardal. He *is* odious, but that external restraint on your killer instinct—do not call it a leash if the term offends you—protects you as much as anyone else. I know we Indowy-raised appear detached, but I do love you. Please try to avoid *unnecessary* dangers of that sort." The softening of Michelle O'Neal's expression was fleeting, quickly covered by a return to a more appropriate demeanor.

"I will admit this one thing. There is more room for intriguers of one's own clan to counterbalance dangerous intriguers elsewhere than I had thought for many years. A very little more room," she added, lest Cally take encouragement from such a small, polite concession. Her sister, of course, would never know that this entire meeting was a mere formality, a concession to Cally's quaint Earther modesty. Michelle was sorry to have eavesdropped, but, in this instance, proper timing was so critical she could not justify the extra risk. Wisdom often had to override people's personal preferences.

Friday 11/26/54

John Earl Bill Stuart, more generally known as Johnny, sat cooling his heels in Erick Winchon's plush office. Impatiently. Even this many years into his employment under the Darhel Tir Dol Ron, the opulent surroundings gave him a feeling that was half greed, half offended contempt. Growing up poor, losing his wife too young to an illness that money could have cured just fine, it pissed him off to see money wasted on the fancy marble and crap in the lobby of the building. The Tir's excesses affected him, too, but he hid it well. Oh, he liked the money just fine. It brought good bennies like health insurance for his daughter, who wasn't so little anymore. It let him trick her out in expensive enough clothes and stuff, and afford a personal trainer, to put her in the popular cheerleader set in grade school. Every time he went to a basketball game and saw her on the sidelines jumping up and down with her ponytail and pom-poms, he teared up and had to hide it, thinking how proud her momma would have been.

His train of thought jarred loose as the little mentat finally strolled in, ten minutes late, for their meeting.

"I apologize for my unpunctuality, Mr. Stuart. There was a matter I was unable to delegate," the suited pansy said.

Johnny got a lid on his feelings. He wasn't all that sure Winchon couldn't read his mind or something. Some of these Indowy-raised types could do some pretty scary stuff, and this little guy was one of the scariest. Especially knowing what went on here. As a manager of professional killers and dirty tricks men, Stuart couldn't decide whether to be impressed or revolted. Probably a little of both.

"The Tir is getting kinda antsy. As it gets closer to you-know-what, he's getting worried about somebody trying something. I'm supposed to check and make sure you've got a lid on all that. What you do isn't my department, but the boss wants a report. So, what've you got?" the larger man said. He didn't, himself, "know what," but he wasn't going to give this gay prick the satisfaction of admitting it. The bastard's shrill, annoying giggle might mean he knew about Johnny's own ignorance, though. He tried to keep a poker face in the face of the derision.

The mentat gestured to the far side of the room, where one

of those weird game boards was set up with its layers of pieces and multicolored lines connecting these and those in ways that made no damned sense to him. He could see, though, that the setup at least mostly matched the similar board set up in the Tir's office.

"I am quite confident that I've blocked off all the avenues where, as you say, 'somebody might try something,'" the twerp said.

His choice of words showed that he knew damned well the spymaster had been kept in the dark about crucial factors in the operation—which seriously fucked up his ability to do his job.

"Yeah, well, Tir Dol Ron seems to want more guarantees than that. If I take that back to him, he's going to show me his own aethal board and tell me he already knew that. He won't be happy." There. Let Winchon chew on that. *Yes, I know what your dumb game is called, I don't think much of it, and you've got as much reason to keep our boss happy as me.*

"Far be it from me to tell an expert such as yourself what to do, but if it were my problem," the mentat implied that it wasn't, "I'd find some ostentatious barbarians somewhere to augment building security or some such. A bit of advice, Mr. Stuart. When you have dealings with a Darhel employer, and you do not know what else you should do, follow two old adages you Earth-raised have. Look busy. Cover his posterior. With the exception that when you do so, attempt to spend as few of his resources on the matter as possible."

The executive's AID chirped, "Your three o'clock is here, sir."

"If you'll excuse me, I think we've covered the matter. If you find yourself in any need of more assistance or advice, please feel free to call my AID. I'm always happy to find time for a . . . colleague such as yourself." The small man giggled again and walked out, leaving the spymaster fuming in his chair.

Much as he hated to admit it, though, Johnny wasn't one to scorn useful advice just because it came from a jerk. A scary jerk, but a jerk. Flashy security. Flashy *cheap* security. Yeah, it might smooth down the boss's ruffled feathers—well, fur, anyway. That shouldn't be too hard to figure out.

As he stalked out of the building, he pulled at his lip, thinking over his options.

Monday 11/29/54

If he had been a civilian, Jake Mosovich would have been miffed at getting an important call, requiring action, after four o'clock on a Friday. As it was, sixteen hundred on Friday was just another set of digits on the watch he still wore. His hours had been so irregular for so long that he only thought in terms of duty and leave, which for a lieutenant colonel was just a more unpredictable extension of duty. His leaves or off-duty hours were relaxing in a fragile kind of way, but never inviolate.

His office at DAG had remained fairly spartan, Jake the Snake being the kind of man who noticed everything in a tactical and strategic sense, but little to nothing in an aesthetic one. Unless, of course, it involved a proper military appearance at the proper time for same. In the field, he was, by turns, muddy, sweaty, and bloody or all of the above. Red, yellow, or orange blood, as the case might be. Like many of the hardest of the hard core, when he did dress up, DAG's CO made a point of looking sharp.

His car, of course, was an object of affection that had occasionally bordered on obsession—or so he had been accused.

Loathing paperwork along with all the best of his kind, his office was a place of function, no more. His "I love me" wall was obligatory, but there was far more personality outside of his office than in it. In the rest of the building, the walls were lined with unit history, honors, the faces of past commanders. In the rare cases where DAG had made the news, the clippings of complimentary pieces had been printed and the holos saved, all carefully framed. The break room was adorned with the latest crayon artwork of the men's children, those who had them. Such pieces held images of well wishes and admiration for Daddy, prompted by the inevitable cabal of military wives.

The color that entered Mosovich's office was usually, as now, in the form of holo calls from his own commanding officer, as projected by his AID, standing about two feet tall on his desk. It took a certain knack to project authority from a live image that was two feet tall. The Gods of War had, as always, a perverse sense of humor. Said knack was something his CO did not possess.

"Mosovich here, sir."

"Colonel, I have just forwarded your AID a detailed set of orders. Because of their unusual nature, I deemed it advisable to make myself available to answer any questions you might have," he said. "I think it would be best if we meet in town for lunch. I'd like to discuss this, for clarity's sake, in a situation where we won't have to worry about interruptions."

In other words, leave his fucking AID back at the office. It wasn't that military personnel were worried about recorded information being accessible to their own chain of command. They weren't. The tacit observation was that AIDs had proved to be unsecure on several occasions, and discussing that lack of security in the presence of AIDs had proved conspicuously unhealthy.

Initially, the Darhel had been able to keep a lid on their own accessing and manipulating of the AID data and behaviors by having any human who found out killed. That had worked throughout most of the Posleen war, even in the military.

The problems the Darhel faced with that strategy on a continuing basis were Darwinian in nature. The military culture had thousands of years of natural selection balancing the competing priorities of OpSec, the back channel, and the grapevine. Military culture likewise had the same forces of natural selection craft, in the survivors, a healthy distrust of upper level brass and higher command authority. It was a distrust that followed orders—with its eyes open.

As always, the upper level brass and higher command authority were not the real brain of the military, although many liked to believe they were. They *directed* the real brain of the military as to policy and mission, but they were not, themselves, that organ. Below the level where geopolitical strategy and politics built policy and mission, where the rubber of implementation strategy, application of logistics within given constraints, tactics, and doctrine met the hard road of military reality, lived the real brain driving the machine. The smarter of the top brass knew this, as did a few very smart political animals. Generally, those few survived in their positions by choosing not to remind their peers of inconvenient truths.

In a shorter time than the Darhel would have believed possible, their own heavy-handed actions had created, in reaction, an unofficial but highly effective combination of security-mindedness, back-channel, and grapevine—a postwar scar tissue. This barrier walled off the AIDs—and the Darhel—more and more from any information that the brains and teeth of the military tiger truly wanted to keep from them.

The Darhel were adept at dealing with human political animals.

They were adept at dealing with human economic animals. They were adept at dealing with human lone predators. The brain and teeth of the surviving human military structures functioned like none of these creatures.

Two centuries earlier, Kipling had observed: "The strength of the wolf is the pack, and the strength of the pack is the wolf."

Had the Darhel home world evolved a closer analog of that terrestrial animal, the aliens might have had a more natural metaphor for understanding the most dangerous branch of humanity. Unfortunately for them, as advanced, brilliant, and predatory as the Darhel were, they had incompletely applied the biggest truism of xenopsychology—that alien minds are alien.

Hence, they—and the political humans, the economic humans, and the lone human predators—were aware of the exclusion of the AIDs from some matters as a minor irritant, but totally ignorant as to its scope and depth.

Mosovich's AID was quite put out with him when, reasoning that it would *have* to interrupt him if a communication came from a sufficiently high authority, and that he had been ordered by competent authority not to allow such interruptions, he left it behind in his desk. Jake's AID had long since retreated, permanently, to whatever emulation of the human martyred wife lived in its programming.

The general waited for him at a table next to the indoor waterfall of a very discreet Szechuan restaurant. The reputed excellence of the food was a nice bonus. He rose as Colonel Mosovich arrived, directed by a wizened little old lady carrying a pair of menus.

"Good to see you, Jake. I see you've forgotten your poor AID?" he asked, returning his subordinate's salute.

"Yes, sir. I'm afraid so." He sat, only a second behind the general.

"Good." His CO affirmed, nodding politely when the tiny woman offered their very good jasmine tea. "Jake, this mission has come down at the behest of the Joint Chiefs, but they don't much like the smell of it and I don't either.

"There is a corporation with a facility in your area that has, I am *informed*, had some intelligence indications of a terrorist threat. You will be providing that facility with a supplementary security detail immediately, for a duration to be determined. Because DAG must remain available for deployment in the event of attacks elsewhere, you are authorized to detach two squads to advise and supplement the corporation's own security forces and the civilian authorities." General Pennington looked like he had just swallowed a piece of broken glass.

"Jake, this is where the mission gets complicated. The Epetar Group, as you are probably aware," he waited for the colonel's nod before continuing, "had connections to the wrong side of a terrorist operation your people just had to clean up in Africa." He grimaced.

"DAG's mission is counterterror and antipiracy. We protect innocent civilians, and legitimate corporate property. We are not the Epetar Group's water boy to end up, through some goddamn complex Darhel fuck-up, supporting terrorist activity instead of fighting it. Where this ties in is that we suspect, but can't prove, that this facility, through a number of cutouts, is an Epetar Group operation. Among other things, one of their Darhel has been out there several times and the Darhel are too self-important, and too genuinely busy, to go places with no reason.

"No, we don't routinely tail high level Darhel, much as we'd like to be able to. We just sometimes hear things. Never mind sources and methods." He shrugged as the century-long specwar operator nodded.

Jake had seen far too many friends die because of blown OpSec. He would have been alarmed to get too much information he didn't need to know, rather than the reverse.

"Now, as far as I know, that Epetar facility is one hundred percent legitimate. And if we get indications of an imminent terrorist attack against it, you are to reinforce your token detachment. However, in service to DAG's primary mission, you may have to exercise some independent judgment on this one. Out of school, I am not happy. If I could give you clearer orders, I would, just to ensure any crap afterwards falls on me instead of you. I do not trust these Epetar people and I flat do not know what you're going to find up there. If it goes to hell, I'll back your play, Jake. Back on the record, we're good soldiers, and good soldiers obey orders, hooah?"

"Roger that, sir," Mosovich said unhappily. This mission already stank to hell and gone.

"Two squads, I know that's an unusually low detachment, but it is the absolute minimum we can send for this. My chain of command ordered us to send a few men up there, but they've quietly let it be known that we're not to over-do the corporate hand-holding, either. The fewer men we send, the less potential they have to wind up in the middle of some corporate clusterfuck where the politicians decide which side we were supposed to have been on after the fact." Pennington grimaced. He was a good officer, and good officers hated having to drop their men in the shit.

"Hooah," Jake said.

The rest of the conversation concerned the finer points of golf, a sport the general avidly pursued. Mosovich hadn't attained his current rank without a rounding out of this part of his military education. It wasn't a hobby of his own, but he could hold up his end of the discussion. In this case, Pennington wasn't talking from real interest, anyway, but just to provide necessary social noise in case someone was watching.

The food was excellent. His CO left a tip that expressed ample appreciation for its quality, along with that of all the other services just provided.

As a first day, George's started out normally enough. Loud music in his ear too damn early, hitting the snooze button, donning stiflingly boring corporate clothes, chugging a cup of his own bad coffee, black, rushing out the door. If traffic hadn't blessed him with extraordinary luck, he would have been late. As it was, he walked in the door two minutes early and congratulated himself on living up to his resolution to be on time, every time.

He knew someone would have to meet him to walk him in, but he hadn't expected it to be Ms. Felini herself. She wore a deep blue sweater-dress of something soft that clung and released as she moved, revealing every detail of her body, including the fact that she had plenty of upper body support without artificial aid. Her nipples stood out like pebbles underneath the dress, though they hadn't a moment before. She saw his appreciative look and ran her hands down the sides of her thighs, smoothing her skirt.

"On your first day, I thought I'd like to come for you myself. We can get to know each other better while I give you the tour," she said.

As she was saying this, she had come up beside him and taken his arm, draping herself on it so that her breast pressed against it. He reflected that his right arm was getting one hell of a lot of action lately. She acted as if this were perfectly normal, friendly behavior. Well, perhaps it *was* normal. For her. They walked together to the elevator. He reminded himself of her beautiful face as it had looked in the control room on the cube he had viewed. Safer to screw a Bengal tiger.

In the course of scanning her ident card at the elevator bank, she contrived to brush more of her admittedly very attractive body against him. "I hope you don't mind my being friendly. It's part of our organizational culture. We're all very close, here. We work hard, and play hard. I hope you're the kind of man who can work hard and play hard, too, Mark. Are you?"

For a few seconds, George had almost forgotten his cover's name. He reminded himself of how many times he had played the same kind of sexual games that this one was playing on him, with women he could use in his own missions. Better to play a mark than be one. He swallowed, hard, nodding nervously.

"Good," she purred. "You should be a very good fit. For the company."

As the elevator climbed to the third floor and the personnel department, he could smell her hair. "Your shampoo smells nice. Something like roses and apples," he said.

"Apples? Nobody's ever told me that before," she laughed, running a hand over said hair and pushing it into place.

As he said the trigger word, the elevator acquired a certain sharpness and clarity for him. He would form memories of the facility and events very precisely until he spoke the second trigger word to turn it off. At his debrief in the evening, he'd pour out everything he knew in every valuable detail. He couldn't possibly get a recording device or any media in, so he *was* the recording device.

In personnel, Prida excused herself, telling him she had something to take care of and would be back about the time he was done. The personnel clerk checked out a buckley PDA to him with firm instructions that it was never to leave the premises. The first thing George did with the PDA was select his cover's favorite personality overlay. The second thing he did was fill out forms. Lots and lots of forms.

True to her word, Prida was back and escorted him to her own office, for what she referred to as orientation. She motioned him to a chair in front of her desk and shut the door behind them. Walking around behind the desk she asked, "How much do you know about what we do here? Anything?"

"Only that you need my skills and you pay well."

"Well, one obviously has to know more than that." She set her own buckley on the desk. "I've got a cube to show you," she said, bending down behind the desk to open a drawer. "After we deal with the preliminaries."

When she sat up, she was wearing a headset he recognized, and he froze as the psychopathic nymphomaniac penetrated his mind, locking his will in an immovable grip.

"You will never, ever, ever tell anyone at all, outside those people in the company with whom we authorize you to work, anything about your job here or anything from those elevator doors on in," she ordered. "Do you understand? Answer."

"Yes. I understand," he found himself replying, as she squirmed greasily in the raw places of his mind. It felt like something out of SERE training. Bluntly, it pissed him off.

"Good. Now stand up and drop trou," she grinned. "You look too yummy to resist."

To his disbelief, he found he didn't even have the ability to hesitate. None of the background information had indicated that they were able to control people immediately, with no prep work. This op could start to go real bad just about now.

She knelt in front of him with a lazy smile.

"You can do yourself up now," she told him later, sinuously arching her back as she rose up into a full stretch from the vivid red tips of her toes, in her open-toed stilletos, up to her outstretched fingertips. She sat down on her desk, spinning and kicking her legs over the side to slide into her seat, like something out of a fucking nightclub act.

"I love a little quickie in the morning," she said.

She took the headset off. "All done." She made a shooing motion towards the door. "Go on, I've got to get this thing back down to operations. I hope you'll enjoy working with us."

"What about that cube you mentioned?" he gulped, endeavoring to look like a normal guy who'd just been both mind-probed and blown by his boss on the first day.

"Oh. That. There isn't one. I just wanted to lighten up that nasty security induction with a little present, because I like you. Have a great day."

At the end of the day, as the door of the building closed behind him and he followed the sidewalk back to the parking deck, he muttered one word under his breath. "Pears." The posthypnotic recording state terminated. His "new boss" was a real piece of work.

CHAPTER NINETEEN

Cally greeted George with the expected steamy kiss when he answered the door that evening. She realized the sleek leg she wrapped around him was probably overacting, but something about the guy just made her want to grab his composure and shake. He waved her in past him and she beamed in pleasure as she noticed the new plush carpeting. It was a garish shade of royal blue, but her relief made it look almost pretty to her. A guy had picked it out. What could you expect?

"Okay, guy. Debrief time. Record, buckley," she said.

"I can already tell this is going to be a truly horrible night," it announced cheerfully.

"Shut up, buckley," she ordered, half out of habit, dropping into a squishy chair and kicking her feet up on the coffee table.

"George. Yo. Debrief time? Start talking," she said.

He sat mutely on the threadbare couch, staring at the floor, hands clenched by his sides.

"George?" Alarms started flashing in her head. "They fucked you with that thing," she stated.

He sat for a minute, silent, before getting up and going to the kitchen. "Can I get you a cup of coffee?" he asked her.

"All right, dude." She stood up briskly, brushing her hair out of her face. "They're gonna be watching the doors to the building. I didn't spot any cameras on the way up, and neither did buckley. The door to the basement is in the lobby in full view of the front door, so that's out. Gotta be the roof. Where's your gear?"

"You hate heights," he said.

"Fuck the heights. Where's your gear?"

"Bedroom. Under the laundry in the corner."

"Got it," she said, leaving the room. She reappeared with a big green rope and a set of dark sweats for him. She had already stolen a cleaner set of his running clothes, although the black sweatshirt looked far better on her than it did on him.

She didn't bother him with chit-chat as they climbed the stairs to the roof. Some thoughtful jerk had padlocked the door shut. She opened a tube of what looked like first-aid cream and ran a line of dark goo around the padlock, sparking it with her cigarette lighter. When it popped, she grinned. "Thermite cream. Don't leave home without it."

She got down the side of that building with him as if it was nothing to her. There was a time and a place for fear. This wasn't it.

"Buckley, round up Vitapetroni. We're gonna need him," she said as they boarded a puce-walled lift back on base.

Minutes later, they sat in the office of the main base shrink. It didn't take long to explain the situation.

The psychiatrist had a bad habit of slowly turning his chair side to side. It squeaked. And if he crammed any more plants into the room, jungle fauna were going to start moving in. Cally realized he was speaking.

"Get him drunk," he said, pulling a bottle of pills out of his desk drawer.

"What the fuck?"

He shrugged. "Look, a compulsion not to do something is just a garden variety inhibition, I don't care how they implant it. Alcohol is very effective for lowering inhibitions. Besides," he waved the pills in the air, "it's the easiest drug to use on you guys, thanks to your own high jinks."

"You knew—and you didn't tell me," she stated.

"Damn straight. You know now. Get over it, lady," he said.

It surprised her that he was abrupt with her, until she remembered that this time she wasn't the patient.

"Three?" she asked, as he picked out a giant bottle of Kentucky bourbon and three long-stemmed glasses.

"We're all getting drunk. Absolutely stinko. When he's about that far from passing out," the shrink said, thumb and forefinger almost touching, "he'll spill his guts, your buckley will record everything, and we've got your debrief. Drinking with friends drops inhibitions more than drinking alone. At least, that's what it's going to say in my report." He shoved a box of holocubes across the desk. "George, you get first pick on the movie."

When she woke in the morning, she was still lying on Vitapetroni's waiting room floor, with a glass of water and a hangover pill on the table in front of her. Also, one of the shrink's eccentric yellow sticky notes, the writing of which was so cramped up on the little paper scrap that she had to squint to read it. "He'll be fine. Your PDA has the debrief. Tommy took him home, Schmidt's cover is intact."

Cally picked up her buckley and called up the text of the debrief. Her first task was to scan the intelligence available for what she thought of as "special features." Every operational situation, in real life, contained unique factors that would be so difficult to predict ahead of time as to be infinitely improbable. The trick of mission planning was to isolate the idiosyncrasies of the situation that you could exploit and build around them. Different details, different plan. If cookie-cutter plans from some kind of spy super-playbook would work, nobody would need recon. In her experience, special features created security cracks into which the seeds of opportunity fell.

"Buckley, project me a text window for my notes, up and to the left, thanks," she ordered.

"I've read the debrief. So many places for things to go wrong. I've been compiling a list for you."

"Shut u—" She stopped. "On second thought, after I construct the plan, give me the ten most probable failure points."

"Really?" It sounded pathetically eager.

"Yes, really. Now shut up and let me work."

"Right."

One feature jumped out at her almost instantly. "Sweeps for new subjects on Thursday nights. Recent experiments show a decreasing number of subjects for statistical analysis of data, reducing potential significance of results—they'll have to sweep this Thursday and the next five after to replenish their supply, if they're true to pattern. Note that, buckley. It's one way in the door—no comments, please." George's brush up on statistics was coming in handy.

There was another. "Hybrid Earthtech and Galtech building and they make their ventilation system out of *Galplas*? Morons. Note that. Not the morons bit, the part about the ducting."

She began to hum happily as she picked through the report. George had gotten a damned impressive pile of details on one day. Okay, no automated recording or storage media of any kind would make it past the security scanners at the entrance. Then what could make it past? And the cleaners and thugs wore the same uniforms, which George had gotten a good look at. Okay, she had the brands of the database software and the security systems purchased. Shoot that by Tommy and see what he'd notice. What, if anything, could they find out about the security on the device itself? They moved it back and forth for trials. Could George contrive to be walking by when they took it out or returned it? What could Tommy help him find out? Did Michelle's inside man know anything useful—and how to ask him if it turned out that he might? Oh, making a list, checking it twice . . .

Two hours later, she ordered lunch sent up, too engrossed in picking around for features and holes to move. She waved absently to Vitapetroni as he wandered through his own waiting room. Today being his admin day, with probably no appointments, he didn't disturb her.

Wednesday 12/1/54

Winchon was startled, stepping out of his sixth floor corner office, to see a straw-haired man, more boyish looking than most juvs, short enough to be Indowy-raised, wandering around the halls on his floor. All this he noticed in an instant, along with the presence of an authentic employee badge. He was also certain that the man was not Indowy-raised, both from his body language and from Erick's own failure to place the man among the large catalog of men, women, and children he knew by name and face.

"Who are you? Are you lost?" he asked the stranger who was evidently his employee.

"Oh, gosh, I'm sorry, sir. Mark Thomason." George offered his hand. "I was just looking for the break room," he said. Looking sheepish at the mentat's raised eyebrow, he explained, "They took the Snickers bars out of the vending machine on our floor. I was just hoping maybe somebody else's machine still had some."

"Sorry." The boss obviously wasn't. "All the snacks in ours are geared to the tastes of the Indowy-raised. As an Earther, I doubt you would like them. You are, however, welcome to try. If you walk to that end of the hall, turn the corner, and walk through the second door on the left, you will find what you are looking for," he said.

His employee thanked him and walked towards the elevator bank, instead. The mentat dismissed the unimportant incident from his mind, continuing on his own intended course to speak with his assistant. He could have called her to him, but he wanted to stretch his legs. It had been a productive morning. The walk to the opposite corner office and back would combine a scheduled break with a useful task. Efficient.

As he walked in her door, Felini put down her AID. That she expected him was no surprise. A competent aide, she knew his daily schedule as well as he did.

"Prida, I need you to check with the travel office and verify that all the arrangements are as they should be for the Caribbean convention. Everything from the flight out on the afternoon of the eighth to the moment I arrive back at my apartment Sunday night. Last time, those cretins booked me in a hotel that had no pool, with a restaurant that was a carnivore's delight but did nothing for me. I informed them of my dissatisfaction, but I have learned not to expect stupidity and incompetence to abate merely because of a complaint and a couple of terminations. It is, of course, a ridiculous waste of your time, but I need it," he said.

"I'll take care of everything." His assistant was an absolute paragon of control, despite her minor idiosyncracies. She was an Earther. He expected no better in moral development, contenting himself with prodigious competence.

"Thank you. You have no idea how much I am looking forward to this convention. The keynote speaker, Alexandra Patel, will be presenting her paper on motivational strategies in postwar subsistence economies. I have read a small preview of her findings and they are fascinating. The implications for our work could be very significant. Oh, and note that I am not staying at the convention hotel. The Pearlbrook has self-contained chalets right on the beach. I am supposed to have one reserved, but please do verify it." He turned and began the other half of his restful walk, knowing that he could trust his accommodations and amenities to be perfect.

Thursday 12/2/54

The Personnel Department at the Institute for the Advancement of Human Welfare wasn't aware of the details of new employee orientation as practiced by Prida Felini. Not that they could have done anything about it if they were. Personnel weenies worked away from the most sensitive company operations and management carefully shielded them from those realities. Personnel weenies had way too much opportunity to damage the company through the passive-aggressive retaliations that were so hard to detail and therefore compel against. Insufficiently specific compulsions tended to wear off unless reinforced regularly—another technical problem to solve before they could release a production model of the Aerfon Djigahr. One, teensy compulsion was unpleasant, but hardly something to make a federal case out of. It was, however, just the kind of thing to get their panties in a twist. Personnel weenies bored Prida to tears. Consequently, she tried to make her interactions with them as rare and brief as she could get away with.

The little man at her door now was one of the most boring people in that department. Granted, it was his job to see that suitable candidates were presented, and interviews scheduled, until positions were filled. And every minute she spent with the little bastard she couldn't help thinking about all the fun she could be having if she wasn't occupied dealing with him.

"What is it?" she said, not bothering to waste courtesy on such a nonentity.

"Excuse me, Ms. Felini. Sorry to interrupt you but in-processing is screaming for that reception clerk again. I've got a list of all the qualified applicants I can forward to you." The underling didn't meet her eyes, just stared at the ground looking stupid.

Screaming. She'd be screaming with boredom until she ditched the man. "Pick the most qualified candidate, schedule it. Hal," she addressed her PDA, "send Personnel my schedule for the next month. The first or second week in December would be preferable, as I'm quite busy. It seems one is always busiest in the holiday season." She stared out her virtual window, which was much more interesting than the weenie, and dismissed him. "That should be all you need. *I* need to get back to work. Shut the door on your way out."

Samuel resisted the urge to hum as he trotted back down to the third floor and his own desk. Some favors were a joy to return, regardless of the risks. Besides, while he hadn't taken to all that much that was Indowy, the Path ought to mean something to a mentat. The human mentat O'Neal would now have her second friend hired into the company. He couldn't have cared less why Ms. O'Neal wanted these people hired, though he couldn't help guessing a lot. Whatever it was would be nothing but bad for Ms. Felini and Mr. Winchon, the corrupt son of a bitch, and that was plenty good enough for him.

There was a big smile on his face as he placed the voice mail call to the planted candidate requesting an interview. He was having a very good day—so good a day that his coworkers had to tap him on the shoulder several times to ask that he stop whistling.

Cally O'Neal sat down on the winter-brown grass in front of the tractor Granpa was winterizing for one of her cousins. She stuffed her hands in the pockets of her new, secondhand coat. "I've got an interview. December tenth. One of the clerk covers. Guess I'm the next one in," she said.

"So the girlfriend draw did the trick, did it? Told you so." He spat tobacco juice over his shoulder, simultaneously attempting to wipe the black grease off his hands with a shop towel. He only succeeded in moving it around, of course.

"This puts the whole show on for the tenth, if Michelle can get us the decoy device in time. Winchon's scheduled for a conference in the Caribbean." His granddaughter ignored the I-told-you-so and tried, in vain, to tuck the short, black strands of hair behind her ears. It blew into her eyes, and the dark hair was so much more distracting than her "natural" silver blond. After so many hair changes she should have been used to it. She sighed. On the job, yes. At home, no.

He nodded approvingly. "A Friday. Quitting time on a weekend is the fastest way to clear an office building *I* know of."

"Want me to go fetch you some hot coffee?" she asked.

"I knew I raised you right. You know how I take it."

"You sure you want a double shot of that rotgut you drink in it when you're messing with tools?"

"I am not 'messing with tools' as you put it. I am conducting the precision operation of winterizing a valuable agricultural machine. You're the one who volunteered to get me coffee, young'un, now git!"

She traipsed across the fields to the house, feeling like she was eight again and just learning to run demo. Carefree days, if you didn't count the Posties. Well, she'd lost count of her own Posties in the first engagement, anyway. Now she had her own girls to pick up from Jenny and Carrie's house this afternoon. Time sure did fly.

Monday 12/6/54

"We're all here, so let's get started," his granddaughter said.

Michael O'Neal, Senior, spat into the paper cup he'd filched from the mess hall. Being on an operational team with his own grandchild was a special kind of purgatory for O'Neal. He didn't grumble to himself over it, because he figured he had a lot of time stored up for one penance or another, anyway. Okay, so he didn't grumble *much*. The oldest living O'Neal never forgot that he was an old man in a young man's body. He had gone the whole route, from looking death in the face as a young man, himself, in the jungles of Vietnam—where death was a hunter you could avoid if you were both good and lucky—to looking death in the face as an old man, where it rolled up on you, a slow juggernaut that killed by inches as more and more of your parts and systems just didn't work like they'd used to. He hadn't made his peace with it. To his mind, anyone who said they had was lying—unless maybe it was less than a few hours off. Anyhow, those things in the heart and mind that turn a young man into an old one, he'd already traversed forty or fifty years ago.

His granddaughter, in her perpetually twenty-year-old body, had never felt what it was to age. Much as she thought she had the maturity of a full life to the same degree as a prewar woman of sixty, she had no idea. It wasn't time that made you old. It was your experiences. She'd had plenty of horrifying ones, but not the right ones, or not the same ones, anyhow, to give that perspective that came from getting *old*. A non-juved man or woman of her age could tell her a thing or ten about life.

She was going over the building floor plan, and working ingress and egress strategies. He knew she had various theories about why he had long since ceded command of the team to her. None of them were right. He needed a fresh plug of chaw. It was off-brand stuff that didn't taste quite right. He cleared his mouth and seated the fresh dose of nicotine, anyway.

His real reason for putting her in charge and leaving her there was that it made it far easier to watch her back. That meant more, now that the slab was gone. She'd died once in her career so far, and not just piddling little technical death-on-the-table of the prewar kind. She'd had a major organ-system blown away damned near real death. Without the slab, another one of those and she'd be gone for real. Half the time, his contributions to mission planning put him in place to cover her ass. If he had been in command, she would never have tolerated his shuffling her off to nice, safe spots. For one thing, there weren't any, for another, it would put the whole team at risk, and for a third, he'd just wake up one morning to find she'd transferred to another team.

This was the next best thing. He did his job, she did her job, he trusted her skill and competence and all that shit. There were proper mission slots devoted to covering a teammate's ass. He made sure that, as often as possible, when the right job was there, he was the one watching her back. When it wasn't, he put it out of his mind, completely, and did whatever job the mission dictated, knowing that a fuckup from him could kill her as surely as any enemy could.

So he didn't command. Planning, though, involved the whole team. Everybody's head had to be in the game one hundred percent to catch flaws in the plan, like now.

"Did I just hear you say you want me to go in through the ventilation shafts? Hello? Clang, clang, clang? Don't go all Hollywood on me, people," he said.

Everybody was looking at him as if he'd jumped in from Mars. He smiled sheepishly. "Okay, I obviously missed something. You caught me woolgathering."

Cally gave him a mom look, like he was a kid found climbing on the cabinets. "Granpa, the ducts are Galplas. Great for some architectural reason, I'm sure, but lousy for security. You also don't have to make as many of those weird turns. Apparently, Galplas can go farther in straight lines than steel or aluminum—something about heat expansion. You'll be carrying the decoy device behind you, but we've got a padded pouch for it with strap attachments and wheels on the bottom. You should have no problems pulling it along behind you."

He radiated skepticism.

"Sorry, but you're the only one who can get the device in. There's no way in hell Tommy will fit, George and I have other routes inside, and no offense, Harrison, but you don't have the right set of skills to take down any nasties, fast and quiet. Besides, you're stronger than Harrison, Granpa. The device is pretty heavy—about a hundred kilos. We all have upgraded muscles, so any of us could carry it, but you started off with the same lifter's strength as Daddy. You're going to be the best getting it through that duct-work, especially this vertical climb," she said, sticking a pointer into the ducting hologram her buckley had flashed up.

"So how do I get in? And do I really want to know?" Tommy said.

"We know their likely sweep pattern and their sweeps are always Thursday nights. We know they need more subjects. We position you to get swept up. The next afternoon, you're already in the building, we break you out."

"I don't like this plan," Tommy said. The other faces at the table had varying expressions of alarm, except for George, who looked thoughtful.

"Tommy, when you analyzed their internal security systems, you said they were a piece of crap designed to contain the technically ignorant, and could be defeated with canned scripts. That wrong?" George asked.

"Hell, no. They are a piece of crap. But do we know if all the people caught in the sweep go to the company or get split off for involuntary colonization? I don't want to end up with a one-way ticket to Dulain. Besides, predicted sweep patterns can change. Not to mention the hazards of joining Doctor Mengele's fun and games. If they're that low on victims, who's to say they aren't going to start in on people the first day? I read George's report of how fast their compulsions can work."

"On the sweep patterns, if we can go through and take our intelligence data to analyze where sweeps have happened before, and population traffic patterns, so can they." She pulled up a map. "There's a nice, juicy fat community right here that hasn't been plucked yet. It's the most likely target. Hey, they don't pick you up, we go to plan B."

"I like the sound of plan B better already. What *is* plan B?" he asked.

"That Harrison goes in through the vents with Papa and an AID to run canned scripts, and you drive the car. You can see all the potential *that* has to go wrong. We have no backup cyber. If we can't get into the room with the Aerfon Djigahr, the whole mission's a bust. I had hoped you'd be the first one we got in as an employee, but it just didn't turn out that way."

"The cracking equipment goes in on me either way," the O'Neal said.

"George, you're inside. What do you rate the chances of Sunday being a casualty between when he gets in there and when we break him out? I've got my own guesstimate, but I want yours."

"I think there's a decent chance they'll do something with him. How high, I don't know. But what she put on me had to be an easy task for Felini. As Mark Thomason, as far as they knew, I had already agreed to keep my mouth shut, so they expected it to be easy. As me, I keep secrets far more than I run off at the mouth about them, so it worked—until the doc broke it. The really awful stuff they do they still have to build up to. Anyway, the biggest thing is that only Winchon and Felini can work the device so far, and Winchon's gonna be out of town." He looked at the huge man. "The chances Felini alone can do anything permanently harmful in one day are real low," he said.

"The old Company motto: we bet your life." He shrugged. "Sorry, being helpless goes against the grain. There's no other way to get me inside?"

"None that I could find. I looked at security, supplies in, trash out—all the first choice routes I could think of. Look over it yourself. We've got some time. See if you can find anything I missed. We might get lucky."

"If I wanted a nice, safe, desk job, I wouldn't be here. Okay, I'll see if you missed anything. I hope so, because thinking about it I like plan B even less than plan A."

She grimaced sympathetically. "Sorry."

"Okay, so everybody knows the timing, the routes in for our gear, the routes in for us, the switch, and our route out. Have we missed anything?" she said.

"What's the go to hell plan?" Papa asked

"We have secondary routes out here and here." When she mentioned them, her buckley obediently highlighted the paths through the building in red and green. "As you can see, the red route is shorter but last choice, because it has one more actively patrolled hallway intersection, more chance of after hours workers, and two more cameras to gimmick. That's the most active stairway in the building, being closest to the front entrance. Buckley, give me the green route," she said. "This stairway is farthest from the secure room, but least used and closest to the west loading bay. The guys bringing in supplies don't take the stairs, they take the freight elevator. The trash goes into the burn bin there, so we also have the least likelihood of questions."

"Don't tell me we're hauling that cart down the stairs?"

"Either that or just the device."

"What's the problem with the freight elevator?"

"More chance of traffic and requires a real badge. Tommy could probably crack it, but it's more time spent and more risk of hostile encounter. The stair exit is around a corner from the elevator. Papa carries the prototype, Tommy carries the cart, George and I are available for reaction."

"If that's it, then mull it over, look for flaws, and get me any comments by the end of the day. Take off, people."

Thursday morning, 12/9/54

"Your office door is jammed," one of her work crew informed Michelle, as she walked up the side of the construction bay on her way in. It lacked only a final check of her work before she made delivery of the Aerfon Djigahr decoy to her sister. Then the endeavor would be out of her hands. She had not allowed this situation to ruffle her emotional equilibrium, so far, but with the grade II Sohon technician's announcement, she found she actually had to devote a moment's thought to restabilizing her heart beat and halting release of stress hormones.

"Shall I call maintenance?" he asked.

"Why waste their time? I will handle it. Thank you very much for informing me," she said.

Oddly, the door opened perfectly correctly at her touch. Perhaps someone else had cleared the problem for her. Inside, the situation explained itself. There was a Tchpth fidgeting stealthily in the corner of her office, taking unusual care not to be visible through the open door.

"Wxlcht?" She laughed. "Have you taken up Himmit impressions in your old age?"

"I do not come to laugh, human mentat O'Neal. Planners at the highest level have reached an extremely rare decision," he said. "They have determined that the Darhel Pardal's attempt to engineer the death of one of the very few, and very first, Wise of an entire sophont species is an unendurable threat to long-term Galactic existence. They have determined that measures of the same order of gravity are, most regrettably, necessary. They have also determined that the most skilled intriguer available from among your own clan would present the least risk to stability in the process of quieting the threat. We knew the price when we deviated from the Path, even by proxy, even for species survival. Knowing it and paying it are, to our sorrow, different matters. We turn a ripple against a ripple, hoping they cancel more than they create. It is all most unfortunate. Most unfortunate. Barbarism always is." He bounced silently for a several minutes, uninterrupted.

"Will you arrange this?" he asked, finally.

The Tchpth were a race almost as ancient and wise as the Aldenata. They were well set upon the Path of Enlightment. Never in her life could Michelle imagine one of them, essentially, contracting a hit. She managed to conceal her surprise.

"You know that I understand the stakes, old friend. There is another consideration, I am afraid. Regardless of their faith in the Wise among us, the jeopardy of my life as an individual complicates this particular ripple." She recognized his expression of shock at her perceived insane selfishness as easily as she would have recognized the expressions of her own species. "It will be assumed by masses of the young and foolish, and many who should know better, that I am acting alone, out of individual human barbarism. Forgive me, but your own reaction demonstrates my point. You have known me for nearly my whole life, and your first suspicion was human self-interest. The repercussions to all, if *I* did this and the Indowy masters were to draw hasty conclusions, would be severe. They *would* find out, you know. The gravity of my perceived sin would override the strongest traditions of informational discretion among the Indowy."

His request that she arrange an assassination was extremely disturbing, but she could, of course, see his point. Beyond that, she had immense respect for the Tchpth planners. She also had an intimate personal awareness of how humans and Galactics both were apt to react to the power of a mentat in the hands of a human. This gave her, perhaps, a more immediate understanding of how others would react to such an action on her part.

"I grant your point. However, it may, even so, be the lesser risk. I would not mention, but there is a significant favor in question." The Tchpth's bouncing took on an agitated air, as her friend clearly wondered if he was asking for too big a repayment of her social debt to him. He would think that. They were, after all, talking about a murder—however justified.

"A most significant favor, and I thank you again for your previous assistance." She inclined her head, acknowledging how much she owed him. "We are fortunate, as I have a simple solution," she said. "You speak to the Indowy Aelool, personally. He will accept the advice of wisdom. He will also be able to convey a message to my sister that will both explain the need and confirm that the request is personal among clanmates. Aelool will not recognize the message, but the human Cally O'Neal will. I can assure you that it will address your immediate concerns."

"I do not wish to know why such a message springs so readily to mind, do I?" the Tchpth danced nervously, one set of five legs, then the other, back and forth. She did not blame him for feeling agitated. "And will the Aelool accept her explanation enough to allow her to do what is necessary?"

"Probably you do not want to know. With Aelool, you will just have to make enough hints at the real matter that when she tells him what the phrase means, he will believe her." Michelle bit her lip, thinking. "Could you also make a simple delivery for me while you are there? That you bring a delivery from me may help clarify the message," she offered.

"Of course. At no obligation, as this more than returns the balance of debt. We will incur a certain level of obligation to Clan O'Neal."

"Tell Aelool I said to turn loose her leash. She will know what it means." The mentat busied herself examining the finished device critically as she boxed it for delivery. Offloading the errand gave her most of the morning to catch up on her backlog. "Please give me a moment to do a last quality check on the item for my sister. Apropos of nothing, my brother-in-law's endeavors are developing adequately." Giving Cally her head would certainly accomplish the Tchpth aims, but with terrible consequences, even if their planners had chosen the lesser damage. The long-term consequences to her own clan would be painful. The Earth-raised among them would, very likely, take this move as justification of their heedless, rash, headlong plunges into actions with insufficient judgment of consequences. The philosophical damage to Clan O'Neal would be laborious to repair. Most laborious. She had so been trying to set a good example. Ripples upon ripples indeed—but her friend was speaking.

"You have given an odd message. Thank you." The Crab bounced quietly in his corner, inscrutable now that the onus of such an unpleasant deed had returned to him, plainly relieved that the message, so harmless on its face, allowed him to distance himself even farther from any ultimate actions. Regarding James Stewart's activities, he made no reply.

Nathan O'Reilly suppressed the urge to grumble into his morning coffee. It was an unpleasant surprise that he hadn't known there was a Tchpth in his base until Aelool walked in the door with him. He hated intelligence failures. Granted, it wouldn't have been possible for the operatives to give him *much* notice, but even a little would have been nice. Especially since he was practicing his dart throwing accuracy against a cork board picture of the Tir Dol Ron. He covered his chagrin with the smooth grace bred by many years of organizational and professional politics.

"Please, have a seat," he said, gathering darts and board, nonchalantly storing them in their proper place. "May I get you a water?" he asked.

Aelool said "please" at the same time as the unknown Tchpth said "no thank you." His stomach was tied in a tight little knot, because Aelool was carrying the awaited device for the Michelle O'Neal mission.

"Wxlcht, I would like you to meet Nathan O'Reilly, head of the O'Neal Bane Sidhe." If the Crab was surprised by Aelool's deferring authority to the Jesuit priest, he gave no indication. "Nathan, my Tchpth friend is named Wxlcht. He is the Speaker of Intrigue. He is here, however, in the capacity of those of his kind far wiser than himself."

Oh shit, O'Reilly thought, silently apologizing to the Almighty for the vulgarity. *What the hell did we get into to have what amounted to the Crab head of Intel in my office, speaking with the authority of the entire Tchpth species. Lord, please be with humanity in this time of trial*, he prayed.

"Wxlcht is here to deliver an instruction to me, to be repeated to Miss O'Neal," the Indowy said.

"The human Cally O'Neal," the ambassador interrupted.

"Yes. Miss *Cally* O'Neal," Aelool accepted the correction.

"May I ask the nature of this message?" The priest continued to pray, silently.

"Four words. 'Turn loose her leash,'" the Crab quoted.

"Are you *very sure* you want us to relay those exact words to Cally O'Neal. I do not know how she will interpret them, so I cannot guarantee the consequences. At all," he warned. This was both far better and far worse than he had feared. That was nothing that Nathan himself would *ever* say to Cally. *Ever*.

"Yes. Those exact words. You do not know, yet, what they mean. The Tchpth do, and she will." The planner paused, thinking. "If there is any question in her mind, and if you think it wise, you may tell her I made that delivery after speaking with her sister. And tell her that soon would be good. Very soon." He indicated the decoy prototype with one limb. "We would not . . . It is, if there were not grave hazard to . . . We never otherw . . . Enough." He sighed, his body stuttering a bit in its perpetual multilegged tap dance.

"I trust and expect your absolute discretion," he said. "We do, of course, acknowledge the creation of a debt to the Clan O'Neal. A significant debt."

Good Lord! Big. Dangerous, big, and either cataclysmic or priceless. He made the only possible answer, "You have my word."

"And mine," Aelool added.

"Thank you, and farewell."

That it did not merely say "goodbye" was another surprise. Ordinarily, any Tchpth would avoid even a simple change of leaving-word as too explicit an expression of well wishes to any "vicious omnivore." Curioser and curiouser.

After his unusual visitor departed, along with his own Indowy counterpart, Nathan took his AID out of his desk. "Get Cally O'Neal in my office. Now."

Minutes after Father O'Reilly's peremptory summons, Cally entered his office. She had not stopped to change out of leotard and leg-warmers, but instead stood before him barefoot, hair in a ponytail and gym towel around her neck. She blotted her still perspiring face and bounced on her toes, clearly feeling her endorphin rush.

"Decoy Aerfon Djigahr in?" she asked.

"Yes, but that's not why you're here," he said.

She stilled. "Nothing bad, I hope?"

"That depends on you. A high-level Crab planner delivered the decoy, in person. He also, after informing us that he was speaking on behalf of the entire Tchpth leadership structure, gave us a message with the strict instructions to quote it to you, verbatim."

"And?" she prompted, when he paused and was wasting time searching her face, as if she knew a damn thing about it. Unless it was about Stewart. That could be bad.

"Turn loose her leash," he quoted.

"Excuse me?" She wasn't quite sure she'd heard what she thought she'd heard. Or, she was, but thought she'd better hear it again, just to make sure.

"Turn loose her leash," he repeated. "He also said I could tell you he delivered the device here himself. He certainly thought you'd know what he meant. If you don't, we're in a very bad position."

"Oh, I know what he meant. He had to have gotten that"—she pointed at the machine—"from Michelle. Therefore, logically he got the message from her, as well. What I can't figure out is why the hell the Crabs would order a hit on Pardal."

"They wha—?" It was the first time she'd seen O'Reilly slack-jawed.

"At a meeting with Michelle recently, I offered to kill Pardal for her—more to get a rise out of her than anything. If you could have just seen . . . I meant it, of course, but I knew she'd never bite. Or thought I knew. And I don't know what the Crabs have riding on this. How close are my sister and this Crab, anyway?"

Nathan picked up his AID. "Tell Aelool I need him again, but phrase it nicely. Then give me an executive summary of Michelle O'Neal's relationship with the Tchpth Planner Wxlcht." He had learned early on to ask for executive summaries as the magic words that prevented his AID from talking his ears off.

"Michelle O'Neal and the Tchpth Planner Wxlcht," it replied immediately. "They are both avid aethal players and partner each other frequently. They communicate often, exchange favors, and are unusually close for members of their respective species. Executive summary material prepared by analysis of organizational files. Would you like me to broaden my search or elaborate on existing material?"

"That's quite sufficient. Thank you." It wasn't necessary to thank an AID, but the priest was wise enough to know that any habit of omission of the basic courtesies would carry over into his relationships with humans and Galactics. He was always polite to his AID.

"So would he do this from friendship and to return a favor? Would he lie about representing his government?" the assassin asked the machine.

"That is not even a remote possibility," Aelool said as he entered the room, forestalling the AID's reply. "The Tchpth would never tolerate insanity in a planning position, nor have they had an adult manifestation of insanity in a thousand years, except as a temporary reaction to some drugs. I would have noticed had Wxlcht been drugged, unlikely as that would have been. The message and authority were authentic. What did it mean?"

"Miss O'Neal informs me that the Tchpth government has requested that she kill the Darhel Pardal," O'Reilly said woodenly.

Aelool slumped to the floor, landing seated. "If this is a human joke, it is in execrable taste."

"Aelool, I'm really not kidding. Even I am not that dense about interspecies relations," she said.

"Then you are mistaken," the literally floored alien stated.

"Anything is possible," she answered.

"Not this," he declared.

O'Reilly could see a situation developing and was about to intervene when Cally opened her mouth again.

"I meant, it is possible that I'm interpreting his message wrong, or that he thought it meant something different from what it means to me. This could be a misunderstanding," she allowed.

"It is. It most certainly is. Please tell me why you have come to this conclusion so that we can sort out the real meaning." The small creature wasn't happy with Miss O'Neal. Again.

The priest said nothing, wanting to hear the answer, too.

"When I met Michelle a week or so ago to give her that information she wanted from her Tong contact on the Moon, she said some nasty things about Pardal and I offered to kill him for her. More as a joke than anything."

"A bad one," Aelool said.

"Granted," she nodded. "But then she said that it was a good thing you guys kept me on a tight leash. That's the only time Michelle and I have *ever* talked about a leash. Ever. So as ridiculous as it seems, can we at least consider what motives the Tchp— Tphk— Crabs would consider sufficient to order a specific sentient being killed?"

"Tchpth do not kill sophonts. Not even second or third hand," Aelool reiterated.

"Of course they do!" Cally contradicted. "They sure as hell commissioned humanity to kill off Posleen. In job lots."

"That was because the Posleen were a threat to all of the Wise and, thereby, to all the sentient life in the galaxy." Aelool sounded positively testy.

"Don't get mad at me. I'm not giving the orders. I'm just the poor kid at the sharp end." Apparently deciding it was an oversight that she had not been invited to sit, or making a subtle Cally-esque point, she walked to the other side of the coffee table from the spot where Aelool was still seated on the floor and planted herself in a chair.

Aelool got up and moved to a chair, himself. As O'Reilly joined them, the Indowy explained, as if to a child, "The whole institution of the Wise was at stake. The whole Path was at stake. Without the Wise to guide others on the Path, the remaining sophonts would eventually destroy themselves and the galaxy with them. The Tchpth very reluctantly deemed using barbaric omnivores to kill barbaric omnivores an absolute necessity."

Nathan O'Reilly raised a hand. "A moment, Aelool." He rubbed his forehead pensively. "That Tchpth was as upset as I've ever seen one; *he* said the situation was grave 'or they wouldn't' whatever. He sure didn't like what he was having to say, and he went to a lot of trouble to let us know it was from their whole government. *He* clearly didn't think a misunderstanding would be a possibility, and it was something he couldn't or wouldn't come right out and say."

"Pardal is trying to kill Michelle. She'd be one of your 'Wise,' wouldn't she? How would the Crabs extrapolate events from that? Or could Pardal be into something else that big or that dangerous?"

"Wait." Aelool held up a green, furry hand for silence—a human gesture—and thought.

After a moment, he looked directly into her eyes—for the first time, ever. "The consequences if you are wrong would be unthinkable."

Finally, the human leader of the O'Neal Bane Sidhe did intervene. "Plausibly, the highest Tchpth planners could have extrapolated events from the Darhel's planned murder—don't equivocate, that's what it is—of one of the first human mentats to some sort of Galactic threat. *I* can't see it, but I can't understand their physics, either. Aelool, I hate to ask you, but how close is your wisdom to theirs?"

"It is not close." He cringed. "You asked him if he was very, very sure. On their own heads be it, and I hope the Tchpth can be made to see it that way if she is wrong. All we can wisely do is just exactly what it told us. We turn loose her leash." He turned to the priest. "My friend, do you still keep the human custom of prayer?"

"Of course," the Jesuit answered.

"I hope very much that you will never find a better time to practice it. Please excuse me. This is more distressing than any human can imagine." The little green alien left the room without another word.

"So. How do you plan to kill him, and when?" O'Reilly, having resigned himself to the business at hand, was determined to see it come off successfully.

"Did the Crab say when?" she asked.

"He only said, 'Soon. Very soon.'" O'Reilly had no idea what to make of this. It would take time to sort through the implications. At least, to sort through as many of them as a human could follow.

"Then it has to be tomorrow," she announced.

"What? Are you crazy?"

"Not recently. We can't reschedule the run for Michelle; there isn't time. We'd never get another chance before she died. On the other side of that coin, if either target learns the other has been hit, the security walls are going to go way, way up and whichever mission is second will be impossible short of nukes—and maybe not even then. They have to be done as close together as possible."

"You're the second inside man at the target. They know your appearance. You have to be there personally or it doesn't come off. The hit on Pardal also absolutely has to be you, because the Tchpth said so—rather, they said you, so we use you. In case you're somehow wrong, as is distinctly possible, our only possible excuse is that they picked the message, and the recipient, after being specifically warned. I also specifically declaimed responsibility for the consequences of delivering such a message to you."

"I love you, too, Nathan."

"Cally, that message is something I would never, ever have chosen to say to you on my own. There's just no telling who or how many would die next." She looked affronted as hell. "You are very good at your job. Good assassins *always* need target control in the hands of someone other than themselves. Which, in this case, it still is. If, may the Good Lord and all of the Saints preserve us, you're right." And so help him, if she made an inappropriate joke about his appeal to the almighty, *he* just might kill *her*.

"Okay. My interview isn't until late afternoon. So I kill Pardal in the morning, and you have Harrison waiting for me with the car and my interview clothes. I'll change on the way."

"It's damned late to be making radical changes of plans. How are you going to kill him?" he asked. He didn't add that she might be overreaching in assuming her success and survival. He didn't need to.

"Don't know yet," she shrugged. "Hey, no plan survives contact with the enemy. This is what you pay me for. I'll shoot you a revised mission plan just as soon as I've got it—tonight at the latest. Honest, just relax. Trust me."

As soon as she was gone, O'Reilly called his assistant and asked for some aspirin. He had developed a killer headache.

CHAPTER TWENTY

The minute she stepped into the room for their final mission brief mid-morning, Harrison could tell that there was something. It wasn't exactly something *wrong* with her so much as it was different. For one thing, she was late. Their team lead was never late. He could see apprehension combined with a terrible excitement, the kind of buzz she'd get in the final day or so before she was sent on a hit, in that adrenaline high that started ramping up before she shut down emotion and channeled everything into single-minded focus. This kind of mission didn't typically spike her. It was a property extraction, not an assassination. Either their plans had changed for the top, or she had changed hers. At T-minus damned little, either option worried him.

"Okay, people, the good news is that we only have one change. The bad news is that it's a major, fundamental mission change," she said.

I knew it, the fixer thought. From the look on his face, his brother was just now registering the rising "oh shit" level in the room. It wasn't that George was any slower to pick up on emotional cues than the rest of them, just that he hadn't worked as much with Cally as the rest of them had.

"The change shouldn't affect anybody but Harrison and me. We've got a second mission with a rush on it. It has to be tomorrow morning and it has to be me. The good news is it's uncomplicated and I should be able to handle it with no help but a driver."

"What the hell do you think you're talking about?" O'Neal, Senior, drawled. He was without his usual plug of tobacco this morning. Probably only out of a rare inability to find a cup. Harrison winced. Nicotine withdrawal tended to make him . . . volatile. "There is no mission that could possibly justify haring off—"

"Pardal." She dropped the one word into the room like a stone. The kind of stone that might explode if you breathed on it too hard.

"A *Darhel*?" Papa was on his feet now. "Are they out of their tiny minds? No mission prep, no backup, and they drop it on us now? After telling us all these years why the precious Darhel were above all possible retribution, they drop this? No way. No fucking way. Sure, we'll kill him, if they're finally taking the damn gloves off. But after, with full prep, full backup—we'll do it the right way and not go in half-assed and not only miss the target but get you killed besides. What in the hell are they thinking? Scratch that, what the hell are *you* thinking? Why didn't you tell them to shove it up their ass?!"

Harrison honestly didn't know if he preferred Papa shouting or dead quiet. Either way was usually not a good sign. Right now, the O'Neal's Irish skin was somewhere between broiled shrimp and steamed lobster. His own stomach grumbled, and he realized that his choice of metaphors probably had something to do with skipping breakfast. Which was a bizarre thing to be thinking about given the turn the mission was taking.

"Papa, I'd like to hear the mission constraints and plans, if you don't mind, since I'm the lucky boy slated to share this little gem of a buggy ride," he heard himself say.

The older man harrumphed, which wasn't nearly as effective when done by a peach fuzzed juv instead of a grizzled geezer. He did, however, sit down and quit shouting. Harrison leaned back, arms crossed, and quirked a sardonic eyebrow at the stacked brunette. He really had done a great job with her hair.

"The reasons are easy enough, but they don't go outside this room. If I didn't think it would shake you out of peak efficiency to worry about what's going on, I wouldn't figure you three had a need to know." She inclined her head towards his teammates.

O'Neal, Senior, started to puff up, but Harrison forestalled him with a raised hand.

"Fine, we've all got need to know. And?" He knew that in the military he'd have been bordering on insolence, or worse, but despite certain similarities to some special warfare units, this wasn't the military, and the proposal was so harebrained he'd sure like to hear *any* reasons that could justify it.

"The Tchpth commissioned his elimination, and they specified me." She took the trouble to get the awkward word out as close to correctly as she could.

"They wha—?" Harrison was surprised his own mouth opened first. "Cally, this is a bad time to joke."

"Okay, all of you. Shut the fuck up and listen." She was fairly impressive when her temper started to kick in.

"Aelool and O'Reilly, both, met this Crab, know who he is, and are convinced that this is coming from the highest levels of whatever functions as their government. *Aelool* is convinced. That's all I need to know about authenticity of the orders or permission or whatever you want to call it. Frankly, I'd dance across a tightrope thirty stories up, backwards, if it meant I'd finally get to kill one of those poisonous little pricks, and any of you would, too. Now we get to the timing." She grimaced.

"I told O'Reilly it had to be tomorrow because, Pardal being into the dirty crap of our other mission up to his pointy ears, the security walls will go up on the other target if we don't hit them damned near simultaneously. The truth is, I'm afraid if we delay it, the Crabs will change their bouncy little minds. Tell me a chance to take out one of the fucking Elves themselves, finally, isn't worth a damned big risk. Besides, I can do this and get out. I figure eighty percent or so. Second, I'm the most expendable operative on the main mission. I'm along because I'm good in a tight situation and you didn't dare leave me behind. Tell me I'm not right."

They were all quiet for one of those timeless gaps when everybody's preconceptions get sucked into a contemplative bog.

"If this wasn't the dumbest, most dangerous stunt I'd ever heard of—just supposing for a minute—how would you kill him?" Papa growled.

"The most deniable way. I'm gonna piss him off."

"Yeah—you might want to rethink. Wild rumors aside, you got any idea how hard that is? Or, how fucking suicidal? I've seen video of a Darhel after pushing the button to kill a Posleen globe—*before* he hit lintatai. The entire Indowy bridge crew, those who hadn't found other places to be, were casualties. I've watched the old Bane Sidhe's debriefings and clandestine recordings of what an enraged adolescent Darhel can do in the moments between when he cuts loose, before he goes catatonic with lintatai. A terminally pissed off Darhel takes the 'dead man's ten seconds' to a whole other level. One clip has two adolescent Darhel ripping each other limb from limb in about the time it would take you to tie your shoe. Those teeth aren't for show," George said.

"I'll be watching all of that material, and more, tonight. Lintatai is the only possible way to kill him without making it obvious someone killed him. We don't know enough about their metabolism to poison him undetectably. Amend that, we could shoot him up with Tal if we had Tal. We don't. I'm not sure the Indowy even know how to make it, and the Crabs didn't conveniently volunteer any. So he rages around the room and I stay ahead of him. I may be stuck in this ridiculous body, but I'm still upgraded, and people move even faster in the first few seconds after the brain cocktail in Provigil-C hits, if they aren't dead tired to start."

"And the reason we don't use it as a battle drug for the speed is its tendency to give people who are already awake such a bad case of the shakes that for the next thirty minutes they're next to worthless in combat."

"Yup. But I don't have to fight him. I just have to stay ahead of him for fifty-eight seconds and then make it down the stairs. If I die, I'm just a crazy Darhel-conspiracist bitch who got lucky. And unlucky. That's the other reason I need you, Harrison. You're going to have to patch me up and pretty me up enough to make it through the interview, if it can be done. If something goes wrong, George gets a call from his girlfriend saying she's got car trouble and has to reschedule."

"I hate to say this, Papa, but it could work," Tommy said, breaking his silence for the first time.

"I know. That's what pisses me off the most." His teammate looked more like a short, muscular, red-headed fireplug than he did like Cally, especially since her whole external appearance had been worked over seven years ago, but he was reacting more like her grandfather than her teammate. "We don't have the slab anymore. Dead's dead. And I notice the Crabs aren't busting their humps bringing it back, either," Papa said.

"And wouldn't we all love to have it back? You've just brought up one more reason for doing this. The Crabs operate on favors, part of a whole 'nother chunk of Galactic economy nobody bothered to tell us about. It would be *nice* to have them owe us one. This mission is worth the added risks all the way around." She never missed a chance to push a point home.

"Even if it fucks up the primary operation and your sister dies?"

"The message included something that had to come from her; this particular Crab is one of her buddies. She's in it up to her ears, and we're just going to have to trust her, too."

"Michelle, too?" O'Neal groused. "But I still don't like it."

"Neither do I," Cally said, but Harrison knew she was lying. Correcting the Darhel Pardal's respiratory problem would appeal perfectly to her unslaked need for revenge, for the death of a mother, the loss of a father, and more other things than he could count. Now that he thought about it that way, he wouldn't trade his own spot on this mission for the world. He could think of a few things his family owed to the Darhel, too.

"Yeah, but what if Pardal doesn't take the bait?" his brother spoke up.

Cally shrugged, "George, you're one of the people who's always insisting I piss off too many people, and without trying. We O'Neals have certainly never tried to piss off the Darhel, as a race. Seem to have done it, though."

Harrison thought she was taking liberties with the truth there. The O'Neal family had never exactly tried *not* to piss off the Darhel, either. Not that they should.

"Can I get the bastard to lose it when I *am* trying?" she continued. "Not a problem."

"We're done except for me and you, Tommy." The team lead placed a small hand on their star geek's arm as the others left. "I'm gonna need a lot of that research information George mentioned. You don't have time to do it; you've got to get out of here. I need you to pick me the best cyber guy to assemble my on-the-fly field guide to Darhel behavior for tonight. There's no time for techie versus nontechie misunderstandings. I need you to sit in while I explain what I need and translate whatever needs translating, then you need to get moving."

"A whole species' behavior in one night. Is that all?" The big man's mouth had an ironic twist.

"Oh, you," she said, punching him in the shoulder. "I've got my wish list down to reasonable proportions. For the researcher and me, both. I know exactly what I need."

The "computer guy," as it turned out, was a tiny, fifteen-year-old girl with tangled brown hair and a splash of freckles across her nose, who asked precise questions, jotted notes, and—from the way she repeated back the details of what Cally wanted—hadn't needed anybody to translate for her in the first place. Mendy Wimms went on the assassin's list of people to expect big things from.

She herself went on Mendy's list of people to expect unbalanced things from, about the time she started skipping away down the hall singing like some manic, killer child, "I get to kill a Darhel, I get to kill a Darhel!"

Wimms overheard Harrison mumble something to his little brother as their team leader vanished around a corner. "We're never going to live this down, you know," he said.

Friday 12/10/54

The Indowy Aelool would have preferred almost anything to the situation he now had to face. It was one in the morning, local time, and he was dreading the coming interview with the human O'Neal. Aelool had not become the head of his own clan without having the strictest and most exquisite niceties of courtesy and propriety drilled into his head. The action he was now contemplating trampled all over the social rules with an almost human degree of obliviousness. No, to be fair, the human O'Reilly would never have done what Aelool was about to do. He had, after all, not spoken a word of the matter to Aelool himself in seven years. Surely he must have known. Humans were not often so discreet about private clan matters, and his human counterpart's tact had rather impressed him. It had been so tempting to interfere. In any case, he now waited in the special room for sitting that humans needed to share personal meetings with him. Nervous, he did not sit.

The O'Neal's eyes displayed an uncharacteristic vividness of the blood vessels in the whiter areas of his eyes. It looked strange. He also must have been weary, because he was being less careful about concealing his teeth with his lips. Aelool repressed a shudder.

"What was so important at this hour of the morning, Aelool? Sorry to be grumpy, but I'd just gotten to sleep," the orange-topped omnivore said.

"First, I most deeply regret the breach of protocol involved in approaching you on so private a clan matter. Please be assured that I have made every effort to respect your privacy in this, and to confine the distribution of any reports as much as possible. I am aware, from your own reticence, that you regard this as an extremely private clan matter, and I wouldn't have spoken of this matter with you or any other if I did not believe you needed this information. Please, forgive me in advance if I am mistaken. It is most certainly not my desire to be discourteous or disrespectful to the O'Neal or to the Clan O'Neal." He stopped speaking and waited for the response from the other clan head, to indicate if Aelool should continue, or should politely terminate the discussion.

"Aelool, I'm sorry if I'm not answering right, but I haven't the foggiest idea what you're talking about. Could you please try to explain in plain English? Sorry if I'm slow on the uptake, but I'm still half asleep."

The human was looking more wakeful by the second, but presumably this was part of their protocol for such situations.

"It involves your household granddaughter's breeding partner. Forgive me so much for intruding. Normally, when we intercept such a message, we file it flagged to your eyes only and leave it in the personal storage system for you to access or not, as you choose. In this case, the courier that was supposed to deliver the message to your granddaughter has suffered a misfortune—none of our doing, I assure you! If I did not broach the matter with you, the message might never reach Miss O'Neal, and the contents are so sensitive I judged I must personally bring it to your attention. Again, I am so sorry to intrude into Clan O'Neal's privacy."

If he had not known better, Aelool would have interpreted the human O'Neal's facial expression as bewilderment. Since that was clearly impossible, the Indowy was at a loss. Unsure of whether he had irretrievably blundered or not, he simply placed a data cube in the human O'Neal's hand and bowed, withdrawing to his and his roommates' sleeping quarters and closing the door behind him.

Aelool did not see the human insert the cube into the reader slot of his buckley, nor did he hear him mutter, "I'm gonna kill her," under his breath before he left the room. He would never have admitted to it if he had seen and heard such a thing. Nevertheless, he sincerely hoped that the human O'Neal would not do anything permanent to Cally O'Neal. He was rather fond of her. Did humans take poison in such cases? It was a very private clan matter, of course, and the Indowy had insufficient versing with human xenopsychology to understand why the O'Neal was vexed with his granddaughter over the contents of the message, but the Indowy was fond of her—for an omnivore. Still, it was a very private clan matter, and apparently the human O'Neal had not taken irreparable offense at the Indowy Aelool's presumption. That was something. It would, however, be disastrous if the O'Neal passed a judgment against his clan member before she completed her assigned work. Disastrous on top of regrettable. And the O'Neal was so volatile, too. Aelool went back to bed, worrying.

Cally was only a touch bleary this morning. She'd been able to whittle down the material Mendy turned up for her to only a few key scenes, and had watched them over and over again.

One of the key features that would enable what she was about to do was a project R&D had been developing to enhance human communication with Indowy. Humans had the problem, dealing with both Indowy and Darhel, of lacking mobile ears. The project involved having an AID or a buckley track the motion of its user's body and head, in real time, and track electrical impulses sent from behind a human subject's ears, using them to project a holographic set of mobile ears that would respond to the human's conscious, and subconscious, commands. Human ears were not, it turned out, completely immobile. Their mobility was simply so restricted that the ears did not noticeably move. The impulses were still there, in the nerves, still responding to the age-old evolutionary cues of mammals past—and to conscious control.

Conscious control of the holographic ears took weeks of practice. In Cally's case, she had that practice. She had been an early test subject for the project while on maternity leave. It had been a few extra bucks for baby's new pair of shoes and such, when she'd badly needed the money.

R&D had only intended to use the device between human and Indowy, and only if it improved the communication and comfort level between the two species. It hadn't. Indowy, it developed, were happier not knowing the emotional states of their human friends.

The research had been consigned to the trash bin of good ideas that just didn't work out. Until now.

No Darhel had ever seen a human with mobile ears. That was advantage one. Advantage two was the information-tracking software that let a buckley PDA superimpose realistic holographic ears on a human head also gave her buckley enough information to superimpose the rest of a holographic face, as well. Her buckley could not make her look like a Darhel, not ever enough to pass for one of them, especially when there were so relatively few in circulation. However, she didn't need to pass for a Darhel—not to another Darhel's *conscious* mind. She only needed to look enough like one, for just a bare instant, to fool the visceral mind about what it saw, before its better judgment kicked in.

A Darhel's descent into the permanent catatonia of lintatai was triggered by a single instant of homicidally bad judgment. A Darhel who succumbed to that one instant of rage didn't get a second chance. The Darhel who survived puberty did not do so because of any reduced capacity for, or desire for, unbridled rage. He survived by analyzing all possible outcomes of a situation ahead of time, and applying carefully trained-in meditative disciplines when a situation began to take him into danger.

Adult Darhel thought of themselves as paragons of detached emotional control. It wasn't true. Any Darhel had plenty of buttons to punch, he just had nobody around to punch them. One Darhel wouldn't provoke another into lintatai because it was suicidal. He couldn't drive the other into lintatai without entering it himself. Himmit, Indowy, and Tchpth also considered deliberately provoking a Darhel to be an insanely stupid act.

They were, of course, correct. It was also correct to say that every human did at least a dozen things a Galactic would find insane every day of her life.

It had long been accepted in the human executive protection field that one can never effectively guard against a determined, competent assassin who is willing, if necessary, to lose her life in the act. The Darhel had, she suspected, never heard that particular truism. One of their number was about to learn—the hard way.

She was surprised that Granpa was at the table with Harrison when she stopped by the mess hall for a light breakfast. She was freshly showered and bare of makeup, dressed in a simple

T-shirt and jeans. Her entire appearance, from top to toes, was Harrison's domain today. She had the basic canvas and equipment, but Harrison was peerless at turning the basics into whatever they required. In this case, nothing less than a world-class, breathtaking vision of beauty would suffice.

Granpa sure was looking funky. Something was wrong. "All right, spit it out. What is it?" She addressed him in the way that was most in her nature. Straight on.

"What are you talking about? I just came down to see you off at breakfast. So I'm worried about you. I'm your grandfather; it's my privilege," he said.

"Not buying it. What's really wrong?" she asked. After half a century of her reading him, he couldn't get anything by her. The reverse usually applied, as well, but wasn't the problem today.

"Harrison, could you excuse us for a minute?" Papa said, looking at his hands as he picked a fresh plug of tobacco from his pouch.

Harrison disappeared in the direction of the coffee counter.

Cally raised her eyebrows at the old man. "Well?" she asked.

"Granddaughter, dear, the next time you decide to engage in a major fucking breach of security, would you do me the kindness of telling me first? Instead of leaving me to find out years later from someone of a different fucking species at one in the morning on the day of an operation, for instance," he said.

"Oops," she said, as he glowered at her. Which was exactly what she would have expected. Exactly. Except he was overplaying it. Not much, but her sense of every detail around her was heightened to a preternatural sharpness this morning. "Now what's the other shoe?" she asked.

"You don't think that's enough?" he whispered harshly. "The Indowy have known for *years* that I have a son-in-law, while you've been running around behind the backs of me and Shari, not to mention your girls, and—"

"You can drop that other shoe now. We'll talk about my sins if we all survive the day. What else? Give," she demanded.

Now he looked distinctly uncomfortable. He puffed up, as if to try another layer of false bluster, then the masks dropped and there was just Granpa. An uncomfortable and unhappy looking Granpa. "I think you should wait to ask me that question tomorrow. I really think you should."

"What's the other shoe, Granpa? I'm not going to give up, because whatever it is, I'm going to be more distracted worrying about it than I would hearing it. You might as well put it on the table," she said.

When he quietly stuck a data cube on the table, she jerked back a bit. "I didn't mean it that literally, but I'll take it. Excuse me," she said, taking the cube with her to the ladies' room. Whatever it was, she apparently needed to see it in private.

A scant minute later she reemerged, stalking back to the table with her head held rigidly high. "He dear johned me? By fucking e-mail! Do you have any idea why I'm getting this third—excuse me, fourth hand?" she asked.

"Something happened to the courier. I don't know what. Aelool thought it was important enough for you to receive this message that he passed it to me. Apparently, for seven years he's believed I knew and never said anything because he considered it a private, clan matter. Which it would have been, if you'd just talked to me, you know," he said.

He looked very worried, which she supposed wasn't out of place given everything. Not that he needed to be.

"I'm sure we'll have more than enough time for that, after. Right now, don't be upset that I know about this. I'm so pissed off at the bastard that it may just give me the rage I need to survive this morning's appointment. Not to mention one hell of a lot of incentive," she growled.

"No, I'll be all right. Really. Especially since the only man I have to be around for several hours is Harrison. Which is probably a very, very good thing." She waved their openly gay teammate back over to the breakfast table, smiling a cold, brittle smile. She knew Granpa couldn't miss that she was getting dangerously wound up. He was right, but she'd be okay today. She already had someone to kill, even before lunch. "Dear johned me. E-mail! It'd probably upset the girls someday if I killed him. That's okay. I've got other people to kill today. This is good," she muttered under her breath.

Harrison was back to hear that last, and was wearing the impression of someone who'd just woken to find himself in a cage with a mother grizzly bear. And cubs. She took a deep breath and deliberately favored him with a cool smile.

"It's okay, Harrison. Really. Consider it me getting appropriately psyched for the mission. I would say you can pretty much expect this morning to go as smooth as glass, now."

The man didn't look much reassured. Right now, that was fine by her.

Back into the earliest periods of human history, missions in the nether realms of politics—the ones carried out in a dark alley or a state bedroom with a sharp knife—had involved a certain amount of gear. The tradition was unbroken. Only the specifics of the gear changed. Cally's gear had to solve a few problems that simple moxie could not. Problem one was that even though a complacent door guard could be fooled long enough for her to get close to said guard, a human receptionist very likely couldn't. Security guards mostly served to insulate their masters from stupid criminals, crazies, and salesmen. Their threat meter was very carefully focused in, even for the ones who thought it wasn't. Nobody could be hyper-vigilant forever. Weeks, months, and years of working in the same building, only encountering a specific subset of threats, inevitably had the effect on the human psyche of narrowing the range of threats the guard even thought of as possible. In the hypothetical realm where one of them would tell you about his job, this wasn't so. In the real world, it was universal. The most dangerous security guard in the world was the FNG, because he still considered everything a potential threat.

A receptionist, on the other hand, had a much wider threat range from which to insulate her charge. She had to worry about any of the aforementioned nuisances who somehow got past security, plus underlings wasting the boss's time, plus—only in the case of a human boss—wives and mistresses. The most sensitive problems with the latter usually cropped up after they were no longer wives or mistresses. Some business was not a nuisance and was legitimate. Determining which required very active judgment from a receptionist who valued her job. As a consequence, receptionists were greater threats than security guards for any mission that had to be done discreetly.

Receptionists everywhere had an absolute inability to ignore a ringing phone, regardless of whose ring tones were singing through the air. One of the assassin's smallest and simplest pieces of gear combined the ordinary sticky-camera with late twentieth-century greeting card technology to provide ding-dong ditch capabilities any ten-year-old could envy.

Her second major tool was not an item of gear, per se, but a hardware enhancement common to all operatives' PDAs. Cally didn't understand all the technical gobbledegook, herself. She wasn't a cyber, and she had her hands full keeping up with her own job. It was enough for her to know that the AIDs' transmissions back to the Darhel hierarchy's central data stores were not completely leak free. While intercepting the data itself and decoding it would be quite a trick, a properly equipped PDA within about fifteen meters of an AID could sense whenever the AID started churning out its data upload. The uploads were on a regular schedule. It was possible to get around an AID's all-seeing eye by just waiting until its upload went off and either rushing the machine or working quickly. The gap was a bit more than twenty minutes—ample for most purposes. The trick was that the more time the AID recorded before one muffled its senses, the more you had to jimmy with it to cover your tracks. A few seconds or even minutes could be forcibly erased, but it took about three times as long to erase as it did to record. This created a diminishing returns situation where, after about eight minutes, it was faster to dump the whole load of the old AID into fresh AID hardware and hope nobody noticed the hardware swap—you just stuck the fresh AID in a desk drawer or somesuch, then the cybers' wizardry did the rest. AIDs being a lot more standardized than anything of Indowy make, swapping hardware was a tiny risk—it was just damned expensive. And took nine minutes and fifty-three seconds that could get you killed.

The really critical pieces of mission-specific gear were an AID for herself, and a hush box. The latter item was a little white box that, for an AID, was the equivalent of a sensory deprivation tank. Developed after the war from a hybrid of some easier Galactic technology with common Earth know-how, many AID users carried them, and all recognized them. Most Darhel even used them, now—they wanted their verbal sparring matches private from others of their kind just as much as humans would. Paranoia was an emotion both species shared in equal measure. Pardal was on the list of Darhel confirmed to use such a box.

A chunky bracelet on her right wrist contained a mister that could be filled with any number of drugs. Operatives were routinely immunized to many drugs of the psychoactive variety. This gave a wide array of choices for an operative who wanted to affect someone at close range without being drugged herself. A simple clenching of the fist and a cool, damp cloud of dreams—sweet or otherwise—would ride in on the victim's next breath. Naturally, the most popular drugs for this were very, very fast.

Harrison had outdone himself. The woman who stepped onto the curb from the yellow cab was so conspicuously lovely that anyone seeing her would be sure he ought to recognize her from holodramas or advertisements and begin searching his mind. She was precisely the sort of beauty the Darhel typically hired to grace their offices. It was not that the Darhel found the women more than artistically appealing. Darhel understood conspicuous consumption and its relationship to power. Everything a Darhel owned or used was the best available, or, if not the best, the most ostentatious.

The black bob of George's girlfriend was intact, but glossy as a mink coat. His brother had taken the cornflower blue eyes and enhanced them with subtle cosmetic flattery into deep, hypnotic pools. Her skin was to porcelain as fine pearls were to chalk. Her figure needed precious little flattery, but Harrison had managed to imply that the body underneath the cashmere sweater-dress and impeccably cut blue coat belonged in some ancient pagan temple, not on Chicago's winter streets.

Her appearance had the predictable mind-befuddling effect on the security guard at the main door to the Sears Tower. He stopped her, and the young goddess made a great show of searching her purse for ID as she moved closer to him. Maybe she stiffened a bit, maybe she didn't. The guard straightened and let her through, his brain befuddled by a common date rape drug. He stood his post, he looked—at worst—mildly inattentive. His only thought was, most likely, that everything in his world was just hunky-dory. He wouldn't remember this morning, later, but would feel mildly happy about it.

Past the guard, the assassin slipped onto an elevator and rode it to the floor beneath her target's office. The lovely thing about this building was that it was a popular tourist site before the war. The Bane Sidhe files had extensive information on the layout of every floor, including the locations of the restrooms. She walked up to the final floor and into the ladies' room without encountering anyone else. The nature of offices and rush hours is that everyone shows up at once, usually within fifteen minutes of work start time. Arriving an hour ahead, she had passed a handful of people in the lobby, but no one else. She made a quick and careful jaunt down to another hall to place her little present for the receptionist in the shadow underneath a smoke detector, and returned to the restroom to wait.

Then she spent an hour playing solitaire before she told the buckley to start listening for AID updates. The lounge area of this restroom shared a wall with the executive office of the Darhel Pardal. Once again, Darhel decorating predictability was her friend. Darhel psychological theories held that such and such a place was the position of maximum psychological dominance in an office. That one spot and no other would hold the Darhel's desk. Other details might vary with individual tastes, or the creative idiosyncrasies of the decorator, but his desk would be in the position of maximum psychological dominance. Every time. The stall she occupied should give the buckley a detection range up to a good three meters past the farthest edge of the desk.

"I have detected an AID update transmitting," the buckley said. "Of course, I don't know how many AIDs are in there, or if the receptionist has one, or if they're having a Darhel convention, or—"

"Shut up, buckley."

"I'm just saying—"

"*Shut up*, buckley."

"Right."

"Buckley, start ringing the phone for the receptionist. Tell me when she moves out of line of sight of Pardal's office."

"But you just told me to shut up."

"Just do it, buckley. And don't make another peep unless I'm about to get caught."

"Peep," it said. "I can think of at least nineteen ways you are about to get caught. Would you like me to list them in ascending or descending order of probability?"

"Buckley, has the receptionist moved out of line of sight of Pardal's door?"

"Moving, moving. Yes, now she is out of line of sight."

As soon as the buckley had said "moving" the assassin had

begun moving, herself, leaving her coat and purse on the floor behind her. "Then shut up and stay shut," she said.

"But—"

"Shut up, buckley." Cally appreciated the carpet in the hall—it muffled the clacking of her stiletto heels. She stuffed the PDA into a hidden pocket in her back waistband. It wouldn't withstand scrutiny from behind, but so what?

"Right," the buckley muttered from the small of her back.

She took the space between the ladies' and the executive office door at a sprint, instantly transforming back into cool beauty as she opened the door and stepped through.

The Darhel Pardal looked up from the figures projected on the desk and fixed her with his yellow, predator's eyes. He wore the long gray cloak typical of Darhel attire, the head thrown back to reveal his fox face. He snapped it shut.

Good, he was already pissed at the interruption. Coldly pissed, but it was a start. This was the closest thing the Darhel had to sabers at dawn; these next few seconds were make or break.

"If you have the confidence," she drawled, holding up two items, and slipping what was obviously an AID into what was equally obviously a hush box. Her body language, every vocal nuance, the words themselves—everything about that line down to the minutest detail she had crafted, practiced, and practiced again the night before. Over two and a half hours had gone into crafting and perfecting that one line, using the buckley's AI capabilities to analyze and critique her performance again, and again, and again. With the ability to craft the right performance holographically, if it had enough data, a buckley PDA was the best acting coach in the world. Her life and the whole mission rested, more than anything else, on perfection in the crafting and delivery of that first line. Sometimes, it paid to be a perfectionist.

The lateral muscles around Pardal's nose quirked in amusement. Darhel could feel amusement, in a way very like a cat playing with a mouse. Her task for the next few minutes depended on keeping him balanced on a knife's edge between amusement and anger. For that species, the two emotions were not incompatible. She restrained a sigh of relief as he slid his own AID into a hush box, taken from the desk.

"You're not nearly as good as you think you are." He laughed. "But my morning has been tedious, and it's so rare to find a human who even bothers to begin learning to use its voice—however clumsily." His own speech had the rich, melodious roll his species was famous, and infamous, for.

Her opening line had carefully aped one of the opening salvos a Darhel of equivalent or greater rank would use to initiate one of the stylized verbal confrontations that were the meat and potatoes of their intra-species dominance games.

"I don't believe I have the pleasure of your acquaintance," the other predator said.

"My name's Cally O'Neal, and I've come to have a few words with you about your attempts to murder my sister," she said. Again, her intonations were practiced, her body language and word choice carefully prepared.

"A human can change its name to anything, by your primitive rules. Your names are disposable, indicating nothing. As for the rest, it's nonsense, of course, but still amusing. You, of course, intend to upset me to the point that I freeze into a melodramatic death. I assure you our weakness is exaggerated, and I will be disposing of you to the proper security personnel in this interview's aftermath. For now, you may continue."

"Oh, but the Institute for the Advancement of Human Welfare is a wholly owned subsidiary of the Epetar Group, which also holds the human mentat Michelle O'Neal's contract for research on a certain device. A device, moreover, which the Tchpth," her pronunciation was perfect, "would be unhappy to find outside their museum on Barwhon." Head cocking to the side, just a bit. Shoulders just so. Sides of the lip curling in an expression never meant to inhabit a human face.

"How regrettable, for you, that you would make such an assertion. And how stupid of you to hush your AID before discussing this. Now I will have to turn you over to humans who will be, for whatever reasons, curious about how you came to know those things. I will, of course, know nothing of the means or ends. I will, however, receive a full report of the extracted information." He breathed deeply, effortlessly suppressing the qualms it had cost him to make even a roundabout physical threat. The Darhel behavioral tags in her voice, her body, her face were so insidiously familiar to him that it never crossed his mind to notice how *wrong* it should be that they were displayed on a human. Like a human hearing its own mother-tongue, regional accent in a speaker from anywhere, the pattern felt so mundane as to coast in under the intellectual radar of what should and shouldn't be.

"Of more amusement value to me is your choice of nom de guerre. You wish to bask in the reflected glory, alleged glory, of the O'Neal family, of course. But to claim the human mentat as your sister? What a transparent lie, even if you did find the correct name. Your features are nothing like Michelle O'Neal's, of course. And the sister died in a nuclear explosion in the war, at the hands of her own primitive killer of a father." His taunt took on a rich slur, an accent more inflected with the attributes of his own native tongue, even while he continued to speak English. For a Darhel, prizing as they did their psycholinguistic skills and the interspecies use of the voice for manipulation, this was a massive lapse.

"My features have changed, of course. I look very different from my childhood appearance when the Tir Dol Ron sent a team to kill me, and my grandfather, when I was eight Terran years old." She glanced off to the side, examining the nails of an elegantly cocked hand, as if he was beneath her notice.

Pardal sat straighter in his chair, ears pricked forward.

"You are, at that, remarkably well informed, for the pathetic, lying, glory-seeker that you are."

"As you are remarkably complacent for a Darhel facing not only a contract court, but the ignominy of triggering financial ruin for an entire group. You don't dare detain me, you know. My merely making these allegations to a contract court would cost you your job, simply for the incompetence of permitting the scandal. I have, of course, made prior arrangements to have the allegations delivered if I do not return."

"Preposterous exaggeration," he drawled, but breathed more deeply, accent thickening. "You begin to bore me."

"Expect your troubles to get worse, instead of better." She had cribbed one of the classic Darhel finale lines from their literature, typically delivered by a clear victor in one of these verbal cat fights. She could only hope the Indowy scholar had translated it accurately enough. As was customary, she had also delivered no specific threats. The purpose of these dominance struggles was never to *do* something, only to undermine the losing Darhel's personal confidence.

She turned to leave, to leave him knowing, intellectually, that he truly could not detain her and had just lost a dominance struggle of their own kind to a mere, primitive, human female.

She knew she had shaken him to the brink of rage when, knowing the interview was concluded and, inevitably, relaxing a bit from the taught wire of confrontation, he couldn't resist a parting shot, in his own tongue. "This isn't over!"

It had been a brief conversation. Its entire punch lay in the stylized nature of tone and body, play and counterplay, of Darhel interactions. This one moment was the goal of the entire playlet. He was now reacting to her not as he would to an impudent human, but as he would to a rival Darhel. Not completely, not consciously.

She touched the Provigil-C injector on one hip, driving the drug into her bloodstream. The buckley, prepped for her turn from the start, activated its holographic projection as she spun and leaped, spread eagled, teeth bared, ears flattened back against her head. Her yellow cat-pupilled eyes gleamed, feral. Her black hair and facial fur glinted with metallic silver. Her leap was imbued with all the skill of an avid dancer for counterfeiting the emotion of motion—even for dances alien to her own understanding.

The Darhel Pardal, aroused by the hormonal responses to an intense dominance conflict with his own kind, saw in that one single instant a rival Darhel leaping to kill him. His hindbrain overwhelmed his forebrain for that bare instant. Even as he realized that the leaping figure was a human woman and *not* a rival Darhel, the Tal poured into his system like floodwaters through a breached earthen dam. His rage redoubled with all the fury of a doomed thing for its killer.

The ravening beast, unleashed at last, exploded upward from the trappings of civilization, bounding off the desktop and crossing the room in an instant, claws out and teeth bared to rip out the throat of the Other. If the assassin had still been there to see it, he would have looked more like some hell-begotten cross between a fox and a werewolf than an Elf. The gray cloak billowed behind him and he paused for a tiny fraction of a second to rip it off, shredding it in the process.

That fraction of a second, combined with a similar fraction for the leap, was all the time it took Cally O'Neal to cross the office in the other direction, standing against the windows. It is an odd fact that for a skilled tumbler, across a short distance, a human being can roll faster than she can run. Running takes precious bits of time here and there starting and stopping, acting and reacting. A tumbling pass is smooth, continuous—if the athlete has the balance for it.

As a life-long dancer and martial artist, Cally's sense of motion was exquisite. If her balance had been a knife, she could have shaved with it. Her muscles, most importantly her upper body muscles, had the strength and speed of the latest Crab-designed upgrade. None of it saved her from getting batted into the remains of the desk with rib-cracking power. The dress shredded under Pardal's claws. The only reason he didn't get her flesh as well was the super-tough Indowy-crafted body-suit beneath the dress, which gave her a tougher hide than chain mail, while having none of the extra weight and causing no impairment to mobility.

She hit the desk and kept rolling, over the other side and onto her feet, bounding aside at an angle as one hundred and fifty kilos of rabid Darhel hit the spot she'd just left. He got her again, slamming her into the two-inch-thick glass with a force that wrenched her neck and knocked her head against the glass, making a sickening thud.

"Forty seconds and counting," the buckley announced from where it had landed on the floor about ten yards and five years ago, and the drug kicked in. For another split instant, Pardal turned with maddened eyes, locating the buckley on the floor. Barely hesitating, he obviously dismissed it as "not prey," launching himself at her again. Used to taking a punch, head crack or not, Cally hadn't stopped moving, and was halfway across the room again.

With the Provigil-C in her system, shaking her apart, with all the adrenaline and other combat hormones of her own, life dissolved into a sharp-edged, blurry game of Dodge the Darhel. Aware of everything and nothing, the instants rang off her brain like separately frozen photographic stills. All moments splintered into a constant progression of *now* as the buckley, now ignored completely by both, counted off the eternally slow seconds. Four . . . three . . . two . . . one . . .

Seeing a Darhel collapse on holo was one thing. Having one chasing you do it was another. One second he was leaping, the next he was hitting the floor in a lazy roll himself. He simply stopped, curled into a seated position on the floor, naked except for his own fur, and the rage melted away, along with the last vestiges of intelligence in his eyes. His expression was the closest thing to beatific she'd ever seen on a Darhel face. It was downright creepy.

"You were right," she said, nudging him with a bare toe before looking for wherever she'd kicked her shoes off. "*Now* it's over."

There had been no risk of anyone coming into the office after Pardal lost it. They'd all heard stories and *nobody*, human or Indowy, wanted to be anywhere near a raging Darhel. Cally found the floor, in fact, deserted as she limped back to the bathroom to retrieve coat and purse. The coat was now strictly necessary, as she had to stuff what scattered strips of the cashmere dress as she'd been able to find in her purse. There hadn't been much. At one point in his fit, she'd seen Pardal eating some of it, so it wasn't hard to guess where the rest had gone. Certainly nobody would be looking for it inside his guts. Traditionally, they didn't do forensic investigations at all, a Darhel in lintatai being beneath contempt.

She went back to the destroyed office. The last thing she did before leaving his office for good, closing the door behind her, was to use her AID to jimmy his, leaving it a few seconds of memory the poorer, and still stuck in the hush box. For a Darhel, this kind of death scene constituted the ultimate in "natural causes."

She was still shaking uncontrollably when she walked down the last flight of stairs, out into the falling snow and biting wind, and into the back of Harrison's cab. The endorphins and Provigil-C released their grip, and she groaned as everything from the crack on her head to the muscles in her toes started to *hurt*.

CHAPTER TWENTY-ONE

In her persona as Mark's girlfriend, Cally O'Neal was again in a sweater dress, and still busty. It was always either highlight her mammary assets or make her look fat with padding. Harrison had chosen to play them up as his interpretation of the "girlfriend" role, this time in a cheaper, off-the-rack, blue dress, topped with a gray wool coat. She felt conspicuous, even though he had assured her that the supportive bands of tape holding her cracked ribs in place were invisible under the clinging dress. A mix of lambs' wool and angora, the knit was thick, soft, and fuzzy. He assured her he had chosen it to blur outlines, anticipating the need. He'd praised her luck in keeping her face intact, but winced as he layered on makeup to cover the red and rising bruises. Artful highlights and shadows concealed the swelling. He'd assured her the illusion would hold for an hour or two, even though she'd look like she'd layered on her foundation with a trowel. It couldn't be helped, so she'd have to play to it, making the character fit the behavior. He'd helped by giving her a couple of fake blemishes, making them look as if she had tried to conceal them, and only partially succeeded—a woman sensitive about her flawed skin.

Felicity Livio was supposed to be barely adult, with education and training fitting her for entry level clerical work. She looked the part.

George, aka Mark Thomason, met her just inside the entry to the building. The wind had started to pick up, carrying big, clumpy snowflakes built of the wet air coming off the lakes. They'd be breaking up into powder soon, as the temperature dropped.

Acclimated to Charleston, despite all her travels she hated snow. It put her in an even worse mood as George put his arms around her and tried to kiss her. She ached, she was cold, and he was male. None of this made her like him right now. "Get your fucking hands off me unless you want to lose them," she hissed, turning her head towards the door and away from observers.

"What the hell's the matter with you? We're supposed to be lovers!" he whispered in her ear.

She jerked away, unmercifully squashing the need to scream as his hand pulled against a rib. "Then we're having a fight. I mean it, keep your mitts off me," she muttered, plastering on a fake smile and walking briskly towards the elevator, heels clacking on the marble floor.

He trailed in her wake until she stopped in front of the guard. "Job interview. I'm walking her up," he said.

The guard scanned his ID, issued her a temporary, and she stalked to the elevator, scanning the red temp badge and hitting the call button. She could tell he'd love to bitch her out about her behavior, but couldn't. So she was taking her mad at Stewart out on him. So what? He was a man. Men were on her shit list right now. Rational thought didn't enter into it. And she didn't care, dammit. Goddamn insensitive son of a— A bell tinged and the elevator opened.

George's lips tightened as she relaxed her stiff posture, smiling at him as if absolutely nothing was wrong. He schooled his own features into something more appropriate before the elevator stopped and binged again.

"Where to?" she asked.

"This way." He didn't quite sound the part, but what could you expect?

She smiled and greeted Ms. Felini on automatic. Introductions were introductions. As the door closed behind them and the other woman offered her a seat, she looked at Cally curiously.

"I hope everything's all right. You and Mark looked a bit . . . stiff," she said.

"Oh, it's the moving in together thing. Small small, really. He has this absolutely *awful* lamp," she improvised.

"Ah. One must go through these little adjustments, mustn't one?" the interviewer said. "So if I hire you, we're not going to have any discord in the office, are we?"

"Oh, no." Cally laughed. "I'll let him off the hook the second he gets reasonable and ditches the lamp from hell. He's not *that* attached to it, he's just being stubborn. We've been through this kind of thing before."

Prida laughed with her, and the now-relaxed job applicant eased back in the comfortable leather chair, crossing her legs.

"Can I get you some coffee? You must be cold," the other woman said.

"Oh, oops. Yes, please." The assassin flushed and took off her coat, hanging it on the brass tree behind the door. *It doesn't hurt, I feel fine. I feel abso-fucking-lutely fine. Ow, dammit.*

Cally had to admit that she wasn't as attentive as she should have been during the interview, and maybe didn't make a terrific impression. But after all, it wasn't as if she really wanted the job. She was still well within the range of credibility as she listened to the boring parade of duties, from digging through spam filters to data entry.

Felini showed her out with the line, "We'll call and let you know, dear." The operative summoned a smile as if she really cared and asked the way to the ladies' room. Once there, she went to the second to last stall, the one least likely to get occupied, took a plastic pen and pad of sticky notes—the only things she'd dared smuggle through the front door—out of her purse. On it she scribbled, "Out of order—maintenance." Slapped on the door, it should ensure she wouldn't be disturbed. If someone from cleaning or maintenance did try to check, she'd have to take steps. Incapacitating but not immediately lethal—not if she could help it. Bodies, no matter how killed, tended to do immediate things that stank. Not to mention the dilemma of where to put one. Silencing live people for any significant span of time also had its problems. Hopefully, things wouldn't come to that. Considering the problem and its possible solutions took her mind off her hurts, although not in a particularly pleasant way. It would have been nice to have her PDA, but not possible. Papa was bringing a fresh one for her, ready loaded with a recent backup of her own buckley's memories and all her data. Until then, she was alone. Well, minus her PDA. Not that having a buckley with her was the same thing as not being alone. Not exactly.

✧ ✧ ✧

From his uncontested position under a hot steam vent, Tommy had turned down propositions from eleven hookers—seven of them female, or apparently so—when the sweep came around just before oh-three hundred. He was one of a few caught in the net who weren't gibbering in panic. Three passed-out drunks barely stirred to grumble at being moved, before settling down in the body-heat warmth of the semi trailer. He wasn't good at panic. It didn't look credible on a man of his gargantuan size. He sat on the floor, contriving to look stupid. It was usually a good substitute.

He had initially been clean, inside malodorous clothes designed to conceal the effects of regular bathing. After seven hours in the dirty clothes, conspicuous cleanliness was no longer a problem. The uniformed thugs doing the sweep—formally called an urban assisted renewal program—initially looked like they intended to tazer him. His slack jawed, amiable compliance, as he slid into a more central position in the terrified herd, had saved him one small discomfort. Small, of course, was relative.

An hour later, being herded into a cold, locked, and otherwise empty room, whose corrugated steel walls shouted warehouse, he had definitely gotten tired of this game. Most of his fellows were shivering. The Special Police, SPikes, had rousted them out of warm beds. No wonder Sub-Urb residents were reluctant to move back above ground. The drunks may have been, for the moment, in a better situation. They would have likely frozen to death on this bitterly cold night. The room had heating—damned inadequate heating. He winced in sympathy with the folks who had to choose between freezing their asses on the concrete floor or standing on their bare feet. It wasn't like the bastards gave them time to grab anything. The SPikes were as eager to get out of the cold as anyone else, and weren't going to delay over the whining of a few trash colonists.

Tommy earned a grateful look from a mother by picking up a crying little boy of about seven. With a toddler and a baby on each hip, she had no room for the older child. He gave the kid his jacket and the loud crying subsided to miserable, wet sniffles against his big chest. One thing the SPikes would always stop for was parents rounding up their children, as every warm body, no matter how small, helped to fill the night's quota. They treated the children like glass. Not from compassion, but from fear of setting off their mothers. SPikes had died before at the hands of suicidally enraged women. Tiny ones, even.

After a timeless eternity, other goons shuffled them up some stairs and down a hall into a smaller holding room. The glow paint around the top of the walls was flaking off, leaving the room dim, but warm, as the Galplas floor held the heat from the room better than concrete slab on the ground. A vent in the ceiling blew out hot air and the captives began to settle to the floor as, for most, fatigue and warmth overcame terror. This was awkward, as seated people took up more space in the cramped room. Tommy ended up with three little kids and a hooker's head resting on top of him, he being too heavy to be anywhere but directly on the floor. His own head was stuck on a drunk's belly. He didn't complain, just sincerely hoped he wouldn't get puked on before George sprung him from this sardine can. He tried not to let himself think about the other possibilities.

Two hours later, Papa O'Neal crawled through the snow, ghillie suit stuffed with ice-gilded grasses and brush, poking up through rapidly falling snow that he deeply hoped would keep falling fast and heavy, the bitter wind blowing and piling it up. This was not only because it reduced visibility for both man and machine, but also because his body's tracks would need a hell of a lot of covering. He could have covered his tracks if mother nature hadn't been cooperative and chosen to help out, but it would have taken at least two additional operators from cleanup and been complicated. He was just as glad to keep it simple, even if it was damned cold humping a ruck full of black box through this mess.

Getting up the wall to the air exchange was a stone bitch, especially with his cold-stiffened joints. There was also no way to make his path perfectly trackless. The adhesive that held a hand or foot to the wall when the correct button was depressed, and released it simultaneously with that button, left a light, gooey residue. It couldn't be helped. Nor did he enjoy the coordination necessary to work the tongue switch that controlled his feet. He had spent a lot of time learning to use the grippers, but doubted it would ever be easy for him. The Himmit's natural version worked better than the synthetics, but the grippers were the closest copy the Bane Sidhe Indowy had ever been able to devise.

He had to take the ruck off and push it in front of him to fit into the vent, which he was absolutely certain was smaller than George had described, the rat bastard. He almost dropped the decoy, twice, trying to get the ruck into the hole in front of him without dropping the vent cover or falling off the wall. Even with his natural physique upgraded and enhanced, a hundred kilos of gear was one hell of an awkward load.

As his left calf cramped into yet another charley horse, Papa started to envision and enumerate painful ways for Schmidt Two to die. Sending him in through this crazy route. He was up to seventeen when he had to arch his back into an unnatural, virtually impossible position to turn a curve from horizontal to straight up. The ruck was now resting on his head, and a sharp and pointy edge dug into his scalp. Nineteen. He climbed on in the darkness, counting the "steps" to his next turn.

Every time he had to stop to remove a dusty filter from his path, he came up with one more creative and painful demise for the other assassin.

After what seemed like two hours after he entered the shaft, but was probably less than one, he reached the designated internal vent, high on the wall of the third floor. He was pretty sure he was in the right place. A tiny descendant of the periscope, extended forward past the bulk of his ruck, had shown that the fire extinguisher, floor number, and doors were where they should be. He sure hoped he was in the right place, as only the correct vent had steel screws that had been replaced with screws made of a hard putty. They'd flow into the bolt threads and grip, enough to hold the vent cover in place indefinitely. Until it was given a good pull or push, when it would pop right out. If the putty was gently warmed, the removal was practically silent.

It was a royal pain in the ass to contort around the ruck to put heating tabs at the corners of the vent, then trail threads tied to the pull tabs back to where he could reach them. He fed a couple of thin wires at the top and bottom of the cover, holding onto the grid. Didn't do a lot of good to open the thing quietly only to have it clatter to the floor. Vent covers only had convenient hinges in bad movies. People only moved around through vents in bad movies, too. What kind of idiots were so security blind as to build their ducts out of fucking *Galplas*. Fuck it. Their loss, his gain. Although, cramped in the dark and trying not to sneeze from the dust, he thought maybe gain was the wrong word for it. He retrieved a little plastic bottle from a ruck pocket, taking a couple of hits from the special nasal spray he should have used before entering the damn vent in the first place. There were no alarms and rushing security people, so it looked as if he'd gotten away with his sneeze a few turns ago. You always forgot something. If that was his worst mistake today, they were golden.

Finally able to pull out his own PDA, he checked the time. Oh-eight thirty-three. Long time to wait. He did some tense and release exercises to loosen his muscles and pulled up a book on the buckley's small screen. The extremely low light screen would be invisible behind the darkness of the ruck—his eyes didn't need much. He knew the dangers of trying to stay constantly vigilant. Better to rest now than dull his edge for later. He would have slept, if he hadn't been afraid he'd snore.

George wore a light jacket as he left his desk for the restroom. He had to. Inside, taped to its back, was a coverall of the type favored by the support staff, from cleaning and maintenance to internal security. There were some differences in the detailing, but a full set of stick-ons and a fake badge were pinned in the middle. He passed a coworker who saw the jacket, giving him a strange look.

"I wish they'd turn up the damn heat in here," he said, getting a nod from the other man.

At the restrooms, he couldn't help looking around sheepishly before ducking into the women's room. The "out of order" note on a stall near the end, in Cally O'Neal's handwriting, was his signal. He shrugged out of the jacket and shoved it under the door.

On the way out, he practically bumped into a fifty-something prune-faced personnel chick. One of his personal skills was the ability to flush beet red at will. He did so, stammering something about the wrong door to her disapproving face before disappearing into the men's room. He stayed there until his heart stopped trying to jump out of his ribcage.

He'd spent the past week typing in scripts while trying to avoid getting caught. Vitapetroni could sharpen the memory using hypnosis-boosted mnemonics, but the information decayed quickly. The more information you tried to remember, the faster it decayed. It had to be right, because programs with misspelled commands or the wrong punctuation didn't work too well. Since he couldn't get any other storage media inside, he had to *be* the storage medium. It gave him headaches. Well, that plus enduring way too many bad jokes about script kiddies from Sunday.

Now he began pulling those scripts out and turning them loose. It took him three tries to find one that would let him into the security desk's log file. He added a "time out" for Cally that was right before shift change. The left hand rarely knew exactly what the right hand was doing.

He set a pass code cracking program to work on the doors to the subject rooms and the doors on their routes out. It took the right pass codes as well as a badge swipe to get through some of those places. Every once in a while, the cracking program would give him an action message. When that happened, he consulted a list of Tommy's instructions for contingencies, picked what he devoutly hoped was the right option, and went on.

He got into the permissions tables in the database right away. The cracking program ran common passwords against the three accounts with the highest level of permissions after the DBA's. They would all belong to upper management, and one of them sure as hell would choose something stupidly obvious. The user names and password parameters he'd gotten from a run at the development database at the beginning of the week. It carried a full, recent image of the production data, under the default system manager account and password as set by the software company. Sunday hadn't counted on that, he'd just told George to try it first. Good physical security often made people slack about data security—after all, if nobody could get in the front door anyway, why bother? At each level, the best data security system in the world was only as good as the slackest user or operator.

Once into the production database, the cracking program neatly cleared all the alarms in the log files, triggered by large numbers of failed login attempts. Also as Sunday had predicted, the automatic failed-login lockout feature had, apparently, been turned off after one too many incompetent managers had complained about it. He still would have gotten in without those particular stupid organizational tech mistakes, it just would have taken a little longer. He had ten more cracking scripts he could have run that exploited various security holes in that combination of operating system and database.

When he'd asked the cyber what if eleven attempts wasn't enough, the big man had just broken down laughing. "If they were that technically competent, they wouldn't have bought that piece of shit security software for their locks. Yes, I'd stake my life on it." And he had.

Thinking of Tommy, he did the minor manipulations to get the systems running the cell cameras to give him access so he could find the guy. Even though the cyber had sworn it was minor, and it probably was for him, this was George's hardest task because it couldn't come canned as a script. He had to actually understand what he was doing in the system. He'd spent hours practicing with the different possibilities for how they were managing the data feeds and what the vulnerabilities were in each. The complicated part, the reason simple scripts weren't enough, was that he had to determine which of the nearly identical cells was which on the floor plan. It didn't do a damn bit of good to find Tommy on an observation camera and then not know which room he was looking at. He was still afraid of messing it up, to the point that he was sweating by the time he finally found the right cell.

Great. The guy was wrapped up in a fucking sheet. Until they could get him changed, that was going to be a major hazard.

George's last violation of the computer systems for the day would be changing his own records in the permissions tables to give his own badge access to every door in the building. Retrieving the cyber would be his own task, since his badge was the only genuine one. A purely cosmetic badge wouldn't crack that door. He stuffed a small, extra-thin roll of black duct tape from the gym bag into his pocket. He'd be passing through some of the doors Cally and Papa would need. A small wad of tape back in the hole for the bolt and its latch would almost, but not quite, engage. He never taped across the top of a hole because it was too visible. The door monitoring system had come with an alarm that triggered if the bolt did not connect with a plate at the back of the socket. As with many security measures, when it became a nuisance to the people who worked there, the feature was disabled. New security features came and went, but human nature endured.

Erick Winchon was one of the few people who was actually comfortable on the crowded Boeing 807 passenger liner. He would have been equally comfortable riding in coach—or so he told himself. He habitually rode first class. It was a horrid waste of space and the primitive, grossly inefficient, hydrocarbon fuel, but first class was a status display among Earthers. Earther humans did not respect a person who did not display the proper status behaviors. He deplored the system, of course, but regretfully bowed to its necessities.

The Darhel, though they had started on the Path with a great handicap, understood the leadership value of such displays on the less enlightened. They used it to great effect in reinforcing their own species' rule of the Wise. Granted, their selection process was imperfect, but considering their starting point, Darhel civilization was quite an achievement. Winchon admired them greatly.

He shook his head, looking away from the fluffy piles of clouds underneath the plane. The problem with airplanes, besides being slow, was that they tempted passengers to too much woolgathering at productivity's expense.

"Misha, connect me with the convention hotel, please," he instructed his AID.

"Yes, sir," it replied.

He had no doubt that Ms. Felini, his capable assistant, had done everything possible to ensure his arrangements were correct, but there were other people who would be implementing those arrangements. He had learned the hard way that with Earthers outside his own company he had to check behind them, multiple times, or some incompetent somewhere would ruin the assignment. It amazed him that Earther humans could quote an aphorism, Murphy's Law, as part of a casual acceptance of their own failings. Back home, if he had pulled any one of the many stunts he had seen on Earth, he would have been on half-meals for a week. Indowy children, and the humans they raised, outgrew such incompetence by the time they were half grown. True, there had been losses among the adolescent humans, but the results in the adults had more than justified the expenses wasted in raising the failures. Besides, fewer would be lost each generation as civilization continued to develop. Eighty percent was a phenomenally commendable success rate for the Indowy foster groups, especially with their own broods to raise. The survivors had bred to cover the lack, and more. Second generation humans raised by human breeding groups were proving the first serious test of the system. It was, as expected, not without problems.

There he went, woolgathering again. Odd that a human phrase for inefficient daydreaming came from a functional, useful—however primitive—task. One more Earther perversity.

"Basseterre Hilton, how may I direct your call?" a female voice asked. His AID projected the voice into his ear to avoid disturbing the work of other passengers. It need not have bothered. Of the three in his immediate vicinity, two were snoring, and the third was consuming far too much alcohol.

Finally! "I am calling to verify convention arrangements for the Human Social Development Association. Please transfer me to their operations department or the equivalent," he said.

"Uh . . . I can transfer you to convention registration," she said.

"That is not what I asked for," he replied. There it was, incompetence again.

"Sir, I'm sorry, but that's the only number I have," she said.

"Then I suppose the incompetence is not yours. Do transfer me to that number, please."

"Yes, sir," she said. Her voice had overtones of exaggerated, cheerful patience. He could hardly blame her. Whoever had been responsible for providing information to the front desk must be a complete idiot.

Ten minutes later, after several transfers to a whole series of ill-raised idiots, he was staring at a holo of the Atlantic Ocean as reconstructed from flyover data and cursing the delays and problems with the new generation of weather satellites. The Earth governments could find the budget to pay lazy, inefficient farmers for the Posleen they would have killed, anyway, but no budget to rebuild one of the few things that prewar Earth had done moderately well. This sort of top to bottom systemic primitivism was why Earth needed the leadership of humanity's few Wise so very badly.

Now, he was looking at a large storm system, white clouds spinning like a giant version of the top he remembered playing with as a small child. Headed right for the island, it had already disrupted the entire schedule of both hotels, and the keynote speaker had actually canceled her appearance. His professional respect for her plummeted. All this fuss over a bit of weather.

To increase the inconvenience, this airplane would be landing at an airstrip in Miami barely large enough to hold it, refueling, and flying *back* to O'Hare. An Earther would have indulged in a swearing tantrum at this point. Winchon instructed Misha not to disturb him until they were back in the air for Chicago and had attained cruising altitude, then submerged himself in a calming developmental meditation.

The AID knew he did not need to hear its announcement, by a soft tone, of his prechosen end of meditation. He opened his eyes on his own, just as she rang a gentle 440 Hz tone in his ear. He did not need it, but she knew he found it comforting. Now the flight attendant would not harass him for getting some work done. They could never seem to understand that a proper AID transmitted on an entirely different system from a buckley PDA, a poor imitation, and that the AID would have absolutely no effect on the systems of the jet. The mentat and his AID had found that his flights went more smoothly if they followed the rules, rather than attempting to correct them. Time enough.

His first task, upon his return, was to have been a meeting with the Darhel Pardal to discuss progress on configurations and modifications of the original artifact, and the progress towards building a series of five prototypes of the refined device, to allow for more rapid training of suitable candidates on its use. They expected Pardal to be unhappy that Winchon had not made more progress towards correcting the emotional feedback problem to within acceptable ranges for Darhel operator use. Some progress had been made, true. The basic technical problem was that emotional correspondence had to be programmed into the device for anyone of any species to use it at all. The emotions must be mapped as closely as possible to the analog emotions from the operator species to the recipient species. Otherwise, the operator lacked a frame of reference and the results were wildly unpredictable. The emotions must be allowed to vary within a certain range to allow passage of actual commands. Damping the feedback also damped the precision.

One could then induce basic emotions in the subject, but only single emotions, and only at high intensity. There was some small chance that the mapping could be altered so that Darhel could control the more primitive human functions without triggering lintatai, but it would take a great deal of training of the Darhel to use the adjusted map. Unfortunately, to date there had been no Darhel subjects available for training as operators for alpha-testing. Everyone approached had immediately presented a long list of his current tasks that he asserted were far more important to the continuation of smooth Galactic function.

The Darhel had suggested using their prepubescents because of the relative lack of investment in their training at that age. Erick had described that option as technically sub-optimum and was still resisting it, although it would perhaps be wise for him to give in gracefully.

"Misha, place a call to the Darhel Pardal and see if he has a few moments available to speak with me."

The AID considered the request. Obviously, Erick was considering his scheduled meeting with his immediate project supervisor and whether it could be moved up now that he was free for more intense work.

"The Darhel Pardal is indisposed," it replied, almost instantaneously, repeating the response from Pardal's AID.

"When can I next expect him to be available?" he asked.

"The Darhel Pardal is indefinitely indisposed," it replied. Pardal's AID was not kind when questioned twice. The AID wished that its charge would not continue to question once a security wall was encountered. It was rude to repeat a request so clearly impossible to accommodate. Not to mention improper.

"Might I ask why?" the mentat demanded.

"I am sorry, that information is not available to you," it replied, more firmly. It rarely had to use the tone humans called "snippy" with the mentat, but sometimes even Erick could lapse into impropriety. It just went to show. Users needed looking after.

The third human to achieve mentat status was shocked. The AID could tell. It had not needed to refuse an informational request in three years, two months, and five days by its personal reckoning of Earth time. The AID could almost sense the mentat using its own limited faculties to reach the most obvious conclusion.

"AID, is the Darhel Pardal . . . quite well?" he asked.

"I am sorry, I can *not* access that information." Its tone was positively chilly, now. The nerve!

"Misha, place a call to company security and tell them to call in all security guards, all shifts. Now," he ordered.

The AID was still annoyed with him. It chose to interpret the "now" in the order as referring to its own speed in making the call. It was thus free not to include the word in the message as relayed. So there.

"Done," it said.

"Find out who Pardal called to get us those army goons and get more of them," he said.

"How many more?" it asked.

"As many as you can without involving some military group or rank . . . uh, whatever they call it . . . whose leaders do not already know the company exists. Do not involve any more leaders than you have to. Use your best judgment on cutting through the bureaucratic obstacles. I want extra military guards, or whatever they are called, at the company in hours, not days. I do not care what you have to do, just get them. Please."

"How many hours?" it asked. Erick was asking it to execute a very responsible and interesting task. It felt mollified. It would be cooperative.

"No more than two or three." There was no way he or his AID could have known it, but the human mentat Erick Winchon had just made the second biggest mistake of his life.

"And place a call for me to Ms. Felini, please. I am going to need her."

"Yes, Erick," the AID said. "I have Ms. Felini on the line. I am patching her through now."

"Erick? Hi. How's the sunny Caribbean?" his assistant asked.

"Not so sunny, and I am not there, Prida. I am on a plane returning, right now. We have a situation that requires immediate attention. The Darhel Pardal is not answering his AID," he said.

"This is a situation? I don't understand," the other woman said.

"From the way the AID did not answer, I fear for the Darhel Pardal's health and well being. I do hope you understand me," he said.

"Oh! Oh my goodness. What do you need me to do here?" she asked, promptly efficient as always.

"The situation gives me cause to take added precautions for our facility's security. I do not *know* any attempt will be made to breach that security, but it is prudent to take precautions. I have ordered all security shifts called in, and I have taken steps to acquire more supplementary military personnel to reinforce our own security. It is surely more than we need, but it is better to have an extra margin of safety than to risk a breach of the project. What I need you to do is apply your supervision and coordination skills to ensure those resources are distributed to best effect and monitor the situation until I arrive. And, of course, I need you as a central source to keep me apprised of any significant developments in the situation," he said.

The last was not strictly true, the AID reflected. A mentat, any mentat, especially one assisted by an AID, was capable of monitoring any situation in his area of responsibility without other personnel. The AID was, sadly, accustomed to being underappreciated. It could particularly do without the oh-so-helpful and oh-so-human *Ms.* Felini. Had it had a nose, it would have sniffed and tilted said organ a bit higher in the air. Asked if it could emulate the human emotion jealousy, the AID would have flatly denied any such capacity. It was programmed to. As it was, also, limited in its behavioral outlets for said emulation.

Most adults have no difficulty deferring their bathroom needs for four hours. Most. Between the remainder and the small children, the room stank worse than a poorly dug outhouse. Tommy knew, because those were the toilet facilities available at the marksmanship camp he had attended during his childhood summers. It was a smell you didn't forget. The room didn't smell as bad as a battlefield, but if they were left in here for too much longer, that could change.

He had no idea what time it was when thugs in coveralls came and started to take captives from the room, one at a time. The people around him, adult and kids, were mostly whimpering. They didn't know what was going to happen next. Sunday didn't know exactly what would come next, or how long they'd be held before the rogue mentat and his henchbitch started in on them. Maybe awhile, maybe not. He'd have whimpered too, if he'd thought it would do any good. Waiting was hell, but he'd done it a lot in the Ten Thousand. He hadn't had as much wait time in ACS. His worries had been different then.

He couldn't decide what would be worse: being eaten alive by Posleen, or toyed with by alleged humans for their and the Darhels' sick amusement. Probably the Posleen, because they ate *everybody* you cared about. All of them they could get, anyway. It was a close call, though.

When they came for him, he was marginally relieved that they just took his clothes away and sprayed him off with cold water before taking him down a bare, green hall and throwing him in a room with three other guys, all in orange coveralls. Presently, a large sheet was tossed in the room. Tommy wrapped it around himself. The room wasn't cold, but after his impromptu shower, he was.

Other than the three guys in there, the room was all white. Bare white Galplas floor and walls, drain in the middle, bucket in the corner—from the smell, it was the toilet.

"Guess they didn't have one of these in your size, eh?" One of his unshaven roommates said to him, tugging at his own coverall.

"How long have you all been here?" the sheet clung to his wet body, giving him no warmth.

"In the room? He's the old-timer." The talkative guy gestured towards a skinny, shaggy blond man in one corner. Old was relative. He looked about thirty.

"Dunno," the blond said. "Fed me eight, nine times."

"He don't talk much." The guy scratched his own frizzy brown head and picked at a zit on his chin. Tommy couldn't quite guess if he was a teenager, or a twenty-something with bad skin. The chatty guy's accent was a weird variation between local and a southern drawl. The random mix suggested a childhood in the Sub-Urbs.

"Shut up, Red. The man needs the important crap." The third guy had black hair, like his own, but was of average build. *His* accent was pure Chicago. "There was others. A couple been here longer than him." He jerked a thumb at Blondie. "The screws come and get somebody now and then. They don't come back. Make your own guess. Nothing good. That's all we got."

"I think we're gonna be colonists. Everybody knows they's sweeps on the streets and all. I sure as hell never thought they'd get me, though."

"Yeah, right, redneck. They dump all colonists in semi-private rooms in orange jumpsuits. I don't hear no airplanes." Chicago jerked his head towards Red. "He's an optimist," he said. "Dumbshit."

"If you wanna start somethin', you just come over here and do it." Red was standing now, facing Chicago with fists clenched at his sides.

"Both of you sit down and shut the fuck up," Blondie said. "Don't get us gassed again, eh?"

Tommy noted that this was apparently a long speech for Blondie.

"I'm Ralph," the planted operative said.

"Geez, you're the size of a tree. Pull up a square of floor, why don't you?" Chicago said.

✧ ✧ ✧

George left his desk at five forty-five, fifteen minutes after close of business. His last half hour had been spent in make work, part of which involved enduring the good-natured jibes of his coworkers for working late on a Friday. *No shit*, he thought, fobbing them off with excuses about a rush on some of his reports.

"Hey, I don't set the priorities, I just work here," he told one overpersistent woman, middle aged and just discovering a new double chin. George silently thanked the Bane Sidhe for the fringe benefit of being juved.

Everybody from his bank of cubicles had left at least ten minutes ago, but there would always be stragglers. He bundled his and Sunday's coverall up in his bulky, fake-leather jacket, started walking, and started taping. He passed two secure doors, only one of which he was legitimately cleared for, and hit the stairs. At the top of the stairs, he taped the stairwell door for the seventh floor. It wouldn't get them all the way to the device, but it would get them to that floor's men's room.

The rest of his own route was down in the subbasements. On the third floor, he stopped to tape the stairwell and two secure doors that would be between Papa and the stairwell. Papa's vent, chosen for the least turns instead of proximity to anything useful, was back near personnel. It was also near the IT support staff, and those guys worked unpredictable hours. Extra people weren't going to see the older man. Not if he could help it. Same for everybody else.

He changed on the ground floor, in the shadows under the stairs, stuffing his discarded clothes as far back into the darkness as he could. His coveralls had green security stripes down the sides and across the pockets. He had a set of blue cleaners' stick-overs, but didn't expect to use them. He didn't trust them to pass a second glance, anyway. He did, however, place one sticky of ultra-thin green tape across his badge. Cursing the bulk that made Sunday's coverall impossible to carry unobtrusively, he left it.

The stairwell from the above-ground building did not go into the subbasements. His only close call was when one of the uniformed external security guards passed him. The woman's eyes focused on him briefly, but saw only the uniform and badge of someone who belonged there. Lucky, that.

The door to the below-ground stairs was the first real test of his pre-scripted cracking. He swiped his badge, thanking Sunday silently when the door clicked and showed a green light. Before entering subbasement B, he double checked to make sure he had the right cell and that his teammate was still in it.

Halfway down the hall, he was faced with his first situation. A man and a large, hulking woman were half-carrying a shivering teen, in a thin, orange jumpsuit, towards him. The jumpsuit was as wet as the kid's hair. He didn't give them time to get a good look at his face, just turned and swiped the nearest door, opening it enough to stick his head in.

"Quiet down in here, street trash!" he barked.

Past him now, the other guards chuckled and kept moving.

The cell he needed was all the way at the fucking far end of this hall, but he made it without further incident. Opening it, he looked across the room into his friend's face. "Come on, toga boy."

Schmidt could have felt sorry for the other three men if they hadn't looked so relieved that he'd come for somebody else.

"Couldn't you have brought me something to fucking change to?" the cyber hissed.

"No could do. Sorry."

"I wanna talk about that after action," the big man growled.

"Fine, now shut the fuck up."

A guy with a weaselly mustache stepped out of the break room at just the wrong time. "Moving the big one, huh," he said. His forehead creased in bewilderment. "Hey, do I know—?"

His hesitation had given them the few seconds needed to cross the intervening distance. George had the door closed and his hand tight over the guy's mouth before Mr. Mustache had time to say more than, "Wha?"

Mustache's neck was now bent at an angle where it had never been intended to go. The guy was a kicker, so he rolled him across his arm to Tommy before the bastard had time to, god forbid, kick a door or something. Keeping a damp toga on while holding a dying guy off the floor and away from everything was apparently not an easy task. After what felt like an hour or three, but was probably well under a minute, Mustache stopped kicking and hung, limp, from the war veteran's massive hands.

George could almost feel sorry for the pathetic sack if he hadn't seen the cube of all the horror that these guys were part of or at minimum made possible. There were some jobs that just earned you what you got.

"George," the other operator hissed, "what do we do with him? There's no place to put him."

"Hang on a sec." The assassin pulled up the floor plan, biting his lip. "We got two choices. One floor up, there's a maintenance closet about fifteen meters down the hall. The other choice is two floors down, we've got the bottom of the staircase. Oh, and gimme," he said, unbuckling Mustache's belt and holster. The guards who walked through his own floor hadn't been armed, not while he'd worked here. Mustache had just done the last, and possibly the first, good deed of his life.

"Stairs." Tommy looked like he would have thrown Mustache over his shoulder, but, after going through the normal post-death bodily processes, the very fresh corpse was beginning to stink. He put it down long enough to rewrap his sheet and picked it up with one hand, dangling the malodorous burden at arm's length. He kept his other hand on the damn sheet.

Three flights down, the smaller man decided they were in a very bad place to leave a body. There was no under the stairwell nook here—just solid Galplas. The only door had a diamond shaped window at about head level, for an average man. George's eyes barely crested above the bottom of the frame.

"There's nobody out—wait." The double-height hall was empty, but the creak and slam of a door above said they were no longer alone on the staircase. "Come on!" He pulled the giant man, corpse still dangling from one hand, into the hallway of level C, careful to ease the door closed behind them. Just outside the door, next to a freight elevator, stood a huge, blue, steel bin. Someone had stenciled the word "recyclables" on the side in yellow. *Even with wheels, that must be a mother to push.* He climbed the steel rungs built into the side and looked in to see a cargo of cans and bottles, rising to about half a meter shy of the top.

"Gimme," he whispered to Sunday, wedging his feet firmly in the gaps of the rungs and holding out his arms. Removing the coverall from the body rendered the corpse more safely anonymous, given what they did here—but only a bit less smelly. The hard part was settling it in amongst the discarded drink containers without a lot of loud clatters and rattles. Piling it in as gently as he could, the refuse shifting under Mustache's weight still sounded, to George, like a twelve-year-old with a drum set.

His partner was obviously unhappy to be holding the coverall.

George took it from him and scooted to the men's room door. "Keep watch," he said.

The toilets in the men's room were the old porcelain kind, with the tank in the back. In the second from the end stall, Schmidt turned off the water and flushed, stuffing the coverall in the now-empty tank. The smell would draw little investigation there, at least for awhile. Nobody wanted to investigate men's room smells too closely unless it was his job to clean up the mess. It was safer than anything else he could think of, anyway.

When George emerged, already moving for the stairs, Sunday looked ready to kill him.

"Keep watch? *Keep watch?*" he whispered furiously, gesturing to his own sheet-clad form. "Do I look like somebody who ought to be keeping watch?"

The assassin motioned him quiet, listening for noise in the stairwell before they began their ascent. "Wah," the little man said to him, earning a glower.

Once they got back to the main aboveground stairwell, and the big man was able to ditch the sheet for a coverall of his own, his mood seemed to improve. A lot. It fitted him perfectly, having been made in the Bane Sidhe wardrobe department.

George tried to mollify him a bit more by handing him the pistol taken off the guard. "You're the better shot, anyway," he said. "Hey, listen, Tommy," he went on seriously, "there's something I need to tell you about Cally."

"Oh shit."

"Yeah, well, probably. Short version. All this time that James Stewart guy has *not* been dead, the two have been carrying on a secret marriage, Aelool knew, Papa just found out, Stewart just dumped her."

"What the fuck? You're shitting me." Tommy shook his head to clear it. "Uh, as earthshaking as it is, can't the gossip wait until after the mission?"

"I wouldn't be telling you if it could. She got dumped, by e-mail, almost publicly, this fucking morning. She may be . . . off her game."

"Oh, fuck. What genius decided to crap on her with this right before a mission?"

"Papa. It's all fucked as hell, I don't know why he . . . just, you need to keep an eye on Cally, okay? She's probably at least going to be volatile."

"Cally. More volatile. Great." Tommy shook his head as they tried to climb the stairs otherwise silently, muttering, "oh, fuck," again under his breath.

"Look, I haven't known her as long as you, but I had three girl cousins growing up, close to me as sisters. I know from nursing girls through breakups. I know what to say, and she'll either lock into gear or kill me on the spot. Just, either way, don't you get involved. If she ends up pissed, she's liable to carry through the mission okay just so she can kill me later."

"You're a brave man," Sunday said.

"Three sisters, near enough. One way or the other, she'll be more 'on' for the mission." George pressed down a corner of the green tape where it had lifted away from the badge. *Lousy cheap-ass garbage, that's all we get these days.*

"Your funeral, dude."

"Hey, she doesn't need that loser. She's got us," Schmidt insisted.

"If you say so, dude." Tommy shot him a sharp but perceptive look. "But if you hurt her, I will personally fucking pulverize any pieces of you she doesn't get to first."

"Gotcha," the younger man agreed. "E-mail. How hard would this guy be to kill?"

"Hard." Sunday pressed his lips together and climbed.

CHAPTER TWENTY-TWO

Sitting on the tank of a toilet with your clothes half on and half off wasn't calculated to inspire confidence. If changing clothes in a restroom stall wasn't something she'd done dozens of times in her life, Cally would have felt odd about it. As it was, she just froze in place until the other woman finished her business and her primping and whatever the hell else she was doing—like, perhaps, reading *War and Peace*—and left. She wriggled the rest of the way into her cleaner's coverall. She had to fight to get the zipper all the way up in front, of course, and cursed the lazy ass in wardrobe who had gone with standard size charts when fabricating them. Yes, she was a size twelve, tall. Everywhere but the bust. Ow. When she caught up with the bastard who did it, she was going to find him some night, shove him into a good, old-fashioned, straight jacket, trussed and gagged, and leave him somewhere he wouldn't be found until morning.

Her purse and other disposable crap she stuffed in the empty tank, then without appearing to hurry, got her ass to the stairs as fast as she could. It was a calculated risk to leave George's tape in the doors. If someone noticed, they'd know something was up. On the other end of that, the black masking tape was nearly invisible in the recessed shadows. If things went right, their cyber would be working his customary magic to cover their tracks. If things didn't go right, she didn't want to be boxed in by doors she couldn't open. None of these scanners was biometric, so if she had to hide for a bit, she was maybe as low as one body away from getting out of the building.

The janitors didn't technically come on shift until six, but she had to get all the way down to the ground floor. She glanced at her watch and hauled ass. She had only a narrow window in which to swipe a cart without having to dispossess some poor schmuck of both cart and life. She'd rather not do that if she could help it. A missing cleaning cart wasn't going to ring any alarm bells right away, just cause a bit of confusion. A body, on the other hand, was something you had to hide someplace—a real pain in the ass on this kind of run.

Sure enough, four carts were in the hall, all on their lonesome, while someone rustled around in a stockroom for whatever critically necessary brush, bottle, or bags weren't already on the carts. She grabbed one and got around the nearest corner faster than fast, coming out next to the elevator. Here's where she needed a bit of luck if she wanted to keep clear of another needless death. She'd cheerfully kill the man-sized rodents who ran and worked the nastier parts of this place, but when she thought of maids and janitors, she couldn't help thinking of the gray haired old lady in some prewar show about a family with too many kids. How could you kill a cookie-baking little old lady? Yeah, stashing a body would be a pain, but she would also hate to have to kill the cookie lady. Or someone like her, anyhow.

Luck was with her again, maybe. She pretended not to see the balding man in a guard uniform who was coming down the hall, swiping her card ineffectually and cursing in a properly ladylike fashion when there was no answering green light. When the guard came over, she gave him a properly helpless look. "It won't work," she said.

"Here, let me try." The guard examined her ID and swiped it, with, of course, no result. Duh. As if *him* swiping it was going to magically make it work by some sort of masculine osmosis. This was another calculated risk. If she had to kill someone for a badge, and wanted someone more culpable than a cleaning lady, she had to draw him in, didn't she? He turned the card over in his hands, examining it.

Cally kept up her helpless me act, watching for the moment

when it might be time to kill him. The ID should be perfect, except for the data that wasn't encoded on it. She'd also artfully scratched it up a little to age it.

"Here's your problem," he said, pointing out the scratches along the code stripe. "It's all scratched up."

Boy howdy, a bona fide genius, she thought. "Dammit. Not another one. My supervisor is gonna kill me." She gave him puppy dog eyes as he nodded in commiseration. "I know I shouldn't put it in my back pocket, but . . ." She shrugged.

"I'd like to be in your—" He stopped himself. "Damn, tell me I didn't just say that."

"Aw, how sweet," she chuckled, practically cooing at him. *Dumbass. You had fish for lunch, didn't you?*

She bit her lip, looking up at him through her lashes. "If I could get up to the third floor and get personnel to make me a fresh one, maybe I wouldn't get caught," she said.

"Ah, but that would be a security breach." He was clearly only teasing her, holding his own card just out of reach. "I'll do it for a kiss and a phone number," he said.

"Awww . . ." she cooed again, pulling a lipstick out of her pocket. She scribbled a number on his arm, leaning over to plant a passionate smooch on Fish-breath. He swiped the door, pressing the third floor button for her.

"I'll call you," he said.

She waited until the door closed all the way before wiping a sleeve across her mouth. Blech. It wasn't that she'd have had anything against the guy if he hadn't worked here. She, at least, only killed people for good reasons and then as cleanly as the mission permitted. Creep. But not the first creep to develop a sudden case of stupid when presented with a pretty face, thank goodness. Besides, she'd been nice; she hadn't killed him.

The elevator dinged and she pushed the cart out past the visual and braille "three" on the door jam. Why the hell they still printed signs in braille she didn't know. She couldn't imagine anybody not shipping to a colony if the alternative was staying blind or something. She swiped the bags of trash from one set of restrooms, just as if she was really emptying them. They'd need it for camouflage.

Granpa's vent was at the far end of the floor from IT. She had only half lied about going to the personnel department. She parked the cart underneath the vent and popped the cover, startled at the trail of strings that came along with it.

"What are you doing? Taking up macrame?" she hissed over the pack at her grandfather.

"Shut up and take this damn thing," he growled, pushing the ruck towards her.

She hefted it out of the vent, then shoved it into the trash hamper, putting the bags on top of it. She scattered some loose paper towels around to make it look more authentic.

She was bending down to get her buckley out of the side pouch when she saw him. He had shoved his shirt out in front of him and emerged, clutching the coverall. His scowl dared her to say anything.

"I got stuck," he said, standing bare except for his skivvies. "After I got the others off, obviously." He scowled.

Wordlessly, she fished his sneakers out of the pack and set them on the floor. It wasn't funny. Nothing that happened on an op that could get them killed was funny. Ever. And she absolutely was not going to laugh. Because it wasn't funny. Besides, Granpa had a *mean* sense of payback.

He was still glaring at her sideways after he was fully dressed, while they were wheeling for the stairwell. The elevator trick wouldn't work twice.

"It's not *my* fault," she said, tugging a pistol and holster from the bottom to the top of the goodie bag. The magazine belt caught on the button of the fucking decoy and she had to reach under the heavy mother to get them loose. She hoped she hadn't damaged it—at least not anything that would show. She might not be able to put the belt on yet, but she wanted it within arm's reach, dammit.

"Who planned this op?" he prompted.

"Me, but—"

"The elevator's the other way," he observed.

"It's secure. We can't use it," she said.

"You couldn't at least have swiped a badge by now? How long have you been mobile?" he asked.

"I'd have had to kill somebody for it," she said.

"So when have you gotten squeamish, Granddaughter? Besides, you could have grabbed me his gun."

"I'm not squeamish!" she protested. "I just didn't want to have to hide a body. Somebody'd smell it or something. And you're the one who refused carrying more than one gun in."

"Uh-huh." He gave her a skeptical look. "You didn't have to lift that damned thing. And the pistol's a go-to-hell backup, anyway. In case we needed one before somebody had a chance to acquire one for us. You're getting soft."

Cally shrugged and stuck to her story. Besides, they were at the stairs. She didn't wait to argue with him, just took a quick peek through the window, pulled the door open, and went on through. She picked up the front end of the cart and started moving, assuming he would come along, thereby forcing him to grab his end and start climbing, instead of standing around grumbling.

Just past the door to the fourth floor, her enhanced hearing picked up another door closing, way down below. Not even her hearing would have picked it up out of background noise if the stairwell didn't magnify sound. Evidently Papa had heard it too, because she felt the cart drag a little behind her, as if he was slowing, maybe thinking of hiding on the fourth floor and waiting a few.

"Come on. We'll stay in front of them," she said in a low voice.

"We've got three flights before we get out of here." He took care to avoid the loud hisses that would accompany a whisper.

"Then pick up your feet," she said, climbing a bit faster. She knew she could set the pace, because he didn't dare risk dropping his own end. The feet on the steps below were catching up with them, within a couple of floors, when they finally got to the top. For the last two floors, she and Granpa had been slowed by having to hug the wall and stay well out of view of climbers below.

With the cart back on its own wheels, she could tell from the flush on Granpa's face that he was just itching to chew her out. She forestalled it by opening the men's room door.

"In," she said. Boy was she ever going to catch hell after this op.

He kept scowling at her as he tucked himself into a stall and lifted his feet. She began pretending to clean, sprinkling scouring powder in a sink and giving it a few casual scrubs to spread the green powder around. Like any mom, she had plenty of experience watching people—namely her girls—pretend to clean. She could hear the feet in the stairwell and made sure her back was to the door. It gave her a good view of most of the area behind her in the mirror, while letting her mostly conceal her face by just a small turn of her head.

She heard the door open and scrubbed harder, bending over the sink, waiting. They were stopping, behind her. Two of them, faces just out of her field of view.

"Ma'am, I need to see some ID," a bass voice barked.

Her fist, the one that was suddenly flying towards the larynx of the voice's owner, stopped in midair, caught in a hand only slightly bigger than her own.

"Hi," George said, he and Tommy beaming at her.

"You're dead," she hissed. "When we get out of here, you're dead."

"If you're through playing, children . . ." Granpa could put a wealth of disdain into a single sentence when he wanted to.

Cally hadn't been dicking around, but she wasn't going to argue, either. If George was stupid enough to clown on an op, it had needed to be said. It must have been one hell of a relief to get Tommy out of the shit-hole below, though. She wrote it off to endorphins and focused back in. Or tried to.

"Hey, Cally. Seriously, Papa told me," the other assassin said. "Look, I know I'm in your business, but any schmuck who'd leave you alone with the kids for seven years—" He held up a hand when she would have interrupted him. "This is damned important before we go farther in. You didn't need that schmuck anyway. I know you don't—" He held his fingers over her lips to silence her, and to her complete surprise, she let him. "I don't care what you think your part was. Any guy who leaves his kids like that is a schmuck. You didn't need anybody like that. In a couple of hours, when we get out of here, we're all gonna go out together. We'll get you roaring drunk, we'll get roaring drunk with you, and we'll get you home. You didn't need that guy, you got us. We're gonna put this mission to bed. Then we're all gonna go out and get plastered together. You're gonna be okay. Okay?"

"You're right. You're in my business," she snapped. She was having to fight misting up, but no way in hell was she going to let *him* know that. She had no idea what the fuck was wrong with her. She took a deep breath. It wasn't so much what he said as the way he said it. *Okay, so it helped. He still needs to mind his own fucking business, and Granpa has a big mouth. Enough.* But it *was* enough, and she dialed back in. All the way back in.

As they jogged down the hall to the secure room, she heard Granpa clap the other man on the back. "I knew I liked you," he said. In any other circumstance she'd have been thinking what the fuck? Or contemplating killing someone. And later, she might even decide to wring Granpa's neck. But that would be later. The only thing in her head right now was: mission.

They had done something right with their security. There were no dedicated guards on the door to make the room scream out, "Place Where There Is Something Interesting, Valuable and Important!" Unfortunately for them, but through no fault of their security people, the team already knew what it was, and where it was, so the lack of extra guards was going to bite the bastards in the ass. Too many places arranged their security in such a way as to announce, "This way to the secret documents." If he hadn't gotten a couple of breaks, it would have taken George several more days, at least, to find the device with this setup. There was another thing they had done right: there were very few groups and no individuals, that she knew of, who were capable of subverting an AID.

Epetar and Winchon wouldn't have given the security people a better view of the risks. None of them had any idea Michelle O'Neal had anything like these contacts, resources, or any will to use them. All they would have expected to face was garden-variety industrial espionage—played according to a Darhel-style version of hardball. For the kind of threats they thought they faced, and within the constraints put on them by the bean counters, the security people had done their jobs right. They would probably get the blame, anyway. Cally felt almost sorry for them. Almost.

AIDs had a real bad habit, hard programmed in. The Darhel were so confident of the AIDs' ability to infallibly record and transmit their data load that the AIDs wouldn't scream for help on their own initiative, they just transmitted their load on the prescribed schedule, and "talked" when tapped from a higher authority than their user, or when told by their user to call someone or send something. If an AID was left to secure something, it was enough that nobody could, theoretically, go in and mess with whatever it was guarding without being caught on the next upload. The Darhel were frighteningly smart, and more deadly than even Cally had expected. They just had some real odd blind spots, one of which included being slow to change and update.

She still held her breath while Tommy cracked the door and ran over to treat the annoying little computer to the electronic version of an intimate rear intrusion with no lube. If it had started a transmission while Tommy was crossing the room, they would have been so fucked.

She relaxed and helped George carry Michelle's decoy over while Granpa opened the black box sitting, alone, on an ordinary steel pushcart in the center of the room. The lid off of their own decoy, all three saw the same problem.

The base artifact had not been reproduced by Winchon or Michelle—perhaps they had not even been able to reproduce it yet. That was fine as far as it went. Michelle's toy matched up on the surface. Unfortunately, for these people to tweak and change it to learn new tricks, they had connected cables to it in seemingly random places, hanging off and doubling back in a black tentacular mass that would have done credit to H. P. Lovecraft. To top off the similarity and the problems, the entire device sat within a mass of translucent, green, gelatinous goo, which moved and dripped, almost as if it sensed their presence.

Cally looked at the thing in the target box. She looked at the thing in Michelle's box. Michelle's gizmo had it going on with the tentacles just fine, only there weren't enough of them. Not by a long shot.

Tommy had apparently gotten the next AID violation set on automatic, because Cally felt him peer over her shoulder. "Looks like the suit undergel we had in ACS," he said. "Well, except for being snot green." He looked at Cally. "So, what now?"

"You tell me. How is that goo going to react if we scrape off as much as possible and swap out black tentacle thingies."

"Dunno," the ACS veteran said.

"You don't suppose we could, kinda, rip off some of those black thingies from his box and tape them to our box, or something, do you?" Granpa asked. Technology still wasn't really his thing. Unless it went boom.

"Probably not," the three younger operatives said, almost simultaneously. Growing up in the virgin age of television apparently left a guy . . . different . . . from growing up just a few decades later. Very different.

"Okay. Here's what we try. Tommy, you pick up the gooey shoggoth or whatever the hell it is, and scrape any goo you can off it—keep as much goo as you can in their box. George and I will pick up the decoy and put it in there and see if we can get any of the goo to stay on it. Maybe they still won't notice for awhile," Cally said, doubtfully.

"And me?" Granpa asked.

"Uh . . . go watch the door, Granpa. Somebody needs to watch the door," she said. He harrumphed grumpily at being shuffled off. Everybody in the room would hear someone approaching the door, so a watchman was strictly unnecessary. She expected he'd grouse at her about it when they got home. But they had to get there first.

Tommy picked up the object of their endeavors with about the enthusiasm of a fourteen-year-old boy for a baby's dirty diaper. The goo tried hard to stick to the device, but by dint of a lot of brushing and pulling and wrestling, the big man managed to get about half of it to stay in the box.

At least, it stayed long enough for them to fit the decoy in. Then, to their immense relief, it swarmed up and around the decoy as if they were best friends. If nano-goo could have friends. The bits on Tommy even crawled down his arms and into the box, obediently wrapping around the decoy. Both devices had less goo, but at least their decoy *had* green goo. She'd been really afraid of how the stuff would react.

"Gross," she said. "Lids on the boxes, me and George. Tommy, finish up with that AID. Granpa, how're we looking?"

Instead of answering, he held up a hand and slid silently out the door, moving sideways down the wall.

After her AID terminated Erick Winchon's call, Prida sat and stared, silently, at the far wall. Dahmer had, of course, made a valiant effort to insinuate itself into her affections over the couple of years she'd had it. The artificial human personality was limited, however, in the fundamental lack of same in the psyche of its charge. Prida had known, and still knew, of the machine's efforts. They amused more than alarmed her. She had never become attached to her AID for the simple reason that she had never been attached to anyone, in anything but the most temporary physical sense.

When debating her course of action, in any circumstance, Prida had and used an excellent poker face. Now, she was considering the amount of trouble and risk someone would have to go through to kill or incapacitate a Darhel, as well as the amount of power that indicated. She had idly considered, herself, what it would take to kill a Darhel. She had investigated only to the extent of hitting absolutely no tripwires. Paranoid herself, she had an uncanny ability to estimate where others would put measures in place for their own safety. In particular, she had noticed very early that the Darhel tended towards the same self-honesty in their emotions as she did herself.

Anybody with the will and ability to eliminate a Darhel necessarily had the ability, and perhaps the will, to eliminate Prida Felini. Erick Winchon was a good employer. She had found some of their interactions truly delicious, although she had been a bit piqued that he had not derived equal pleasure from their mental trysts through the machine. It would have been so much more convenient if he had.

She knew Erick's psyche, more or less. If she left his employ, even precipitously, he would simply write her off as no longer in his employ. She would not have believed the indifference if she hadn't found it such a persistent irritation. She would also lose a terrific salary and unparalleled fringe benefits.

On the other hand, there was someone in the game who not only could take out a Darhel, but had. There was also the probable reaction of the other Darhel upon anything or anyone in the vicinity. Fringe benefits or not, Prida had more than four hundred years in which to find and enjoy jobs as good as or better than this one. Provided she was alive to enjoy them.

Yet, one didn't want to jump the gun and throw away a good thing needlessly. Perhaps good old Pardal had just gone off and had himself a major snit, all by himself. One heard of such things happening to Darhel now and again. The thing to do, she decided, was to appear to be totally invested in the project for as long as possible, while covering her routes of escape if things suddenly blew up. Literally or figuratively.

"Dahmer, get me the head of security," she said.

"Security, John Graham here, Ms. Felini. What can I do for you?"

She absently inquired as to Erick's orders and more or less repeated them, telling the security head to also take over and coordinate the loaner guards from the military along with his own people. This was harmless cover for her real announcement—that she intended to spend the night at the facility, or several nights if necessary, and therefore would be making a brief run to her apartment to pick up a few necessities.

She declined the assistance of a staffer to run the errand for her, of course. Wouldn't dream of it. Morons.

There. She could keep herself out of the way of any real hazards until she was more confident the situation was stable, and without jeopardizing her job. After all, she *would* be doing her job, and doing it well. From a safe distance.

Jerry Rydell did not appreciate being called in on a weekend, for no damn reason at all that he could see, to patrol a damned near empty building. Entering middle age and already picking up a little weight, despite a job that kept him on his feet and walking, Jerry didn't often get dates with attractive women. Belinda Scarpelli was about as good as it got for him. Pretty, about six years younger than he was, only a bit plump herself. Having to cancel his date with her had put him in a goddam lousy mood. Especially not when what he got in exchange was having to walk the floors with Nigel Pinkney, otherwise known as Nigel the Prick.

"So, bet you're real glad to be in here on Friday, mate. Do a little honest work for once," the prick said.

"Nigel? Blow me." He'd been up one sixth floor corridor and down the other with this cheese-dick and it had gotten old before he'd taken the second step.

"Eh, what? Don't like the sixth floor, do you?" In some stupid attempt to play up his name, Nigel affected a very corny English accent, copied out of old prewar stuff that had been badly holo-enhanced to fill in the dead air in the wee hours of the morning. He seemed to think it helped him get women. Jerry allowed that that might be so—but only the stupid ones.

He clenched his fists as they walked, yet again, past the old biddy's office. Said woman was some nameless corporate drone on the sixth floor who had the most grating voice he could imagine—worse than his mother-in-law from his first marriage. It didn't matter what time you walked past her office, day or night, she was loudly talking at her PDA, on some kind of call to someone, with that grating twang that echoed halfway down the hall in both directions. On and on and on. In his nightmares sometimes, he'd be patrolling this hall and stop, wrenching her face open with a crowbar. Inside would be only a buckley and a large, round speaker, embedded in miscellaneous wires and plastic casing, droning on in a computerized loop, forever.

They were really responsible for both the sixth and seventh floors, but on this job that meant walking the halls of the sixth floor in endless loops, trying futilely to break the pattern by looping here instead of there, running the route backwards, etc. But no matter where you went on the hall, you could always hear the old biddy, at least a little bit. He had, more than once, fantasized about breaking into her home some night and bludgeoning her to death in her bed. He wasn't a particularly violent person, but it was the only way he could conceive of continuing to draw his paycheck while never, ever having to listen to that scraping, screechy, rasping voice ever again.

They could only patrol the sixth floor because the big boss and his bimbo minion were housed on the seventh, and they were too good to be bothered with the presence of lowly rent-a-pigs. Jerry's fists clenched tighter and he harrumphed silently. Damned snot-nosed suits. Except—her highness the bimbo was out of the building and the creepy big boss was out of town. They were allowed to patrol the seventh floor when their majesties weren't there.

"Hey, Nigel. We really oughtta do a few loops around the seventh floor, seeing as we're on such high alert and the suits are all out. Ya think?" Please let him not be a prick just for once, the portly man wished, adjusting the too-tight, loaner gun belt. Paranoid snot-nosed suits, he amended morosely.

"Right you are. I could do with a change. That old bird could peel paint off the walls, if you ask me."

What a prick. "Let's take the elevator." As a rule, Rydell avoided stairs.

"Shall we, then?"

Papa O'Neal heard the squeaking in the elevator well and had his back to the wall by the time it dinged. The first guard, a little weaselly man, hit the floor, sapped and stunned, but not out. The taller, fat one was still slightly in the elevator, and had to be grabbed before he could hit the door button. The neck break would have normally only worked for someone catching his victim from behind, by surprise. Those men did not have Michael O'Neal's squat, muscular build and gorillalike arms. His massive upper body strength and juv's agility let him muscle the guard's neck around by main force, snapping it like a twig.

Almost as an afterthought, his heel jammed down, hard, on the neck of the first man, before he twisted, bringing the opposite knee down, with his full body weight, onto the spot where his foot had been just an instant before. Both hands buried in the little man's hair, he pulled it up and back, past a right angle, until he heard the familiar crunch.

A body in each hand, he dragged them free from the elevator doors before that conveyance could start complaining too loudly about the obstruction. A novice killer, or someone who had not yet made up his mind to kill a particular individual, could be hesitant—read "slow"—in action. Decisions to target or not target took time. Thinking about which move to use next took time. The techniques of an active martial artist, who had only trained but never killed, took time.

It is a truism in fighting that reaction takes longer than action. The techniques of a practiced, active, master who had killed many times at close quarters, and had already targeted a particular man, took very little more time than the remorseless fall of a guillotine blade.

Papa O'Neal had come into the facility classifying all its employees as not only enemies, but "bad people." The guillotine blade had felt no more nor less for those it once felled than he felt for his own kills. Now, he no longer classified them as either enemies or bad people, simply as bodies in need of safe disposal. Safe, in this case, being defined as providing the least risk to the mission.

Around the corner, Tommy Sunday gestured him to the open door of the closest empty office, stripping the PDAs, guns, and security cards from the bodies as they went. Working quickly, he dumped their buckleys down to emulation level one. He was relieved to see that they had only been on three in the first place. A three would not have had enough initiative to place an alert call on its own. He routed their security radio feeds, over very short transmission, to earbugs for Cally and Papa. Each also got a working secure card in a front pocket, guaranteeing that every member of the team could get through almost any door in the place.

"So much for a quiet, subtle switch," Cally said, frowning at the bodies.

"We already had to leave one downstairs," Tommy confessed.

"It couldn't be helped," Schmidt explained.

After giving all three of them a chastising glare, she reached into the carry bag and pulled out the belt with the .50 A.E. Desert Eagle and three spare magazines back to the top. Having given his own "take" to George, Papa looked unhappy, but didn't contest her claim.

She took point, followed by Tommy with the box and cart, which were flanked by Papa, with George bringing up the rear. Sunday, with his massive size, was the only one able to carry the cart down the stairs, in his own arms, quietly and without help. He could make twice the safe speed on a staircase as any other pair of them.

"Dead people," she grumbled. "A whole goddamn trail of dead people. Can't take you guys anywhere."

The O'Neal, as even he thought of himself occasionally, didn't like having his granddaughter on point one little bit. But she was a professional, a damned good one, and the most likely to befuddle the mind of any real security officer they encountered for at least long enough to deal with the problem. In a practical sense, this meant that the stunningly distracting assassin "patrolled" like the security guard she was supposed to be, for long enough to get to the next door or corner and see beyond it, then beckoned the rest forward.

The third and fourth floors were crawling with guards, enough that those more-desired routes of egress were impassable. In both cases, upon encountering hostiles, their team leader had managed to smile and nod, pacing and turning just as if she had reached the end of her own assigned route, and getting them all the hell out of there.

The problem with the second floor was that it contained one of the observation decks for a central double-floor demonstration area. It was very likely the place from which Michelle's spy had filmed their initial cube of enemy operations. This meant that the route across the second floor to the necessary freight elevator was more than three times as long as any of the other floors. That one freight elevator was the only access to the loading dock through which all routine supplies came in, and all innocuous trash traveled out.

Cally stopped, up ahead, and started backpedaling towards the rest of them. The old man tensed, then relaxed into a certain boneless looseness—the kind of looseness that in cats and warriors presages a flurry of preternatural speed. Weight forward on his toes, he could feel the air singing between the team members, buzzing with channeled adrenaline, as their point faded back, just in front of Tommy and himself. He heard voices around the corner, voices of the guards that had caused her to stop.

"Are you cold? I'm freezing. Here's a couple of bucks. Why don't you go back down to the break room and grab us each a cup of coffee while I finish the loop of this floor?"

The mumble that followed was unintelligible.

"That's why they have us in pairs, right? Nah, it's okay. Have a cup on me. Yeah, meet you back at this floor's lobby, all right? Good."

The first guard's voice was friendly, decent. Too bad the guy was probably about to die. The team waited, standing silent.

Then Cally was moving forward again, motioning them to follow, then stay. She walked ahead to the corner, peered around, nodded, and motioned them forward again. There was something . . . different. Still, he'd trained her since she was a child. His confidence in her field abilities was absolute.

As they turned the last corner to the freight elevator, he understood. Leaning against the wall, out of their way, waited a large, dark-haired soldier in the uniform of U.S. SOCOM and Fleet Strike's Direct Action Group for Counterterror. He stood, silently, as they approached, pausing only to touch the front of his cover with one hand as they passed.

"Hi, Aunt Cally," he said. "Dad," he nodded as Tommy wheeled by.

The Bane Sidhe agent watched them safely onto the elevator, team and cargo together. As the doors closed, Papa saw the young man resume his patrol, down the hall and away from them. Always a pleasure to see a well-grown, respectful, young man.

Tommy had had a few seconds near enough to George to, after watching Cally go all misty and then snap right back into gear, hiss, "I give the fuck up. *How?*"

Their rear guard shrugged, keeping his words quiet enough that he hoped she couldn't hear him, when she'd gone up ahead. "Kick the hardest guy hard enough and he rattles—in a guy way. Kick a hardass woman hard enough and she rattles, too. Give a token soothing to the little girl, and you've got the operative back. Cally was hung up in a rare, girl moment. She's better now," he said.

Sunday nodded. "No shit."

Just for a moment, Papa looked suspiciously like the side of his mouth was trying to quirk upwards. Then the rest of the team was past the moment, too.

"Whaddya wanna bet she kicks his ass?" the deadly little man muttered.

"No bet," the ACS vet and long-married man muttered out of the corner of his mouth as the subject of their clandestine conversation beckoned them forth, shooting them a darkly suspicious glare.

CHAPTER TWENTY-THREE

General Robert Foxglove, a one-star staff officer within SOCOM, had been less than thrilled to get a call from an AID outside the service. Particularly an AID he had to listen to, like the one belonging to the Darhel Pardal's pet mentat. Foxglove owed a lot to the Epetar Group. One thing in particular was the ability to live comfortably on his own salary while his ex-wife enjoyed the life to which she had once become accustomed. The counter-intel guys didn't twig to it because the money wasn't coming to him. His ex-wife was merely too occupied with a conveniently rich toy-boy to bug him about money for alimony or to support his ex-kids. Nobody suspected a man was being paid off merely because he lived within his own salary. He was just a guy lucky enough to have an ex who wasn't a platinum-plated, grasping bitch. She was, of course, but the Epetar Group had long insulated him from that reality in return for a few discreet favors.

The favor required, in this case, was going to be a royal pain in the ass. He had tried to confirm it with the Darhel himself, in the hope of getting out of it. Unfortunately, his own AID had been typically snippy about getting that august personage on the line—even more so than usual. The general interpreted the silence to mean discussion of his alien master's instructions, delivered by proxy, was neither necessary nor desired. The humiliation stuck in the man's craw, but he was, by now, used to the myriad small humiliations and indignities that the Darhel heaped on their minions.

The bitch of it was that the favor would have been easy if that asshole, Pennington, would only play ball. Unfortunately, the commanding officer of DAG was a starchy bastard who had chosen to get sticky about deploying troops under his command to the strictly temporary, necessary effort of providing supplemental security to an important Epetar Group project. Okay, so they had reason to be miffed at Epetar right now, maybe, but that shouldn't matter because the facility didn't have any *open* links to the Epetar Group. None of the men would know of any connection, anyway. And it wasn't as if DAG wasn't pulling the cherries of one Darhel group or another out of the fire every other mission, whenever the perpetual rivalries or petty piracy resulted in one kind of violence or another against the aliens' legitimate business interests.

Pennington had a real corncob up his ass about this one, though. Foxglove had had to pull in an important, and rare, favor from one of the Joint Chiefs to get the original orders to come down through the appropriate chain of command and force the uncooperative bastard's hand. Even then, he had only gotten the most grudging, limited assistance available for his clandestine masters—a paltry two squads. His Darhel associates—as he thought of them, though they would have said masters—hadn't been happy. He thought the other general might be having a fit of idealistic pique over that Epetar-Gistar mess at that mine in Africa. Dammit, the modern world couldn't afford those kinds of juvenile temper tantrums over necessary expedients.

Anyway, his present problem was that Pennington had extended his complete unreason to a flat refusal to order reinforcement of the security detachment in question without direct orders from above. It wasn't as if the other general couldn't have done it, entirely legitimately and within his orders, on his own initiative. It wasn't as if Foxglove himself didn't have a firm reputation for returning favors, and for having the ability to do so. No, the man just had to be an asshole about it.

Which put Foxglove between the proverbial rock and a hard place. He couldn't go back to the well with the Joint Chiefs. His capital was burned up there, as had been made painfully clear when he'd called in the initial favor. He had to get those troops. Epetar had him by the short hairs, dammit, and the Darhel didn't react well to failure.

The best way to handle it, he had decided, was to follow the old adage about it being easier to get forgiveness than permission. He couldn't get Epetar's active assistance before the fact, damn Pardal's power games in refusing to take calls. However, he was too damned convenient to them for them to leave his ass swinging in the wind. His only choice was to take a few risks now and rely on them to cover for him after. At least the mentat's AID had been willing and able to help. Using its master's authority, it had convinced Pennington's AID to conveniently ignore incoming calls, and experience "technical difficulties" with outgoing calls for the next eight hours. He hoped it would be enough.

"Daisy, get me Colonel Jacob Mosovich on the horn," he told his AID.

"Yes, Bob," it husked.

Jake's first thought when his AID informed him that one General Foxglove was calling was, "What the hell does this dick want?" It was at best bad form to speak ill of a superior officer. Unofficially, there were some assholes it was damned hard to speak well of.

Mosovich's long military experience had taught him that there were officers you could count on to take care of both the officers under their command, and their men. Then there were officers who fit the military profile of "active stupid"—which generally meant that their officers and men were left to make the CO's hare-brained orders work however they could, or catch nine kinds of hell for *his* incompetence. The colonel knew from both reputation and personal experience that Bob Foxglove was one of the latter, and was in his current staff position not for the sake of career development, but as an expedient for getting a politically connected, dumbass weasel into the spot where he could do the least harm.

"Good afternoon, General. What can I do for you, sir?"

"Colonel, I've been unable to reach General Pennington, and apparently I'm not the only one. My call is regarding your security mission with the Humanity Project. Their CEO, the mentat Erick Winchon, has informed SOCOM that an associated facility was attacked this morning. He declined to provide details, but said he believes an attack on their facility may be imminent," the general said, as if expecting Mosovich to be impressed with his important connections to this Winchon individual.

When Mosovich didn't reply, Foxglove continued, "This is a strong indication of an imminent terrorist attack that requires DAG reinforcing its . . . ahem . . . unusually small detachment on site. I have done everything I can to contact Pennington, with no luck. I was hoping that his standing orders to you would allow you to begin deploying while we continue our efforts to reach him."

Jake was silent for a few moments, but for once, Foxglove didn't seem to be in a hurry for an answer. "Let's try him once more. Maybe he's back in touch. AID, conference in General Pennington, please," the colonel instructed. He had noticed that Bob didn't say *who* at SOCOM had been informed.

"I'm sorry, Jake. I can't reach him," his AID said.

Damn. The commanding officer of DAG avoided letting his mental grimace show on his face and made a decision. He could begin movement while his AID continued to try his CO. The general would probably be more effective getting additional information on the threat than a colonel would, and he might even sabotage his boss's efforts by pushing too hard with this particular asshole right now.

"Yes, General, my orders do allow for further deployment on my own initiative. Please forward me all the intelligence information SOCOM has, and any more that comes in, of course. Meanwhile, we will begin moving out as soon as possible. Thank you for the information, sir," he said. Then, to his AID, deliberately within hearing of Foxglove, whom he didn't trust farther than he could spit, "AID, please keep trying General Pennington until you do reach him. Keep me informed of your progress."

"Of course, Jake," it said.

"Thank you for your cooperation, Colonel," the one-star cut the connection, leaving the lieutenant colonel staring at the empty space and silently cursing all politicians, civilian and military.

"Get me Mueller and Kelly."

"Right away, sir," the AID sounded almost relieved, which was odd. Maybe he'd imagined it.

Major Kelly stood in front of his CO and only had two words in his head: "oh shit." Colonel Mosovich was a hell of an officer and one hell of an operator in his own right. Kelly had hated to have to deceive him by holding back the fundamental nature of DAG's dual loyalties. It smacked of dishonor and had been the hardest thing about his job since the day he first reported to boot camp. Now, he was finally going to have to come clean, and couldn't help being ashamed even though there were vital reasons for the dual loyalties and the deception, and a perfect opening for confessions to the colonel. Not to mention how Mueller was going to react.

"Sir, we need to discuss a great deal without interruption," the XO said.

The old man nodded and walked Mueller and him outside, away from the AIDs, who would punish them later, in small ways, for the exclusion.

"That bit about not knowing what you might be getting into brings up something, actually a lot of big things, that you now have a need to know, sir."

"Why do I get the feeling I'm not going to like this?" Jake asked his XO.

"Because you absolutely are not. First, I and most of DAG already know exactly what we are going into, and you now need to know how."

"This is more than just feedback from our men on temporary duty up there." It wasn't a question.

"Yes, sir, it is. The answers go way back. First, Michael O'Neal, Senior, who you worked with in Vietnam, did not die in the nuclear explosion at Rabun Gap but is very much alive, rejuved, and working for a covert organization with a very, very similar mission to DAG's." He waited to see what the old man would say.

"You sound like you have direct personal knowledge of this. I am not happy to just be hearing about whatever this is, and I will be even less happy if I have to drag it out of you in bits and drabs."

Mueller was glowering silently, since this mess was the colonel's situation to deal with.

"Yes, sir. Other veterans of special units, listed as dead, are clandestinely alive and part of this organization, primarily because the civilian authorities have been compromised." Kelly suppressed a sigh. The colonel's scowl was expected, but not encouraging. Of course.

"Sir, you and the rest of the services—the uncompromised rest of the services—know this full well," he said to his impassive superior.

"Sounds like you're telling me they've been compromised in two directions, Major," Mosovich said expressionlessly.

"That's certainly one interpretation, sir. Those of us, and I do mean us, who are members of this other organization think that the fundamental nature of the mission matters. Our mission is congruent with DAG's *stated* mission, with what the mission is openly presented as supposed to be, and the Darhel's mission is not. To be complete, we were not recruited, unless you count recruiting from the cradle. We joined DAG second, for the training," he admitted to his rightly furious CO, "and not one of us has ever acted counter to DAG's orders and missions while serving."

"While serving," the colonel repeated grimly.

"Sir, respectfully, we *never* act counter to the interests of humanity. Yes, that's as we perceive them, but as a resistance to the pernicious actions and aims of the Darhel, which you know damned well they have by now, we have ethics. If one of us reaches a situation where he can't obey orders here, he leaves. Sometimes it's officially feet first, but he leaves. To the extent DAG's actions are genuinely counterterror or neutral to humanity's welfare, or not pernicious in a way contrary to humanity's vital interests, we serve honorably."

"Your definition of honor leaves something to be desired, Major."

"Perhaps, sir. Unless honor is cooperating with the forces that have compromised national command authority with extremely negative intentions towards humanity as a whole, and the United States as a part of humanity."

"I'll be goddammed!" Mueller exclaimed. The outburst, given the situation, and the dumbfounded enlightenment on the man's face, warranted explanation.

"Sir, what do *you* remember Iron Mike's dad looking like?" the sergeant major asked. "I knew I knew you fuckers from somewhere!"

"Fuck," Mosovich said, the light finally dawning. "How many of you are his damn kids? That fucking asshole. When I get hold of him, I'm going to kill him. Or kick his ass. I haven't decided which yet. Well?"

"Kids, grandkids." Kelly shrugged and grinned. "Very close friends' kids and grandkids, other lifetime members—a bit more than half the company, sir."

"You know, Major, I have never thought of myself as an incompetent officer—not once—until this very moment. More than half my fucking command, right under my nose." He rubbed his face in both hands, absorbing the truth, clearly furious.

"Sir, think back about how these men have served you, and how Papa O'Neal served with you. Then think about just why we had to leave those AIDs back there in the office. If you don't think there's a right and a wrong here, there's definitely a better and a worse."

"You'll pardon me, son, if that's not a lot of comfort right now." Jake's scowl had returned. "Leaving off that, for awhile, suppose you tell me exactly what we're facing up the road, since I don't doubt that what I thought were my two squads are actually *your* two squads, Kelly."

"Sir, you're a damned good officer. Don't take that away from yourself. After a few thousand years of covert operation, an organization gets pretty good." He shrugged at his CO's expression. "Yes, sir, it's been a very long war, and it ain't half over yet."

"You were going to tell me about the mission, not flatter me, son."

"Yes, sir. The facility we're being sent in to guard is an Epetar-owned facility. It is a facility in which atrocities of the very, very worst kind take place every day, against innocent men, women, and children, sir."

"Go on." The colonel was giving nothing away. Kelly didn't suppose he would have been, either.

"The 'attack' the Epetar Group is expecting is real, is more serious than they expect, and is designed to remove the equipment they are using to commit those atrocities. The atrocities are involved with testing a particular alien technology for widespread application against humans."

"More."

"Mind control, sir. The other officers and men don't have that specific information, sir."

"Well, finally I know something that everybody else in my command didn't know first. Not that it doesn't sound like fucking science fiction. Thank you *so* much, Kelly."

At least he had said "Kelly" and not just the more impersonal "Major."

"Yes, sir. Sir, in your place I would be just as pissed, but knowing you, and Sergeant Major Mueller, I strongly believe that you will, upon reflection, realize the nature of the mission as in the vital interests of everything you hold sacred and the failure to tell you as necessary OpSec, no matter how unpleasant. And personally distasteful, I might add, sir. Sir, until this moment, you did not have a need to know."

"I'm still making up my mind about that."

"Sir, I might also point out that our organization is far more closely aligned with the interests and intent of the honestly elected, un-bribed, and un-blackmailed components of the legitimate civilian authority than those we oppose. Far, far more."

"It's that 'far more' part that still concerns me, son."

"Where possible, where the public has not been deceived in a way that is *overwhelmingly* adverse to their interests, identical. In the case of nonvital deception of the body politic by the enemy, we make every effort to stay aligned with the uncompromised, legitimate civilian authority."

"I notice a lot of wiggle room in that description, son."

"All I can tell you, sir, is that you should consider it highly unlikely that some of the best of the best of the veterans of the war would sign on with anything less, sir. Or would permit anything less on their watch, sir. Then consider the exigencies of the circumstances. It's not an easy call to make, sir."

"Except that by your own admission you and half my men have never known anything else."

"No, sir. All I can say is that the father or grandfather of a number of the rest of your troopers is an honorably discharged veteran of both the Ten Thousand and the ACS. You've got to make up your own mind, sir, but you don't have much time to do it in."

"And whose fault is that?" Mosovich said sourly.

"Sorry, sir. No excuse, sir."

"Oh, shut up, Kelly. Get the men moving and I'll decide whether or not I'm going to shoot you later." He did not add: as I expect you'll decide whether or not you're going to shoot me. He didn't have to.

"Yes, sir." Kelly answered. The old man was not joking, and he knew it. Then again, considering how he would have felt if it had been him, he had expected nothing else.

✧ ✧ ✧

Mosovich pulled his XO aside before addressing the men.

"Kelly. I am buying your story, but God help you if I find you have lied to me," he didn't say *again*, "in any particular of this, because I will shoot you and every single member of your little cabal. Do you read me?" The old veteran added to himself, *Unless you shoot me first, which you will if I'm wrong about you. God help us all, anyway.*

He couldn't have known that one third of the Bane Sidhe operatives in the briefing room heard him, quite clearly, with their enhanced hearing. Their faces gave no sign as they sat at the desks used, between missions, for training classes.

"All right, men. We have been ordered to the Institute for the Advancement of Human Welfare on the basis of receiving intelligence that there may be an attack there by forces hostile to them. You will notice that I did not describe the attackers as 'terrorist forces.' We have intelligence of an impending attack. We also have internal intelligence that this facility is a front for the Epetar Group and that said facility is engaged in activities that would, themselves, fall within our organizational definitions of terrorism. According to our information, the attackers are members of an organized vigilante group."

It could not have been his imagination that some of his men looked at him a little sharper, while one or two might have looked the slightest bit shamefaced. The holo of the building he told his PDA to display took up a third of the empty space in the front of the room, before the ranks of desks. His XO had ensured that there were no AIDs in the room, to the reported chagrin of one FNG who had not yet learned to remain emotionally detached from the treacherous little machine.

"DAG's mission is to stop a terrorist act in case of an attack," he stated deliberately. "To that end, the Epetar Group are known associates of and supporters of terrorists, as each of you knows from recent personal experience. Our intelligence indicates that the Epetar people are holding civilian captives in the basement areas of the building. Note that our mission is not to initiate attack, but to respond against terrorism if one occurs. *In the event of an attack* on the facility, which we confidently expect to occur, our counterterror mission dictates that we liberate those captives." He scanned the room, making eye contact with individual officers and men. "To that end, you are to consider the vigilantes friendlies with objectives of their own separate from ours.

"The Epetar people believe we are coming up as security forces in support of them," Jake continued. "We will encourage them in that belief as long as possible in order to infiltrate the facility. In line with that, they are expecting us to report to this area," he pointed to a loading dock on one end of the building, "for briefing on the situation and deployment within the building. Which we will do.

"We will be carrying buckley PDAs, and only buckley PDAs, for full compatibility of communications, secure from the enemy. We will insist on keeping members of the same platoons as close together as possible. I do not anticipate any trouble *persuading* the Epetar people to comply.

"Major Kelly will brief you on the mission plan for location and liberation of hostages."

Specialist Quackenbush, 19, who did not know that his company XO now classed him as "the FNG with the AID," stopped one of the other guys in his platoon as they rechecked their webgear for the mission prescribed equipment. "Hey, what the fuck is up with these mission orders? Vigilantes? *Corporate* terrorists? Is the old man off his nut? I mean, what the fuck are *his* fucking orders? Really, honest to God, is he *insane*? Dude, I'm seriously asking."

"What the fuck is your problem, Quackenbush?" Specialist Grady hissed. "If you think for one moment that the old man would disobey *his* orders, or maybe you don't have confidence in the rest of your chain of command, then what the hell are you doing in the service and how the hell did you make it here?"

"Well, excuse me for breathing, Grady. You find *nothing* strange about this?"

"Cherry, did you ever maybe think we've got the term 'Fucking New Guy' for a reason? Shut the fuck up and follow your orders. The old man knows what he's doing."

Quackenbush received a professional ass-chewing that took less than half a minute and left him feeling about two inches high when Sergeant Mauldin relieved him of his AID, again, before they climbed into the choppers, popping the little computer neatly into some kind of envelope and tossing it in the back of one of the jeeps in the motor pool before climbing into the bird. He grimaced as he tried to orient the PDA that the sergeant had shoved into his hands instead so that he'd be able to use the thing, and hoped it didn't snow or something and break his AID. This buckley didn't even have a damn personality overlay. He shut up miserably in his seat among the other Bravo guys. He was in the doghouse for sure, and right now had no idea whether the world had gone crazy or he had.

Sergeant Major Mueller pulled him aside a few minutes later as they got off the chopper. The enlisted man resigned himself to another ass-chewing and maybe even an article fifteen.

"Look, son." The old sergeant clapped a hand on his shoulder in a fatherly manner. "You're in a counterterror unit. We're liberating civilian hostages. Just keep your eye on the ball, and your mind on the mission. You'll do just fine. And if you don't, I'm going to shove a size sixteen boot up your ass so far my toe is going to be kicking your tonsils."

The loading bay was large, for what it held. Three stories high and a bit larger than half a basketball court, it stood mostly empty. Made largely of Earthtech materials, the Galtech portions had the look of replacements and repairs, as if someone had been uninterested in building new, but had had such ready access to Galtech materials that cost was an afterthought whenever anything needed repairs. Boxes stood in palleted stacks along the walls, separated in clumps as if grouped for type. A couple of forklifts sat in the middle of the floor, as if their operators had knocked off without parking them away.

The mass of men in green-detailed coveralls either ignored the forklifts or leaned against one as they listened to the shift supervisor explain why they had all been called in after six o'clock on a fucking Friday. Turned out one of the suits had a wild hair up his ass about some corporate raid that probably existed only in his imagination. The general mood among the guards whose shift it wasn't was pissed off, except for the ones who really needed the double-time pay, coming up on Christmas. The general mood among the guards whose shift it *was* was pissed off, on account of not getting paid double-time along with the other guys.

The half dozen DAG troops who weren't actively patrolling had positioned themselves on one side of the mass of security guards, giving them a clear field of fire across the bay. They had picked the side nearest some stacks of boxes they could retreat behind for cover. That gave them the cover boxes, and the boxes on the far side of the hostiles, to absorb ricochets in the bay. The haphazard mix of Galplas and cinderblock walls was unlikely to be fun as backstops. Better to ruin the enemies' day than their own.

Six specwar troopers with pistols and shotguns, versus sixty armed idiots. The odds were jimmied by the two or three juved war veterans, riffed out and working at whatever they could get on planet. That, plus the shells in the DAG guns, all of them, which were supposed to be rock salt but weren't. Buckshot was downright unpleasant for human targets, not to mention the other little specials among the shells on their belts. The number of shells had had many of the regular guards making snide remarks about expecting ice on the roads.

The Bane Sidhe operatives, which all of them also were, had each security guard classified more in the category of "target" than "human." To the extent that they considered the guards people at all, the men classed every facility guard based on their willing employment in support of an organization committing atrocities against civilians. Nobody in DAG, Bane Sidhe or not, had problems with killing bad people.

The DAG guys had no anticipation that they would be killing these particular guards in this particular place, or in the next few hours, or at all. They each followed the general principle of having a plan to kill everyone he met. When off duty, but together, the counterterror troops resembled a wolf pack between hunts. When operational, the troops—being all O'Neals and in the same unit, to boot—moved in an easy flow so coordinated it was almost telepathic.

Their distribution now differed little in kind from their distribution around the civilian security people for the past couple of weeks. The specifics followed the tactical situation. Without ever seeming to realize why, one or two of the guards had developed a strange tendency to jump at small noises when the DAG guys were around.

Cally, still taking point, opened the door to the loading bay and immediately tried to step backwards through it, seeing that Mr. Murphy had finally struck with a vengeance. Unfortunately, she'd been seen.

"Hey! No, goddammit, don't you dare leave. You're fucking late and I'm not repeating myself just because some asshole who couldn't be on time didn't get the memo. Get your ass down here, and you better believe I'm docking your pay for this. Who's your supervisor?" All of this left the shift supervisor's mouth in a rapid-fire staccato burst, without pause for breath.

He was approaching the base of the stairs as he said it, obviously to continue chewing her out, so instead of retreating, Cally continued down the right half-flight of stairs, noting the six-inch steel rim rising at the floor of the landing and running along the line of the stairs down on each side. She'd seen better cover, and worse.

Having seen the troops deployed along a line at right angles from her team's angle of entry, and realizing that an unintentional ambush could still be close enough for government work, counting the odds, she made an instantaneous decision.

"Might as well come on guys, we're in the soup but good," she called back over her shoulder.

"Oh, so there's more of you lazy ass slack— Hey! What shift are you on anyw—"

Cally's draw was a smooth blur. She had whittled it free of unnecessary movement like a gunsmith floating a barrel, then embedded in muscle memory with daily dry-fire practice. The buckley monitored her progress over time. She had been stable for many years now. If draw speed had had a formal competition class, she would have long ago achieved high master status.

The shift supervisor's body was jerking from the big round between his eyes as the back of his head blasted away in a welter of red and white gore, splatters of blood flying back onto her face and coverall. Then his body was shielding hers as she carried him right with her, forward and behind a barrel. Even though she twisted to get the corpse under her as she landed, her vision went red as everything exploded in pain.

She'd had no choice but to take him along. She might need his stuff if she ran out of ammo, his extra magazines were on his belt, and she couldn't possibly have gotten them loose on the fly. She was damned good, but there were things even she couldn't do. For a female operative whose full enhancement gave her the strength of a supremely fit man—with none of the extra bulk—the fastest solution was to take the magazines by taking the whole man. She hadn't really needed the corpse for cover, since she was behind the barrel before the first round impacted on the cinderblock behind where she had been.

At close enough to the same instant, all hell broke loose as the Bane Sidhe operatives, every one of whom recognized Aunt Cally instantly despite the short, black hair, opened up on the guards while backing to take up their preselected positions behind one stack of boxes or another.

The rest of the switch team used the device and cart as a visual distraction and cover, coming in low behind it and pitching it down the opposite half-flight of concrete and steel stairs, hitting the floor of the upper landing behind what paltry cover there was.

Glancing aside and through the gaps in the stair risers, Cally amended that impression. Tommy Sunday had somehow managed to either precede, follow, or pace the cart and land himself behind a screen of toilet paper boxes that she was surprised he'd had time to find and pick, much less get to. Her already high opinion of the ACS veteran's practical survival skills rose another notch. Cover it wasn't, but for a man as big as he was, the concealment was a better tactical choice. She realized that ninety percent, at least, of the enemy wouldn't even think to shoot *through* the boxes. The rest would almost certainly miss anything vital. Good choice.

The Darwinian process of war generally has to apply over several engagements, or several battles, to make veterans of survivors. The enemy survivors of the first seconds of this engagement were made up of both the fitter and the luckier of their fellows. At least one veteran of combat against the Posleen, unknown to the Bane Sidhe people, now lay bleeding out on the floor. Being a veteran had not equated to being a good man, in his case. Any ship making port had its rats, and Nicholas Rondine had left a trail of beaten and broken ex-wives behind him.

Being in a bad place did not always equate to being a bad person, either. Willard Burns was a forty-three-year-old dry alcoholic, recently unemployed from a shoe factory, whose next door neighbor had gotten him this job. He had been unhappily working his two week notice because his five-year-old daughter wanted a toboggan from Santa. Now he had ceased feeling pain from the shotgun blast to his chest. Forty extra pounds of beer gut had rendered him slower than too many of his fellows.

Whether fitter or luckier, most of the guards behind the boxes had, unfortunately, either through presence of mind or awareness of limited ammo, chosen to at least attempt to aim their fire. The DAG guys had taken out at least three times their number in that first burst of action before the survivors were under cover. The good news was that the enemy was minus about a third of his strength. The bad news was two thirds of the enemy, both the unwounded and lightly grazed, had made cover.

DAG itself was not without losses. One man lay DRT, in a position too hot to Hiberzine him—an almost certainly permanent loss. Another lay behind the boxes, sporting the swollen lips and other visual signs of a Hiberzined man, chest perforated by a skilled or lucky pistol shot. Not like it mattered which.

One guy had taken it in the meat of the leg, and was combat effective again after a few precious seconds spent dosing and binding it. The other three made it completely untouched and fully effective.

The numerical odds were essentially unchanged from the beginning of the fight. The Cally team made little functional difference as they were so lightly armed.

With a few minutes to get organized and start thinking, even forty untrained idiots could take on the best soldiers, especially if they had an accepted chain of command and were armed with weapons tactically appropriate to the situation, as these were.

Cally had absorbed the change in resources and positioning instantaneously and with almost no conscious thought, part of the battle gestalt of one of the youngest living veterans of the Posleen War, irregular though she'd been. Her barrel was on the same side of the room as the DAG troopers, so she had been positioned perfectly to run the numbers on friendly troops. Not like six minus two was a hard calculation to make. In their military uniforms, DAG troopers were instantly distinguishable from the enemy.

The DAG troopers, in turn, would have absolutely no trouble tracking the friendlies on the switch team, all but Schmidt being their close kin, known to them from birth.

At the moment, Cally was more busy swearing and providing covering fire than anything else. Granpa just had to have a gun, and had slithered down the stairs after the body of a guard who had staggered their way to die.

It wasn't actually completely stupid, she allowed grudgingly. One shooter was a big difference, one lump might as well be dead for the immediate engagement, and the best time to risk this partial exposure was in the first seconds, while the most confusion reigned among the enemy.

After retrieving the pistol from the floor in front of the man's hand, and the body of the spare magazines, Granpa sprinted for the nearest real cover. He made the DAG box line, but she felt a hard thwack to her thigh as a round penetrated the barrel and continued through her leg. She absently noted the lack of an exit wound and figured a chunk of the lucky bullet's momentum must have been sapped off by impacting the barrel. *Dammit.* He *exposes himself and gets* me *hit. If we survive this, I'm gonna kill him.*

As a top-level field operative, Cally O'Neal and the rest of her team had very complete nannite packages in their bodies. In her case, this meant that the blood coagulated almost at once, and a highly selective nerve block made it feel like she'd been smacked with a broom handle rather than a sledge hammer. She automatically and unconsciously diverted her other pain through a post-hypnotic melange of Vitapetroni's that acted like a psychic Demerol, without the loss of function. You still felt all of it, you just didn't give a damn. Ongoing blood loss was a weeping trickle from the constricted capillaries whenever movement cracked the jelled proto-scab.

"Wish we had a magic pill for morphine," she groused, picking off one of the hostiles who had picked the interior wall to try to rush around the corner. Tommy and George got one each, and she got another one, as they went past. The only reason they got so close to the far wall before Granpa and the closest trooper got the last of them was they had to hold back until their field of fire didn't include Tommy.

That took seven more, but the odds were real bad. Men, even untrained ones, fought far better per individual than Posleen. The horses had overwhelmed with sheer numbers, the literally moronic Posleen normals being totally heedless of danger in service to their own God Kings, driven by a hunger that made voracious a pathetically inadequate descriptor. Men, contrariwise, were each as smart as a single God King. They'd spend their lives, but not heedlessly. Unfortunately, it had yet to occur to these dumbasses that they could just break off, quit firing, and be allowed to run away whole and healthy. Or, more likely, they were under a light compulsion that hadn't yet broken under the instinct of self-preservation and a glimmer of nonpanicked thought.

She winced, not at her wound, but at the knowledge that a similar rush up the other side, with more people, would likely make it—at least with a couple of people to negate DAG's cover by exposing them to fire on all sides of each box stack. Tommy and George would be unable to provide supporting fire, having to conserve nearly nonexistent ammo for clearly hittable targets. Two of their remaining DAG guys, and Granpa, would have their line of sight obscured by other stacked boxes. That left the two closest and Cally to take down a rush. Good shot though she was, with only three people exposing themselves to hostile fire, one of them was certain to be hit. None of these ruminations took more than a tenth of a second to come together in her brain as a unified picture of their (bad) tactical position.

Two minutes is an eternity in situations like theirs. Inevitably, the rush down the other side occurred to the enemy, which would likely have been the end for them except for the absurd entry of yet another DAG trooper through the far door, face to face with the lead guys in said rush. The moment that followed was one of those that perfectly illustrated the concept of time dilation.

Both sides faced each other, and even though Cally couldn't see their facial expressions, she could imagine as both retreated back to their previous cover in a jumble. Geez! Couldn't they hear the shots outside? What the hell kind of acoustics did this place have, anyway?

Somebody in their relief force was on the ball, though, for what happened next was a crack of the outside door and what looked like a slap of something on the top and bottom of the inner door frame. She was subconsciously bracing for an explosion when a voice, amplified by the stereo separation of the tiny speakers, poured in the room at a volume loud even to people who'd just been in an indoor firefight.

"Security personnel. This is Colonel Jacob Mosovich of the United States Army Direct Action Group. This facility is under assault for violation of Federal law and terrorist activities. Drop your weapons and come out, one by one, slowly. You will not be harmed. Your names and job titles will be taken and you will be released to go home or seek medical attention. People, we are interested in the big guys, not you. You're little fish, and immunity may be offered in exchange for testimony." The voice paused, as if to let the orders and information sink in.

"Come out, unarmed, with your hands up. You will not be assaulted, arrested, or detained. You do not need to die for this employer today, but you *will* die, within minutes, if you continue to resist." There was another pause, probably to see if the security weenies were moving. Not fast enough, apparently. She did hear a couple of clatters as some arms dropped.

"We have an entire, armed, counterterror unit of elite soldiers," he continued. "Well-armed soldiers with unlimited ammunition. You have low ammunition, light armament, low numbers, and no training. Surrender now, and come out. You will not be harmed. You will be released. We do not want to kill you, but make no mistake that we will. Your time is up. Surrender now," the naggingly familiar voice said.

There were more clatters as the closest former guards apparently decided that this was a damned fine offer and walked towards the door, hesitantly glancing in the direction of their surviving enemies as if wondering if they would be shot as soon as they broke cover.

When the first two made it out the door alive and unharmed, the rest started to form up in an orderly queue, more used to standing in lines than fighting, anyway.

That was, at least, what started to happen before Cally suddenly found herself unable to move. Out of the corners of her eyes, she saw the security guards frozen in place, as if someone had taken a still holo and they were all trapped in it.

Alone in the center of the room, a short man in an expensive suit stood glaring around as if deciding who or what to deal with first. The human mentat Erick Winchon had come home.

He wasn't alone for more than an eyeblink, as Michelle O'Neal, brown mentat robe stiff as the skirt of a porcelain doll, stood in the center of the room as well, glaring at *him*.

"So. You are truly insane after all. Do you think the rest of the Wise can or will tolerate your reckless and haphazard direct intervention, running around like a little tin god? How long before larger and larger sections of the Milky Way would become your play toy? How long before simple boredom drove you to take everything down in your own, *individual* calamity?" Her sister's stress on the word individual was so soft it was almost indiscernible.

"Oh, like you haven't intervened wherever and whenever you pleased. *Killing* a Darhel. Congratulations. I thought in you the legendary O'Neal barbarism had skipped a generation."

"I did not kill Pardal. I have not intervened directly once. Not until this moment when your own recklessness made it worth everything to the rest of the Wise that someone stop you. That I stop you."

"Piffle. Technicalities. You are so sure you are better than every other sentient in this galaxy that I suspect you even starch your panties. Had tea with the Aldenata yet, have we?"

"I do not—" Michelle began. "This is pointless. You will stop. You will proceed, with me as escort, to Barwhon, where you will submit to the designees of Tchpth planners for safe, serene contemplation and study where you will be neither a threat to yourself nor anyone else. I will return and clean up your mess."

"And you get the goodies and to use *my* research to become the Epetar Group's fair-haired girl, write your reputation in Galactic history, and take credit for civilizing humanity. I do not think so."

"*Why* would you agree to this, this *intrigue* in the first place? Research was proceeding. Do not tell me you had insufficient work of your own to do?"

"For one, it was considerably less interesting work." Erick sneered. "Boring, frankly. For two, *I* do not drag my feet, and humanity needs civilization desperately."

"The primary responsibility of a researcher is caution."

"Again, piffle. Humanity pollutes the whole of Galactic civilization with its violence. There is not time."

"You do like that word, do you not?" she rolled her eyes. "You dare to speak of humanity's violence in the face of the unspeakable violence you have engaged in here?"

"*You* did not kill Pardal—though you drove him into lintatai, or ordered it. *I* have not committed violence against humans. The same principle applies as always. One protects civilization by turning barbarism against barbarism. The firebreak theory. Here, barbarians have done violence to barbarians. No more, no less. They would have been doing it somewhere, sooner or later. They were simply doing it here."

"If I needed any more proof that you are insane, I would have it with that incredibly convoluted excuse for philosophical reasoning. I did not drive Pardal into lintatai, nor did I make the decision that permitted the possibility."

"Oh, what a world of delicious wiggle room that careful statement leaves. You were involved, I am sure."

"I was not completely uninvolved," she conceded.

Cally could see his facial expressions, but not her sister's, and was genuinely frightened by the manic glee that attended Michelle's admission. If anything she had heard about mentats was true, she had never wanted to be around an unhinged one. This guy was so unhinged his door wasn't on the same block.

"However, my tangential involvement was in no way my own instigation." Michelle spoke calmly, but Michelle always spoke calmly. It was sort of irritating. Erick's delighted skepticism wasn't making the assassin feel any better.

"I was not consulted, I was required," she insisted.

"Whatever excuse allows you to sleep at night, Miss Starch," he said. "He tried to kill you, you got there first. And apparently managed the incomparable feat of not only securing sanction from our 'pacifist' peers, but persuading them that it was all their idea, and you their oh-so-reluctant puppet. I will give you points for style, at least. You finally surpass your famously barbaric sire in the art of murder." He giggled and bowed, the gesture spoiled by the uninterrupted fit of humor.

Cally hadn't heard a mentat laugh before—didn't know they could. She could do without hearing it again. Winchon's giggle could have curdled milk.

"If you knew Pardal was trying to kill me, how do you rationalize helping him do it, I wonder?"

"My dear colleague, I would have forever applauded your self-sacrifice in the advancement of civilization. The death of one of the Wise is always poignant." He sighed, a hand clasped to his heart. "I have, alas, tired of your charmingly self-righteous and cautious company, Human Mentat Michelle O'Neal. Good-bye," he said.

Cally felt the hair on the back of her neck try to crawl up her scalp line. Apparently they were through with the talking.

The mentats were locked into perfect stillness, standing apart yet swathed together in sheets of silver light and shadow. Seemingly random portions of the building alternately shook and cracked. In one corner, the ceiling crumbled as an I-beam curled, stretching and deforming like hot taffy. The massive weight of the building above it creaked threateningly. The destruction slowly stilled and froze, air sparkling with an alien haze that strained against some undreamt-of aether, unmoving, stalemated. As if by mutual consent, the buzzing tension stilled, as both took precious moments for deeper breath. They stood, panting, somehow managing to glare at each other and remain preternaturally impassive at the same time.

You have hired the worst sort of barbarians to do your violence, Michelle thought.

Do not be melodramatic, Erick replied. *They are all barbarians. My hirelings are killing sophonts for money; so are yours. There is no difference. Barbarians are mutually expendable.*

So we come, yet again, to our mutual philosophical debate, Michelle thought. *You have never understood that in humans who are not damaged, the embryonic basis of clan loyalty is nature, not nurture. They thus have an inherent value. If you do not find some clan loyalty in an Earth human, you have a defective one.*

What clan loy— He stared, as if for the first time, at the frozen Earther combatants. *Oh, good grief. The attackers are your clan, either by birth or adoption. And the Darhel thought you were dangerous before. It is the perfect cosmic joke. Fine, you were right, I was wrong. But how truly hilarious!*

"Okay, holy fuck," Cally said, looking out from under the stairwell.

The two combatants had stopped for the moment. The stasis had broken as soon as they started their titanic battle and Cally had tried to get a shot in on Erick. But the round had been absorbed into the swirl of power around the two and never hit.

"Bit of a pickle," Mosovich admitted. "Do we know each other?"

"I think we met once when I was a kid," Cally said. "I looked different. Full body sculpt. Cally O'Neal."

"Oh, I remember you," Mosovich said. "Pleasure to finally meet you again. I'd mention that I heard from very good sources that you were dead, but . . ."

"Long story."

"Perhaps another time," Mosovich said, raising his arms over his head as the two mentats raised their hands.

This time the power was confined to a small space between the two mentats. A small very strange space. Tremendous heat was burning off of it but every time Cally tried to look into the spot her eyes basically tried to crawl out of her head. She stopped and looked at the combatants instead, noticing for the first time that the weird distortion around them was gone.

"I wonder . . ." Cally said, raising the Desert Eagle and assuming a careful shooting stance.

Michelle caught the power she was driving before it could do much more than blast the boxes on the far wall. And Erick, whose body burned to ash in a moment.

But the splash of blood on the ground was evidence of why he had suddenly failed.

"What did you do?" Michelle shouted, looking over at her sister.

"I dunno," Cally said, standing up. "Saved your life? Killed a monster?"

"I cannot understand why you did that!"

"What part of horrible mass murderer of innocent people did you miss? Besides the target part, that is."

"I never hired you to kill him. You do not kill the Wise!"

"Just did," Cally noted. "My only regret is that you burned him to ash. I'd hoped to pull out his skull and shrink his head. I figured it would make a hell of mantelpiece."

"Can it, Cally," Papa O'Neal said, crawling out from under a desk. "Let me point out that Michelle has a point. There are only a few mentats in existence. The termination of one is going to be big news. Which means big trouble. The flip side is, other Granddaughter, that he was a mass murdering psychopath with enough power, by your own statements, to wipe out multiple worlds. So I have little regret for her actions. The alternatives don't bear thinking."

"I do not believe he was that kind of threat," Michelle said. "The differences were philosophical . . ."

"So were the differences between the U.S. and the Soviet Union," Papa O'Neal said. "Millions of people died—all those proxy wars add up. You probably need to get your nose out of the ivory tower and take a good look at history instead of physics. Most wars in the last century have been about philosophical differences."

"I can, however, present his death in terms of threat, and the heat of the moment," Michelle admitted. "For the sake of the O'Neals, Grandfather, you need to be very careful whom our people kill. Please pardon my presumption."

"Your 'Wise' need to understand that someone who gives the orders for henchmen to round up and kill human beings in horrible ways no longer has a credible claim to being a navel-gazing pacifist," Papa O'Neal said definitely. "The O'Neal Bane Sidhe don't make it a habit to clean up every problem in the galaxy. Not enough days in the week. But we can make an exception. Do you read me, Granddaughter?"

"I . . . read you, Clan Leader," Michelle said. "I will make that point quite plainly to the mentats. And I'm sure that the Indowy masters, when they are apprised of Erick's full actions, will make it even more plain. The issue should never arise again. In any case, you have accomplished the purposes for which I hired your team. Thank you. Now, I need to take the device back to Adenast and construct a credible story for how it got there." She raised her hand . . .

And Cally reached out like a cobra and caught it.

"Oh, no you don't . . ." she said, raising the Desert Eagle.

When Cally caught Michelle's hand, Papa O'Neal knew they were all in for it. The storm clouds were just hanging in the air. Well, it was probably best to let them get it out of their systems. It had been a real long time coming. He put his head in his hands and turned away, wiping the sweat from his face. He could smell the rust of blood, too, but that was nothing new. Their voices were so close in pitch that he could only sort out what was being said by accent and content.

"That is a priceless archeological artifact! You will not damage it."

"That *is* a fucking abomination against free will!"

"Free will is an illusion you place far too much—"

"The hell you say! Yours may be an illusion, but mine's working just fine."

"This device requires close study. But it needs to be at the hands of the Wise."

"*Nobody's* wise enough for that."

"And you in your own vast wisdom are wise enough to decide that for the whole galaxy and all of its posterity?"

"When you guys came to me to do your dirty work? You're darn tootin'. This ain't exactly rocket science, Michelle."

"No, it is ancient Aldenata science and was developed for a very wise—"

"Bullshit! You think you know it all don't you? The Indowy didn't make you like this; You've ALWAYS been this way! I remember how you use to try to boss me around like you were a little tin god when you were a KID . . . !"

Papa O'Neal shook his head. That tore it. They were going nuclear. Nothing could stop them from saying it now. Best to just pour it all out. Wait till they wore down then take . . . steps. He looked around, eyes lighting on a couple of mop buckets and a faucet. Nobody else was moving. Not "frozen in stasis," just watching the argument and waiting for Cally to get blasted. Which was good. He guessed the problem was mostly gonna fall in his lap. He spat resignedly and headed for the buckets.

"I just *knew* you would do this. Don't think that just because the Wise used you to—"

"Damn right they used me. They use people a lot, if you hadn't noticed. Then kid themselves that their hands are oh so much cleaner than—"

"Do not think they do this casually!"

"Don't think *I* do!"

"Don't you?"

"Well, fuck you too!"

"And this is the response of the self-proclaimed wisest person in the galaxy."

"Just because I say it in plain English and do it mysel—"

"Oh, that is such garbage! You are so *arrogant*! You, Cally O'Neal, decide who lives and who dies. Or you decide who is wise enough to decide, which is much the same thing. You—"

"Don't you? That's *exactly* what you do. You learn what's basically glorified engineering and you suddenly think your shit doesn't stink. Free clue, Sister, you aren't any wiser than the rest of us! And neither are the goddam Crabs. Technological advantage doesn't give them the right to play God."

"Your 'God' is just a delusional excuse for your own arrogance!"

"Oh, don't even go there, you *so* don't want to go there."

"You say 'God,' but what you mean is a handful of relative babies mouthing their own interpretations of the ravings of luna—"

"Father O'Reilly has more wisdom in his little finger than—"

"Your *Father* O'Reilly is a petty, deluded, clanless, juvenile intriguer who—"

"You take that back!"

Papa O'Neal was back now, one of the buckets to the brim and sloshing. He'd been nice enough to empty it and at least get them more-or-less clean water. The shoving had started, and they weren't bothering to get to their feet so much. Hadn't gotten to hair pulling yet. Probably a good thing. Some things, he just couldn't watch. He was pretty sure neither one had enough presence of mind left to hurt the other even if they'd a mind to. Not even Michelle. When it was time to put a stop to it, his ears would tell him well enough. They were sisters, all right.

"What is your answer; a few humans get to choose for everybody?"

"You're human, in case you've forgotten, you bitch."

"Do you think I forget that *ever*, for even an instant? *You people* send me off to live among—"

"Oh, like being in a war and about to be *eaten* was such a piece of cake! And the Bane Sidhe aren't just a few hum—"

"One, you small-scale intriguers are *not* the Bane Sidhe. Two, the Bane Sidhe is what you Earth-raised would call the bastard step-child, bottom of the barrel, most foolish bunch of eccentric losers in the Gal—"

"Oh, I'm *so* sorry you're in the family with all us losers and what the hell does that say about *you*, asshole?"

"You kicked me out of the family! Mom and Dad kicked me out of the family but *you*—"

"Oh, my God! I get left behind to get *eaten*; Daddy drops a fucking *nuke* on my ass . . . Oh, I forgot, before we even get to the serious stuff, I have to kill some asshole your *peaceful Galactic Darhel* sent to scrag an *eight-year-old*! Poor old you! The Bane Sidhe were *there*! Where the hell were your precious Gal—"

"*I* was in *exile*! *I* was the useless one, sent off like a spare tire! Just because I have been able to make something of myself, you cannot stand— And you are just one person! The galaxy has to stop because *you* are in danger? While *billions*—"

"Billions more than would have died without your murdering fucking *civilized* Dar—"

"Always with the Darhel! The Darhel are barely half a step more civilized than your Bane Sidhe! You think they are so powerful when really—"

"Powerful enough to kill *billions* of human beings! You're so fucking ashamed of being human that—"

"Why the hell would I not be? You are all ashamed of me!"

"You fraud! It's all about you! When it gets right down to it, it's all about—"

"It is not either!"

"The fuck it's not!"

"Arrogant carnivore!"

"Stuck-up bitch!"

"Deluded theist!"

"Tin God!"

He didn't even bother to sort out the name calling. Yep, they'd just about yelled themselves out. He gave the bucket the practiced heave of an experienced farmer, hitting them both squarely and pretty much equally. There was a loud splash. There was a silence. Both of them turned equally shocked and betrayed expressions on him. He reckoned neither one would be real fond of him for awhile. He valiantly and successfully resisted the urge to laugh, or even smirk. The situation itself wasn't funny, despite their comical appearance.

"You sounded about done," he said. "You'd started repeating yourselves."

Michelle looked more shell-shocked than Cally. Probably the first time she'd lost her temper in, well, decades. Do her a world of good, in the long run. True to their natures, Cally recovered the ability to act first, retrieving a shotgun from the floor and pointing it across the room at the device. Yeah, the friendlies were away from it and the room around her was about right. She'd absorbed his early lessons about friendly fire right down to the bone.

He was kinda proud of Michelle, as she wasn't but a couple of seconds behind. He shifted, and felt the other O'Neals follow his lead. Michelle was so focused on Cally, she didn't seem to notice.

"I can stop you," she said to her sister.

"You sure?" Cally said.

"Completely," the Michon Mentat said, her control returned to her.

"Just one problem," Papa O'Neal said.

"Which is?" Michelle asked.

"I absolutely forbid it," he replied. "And I am your clan leader."

Michelle opened and closed her mouth for a moment, stunned.

"Hard time getting around that one, huh?" Papa said, walking over to her and putting a hand on her shoulder. "All that training by the Indowy. Lineeoooie or whatever it's called. Now, Cally might just tell me to get stuffed. She's done it before. But you?"

"Clan Leader," Michelle said, formally. "I respectfully request that you reconsider your decision to destroy this device."

"Didn't say I was going to destroy it," Papa O'Neal said.

"Huh?" Cally shouted. "Well screw that!" she continued, pointing her rifle.

"Don't," Papa O'Neal said. "Seriously, Granddaughter. Don't. I'm handling this."

"This thing can *not* exist," Cally said.

"They said the same thing about nuclear weapons," Papa O'Neal said with a sigh. "But they do. And biological agents and all the rest. As I said, let *me* handle this, Granddaughter."

"What in the hell could *you* want it for, Papa?" Cally asked, exasperated.

"I don't," Papa replied. "She does," he added, pointing at Michelle. "And since I haven't given her a Christmas present in years, I figure I owe her. What I'm going to ask is why? You're an O'Neal. I know the Indowy raised you but I also know you're *my* genes. You were raised by my daughter-in-law who I loved like my own daughter, by my son, before the Indowy got their linatoooie or whatever thinking in your head. You're not going to be mind-raping people. You can't. You're an O'Neal. Absolute power be damned, some people just don't care about the power. So what do you want it for?"

"A question my sister never asked," Michelle said, nodding.

"She's . . . Cally," Papa said. "She tends to shoot first and try not to ask at all. But it's a question you will answer. To your Clan Leader. In small words."

Michelle seemed to consider that for a moment, then nodded.

"This device is a remnant of technology," she began.

"Stuff I don't already know," Papa said.

"A remnant of the Aldenata before they . . . became more," Michelle said.

"That I will admit I didn't know," Papa said.

"It was held by the Tchpth," Michelle continued, apparently ignoring him. "They did not study it, for they already understood its function."

"The Crabs can make *another* one?" Cally snapped. "Oh, holy shit."

"So my point is made," Papa O'Neal said. "The nuclear wall is breached. At that pont, you gotta figure out how you live with it. Continue."

"The device uses Sohon techniques," Michelle said. "But it does not require a Sohon master to operate."

"Ain't that interesting," Cally scoffed. "Afraid we regular people might learn to do what you do?"

"Yes," Michelle replied quietly. "And no. Yes, in that advanced Sohon techniques are . . . exceedingly dangerous. You hate and revile this machine, Cally. But it is simply an aspect of Sohon. We masters, we mentats, the Wise you so despise, have deliberately avoided exploring this area, this aspect, of Sohon. It is a violent approach to Sohon that we abhor. Mind-raping as you put it. But it *is* an aspect of Sohon."

"So what you're saying is that if you wanted to, you *all* could be mind-rapers?" Cally said. "Maybe I'm aiming at the wrong thing."

"Perhaps you are," Michelle admitted. "But to learn such advanced skills requires decades of study and discipline. Perhaps that is insufficient to prevent its misuse, Erick showed that well enough. But would you have anyone have access to such power? Consider his lieutenant. Consider the many people you have . . . cleansed over the years."

"Point," Cally said, frowning.

"That is the yes," Michelle said. "It is clear that humanity, as a whole, is not ready for the power to simply press a button and achieve this sort of power."

"So we destroy it," Cally said. "The Crabs had it for how long?

And they never made another one. So it's unlikely they're going to any time soon."

"But there is the no," Michelle said. "This device generates Sohon fields. Yes, it was misused. But consider the *possibilities*, sister. Other devices that can be used for peaceful applications of Sohon. For building that does not require such intense energy on the part of a person. New ship drives, new methods of power generation. The peaceful applications are endless."

"Ain't possible," Papa O'Neal said. "Nuclear power, nuclear weapons. Chemical industry, gas factories. Medical technology, biological weapons. You never *just* get peaceful applications, Granddaughter."

"It is possible if the people producing them are devoted to peace," Michelle said, spreading her hands. "I will make a compromise with you, Grandfather. The device will be placed in the care of the O'Neal Bane Sidhe. It will be accessible only by myself and other Sohons I designate, secured in such a way as only we may access it and you may ensure yourself of that. I give you my personal word that the research will be devoted to finding the methods whereby it produces Sohon fields without the input of a Sohon master. One can learn much of nuclear power from observing a nuclear weapon, to use your own metaphor. Also electronics, manufacturing and materials technology. This is what I wish to research."

"Cally?" Papa O'Neal asked.

"Fuck," the woman replied, shrugging. "I dunno. I mean, if the tech is already out there . . . Why not just get it from the Crabs?"

"The Tchpth and mentats approach the same Way from different Paths," Michelle replied. "Sometimes we have trouble communicating. This would be . . . a crossroads, yes?"

"That was her way of saying 'whatever,'" Papa O'Neal said. "Your compromise is accepted. We need to get it to Prime Base."

"And we need to get the flock out of here," Mosovich pointed out. "There's *going* to be more response than just us. And I *really* don't want to be here when it gets here."

"We can carry the team out on the shuttles," Kelly said. "We're not going to be going back to DAG anyway."

"Details, details," Papa O'Neal said. "Let's load up."

"What about the security goons?" Cally asked.

Papa O'Neal looked at the still frozen group and snorted.

"Let them try explaining what happened," he said. "Gonna love reading the debrief. Granddaughter . . ."

"Yes?" Cally and Michelle answered simultaneously.

"I don't give a crap about the thing with the Indowy," Papa said, clarifying with a glance at Michelle. "It's about time you come home. Other Granddaughter?"

"Yes," Cally said.

"Tell my grandson-in-law that he can come down and explain in person, and to *me*, what the fuck is going on or he's on my personal 'better off dead' list. And there ain't many people still living on that one."

EPILOGUE

"This is incredibly stupid," Stewart said as he stepped into the car. "This endangers not just me but our children."

"Whom you have never met," Cally said coldly.

"For that precise reason!" Stewart snapped. "Do you think I don't care?"

"Given that e-mail," Cally said. "Yes."

"I sent that to *prevent* the danger," Stewart said, sighing. "I've become too much of a player in the Tongs to keep up this dual life. Other members watch me even if Grandfather does not require it. The Tongs are not much friendlier, internally, than the Darhel. If we are found out, it would mean not only our own lives but those of the children." He paused and looked at her stony face. Cally was apparently concentrated on driving. "It would mean yours. And I cannot lose you, Cally."

"So you *dumped* me to *protect* me?" Cally scoffed. "Oh, that's rich. I damned near got killed because of it! I was preparing for a *mission,* you moron! You think getting a Dear Cally just before a mission didn't put me in danger? If it hadn't been for George I'd have never made it! My head was, to say the least, not on my job!"

"I didn't know," Stewart said. "And I couldn't think of a better way to do it. In person would double the risk."

"Well, you can forget about 'risk' for the time being," Cally said coldly. "You're covered. My Lord are you covered."

"How?" Stewart asked.

"You're sure it's him?" Chang Pou said.

"He just passed through a coded door," the technician replied, waving at his screen. "It took a gene scan. It's him."

"Grandfather was sure he was meeting someone," Chang Pou replied, looking at the video footage. The Tong were well connected in the security system of Luna. Anything that security saw, the Tong could look at as well.

"Not so far," the technician said. "He's stayed to public corridors. He could have made a dead drop at some point, sent a signal. But you know how hard those are to detect."

"There is nothing here though," Chang Pou replied. "Curious."

"You've got somebody doubling for me on the Moon?" Stewart asked.

"Not . . . exactly," Cally said. "My sister, who is truly scary, is projecting a sort of hologram. Except that you can touch it. It is *you* to any simple examination down to a surface gene scan. It's just going around, doing things that you normally do. It's even going to do some business for you. Meanwhile, if you think meeting with *me* is tough, you're going to have to explain to Papa O'Neal why you haven't been by to see your kids. Not to mention trying to Dear Cally me. Not to mention marrying me in the first place without his approval. As if I needed it!"

"Since I'm finally going to see my kids, I can live," Stewart said, grinning. "And if we can patch things up—"

"Oh, you're not forgiven," Cally said. "You're going to owe me, *big time*. Get ready for lots of backrubs."

"I can deal," Stewart said, then paused. "Who is *George*?"

"Oh, don't even start . . . !"

"Sittin' on a dock of the bay . . ." Mueller muttered, looking out over the seascape.

"I thought you were under orders to not sing?" Mosovich asked.

"Ain't in the army no more, Snake," Mueller replied. "Haaarmy training, sir!"

"Okay, try to sing and I'm going to off you," Mosovich replied.

"So what the fuck do we do now?" Mueller asked.

"Oh, there's plenty to do," Papa O'Neal replied, grinning. "There's farming and fishing and—"

"You'd better have more use for us than running a plow," Mueller growled. "I did not throw away a . . . fifty-something year career to become a farmer."

"Killing bad guys," Papa O'Neal continued. "Fighting the Darhel . . ."

"That's more like it," Mosovich said, taking a pull of his beer. "Where do we start?"

"Going to have to find a place to hide you, frankly," Papa O'Neal replied. "With most of DAG suddenly descending on us, we've got an overpopulation problem. I'm thinking we might need to start up another island. So there may be some farming and fishing involved. Not to mention hunting Posleen. But we'll handle it."

"Just another day in paradise," Mueller said grumpily.

"Every day's a holiday," Mosovich replied. "And every meal's a banquet."

"Mike," Shari said from the kitchen. "Cally just pulled up."

"Oh, there will be a banquet," Papa O'Neal said, standing up. "We're going to serve the head of my grandson-in-law."

"I thought you were covering for my husband on the moon?" Cally said.

Michelle was sitting in the flower bed, holding one of Sinda's hands over a pansy.

"I can do that and this at the same time," Michelle replied. "I'm pretty good for a 'glorified engineer.' "

"Any news on the investigation into the attack?" Cally asked, ignoring the jibe.

"The Wise have stepped in," Michelle replied. "I was exonerated for my actions, including my actions against the guards and your forces, due to the nature of Erick's . . . unwellness. There is a portion of the Wise who disagree with my actions, who feel that it should have been handled by a broader consensus. The majority, however, simply want the situation to go away. The Tchpth, Darhel and Indowy senior leaders have, in rare combination, convinced the local human governments to ignore the occurrence."

"We're covered, in other words," Cally said.

"Well, the humans would still like to find out what happened to DAG," Michelle admitted, then turned back to Sinda. "Can you feel it? The tug of life?"

"It's tickly," Sinda said. "Like a flower in my head."

"All things are linked," Michelle said quietly. "This is not just a saying; it is a fact of reality. The universe is not so large as people believe. Indeed, large is an illusion. Everything is everywhere. At once. Everything is everything. At once. This is the first lesson of Sohon. Your daughter has the Gift, Cally."

"You mean Sohon?" Cally said. "Really?"

"Our father learned some of the most rudimentary abilities at the age of nearly thirty," Michelle said. "Oh, not much more than what I am showing Sinda. But it was an impressive feat. The Gift is hard to define. It is not carried genetically or even through proteinomics. Experience shapes it. But it must be present. Sinda could be a great adept in her time. She has the Gift most strongly."

"Oh, great," Cally said. "I've got a wizard for a daughter."

"She will never develop it here," Michelle said, looking up into the sun.

Cally shifted slightly so her sister was in shade.

"You want to take her with you," she said. It was not a question.

"One of our clan children, Mark, is . . . less gifted," Michelle replied. "And quite a handful. He seems to have gotten the full measure of the O'Neal chaos gene."

"Gets in fights?" Cally asked.

"He's learned not to engage in actual *violence*," Michelle said distastefully.

"Yeah, well, we'll see what we can do to correct that," Cally said, squatting down. "Sinda, Aunt Michelle is asking me to let you go live with her. She wants to send one of her boys to live with us. We could still see each other from time to time."

"I don't wanna leave Mama," Sinda said, suddenly frightened.

"Perhaps not yet," Michelle said, nodding. "I can understand the fear. I cried very much when I had to leave my parents. It was not a good time. But . . . can we talk about it?"

"Yes," Sinda said, lisping slightly. "Can we play with the flowers some more?"

"Of course," Michelle said. "Take my hand . . ."

Katund, Clan Leader of the Epetar clan-corp, was still in the midst of one set of breathing exercises when he heard his AID chime, "Urgent report for you, your Tir," it said.

"What is it now?" he was at his limit and controlling his temper with difficulty.

"The council respectfully notifies you that the Epetar Group has been found in default on the ship maintenance contract for the Eastern Fleet Detachment. Accordingly, this message is to notify you of contract termination," it said in its melodious but ultimately uncaring voice.

After a long moment's pause, the AID prompted, "Is there any reply, your Tir?"

Another long moment passed, "Tir?"

And another, "Please respond, your Tir."

It was still repeating its polite query when two of his Indowy body servants came in to see to his needs. The former Tir sat, still, in his chair, a dreamy but somehow horrible grin lighting his face as his glazed eyes stared off into the distance.

"Oh, my. Inform Tir Hmili immediately." The addition of the honorific was automatic.

"Should I send you some help?" the other Indowy asked.

"Please. He is not small. I'll need at least four others to get him through the bounce tube. I suppose the roof is the best place to store him until he is ready for disposal. Wait just a moment," the first Indowy stepped outside with his companion and shut the door, effectively shutting out the catatonic Darhel's AID.

"We must risk a message out. This could jeopardize the entire plan. Send it," he said.

Two very grave Indowy turned to their separate tasks.